The Price to Pay

Euan B. Pollock

© Euan B. Pollock 2018

Euan B. Pollock has asserted his rights under the Copyright, Design and Patents Act, 1988, to be identified as the author of this work.

First published in 2018 by Endeavour Media Ltd.

Table of Contents

Chapter 1	7
Chapter 2	10
Chapter 3	12
Chapter 4	17
Chapter 5	21
Chapter 6	25
Chapter 7	30
Chapter 8	36
Chapter 9	40
Chapter 10	44
Chapter 11	48
Chapter 12	52
Chapter 13	55
Chapter 14	59
Chapter 15	64
Chapter 16	72
Chapter 17	78
Chapter 18	85
Chapter 19	91
Chapter 20	96
Chapter 21	101
Chapter 22	109
Chapter 23	118
Chapter 24	121

Chapter 25	128
Chapter 26	133
Chapter 27	138
Chapter 28	143
Chapter 29	149
Chapter 30	156
Chapter 31	160
Chapter 32	163
Chapter 33	169
Chapter 34	176
Chapter 35	180
Chapter 36	185
Chapter 37	189
Chapter 38	191
Chapter 39	196
Chapter 40	199
Chapter 41	205
Chapter 42	209
Chapter 43	215
Chapter 44	222
Chapter 45	229
Chapter 46	234
Chapter 47	237
Chapter 48	239
Chapter 49	242
Chapter 50	246
Chapter 51	253
Chapter 52	254
Chapter 53	263

Chapter 54	270
Chapter 55	273
Epilogue	277
About the author	278

Chapter 1

Stewart Scott stared at the phone on his desk, its shrill ring loud in his ears. His hand hovered over the receiver, frozen in place as he stared at the name of the caller.

'*Sudgeon*'. The name of one of the partners at his law firm appeared in the text screen on the phone in small, old-fashioned text letters, with a vast power behind them.

He took a deep breath and grabbed the receiver.

"Hello, Mr Sudgeon, this is Stewart Scott."

"Stewart, good fellow! I'd like you to pop along, for a quick chat." Sudgeon sounded jovial, but that meant nothing. Sudgeon sounded just as jovial before he fired people.

"Eh, yes, right. I will. Eh, to your office, Mr Sudgeon?"

"Yes, that's right. My office."

"Ah, yes, okay. No problem, Mr Sudgeon. And, eh … Now?"

"Yes, that's right. Now. Right now, in fact." The voice was becoming less jovial with each question.

"Okay. Right. I'll be there. Right away."

"Capital!"

The line went dead. Stewart looked at the receiver in his hand for a second, then put it down slowly. He looked at Michelle and Jennifer, the other trainees who sat with him in their office.

"I've been summoned. By Sudgeon."

They nodded in unison, both equally dubious, and Stewart knew they were all thinking the same thing. Being summoned by a partner was news. It could be good, or bad, but it was definitely something. Unless you were Hamish, of course, the other trainee, who excelled in ingratiating himself wherever he went. He always got good news.

"What about?" Michelle asked.

"He didn't say."

"You've been working really hard recently on the Raker file. And it's going really well, isn't that what Mark told you? So maybe it's to say thank you?" Jennifer tried a smile.

The Price to Pay

Stewart shrugged. "Maybe." Except that it wasn't even a maybe. There was no chance that Sudgeon was calling him up to give him a pat on the back, even if he'd done the most sterling work. That wasn't the way it worked.

"Maybe there's news on the job positions for us at the end of this year? Maybe a third one has opened up? They did say that there might be more." Jennifer again. She was still trying for that smile, but it was more wishful than certain.

"Yeah, could be, I suppose. But I don't know why he would give me a summons for the news. And then just me as opposed to all four of us. And I definitely can't imagine any of us being told before the golden boy." Stewart paused as he put on his suit jacket, his voice quieter when he spoke. "I'm just hoping it's not the firing squad."

"Of course it won't be!" Jennifer spoke immediately, the sound of her voice loud in the small room.

"Stewart, they're not going to terminate your traineeship." Michelle's tone was gentler.

"It happened to Belinda two years back. She's working as a waitress now. She can't even get another firm to take on her traineeship."

"Yes, but we're second years now. She was cut after a few months of her first year. I mean, they said she got so stressed so quickly she couldn't do anything except cry in the toilets. You don't do that." She tilted her head, and gave a mischievous smile. "Do you?"

A smile broke out on his face as he snorted. He walked over to the mirror in the office, pen and notepad in hand, as he did every time before going to see a real, bona-fide lawyer to make sure he hadn't spilled something on his tie. He had to skirt the papers and folders lying in piles on the dull green carpet, placed there because the solid wooden desks were already overflowing. There was talk about it becoming a paperless office, more environmentally friendly. And maybe it would, on the day the Devil skated to work.

He patted down his shock of dark hair. Tall, dark and handsome, wasn't that it? He had the dark bit down, at least hair-wise. Although it had the unfortunate consequence of accentuating the natural paleness of his skin, making him look even more peely-wally. He was struggling with the tall part, aiming for six foot but always falling just short.

As for handsome, well, his mum always said he was handsome. That would have to do.

His brown eyes looked a bit tired. They always seemed to be, these days. He tugged on his cuffs. He felt odd wearing suits, with his thin wrists and neck poking out, and his boyish face. It always reminded him of the days when he used to dress up in his father's suits, when he was eight or nine.

But still. He was getting there. He was getting there. His first year had been a roller coaster ride, lows with people shouting at him and messing things up, and highs when contracts were signed and pats on the back were handed out liberally. He could practically feel himself getting more professional, learning more each day. And getting the Raker file … that had been great. All to the good, in fact. So long as he wasn't cut off early.

Stewart checked his tie in the mirror. If it was indeed the firing squad, he would at least look smart.

"If I'm not back in an hour, send a search party. I'll probably be crying in the toilets …"

Chapter 2

Stewart's battered black shoes sank into plush, thick carpets of reds and golds in the partners' corridor. Paintings adorned the walls here, grand battle scenes alongside flowers and fruit. Fresh flowers and the occasional small shrub here and there gave a real life to the place, their smells wafting in and out of the art.

Stewart tugged on his cuffs again as he walked. The trainee and junior associate corridor where he worked was far drabber – white walls and worn carpet, paying the price for being host to those at the bottom of the legal food chain.

There had been a time when he'd been scared of these rich surroundings, but then he'd discovered, chatting with a secretary, that the artwork was all rented. For some reason that made him feel much more relaxed, as if knowing the company was only playing at being cultured made him feel better about playing at being a proper lawyer.

Sudgeon's door was ajar. There was talking inside in low voices, Stewart unable to make out any of the words. He checked his tie one last time, then knocked. Sudgeon appeared through the crack in the door, rolling his black leather seat across the rich cream carpet. Stewart gave him the awkward smile his face made when he was worried that he wasn't meant to be wherever he was.

"Ah, Stewart! Come in, my boy, come in!" Sudgeon boomed the words. Stewart stepped into the room, slipping into the corner with his back to two walls. It was a large space, with lots of light entering through big windows. They lined up behind a beautiful oak desk that commanded the room. In front of it was a long wooden table, with chairs down the length of it.

Sudgeon often spoke in this bombastic tone, as if his volume was set a couple of notches higher than everyone else. It was in contrast to his appearance. Sudgeon was slim and bald, with circular glasses dominating his face. He reminded Stewart of the clever but weak kids who were bullied in school.

Richard Green, an American partner, was sitting at the table beside Sudgeon. Stewart felt himself shifting under the man's bright, cold eyes.

Green had never so much as smiled at Stewart, and it didn't look like he was going to start today.

Hamish, the other trainee, sat beside Green at the table. He was looking down, not meeting Stewart's eye. That was unusual enough, but besides that his face was oddly petulant, something Stewart couldn't remember seeing before.

Opposite them sat a bald man, with his back to Stewart. Before Stewart had a chance to get a good look at him, Sudgeon had rolled his seat back to the table. He motioned Stewart towards the table.

"No, no, please, come in and take a seat! Don't stand back there!" Sudgeon spoke, before turning to the table. "Hamish, my boy, that will be all. You may return to your duties."

Hamish looked at Sudgeon for a second, like he was thinking about arguing – arguing! – but then stood up and marched towards the door. He didn't so much as glance at Stewart on his way past, instead just stomping out, eyes fixed on the ground.

A flash of schadenfreude warmed Stewart's mind. Hamish in the doghouse. Happy days. Although that was pretty unusual. And maybe, just maybe, whatever happened to him was about to happen to Stewart...

But before Stewart's imagination could really get going, the bald man stood and turned.

"Hello again, my brother."

Chapter 3

Sebastian Dakar wore the same gentle smile Stewart remembered. His hand moved to his heart as he spoke, and he gave a small inclination of the head with eyes closed.

Stewart looked back, no words coming out. He hadn't seen Dakar for months. After the events at Hanover House, where they had been investigating a suspicious death, he wasn't sure he was ever going to see him again. He found himself smiling back at Dakar as he eventually put out a hand and his brain connected with his mouth.

"Hello, Dakar."

They shook hands before Dakar sat back down at the table, Sudgeon glancing between them.

"I see you remember each other. Stewart, the firm is hiring Mr Dakar to conduct another investigation, across three days. He has requested, aha, that you personally be the firm's representative, as opposed to anyone else." Sudgeon coughed delicately.

Stewart stared mutely at him. He hated that 'aha' that Sudgeon made, pulling out the second 'a', as he pretended to deliberate over his next words but really just wanted you to wait for what was coming.

"Richard and I ..." Sudgeon shot a look over at Green, but the man's eyes remained fixed on Stewart, "... thought we should consult with you about whether you wished to accept this assignment. It would take approximately three days."

Stewart waited for more, but Sudgeon seemed to have finished. "Right. Yes. What's the investigation about?"

"I'm not at liberty to divulge that information until you let us know your thoughts."

Stewart nodded at this legal equivalent of 'I'm not telling'. He wouldn't have expected anything else from Sudgeon.

"And, aha, we would probably have to re-assign the Raker file. Perhaps give it to Michelle."

Stewart's eyes widened, and he breathed in sharply. "But that's my file, Mr Sudgeon. It was given to me—"

Sudgeon cut him off with one upraised hand. "I know it's the first time you've been trusted with your own contract, with only the final sign-off required from your superiors. And Mark tells me you've been doing good work on it. But no-one in the firm is irreplaceable."

"Especially not a trainee." Green's tone was laconic, his eyes looking unblinkingly at Stewart.

Stewart swallowed hard, his cheeks beginning to burn at the rebuke. But even that was overruled by the thought of losing the Raker file. He remembered lonely, long, late nights working on it on his own, his pride at being given his own file and of the praise he was getting for the quality of work and the hours he was billing. He'd felt, for the first time, like he felt a proper lawyer ought to feel. To lose that …

Stewart looked at Dakar. New images flooded his mind, of yoga lessons at a place in Morningside, a police file on a man's death, and the rooms of Hanover House, where Stewart watched Dakar as he figured out how a man had died. He remembered people shouting and screaming at Dakar, the police, a poisoning. Mysteries and obstacles, but triumph in the end.

And then nothing. Nothing from Dakar for months – four months. Radio silence, almost like he'd done something wrong. Instead, back to SSM, slowly building up his reputation for good, hard work, for reliability, being the safe pair of hands. Nothing fancy, everything solid, preparing the ground to fight for his place at the lawyer table at the end of the year, with weapons like the Raker file.

And now Dakar was back, wanting him to help.

Stewart looked back at Sudgeon, into the man's eyes. There was movement there, a constant movement. He could practically see the machinery of Sudgeon's mind, shifting, analysing, reacting, and always, always, calculating. Constantly predicting the future in order to put himself in the best possible position, an ability honed through life as a lawyer, a shark in human clothing. And he'd surrounded himself with people like Green, and patronised people like Hamish.

Stewart looked over at Dakar, seeking his eyes. Nothing seemed to be moving below the surface there, no complex plots or deep thoughts. No analysis, no readiness. But there was a depth there that was hard to penetrate.

He could hear his own thoughts as he looked between them all, as if someone were whispering them in his ear. Sudgeon and SSM represented his future. The Hanover House investigation had been an anachronism, albeit an exciting one. But if he wanted to get on in life he had to be like Hamish. That was the key. Working with Dakar again would be a waste of his time, valuable time that he could bill to clients. It wouldn't look good. This was a test, and Sudgeon was making sure he was truly a safe bet.

He had to be like Hamish. So he could end up like Sudgeon. Or maybe even like Green.

There was a seat beside Dakar at the table. There was also the seat that Hamish had vacated, on Sudgeon's side. Stewart looked at Sudgeon, then at Green. Then at the spot Hamish had vacated. Very slowly, Stewart walked over and lowered himself into the seat beside Dakar.

Sudgeon's smile didn't leave his face, but it did twist slightly, becoming uglier.

"Capital." Sudgeon spoke coldly. He got up and walked over to the door, closing it firmly before returning to his seat. "One of the partners at the firm would like Mr Dakar to investigate a crime for him. A murder."

Sudgeon paused after the last word, saying it distastefully. Stewart looked at him incredulously.

"A murder?" His fingers gripped the edge of the oaken table.

"Indeed."

"Aren't the ... Well, you know, the police ...?"

Sudgeon shook his head. "It appears they have concluded their investigation, without making an arrest. They are apparently perplexed. Mr Dakar is going to re-investigate."

Sudgeon held up a newspaper, a broadsheet. It was open at an inside page, a headline screaming 'Police still baffled over murder of dentist'.

Sudgeon placed the newspaper down. "Rather dreadfully, the victim is actually Tom Mannings' son, Daniel. The poor man found the body himself. Awful. Simply awful."

Stewart nodded, trying to keep his face professional. Tom Mannings. Also a partner at the firm. Stewart hadn't had much interaction with him, what with Stewart being a trainee and him being a partner. Tax specialist, from what Stewart remembered. Bit of an oddball. No, wait, plenty of money. Eccentric, then.

"Tom had a heart attack when he found his son dead. Almost died as well, poor chap. Although thankfully he survived. Very fortunate. In some ways, of course. Perhaps better if, well ... Well, no. No. Of course not. But dreadfully hard to put one's own son into the ground, as it were."

Stewart watched Sudgeon speak, but for the life of him couldn't work out if the man was being sincere.

"Tom is in hospital. Private, naturally. The Squareglass, just past Morningside. Recuperating."

Stewart sat back. Now he thought about it, he did remember something about a murder, about a week back or so, in one of the nicer areas of Edinburgh. Somewhere on the outskirts.

"Mr Dakar has already agreed to undertake the investigation. Turning to the brass tacks for you. Stewart, my boy, if I may, your report last time was … how can I phrase this? Not quite satisfactory?"

Green leaned forward across the table, head seeming almost to wave on the end of his slim neck as it struck out towards him. Stewart had never seen him so close before. He had little pitted grooves scarring the skin on his face. His American tone was like an iron fist in a velvet glove, softly spoken but hitting like a wrecking ball.

"Scott. Take notes, okay? Proper notes. And this time, bill your time, every six minutes. Include a breakdown in your report. I know you're only a trainee, but try and act professionally. You get me?"

Stewart felt transfixed by the eyes a few inches from him, a hot flush breaking out at the word 'professionally'.

He swallowed, then nodded. "Yes," he managed, but it was barely a whisper.

Green stared at him a moment longer, then retracted his head back across the table.

"Yes …" Sudgeon said, elongating the word into three syllables. "Well, excellent. I have no doubt your product will be superior this time. As I said, Mark has remarked, aha, on the improvement of your work and, indeed, attitude, of late."

Sudgeon smiled. Stewart felt approximately two inches tall. He looked down at his notes, cheeks still burning from Green's remark.

Bollocks to them. Bollocks. To. Them. He felt like screaming the words. If they wanted a professional report, they'd get one. Come hell or high water. Fully itemised in terms of billing, and with every last note in there.

Oh aye. He would stuff it down their throats and then some.

Stewart looked back up, the fire in his eyes now. "I'll get you your report, Mr Green. Fully detailed."

Green leaned forward again, bright eyes glittering. "Good. After all, you only have to trail around after Mr Dakar here and take notes. It shouldn't be too hard."

Stewart gripped the edge of the table hard, his fingers turning white.

"I found Stewart's aid very useful at Hanover House." Dakar spoke into the silence between Stewart and Mr Green.

Green's eyes flicked over to Dakar. "I've no doubt you did, Mr Dakar." Green spoke in a scathing tone, a heavy emphasis on 'you'. Dakar smiled back at him, demeanour unchanged by Green's look.

Stewart glared at Green. He wouldn't just trail around behind Dakar like last time. Hell no. He could be a detective too.

Sudgeon put up a hand, his eyes casting back and forth between Dakar and Green. "Yes. Well. Gentlemen, no firm likes to be linked to this kind of incident. Obviously the victim was a partner's son, that is one link. But Tom was present that night and therefore, absurdly, may be a suspect. Obviously, if there is any indication an employee was involved in, aha, any kind of criminal activity, we should appreciate knowing before the police. To take any necessary action."

Pause. "We shall let you know if we suspect Mr Mannings murdered his own son." Dakar looked at Sudgeon now. Green was still fixated on him, but Dakar didn't seem to notice.

Sudgeon coughed delicately. "Tom Mannings wasn't the only firm employee there that evening."

Chapter 4

Stewart's eyes widened. A partner's son murdered, while both the partner and other employees were there. Scandal indeed.

"What are the names of the other employees who were there?" Dakar spoke gently, and Stewart grabbed up his pen and notepad, looking grimly for a second at Green. The man ignored him.

Sudgeon put up his hands hurriedly, as if Dakar had asked something outrageous.

"Only one, my good man, only one. Aha. Charles Robbin, one of our junior associates in the tax department. A bright young man. He'll certainly be a mover and shaker one day. Unless, of course, he's been involved in any, aha, unpleasantness."

Stewart wrote down Charles's name, looking down so that his sour expression wouldn't be seen by others. Stewart had had to work with Charles a few times, experiences he remembered for their unpleasantness rather than inspiration. He certainly wouldn't mind seeing Charles quake a bit under interrogation.

Not that 'fear' was the word that sprang to his mind with Dakar's questioning, though. He'd come across sheep that were scarier.

"Tom Mannings wants to see you as soon as possible. As you are here, though, well, it may be more convenient to speak to Charles first. I have made him aware that you will be calling on him at some point, and he has instructions to answer all your questions."

Pause. "We shall speak with Charles first."

Stewart wrote his notes, savouring the pause. He'd forgotten about it, Dakar's odd method of pausing before he spoke, no matter how simple what he was going to say. It was really handy for catching up with taking notes.

"Very good. I'll have a receptionist get a taxi for you in, let us say, half an hour, outside the front of the building. But take as long as you need with Charles. The taxi will wait."

Pause. "Are the police aware of this concurrent investigation?"

"Mmmmmm, yes and no." Sudgeon smiled at his own words. "Tom has requested the police file, although they are resisting handing it over. I understand he is phoning some acquaintants higher up the chain, as it were. But so far as I know, they are unaware that SSM is contracting a private investigation, and certainly not who is doing the investigating."

Sudgeon looked over at Green, and nodded once, before he turned to Dakar.

"Now, in terms of payment, will the previous contractual terms suffice?" Sudgeon sounded happier now, talking contractual terms, his tone smooth.

Pause, smile. "They will, thank you."

Green handed over a stapled set of papers to Sudgeon, who slid them over the table to Dakar. Dakar picked them up and read through them, carefully turning them over.

Sudgeon turned to Stewart. "Stewart, I trust you remember the office party is taking place tomorrow evening."

"Yes, Mr Sudgeon."

"Such opportunities to meet and discourse with the leading partners of the firm are extremely rare, and therefore extremely valuable. Particularly to a young man such as yourself."

"I'll be there, Mr Sudgeon."

Sudgeon tilted his head down, looking over his glasses at Stewart. "See that you are. The firm, while robustly healthy in financial terms, is, as you know, growing at a sufficient rate only to take on two of the four trainees this year. There will be some who are regrettably not offered employment. I should not like you to be among them."

Stewart's smile became grim.

"I believe you could be an excellent addition to this firm, Stewart. With the right training and guidance." Sudgeon put a heavy emphasis on the word 'I'. Stewart snuck a look over at Green. The man was looking back at him, slow, languid blinks.

"I understand, Mr Sudgeon."

In the silence, Dakar handed the signed papers back over to Sudgeon.

"Excellent. Stewart, you will work exclusively on this delicate matter until it is fully resolved. In the meantime, Michelle will take over your work on the Raker file. Please transfer it to her."

Stewart nodded, a hard lump appearing in his throat for a second. He'd forgotten about the Raker file, and a sudden feeling of guilt washed over him, like he'd forgotten a good friend's birthday. But the choice was made now. And in any case, better Michelle than Hamish.

"I will, Mr Sudgeon."

"Very well. And one last thing. No-one else is to know what you are working on. We would rather keep the firm's involvement in all of this unpleasantness, both regarding employees there on the night and that the firm is conducting an investigation, out of the rumour mill. Do you understand, Stewart?"

Sudgeon tilted his head forward once again, looking at Stewart over his glasses, while Green also leaned forward. Stewart found himself nodding quickly.

Sudgeon's face tilted back to its normal angle, his smile re-establishing itself. "Capital! Well, gentlemen, if everything is as far as we can advance it, for the time being, of course, then perhaps we can adjourn?"

Dakar smiled, nodded and stood up. Green, however, leaned further across the table towards Stewart, neck sliding out. Stewart's chair creaked ever so slightly as he leaned back.

"We want daily reports this time, Scott. In the evening. Starting tonight. Email them to me. I'll pass them on to Mr Sudgeon." He paused. "If merited."

Green took out a thin case from an inside pocket, slender fingers grasping it strongly. He flipped it open, and slid out a business card with his thumb, all without breaking eye-contact.

Stewart looked down, and took the card hesitantly. It felt deep and rich and luxurious as he held it between his fingers.

"And before you do anything, sort out your files first, for … Michelle, was it?"

Green swivelled to Sudgeon, who nodded. Green swivelled back.

"Get them to her first, before you begin to work on this. You get me?"

Stewart swallowed loudly. "Yes."

Green gazed at him a second longer, then curtly nodded and retracted himself.

"Thank you, my brothers. I wish you both a happy day." Sudgeon responded to Dakar's words with a lopsided smile, although Green's expression looked like Dakar had just suggested they all forget this work thing and go and have tea and cake somewhere.

Dakar put his hand on heart, bowed, and then headed for the door. Stewart got up behind him, a bit less smoothly, and nodded to both men in as respectful a manner as he could. Their expressions of bemusement and displeasure did not change.

Chapter 5

Stewart looked Dakar up and down. Incredibly, the man was wearing pretty much the same clothes as the last time Stewart had seen him. The light-coloured shirt – a salmon colour this time – the same grey checked trousers and brown loafers encasing his feet. His cream jacket hung over one arm. Eye-catching, although perhaps not in the best way.

"So, eh ... How's it going?"

Pause, smile. "I am well, my brother. And you?"

"Eh, aye. Doing well. Well, well enough. If you know what I mean. And you, have you been up to anything exciting since Hanover House?"

Dakar shook his head. "Certainly nothing that has been reported in any newspapers. I continue to speak to those who come, whilst trying to defeat my own ego."

Stewart nodded. Right. The Dakar code. His flatmate Beth had warned him about this the first time he'd worked with Dakar, about how Dakar spoke in an odd way. She'd even offered to translate.

"So the lessons you give out in Morningside are going well, are they?"

Pause. "Very well, thank you, my brother."

"And, eh, the books? Still selling, are they?" Stewart had actually borrowed the first of the three books Dakar had written from Beth, determined to read it after having seen Dakar in action. He'd lasted about twenty pages before his willpower collapsed.

Pause. "So far as I am aware."

"Okay. Great. That's great." Stewart looked around quickly. They were standing in the partners' corridor, but no-one else was there. He lowered his voice anyway. "So, well, a murder! Eh, we'll away and talk to Charles then?"

Pause. "I had understood that the first thing to do was to hand the Raker file to Michelle?"

Stewart froze as Green's bright eyes arose in his mind.

"Christ. Yes. Thanks for reminding me. Eh, do you mind waiting here? It'll only be two minutes."

Pause. "By all means, my brother."

Stewart ran back to the lift, taking it down to his office. He burst in to the surprised looks of Jennifer and Michelle.

"Is everything okay?" Michelle asked.

"What? Oh, aye. Yes. I'm not for the high jump." He hesitated as he remembered Green's face. "At least not yet."

Stewart reached his desk and gathered the various documents that made up the Raker file. He pulled together his drafts, automatically slowing his frantic pace as he gathered each one, making sure they were chronologically ordered.

"So what was it about?" Jennifer asked.

Stewart looked up from his search. "Oh, eh, just a new assignment I've got to do. And, well, I'll be away from the office for a couple of days, so the Raker file is going to Michelle. I'm just pulling it all together now."

Michelle raised her eyebrows. "You have to give up the Raker file?"

"Yeah. I know. It's a real pain. But it can't be helped."

"Stewart, that's your own file. Your first one. I don't even have one yet, and they're making you give yours up? How can they make you do that?" Jennifer sounded outraged on his behalf.

He opened his mouth, then closed it again. "I can't actually say. Sudgeon told me not to. Sorry." Michelle and Jennifer both looked mystified by this. "I'd tell you if I could. You know I would. But I can't."

He finished pulling the rest of the documents, and slid them into a folder, taking it across to Michelle's desk.

"So the client is due to call on Friday for an update. Everything's going to plan, and it looks like we should have a contract signed on schedule. The proposed contract is still with the buyers, but my negotiating partner over there has indicated that they haven't seen any serious issues as of yet. Tell them I'll give them a ring the minute I'm back."

"Okay. Thanks. Why aren't you more bothered by this? You've been working your arse off, and now you're just giving it up?"

Stewart put the folder down on Michelle's desk, having located an empty spot, keeping one hand on top of it for a few seconds as he looked at it.

"I'm not happy about it. But, you know, sometimes …" He shrugged. "Something else has come up."

"And you want to do whatever it is more than work on the Raker file?"

Stewart looked at her for a second. "Yes. I suppose I do."

"Must be something good."

Stewart nodded, then tapped the file. "If you have any issues, any questions, just give me a shout. I'll have my phone on all the time."

Michelle just nodded.

He turned to grab his long, black coat. He had bought it before he started work because he felt it looked very impressive. The designers hadn't reckoned with the Scottish weather though, where the swirling wind spirited rain past umbrellas and soaked coats. A Macintosh would have been far more appropriate. But the black coat was part of the lawyer uniform.

"Okay. Well, see you later. Not sure when I'll be back."

"Will you be at the party tomorrow night?" Jennifer asked.

"Yes, definitely. Sudgeon reminded me how important it was to be there." Both Jennifer and Michelle's faces immediately creased in pain, as if they had both contracted a simultaneous headache. "What?"

Both of them shook their heads. Stewart eyed them both, but there was no break in their expressions. "Did we ever find out why they moved it to a Thursday night?"

A silence, broken after a second by Michelle. "Yeah. An associate told me that last year, when it was on the Friday night, some of the staff, partners included, got a bit too wild. Bit of a mess afterwards. So they moved it to the Thursday night to try and rein it in."

"Well, it'll be a good night anyway." Beth flashed into his mind. "And I'll definitely be there. I'm going to head out afterward with my flatmate to catch a gig as well."

"Who's playing?" Michelle asked.

"A singer-songwriter. In the Royal Oak. You wouldn't have heard of them."

Stewart had only hesitated for a split second, but it was long enough. Michelle smiled in triumph. "You don't know, do you?"

Stewart opened his mouth, then closed it again. He shrugged in defeat. "My flatmate organised it. It's more her type of music than mine. Listen, anyway, I'll see you both tomorrow night. Have a good one."

Stewart looked towards the Raker file one more time, then took a deep breath and turned away. He went back to the lift, and headed back to Dakar, passing from a world of dull shades to one rich in colour and life.

Stewart found Dakar where he'd left him, sitting upright in one of the comfortable chairs in the partners' corridor. The man stood up as Stewart arrived.

"Right then. Time to get started, I suppose?"

Pause. "Indeed, my brother."

Stewart checked around them in the corridor. "Before we speak to Charles, eh, do you know what actually happened on the night? Of the murder?" He kept his voice low on the last word. "Just so I know roughly what we're talking about."

Pause. "I only know what Tom Mannings has said to the partners. There was a party at his son Daniel's home. Everyone was outside watching some fireworks when Daniel appeared at an upstairs window, banging on it. He disappeared, and there was a crash. Everyone rushed to the room. They found signs of a struggle, but no body. An hour or so later, Tom Mannings's found Daniel's body in the cellar. He'd been stabbed numerous times."

"Right. Wow. Okay. But, eh, how come the police haven't arrested anyone? There must have been plenty of people there."

Pause. "There were. But from what I understand, it appears none of them could have done it."

Chapter 6

Charles Robbin looked at them with his goblin smile, a weird, creepy thing that seemed to spread over his face and distend his mouth in a strange way, as if he was constantly sucking on something sour. Stewart had quivered under that smile before, but now, now the tables were turned.

"How are you today, my brother?"

After introductions, these had been Dakar's opening words. The goblin smile had twisted even further, the sourness taste getting stronger.

"I'm fine, thank you."

Stewart checked the time and date, and made a note of it. First interview, the case officially begun, at twenty-five past eleven. Charles glanced over at Stewart, armed with his pen and notepad, looking down his nose at him. A small part of Stewart was already hoping that Charles did it.

"On Saturday 30 September, eleven days ago, you were at Daniel Mannings' house?"

"Yes, that's right. It was Daniel's birthday, and his wife was throwing a surprise birthday party."

Pause. "You knew Daniel well?"

The smile soured further. "Not really. We met at a party a year ago. Since then, we've had the occasional drink together."

Pause. "How occasional?"

"Somewhere between once every couple of weeks and once a month, I'd say."

Pause. "Did you invite Daniel to these occasions?"

Charles shook his head. "Vice versa."

Pause. "You didn't enjoy them?"

Charles's eyes widened. His goblin smile became large, like a puppet master was pulling the muscles in his cheeks to make his lips move upwards. "Yes, yes I did. Of course I did. Daniel was good fun." A pause. "Once he got going."

Dakar had a long pause now, but Charles didn't elaborate. "Who invited you to come?"

"Daniel. My fiancée and I ... She's a lawyer as well, works over in Q&T." Charles vaguely waved at the wall behind him, although he didn't turn around. There was a photograph of a woman there, with Charles, on a beach somewhere, mountains cascading down to the sea in a tide of green trees visible in the background. It and a calendar of Scottish scenery were the only decoration on the otherwise white wall, and nothing except for work papers and Charles's mobile phone adorned the desk.

"Family law, mainly, as most women do. Ghastly stuff. Well, anyway, we had planned a night at the theatre. But it's not every day that you get the chance to go to your partner's house and have dinner with their family. These opportunities have to be taken, you know."

Pause. "Your fiancée came as well?"

"No, no. No, I needed to be undistracted in such an important setting. I couldn't play nursemaid to someone who didn't know anyone else there."

Pause. "And did you know Daniel's wife?"

"Only by name."

Pause. "Who was there that night?"

"Daniel, of course. His wife, Sarah-Anne. And Tom, naturally, Tom Mannings. He's my partner. That is, he's the partner I work for. We specialise in tax, as Stewart knows. And Daniel's stepdaughter Sandra. She had a couple of her friends with her, Jane and Russell. Russell is Sandra's boyfriend. Jane was her flatmate, I think, or something along those lines."

Pause, nod. "Anyone else?"

"Well, there was some woman called Martina who was there. Fine-looking creature, although getting a bit long in the tooth. Her son was also there, can't recall his name. He looked, how can I say ... a bit unkempt. Rough and ready all round. Like he'd just got over being a teenager."

Charles stopped, waiting for his audience to smile. Stewart cast his eyes to his notes, until the moment passed.

"The only other people there were an older couple Daniel worked with. Daniel was half of a dental partnership. Eleanor, the woman, was his business partner. She's incredibly plain, in looks and in conversation. Her husband is a balding, plain little fellow. And more than a little rotund. He's the secretary, of all things, of the dental partnership."

Stewart looked at Dakar, but his expression hadn't changed. "What time did you arrive?"

"About half past seven. I was almost last. The dentist couple turned up about fifteen minutes later. I met everyone. A bit of desultory small talk later, it was time for dinner so we all trooped through to the dining room."

Pause. "Did anything happen during the dinner?"

"Nothing special. I was sitting between the dentist secretary, whose name escapes me, and Eleanor. David, perhaps? Something beginning with 'D' anyway. We spoke about inconsequential things, like the weather. We didn't have much in common."

Pause. "Where was Daniel sitting?"

"Up at the head of the table, of course. It was his home. He was chatting to Tom, mainly. They were sitting next to each other."

Pause. "What happened after dinner?"

"Well, I ... Look, something a bit embarrassing. Something I'd rather the rest of the firm didn't know."

Pause. "Mr Sudgeon has requested that Stewart give him and Mr Green reports."

Stewart's heart began to beat faster at the mention of his name. But Charles just waved a hand. "Yes, yes, I understand that. They already know, of course. No, I mean, I'd rather it didn't get out amongst the ... Well, you know. The trainees. Paralegals. That sort."

His eyes flicked over to Stewart and away again. Charles' last words were laced with distaste, as if he had popped into the legal world as a fully formed lawyer, never having had to go through the disagreeable embryonic trainee stage.

"I won't tell anyone, Charles."

Charles' eyes lingered on Stewart for a second or two, but eventually he nodded.

"Well, during dinner I had some wine. Perhaps too much. And I was animated, you know, what with being with my partner's family. Anyway, I ended up discussing things with Russell. He's rather liberal, you understand. No life experience. Anyway, because he was floundering on the technical points of our discussion, as these people always do, he decided to claim he could drink more than me."

Charles began playing with a pen, holding it between fingers of either hand. He focused on it as he spoke.

"Well, after that much wine, I accepted. More fool me. We went to the dining room and began drinking beer. I had brought some imported stuff, a champagne bottle of Belgian beer. It's strong stuff. And we began doing shots of vodka. The girls tried to stop us, but, well, a long story short, both Russell and I had to be carried upstairs to the spare bedroom."

Pause. "And so you did not see the fireworks?"

Charles shook his head. "Didn't see them, didn't hear them. In fact, my memory of the evening goes from getting drunker and drunker with that fool Russell to waking up in the morning with a police constable on the door."

Pause. "And then?"

Charles looked up from the pen to Dakar. "Then? Then I was interrogated, like a common criminal, by some idiot of a policeman. They even brought in a police casualty surgeon to take some of my blood, after threatening me with a warrant. It's outrageous, really."

Pause. "Do you recall the police officer's name?"

"Thomas. A Detective Inspector, so he claims."

Stewart was halfway through writing the name when his stomach sank. He looked up at Dakar, who was already looking back at him.

"What?" Charles interrupted their shared glance.

Pause. "We know that officer."

"I see. Well, no doubt you know exactly what I mean."

Dakar paused for a few seconds longer than usual. "You were invited by Daniel personally?"

"That's right."

Pause. "I had understood it was a surprise birthday party?"

"Yes, that's right. I suppose it was one of those surprise birthday parties which aren't really a surprise."

Pause. "Do you have the message from Daniel inviting you?"

"Yes, of course." Charles reached for the phone lying in front of him on the table then stopped, his hand hovering over it. "No. No, I don't." He took his hand back, holding it up awkwardly in front of him. After a few seconds he held up his index finger. "I deleted it. Yes. Sorry."

A long pause. "Why did you do that?"

"Why? Is that what you asked?" Dakar nodded once. "Well, I, it's something I do regularly. Space. For apps. On the phone, you know." Charles was turning red.

Dakar waited for a long time, gazing at Charles gently. Charles, his eyes darting back and forth between Dakar and Stewart in the silence, suddenly gestured towards some paperwork on his desk.

"Look, I have quite a lot to do, so if that's all, well, duty calls and all that. So perhaps we can wrap this up?"

Another pause from Dakar. He looked down at Charles' phone, then back up at him. The lightest bead of sweat had appeared on Charles' brow, even though the room wasn't warm.

"I have nothing further. For now." Dakar spoke in his normal gentle tone, but somehow the last two words sounded ominous.

Chapter 7

Stewart stood outside the Squareglass Hospital, beside Dakar. It was a beautiful October day, and the morning had given way to a splendid afternoon. The sun shone in a blue sky, making vibrant the autumn yellows and browns of the trees and picking out individual blades of short, well-trimmed green grass in the tree-lined avenue on which they stood.

But only a foreigner would be fooled by such weather in Scotland. In spite of the sunshine, Stewart had to turn his coat collar up against the chill invading his bones.

Squareglass Hospital looked magnificent in the light, like an old Victorian home. It was built from grey shaped stone, sitting amidst well-manicured gardens of grass and trees. A small wall, made from the same grey shaped stone, ran around the gardens. Aside from the sign on the wall, you wouldn't have known it was a hospital at all.

Stewart looked around. The area epitomised what he thought of as Edinburgh proper. Grand old buildings faced each other across wide, tree-lined streets, broken only by a multitude of green spaces. It had been like this for a long time, the upgrades and maintenance only accentuating the riches and opulence the area represented. Had always represented. If you threw in the castle and Princes Street Gardens, maybe the Scott monument, this basically was Edinburgh. Or at least the one on the postcards.

They started towards the building, Stewart carrying his work bag in one hand as he walked.

He shifted his grip on it, trying to find a comfortable one. It was actually more of a satchel, an over-one-shoulder job. His mum had given it to him, as a present for landing a traineeship. And it was a quality bag, no doubt. Lovely leather. Kept stuff dry on the dreichest of dreich Scottish days, when no matter what you did the rain somehow got in.

But in spite of these qualities, he'd got a ripping from his mates as soon as he'd put his bag on. Digs about wearing a glorified handbag, and being labelled that all-purpose insult, gay. So he'd taken to not wearing it at all, but rather carrying it briefcase style, looping the wrap around his hand.

But he was with Dakar now. Stewart took a quick look at him, then put the satchel shoulder strap over one shoulder and let the bag fall to his side, the way it was meant to be worn. He looked again at his companion. Dakar didn't even seem to notice, much less comment.

They strolled in through the open doors, Stewart adopting Dakar's slow pace. He stopped as he saw the corridor. It was all black and white, little tiles on the floor of the alternating shades, then white paint on the walls interrupted occasionally by black and white photographs, like something out of *Alice in Wonderland*.

Dakar had gone straight to the reception, a hole in the wall to the left just beside the entrance. A young woman, no more than 20, sat there, looking sprightly in a white coat and suit trousers. Dark hair spilled in curls down over her shoulders. She smiled at them, although her expression became amused for a split-second as she looked over at Stewart.

Bloody satchel.

"Good afternoon, and welcome to Squareglass Hospital. How can I help you?"

Stewart, whose face had contorted into a frown when he first saw the corridor, kept on frowning. He always did when people with Scottish accents sounded genuinely happy. It wasn't natural.

"Hello, my sister. My name is Sebastian Dakar. I believe Tom Mannings is expecting me."

"Of course. Just give me one moment ..." She picked up a phone and consulted a list of numbers. Stewart looked around at the corridor again, studying it in an attempt to explain its existence.

"I've got a Mr Dakar here, to see Mr Mannings?" ... "Yes, that's right." ... "Okay, no problem. Yes. Okay."

She turned back to them, the genuine smile in place. "Would you care to take a seat in the waiting area? Sister Agnes will be with you in a moment." She indicated the door next to the reception.

Pause. "Thank you, my sister."

"Oh, I'm not a sister, I'm just the receptionist."

Pause, nod. Dakar turned and walked through the door the woman had indicated, Stewart slowly following him. They entered a deserted room with a number of couches and comfy chairs, and reading material scattered around various grand tables. Large windows allowed those waiting to see out into the gardens.

They had barely sat down when the door opened again and a grey-haired woman walked in, dressed in the blue top and trousers of a medic. She was carrying a clipboard.

"Mr Dakar?"

Pause. "My sister?"

"I'm the sister, yes. Mr Mannings is expecting you." She frowned at Stewart. "Will your associate be joining you?"

The woman's tone was clipped as she looked at Stewart, as if he was some untidy loose end, a little bit of soon-to-be-eliminated chaos in an organised world. Stewart did his best not to look shifty.

Pause. "He shall, yes. His name is Stewart Scott."

"Mr Mannings was quite clear he was expecting a Mr Dakar, and only a Mr Dakar. I'm afraid your associate will have to remain here."

Stewart looked at the sister, who looked back at him. Her expression didn't show an ounce of sympathy, much less fear.

Pause. "My sister, I would prefer if Mr Scott joined me. My preference is sufficiently strong that I will not see Mr Mannings without him."

The sister frowned as she looked over at Dakar, her fingers gripping the clipboard tighter.

"His instructions were very clear."

Pause. "I have no doubt, my sister. And I have no doubt that you have ignored his instructions in the past when you think best. For what it is worth, I do not think he will care that Mr Scott here accompanies me. Certainly, I imagine he will be more irritated if Mr Scott, and therefore I, are turned away."

The sister looked back over at Stewart for a second, the nodded reluctantly. "Mr Scott. Yes. Then if you'd both care to follow me, I'll take you to Mr Mannings' room."

They followed her in silence back out into the black and white corridor, to a spiral staircase at the end. They climbed up, coming into a corridor that was, while geometrically identical to the one they had left, different in all other respects. The floor was polished wood, overlaid with oriental rugs down its length. The walls had been painted a rich green, portraits and paintings placed generously along them. Stewart let out a deep breath as they walked along.

They followed the woman to one of the doors. She knocked sharply, two taps, before opening the door immediately.

The room was smaller than Stewart expected when he first heard the words 'private hospital'. It was old-fashioned, from the screens that hung down over the window to the iron bedstead. The bedsheets had a rough woollen shawl on top of them. A wooden table with a couple of chairs beside the window completed the furniture, while the window provided a view over the garden, trees and wall into Morningside.

It reminded Stewart of the rooms you saw in films about the first and second world wars, where pretty nurses tended wounded soldiers. The only recognition of the 21st century was a flat screen TV, stationed high on the wall opposite the single bed.

Tom Mannings lay on the bed, hooked up to a monitor. As soon as they came in, he began speaking in an aggrieved tone.

"Sister! What's this? I just … Read … If I need … MRI … I go to … Royal Infirmary."

The sister stood by the bed, looking disinterested.

"That's right, Mr Mannings."

"But that's .. NHS. I pay … For private!"

"We don't have an MRI machine, Mr Mannings. It's too big for the hospital. So we send you off to get an MRI, then bring you back."

"Bloody disgrace!"

"It's standard practice for this hospital, and most UK private hospitals. And it's in your contract, Mr Mannings. The NHS does a number of our operations." The sister's tone was firm, a warning note underlying her words. "Now here's Mr Dakar and Mr Scott."

The sister turned to leave, Mannings muttering under his breath until she had disappeared and the door was closed.

He took up the entire single bed, his body fallen across it. He still had the wild hair Stewart remembered from the firm, and his bushy, untamed beard, which had started to grey, now crept down onto his chest, stretching down to meet the blanket. Even his eyebrows sprouted out, striking away from his face like so many intrepid explorers. His red nose was large and bulbous, combining with the hair to make him look like a drunken, angry Santa Claus who brought bones rather than presents.

"Who are you?" Mannings said abruptly, and Stewart realised with horror Mannings was staring at him. "I wanted … Dakar here … Only."

"Eh—"

"This is Stewart Scott. He is a second year trainee at your firm, my brother."

The Price to Pay

Mannings glared at Dakar, then back at Stewart. "Ha ... Right. Yes. Firm representative. Piece of ... bloody nonsense." He glared at Stewart for a second longer. Stewart looked down at the floor, his cheeks on fire, as if being forgotten by someone was a sin.

"Now listen," Mannings divided his glare between them both as he lay incapacitated in the bed. His tone was severe, like a rock face stripped by the wind. "Both of you. Sensitive matter ... I don't want ... any rumours ... Not friends ... Not family ... Not wives, girlfriends. No-one ... at the firm ... Except Charles. He knows ... already. Yes?"

Stewart nodded. He'd forgotten the way that Mannings spoke, as if he ran out of breath after a word or two. It gave him a brusque, halting manner. He slid his notepad out.

"Mr Sudgeon and Mr Green have requested that Stewart provide them with reports detailing our progress."

Mannings grunted angrily, and one of the monitors beeped more urgently. "Stuff and nonsense! They want ... Rumours ... Gossip. No reports ... to them. Reports ... to me ... I'm the one ... paying. Yes?"

Stewart looked at Dakar, but the man just looked back at him. Stewart turned back into the intense glare of Mannings.

"Right. Eh, yes, Mr Mannings. No problem."

Mannings grunted again, in acceptance. Stewart sat with a horrible sinking feeling in his stomach as he realised he'd agreed to both send and not send reports to Sudgeon and Green.

Bollocks.

"Good. The issue ... My son. He's dead. Murdered .. Stabbed. By some bastard. Want you ... to find out who. "

Stewart was ripped back to the present by Mannings' voice, a raw mixture of anger and pain. He picked up his pen and wrote down the time at the top of his blank sheet, his pen poised.

"I'm full of sorrow for your loss, my brother."

"Don't be ... sad! Just ... find the bugger ... Killed him. Killed ... my son. Ask me ... whatever you want. Just find ... murderer." His eyes were glinting in the light of the room, watering as he focused on Dakar.

Pause. "Who else was there?"

"Sandra, Sarah-Anne's daughter. Daniel's stepdaughter. She came next ... With a friend ... Girl ... Good-looking ... young thing. And her boyfriend. Then Martina Donaldson ... Fine-looking ... filly. Childhood friend, Daniel ... Brought her son. Young thug. Then Charles came."

Mannings paused, and took a drink of water. Some of it spilled into his beard, and stayed there, caught up on the greying hairs like flies in a spider's web. "Bright young spark ... Charles. And last ... the dentists. Well ... female dentist, Eleanor. Her husband, Dennis ... Secretary." Mannings snorted at this last word.

Pause, nod from Dakar. "It was Daniel's birthday?"

"Yes. A surprise. That's why ... celebration."

Pause. "And what did you and Daniel discuss at dinner?"

"Work ... mainly. Awful state ... Tory party ... at the moment. Get power ... Still ... bloody useless."

Pause. "And did you notice anything unusual at the dinner?"

"Not really. Well, one thing. The young girl ... friend of Sandra ... She was looking ... Looking at Daniel ... Very feisty. Sarah-Anne ... One foot away. Looked ... annoyed. That was all."

Pause. "What happened after dinner?"

"I went ... to prepare fireworks." Mannings's eyes lit up as he said the last word. "Had some ... big ones ... Big bangs."

Pause. "Do you always have fireworks when you have a party?"

"No ... No. But special occasion ... So ... fireworks."

Pause. "And everyone came out to watch the fireworks?"

Mannings nodded, then stopped, his eyes screwing up as he frowned in recollection. "No ... Almost. Charles ... Young idiot ... Got too drunk. Sandra's boyfriend ... the same. Some kind of ... drinking game ... Fools. Rest, yes. Great show. Well ... the start, anyway. Sandra's friend ... Bloody idiot. Crappy little bangers. Let a couple off. I told her ... Fireworks ... Proper show."

Pause. "And what then?"

Mannings took a deep breath. "Banging ... at the window. Turned ... Daniel up there. In his bedroom. He disappeared ... A crash ... We ran upstairs. But there was no-one ... in the room ... No Daniel ... or anyone else. Nobody."

Chapter 8

Pause. "You saw Daniel in the room and heard him bang on the window, but by the time you arrived, there was no-one there?"

"No-one."

Pause. "How did you know it was Daniel?"

"He's ... my son! Think I ... can recognise ... my own son."

Pause. "You saw his face?"

"No. But he had ... jacket. Suit jacket."

Pause. "Suit jackets can be mistaken, my brother."

A smile of victory lit up Mannings' face. "I bought it. For Daniel. As a ... birthday present. From ... my own tailor. Lovely turquoise. Daniel wore it ... all night. Was wearing ... at the window. Unique. Unique."

Pause. "Daniel was outside with you when the fireworks began?"

"Yes ... Right beside me. Didn't realise ... he had left ... at all. Until saw him ... at the window. Was concentrating ... Watching the fireworks. Big bangs." The manic gleam reappeared in his eye.

Pause. "And did you see anything out of place before the banging at the window?"

A shake of the head. "Concentrating. On the fireworks."

Pause. "What did you do when you heard the banging?"

"Went. As fast ... as I could. Heart condition ... You know ... Can't run ... Not fast."

Pause. "And what exactly was there?"

"Nothing! Well ... There had been ... a fight ... Of some kind. Some things ... on the ground. A knife. And blood." His voice, like wind scouring through heather, lost its strength at this last word.

Pause. "Blood?"

"In different places. Some leading to ... the en suite." His voice was low now, eyes sunk in their sockets. "It was. Locked. Everyone was ... Shouting. Screaming ... Broke the door down. Before I got ... there. Lots of blood. But no ... body."

Pause. "What was the knife like?"

"A ... kitchen knife. Blood all ... over it. Just lying there ... Middle of the bedroom."

Pause. "Do you think there was enough time for the murderer to remove the body?"

He shook his head vigorously, energy returning. "Definitely not time."

Pause. "What did you do after you arrived on the second floor?"

"I went to ... Daniel's bedroom. Stayed there. Sandra's friend ... Began shouting about Charles ... And the other boy. Dead. Everyone ran ... to their room. Rubbish. Not dead. Drunk."

Pause. "You did not go?"

He shook his head, eyes closed, lines of pain and weariness traversing the old skin. "Daniel had been ... in his bedroom. That's where ... blood was. Stayed there. Looked. Properly. But didn't find ... anything."

Pause. "Do you remember who was all in Daniel's bedroom when you arrived?"

"Everyone. I think. I don't know. I went ... to Daniel's bedroom. I heard Sandra ... Her friend ... in the en suite. Think the young thug ... was there too. Martina was in ... the bedroom. Sarah-Anne ... Came into the bedroom after me ... at some point."

Pause. "And the dentist couple?"

He shrugged. "In Daniel's bedroom ... When I got there."

Dakar leaned back, nodding once or twice to himself, then forward after a few seconds. "And after they discovered that Charles and Russell were not dead?"

"The rest ... Came back. And we looked. In the other rooms upstairs ... Nothing. Began to think ... A joke. Daniel had said ... something ... to Sandra's friend ... The young girl ... about his own surprise ... that night ... She told us. Thought maybe he meant ... Disappearing ... from his own ... celebration. Like Tom Sawyer, Huckleberry Finn. Late ... for their own funeral."

Mannings paused for breath here at the effort of all the words, heaving the air in through his mouth.

Pause. "Did you see any blood anywhere else when you searched?"

"No. No more blood ... Nowhere."

Pause. "And what took place after Sandra's friend spoke about this joke?"

"Sarah-Anne ... Furious. Took Sandra's friend. Into the en suite. Sent rest of us ... away. They came out ... few minutes later. Angry. People left. Sandra ... Her friends ... Young thug ... To the local pub ... See ... if Daniel ... was there. Then dentist and secretary. They left ... Quickly."

Pause. "You don't know what they discussed in the en suite?"

"No."

Pause. "And Charles and Russell?"

"Couldn't wake ... either of them."

Pause. "What about Martina?"

"She stayed. I was going ... to go. Leave. Sarah-Anne suggested ... one more drink ... But then ... Found the body ... Stabbed ... In the cellar." Mannings's voice became flat as his chin fell to his chest, battered unceasingly by a whirlwind of emotions that stripped away not just energy but also hope. "On the ground ... Lying ... Face up. Like he'd fallen ... Blood ... On the steps down ... Bright red ... On the wood. Terrible smell, death ... Stillness ... In the air. Still."

Pause. "I am full of sorrow about what happened to your son, my brother."

Mannings's eyes glinted as he brought his head up, his glare refracting through tears. "Told you. Don't be sorry. Find bastard ... who did it."

Pause. "And the turquoise suit jacket, where was it?"

"Still ... wearing it." His head fell back, his voice directed into his own chest.

Pause. "What happened after you found the body?"

"Felt pain ... Fell ... myself ... Next thing, an ambulance. Remember the lights ... Hospital ... Then here." Mannings hit the bed, glaring at it as if it was somehow responsible for his plight.

Pause. "Thank you, my brother, for talking about this night. It must be hard."

Mannings grunted at him, and hit the bed again.

"I would like to speak with Sarah-Anne. Do you have her address?"

Mannings's picked up his phone, a tiny thing in his huge hand, swiped around it before he handed it over to Dakar. "Here."

Dakar looked at the phone, then passed it to Stewart. He copied down the address before passing it back. 'Colinton.' The name rang a bell with him. A suburb of Edinburgh maybe? Something like that.

Dakar looked over at Stewart. Stewart looked back silently, before he suddenly remembered, the first time he'd worked with him down at Hanover House, that Dakar would always wait at the end of interviews to see if Stewart wanted to ask anything.

"Eh, nothing from me," he said, snatching at the words. He felt his face warm up. Dakar nodded, and turned back to the man in the bed.

"Thank you, my brother."

"One more thing. For you." Mannings spoke as they got up to leave.

Pause. "My brother?"

"When you speak … With Sarah-Anne." Dakar and Stewart both nodded. Mannings took a deep breath. "Don't believe a word that hippy bitch says about me."

Chapter 9

Dakar and Stewart stood outside the hospital, waiting on the taxi the receptionist had called. The afternoon was getting older now, more mature, the vibrancy of the sun waning as it fell from its zenith.

They hadn't said anything to each other since Mannings' last words. Stewart was pretty sure his shock showed when Mannings spoke – in fact, he was certain it was written clearly all over his face – but Dakar had just nodded once at the man, imperturbably.

"Pretty mental, eh?"

Pause. "Indeed."

Stewart stood, waiting for more, but nothing more came. "No love lost between those two by the looks of it?"

Pause. "It would appear not."

Stewart waited again, but it seemed like Dakar had finished. If Dakar was a normal person, Stewart would have guessed this was something he didn't want to talk about. But Dakar wasn't a normal person. Stewart couldn't really remember how to interpret Dakar's answers from the last time they'd worked together. If he'd managed to work it out at all.

"I suggest we go to Sarah-Anne Mannings' house, to see the murder scene and speak to her. What do you think?"

Stewart hesitated. Green's eyes came to his mind, the words 'trailing around' bouncing around Stewart's skull in that sardonic voice.

Stewart shook his head. Bollocks to Green.

Go and see the murder scene. It seemed the logical thing to do. Seeing the murder scene was important. He wasn't sure why, but that's what everyone on the TV did. Plus they could talk to the wife, an important witness on the night and someone who could give them background info on the victim.

Stewart examined it every which way he could for a few seconds, then nodded. If he were a proper detective, that's exactly what he'd do.

"Sounds good to me."

"Very well. For this investigation, I suggest we drive. I have access to a car we can use."

Stewart frowned, his imagination conjuring up a big 4x4 squeezing through the narrow streets of Edinburgh. He shook the thought away. Dakar didn't seem the type to try and get attention through such desperate measures.

Dakar checked his watch, an old, black plastic thing, as the taxi pulled up. "It is now just after two thirty. I can pick you up at three thirty at the firm. Does that work for you, my brother?"

Stewart, still think about the type of car Dakar would drive, nodded his head absent-mindedly. "Aye, right. Yes. Good idea."

Pause. "I shall ask the taxi driver to send another taxi."

Dakar went to do his hand on heart thing, but a sudden thought grabbed Stewart's attention. "Eh, actually, could you pick me up at my flat?"

Pause. "Of course."

"Great. 180 Summerhall Place. And, eh, you'll be wearing what you're wearing now, will you?"

Dakar looked down at what he was wearing, then back up. "Indeed."

"Eh, right. Well, I was just thinking, I might join you. In what you're wearing, that is. I mean, not what you're actually wearing, like, those precise clothes. My own clothes, obviously. I meant the style. Well, maybe not the style, actually. But the, eh, the formality. Aye. Well ..."

Stewart trailed off. He had forgotten about Dakar's lack of desire to interrupt others, which had left him drowning in his own verbal diarrhoea on a few occasions the last time they'd worked together.

Dakar smiled, then put his hand on his heart and did his nod thing before he strolled to the taxi, hands in pockets. Stewart watched the taxi pull away and disappear.

He was about to pull out his phone and start a Sudoku, but stopped himself, remembering his vow that morning. Instead he pulled out his notes and leaned back against the wall, studying what he had written down until the taxi arrived.

He gave the address, received the taxi driver's grunt in response, and in silence they drove back. As they returned back via Morningside, Stewart remembered the taxi ride he and Dakar had shared from the train station the first time they'd worked together. Dakar and the driver had bonded over the taxi driver's family, or something like that.

Stewart shuddered at the memory, his feeling of crawling up the walls with embarrassment re-emerging for a moment. This taxi ride was much more his cup of tea, driver and passenger ignoring each other as one undertook a service for the other for straightforward cash in hand. An entirely non-intimate experience.

The taxi arrived, and Stewart paid his money and got out.

He walked up the stone steps of what he would have called, if he were back in Mother Glasgow, a close. He could feel the bounce in his step as he thought about the murder – a murder! Of a partner's son! And one that had the police stumped to boot. He began whistling.

As he walked up the steps, his mind passed from the murder to Beth. She wouldn't be home just now, but just wait until he told her about this. She'd be mightily impressed that he was working with Dakar again. His heart thumped as he thought about her, the blood pumping around his body as her image appeared in his mind.

Stewart still remembered when he had first told Beth he was working with someone called Sebastian Dakar, regarding a death down at Hanover House. Stewart had never heard of the guy. But Beth had known so much about him she was basically able to give him Dakar's shoe size and favourite holiday destinations, simultaneously conveying the impression that she'd love to cover him in crushed avocado and lick him clean.

Stewart reached the door, and felt for his keys.

And as night followed day, Stewart once again remembered confessing his love for Beth to her. Well, asking her out, anyway. It was Dakar's fault. After everything had been said and done at Hanover House, Dakar had given Stewart the advice to tell Beth that he, Stewart, fancied her. Big time. It had backfired pretty spectacularly, Beth swiftly rejecting him.

He opened the door and went inside, his face wearing the concentrated expression of a person focusing on the past rather than the present.

Except weirdly, afterwards, their normal relationship had almost reversed. Beth, determined and fierce about things she believed in, had become almost shy around him. Stewart, on the other hand, with his cheeks always ready to blaze red, had become more confident around her.

It was funny, the way life worked.

He took off his coat and hung it up.

But that was the past. Now, after letting time carry the worst of the awkwardness away, there was a future. The gig tomorrow night was the first time he'd be going out into her world of trad singer-songwriters. And then, at the gig, he could impress her by telling her he was working with Dakar again.

Yes, it was all coming together.

Stewart closed the door, and looked with satisfaction around the empty flat. With the door closed, the world was shut out, like he was in his own private fortress where he could do what he wanted and be what he wanted. He sighed with contentment. Then almost jumped out of his skin as the sound came to his ears.

"Hello?"

Chapter 10

It was a female voice, calling down from upstairs. The tone was that of someone who is pretty sure they've just heard their front door open, but that no-one was meant to be doing that right now.

Stewart frowned. "Hello?"

"Stewart?"

"Beth?"

There was a bit of noise from upstairs and then Beth appeared at the top of the stairs. She was covered in sweat, her hair either plastered to her head or sticking out at random angles. She was decked out in running gear, the crazy neon colours alternating with her skin, which was a patchwork of sweaty red and drained white.

Stewart thought she looked magnificent.

"What are you doing back?" She smiled at him, and his heart soared.

Stewart opened his mouth, then closed it again.

"Eh … the firm has given me a new assignment today. A new client. Yeah. New client. So I've just come back to get changed. Into something a bit more, eh, informal …"

"That's cool! But don't you need to wear a suit for a client?"

He looked at her with his mouth open. "Ha, aye. You'd think so, wouldn't you? And, well, yeah, normally. But, it's more of an informal chat. Not necessarily a client yet. Anyway. Yeah, informal. The client's informal. Well, in what they wear. But you know, that's life, I guess." He shrugged desperately.

"Wouldn't you want to be more formal then, to try and impress them?"

The lightest of light sweat broke out on his forehead as he found himself straining for words, any words, once again.

"Ha, yeah, well, normally. Normally, that's very true. But this client, or, eh, potential client, they're one of those techy companies. Everyone wanders around in t-shirts and jeans, that kind of thing."

"What's the company's name?"

He hesitated for the third time. "Eh, do you know, I can't tell you. Commercial secrets, and all that. Apparently. So I'm told. I just got told to accompany ... Eh, a more senior colleague, to the place. The company. The tech company. Techy."

Beth looked at him. Eyes narrowed, one eyebrow arched.

"And are you going to get to do anything interesting?"

"Nah, not really. Just the usual trainee crap, you know how it is. Take minutes. Double-check contract offers." He breathed out again, his racing heart beginning to calm down.

Beth hesitated for a second, and Stewart managed to go on the offensive.

"So, eh, you've been running?"

Her eyebrows pulled together. It looked like she was trying to work out if he was taking the piss. "Yes. The half marathon was today."

"Right! Right, yes. To raise money for orphans, wasn't it?"

"Breast cancer. You sponsored me, remember? Twenty quid."

"Right! Right, yes. That's right. Orphans was the last one?" He tried a smile.

She gave him a wan smile in return, and pulled one sweat-caked bit of hair away from her face.

"So how was the run?"

A radiant smile appeared on her face, like the sun shining down on him, arched eyebrow becoming unarched. "It was really good. It's so amazing that they set up a half marathon especially for breast cancer. I didn't get the time I was aiming for, but I came close. I feel great now. Plus of course, a bit more money for charity, paid for by us rich legal types!"

"Nice one. Did you raise a lot then?"

"Nine hundred pounds, I think. Somewhere around there."

Stewart whistled. "Good work."

"Thanks! And thanks for your own contribution."

"No worries. Impressive you got out there and did a half. I've never run anywhere near that far in my puff."

"No, but at least you get out and do some exercise, like the five-a-side football you play."

"Sevens."

"What?"

"Seven-a-side. I play seven-a-side football."

"Right, sorry, seven-a-side. At least you're doing exercise. So many people now just seem to sit around, and then they wonder why they become overweight. And look at the diet some people have. I mean ..."

Stewart recognised the serious expression that settled on Beth's face, one he'd seen already during previous monologues about the iniquities of modern life.

"Right, yeah, I totally agree. It's shocking, really. But ah, I have to be heading now, I'm afraid. At …" Stewart checked his watch. Christ, quarter past three already.

"In fifteen, I'm meeting Da … vid. The colleague. Eh, well, I need to be out of here. Downstairs, ready to go. Getting picked up. By my colleague. By David. Don't know if you know him? No, why should you. Ha. And, eh, anyway, shouldn't you jump in the shower? I mean, I've heard it's not good to let sweat cool on your body. You might get a cold, you know, or eh, yeah …"

She smiled again, and for a moment, Stewart thought that maybe none of any of the rest of it really mattered. "Yeah, you're right. Before I give another lecture on things wrong with the world? How did you put it? Go off on one?"

"You're never going to let that go, are you?"

She shook her head, smile turning impish. "No."

"You weren't meant to hear it."

"Then you shouldn't have been bitching so loudly to Saz, and definitely not in the living room!"

He shrugged, smiled back. "Touché. Not bitching though, just an observation. Eh, we still on for tomorrow night by the way? The gig in the Oak?"

She nodded enthusiastically. "Yeah. It should be awesome. I think you'll really like her."

Stewart nodded equally enthusiastically, and gave her a smile back, all the wider with his secret knowledge. He'd drop it in casually, that he was working with Dakar again. As if it didn't matter. Yes. Perfect.

"Okay. Listen, have fun with your informal chat with your client who isn't a client." She smiled wickedly, before turning and walking away. A second later Stewart heard the bathroom door shut.

He hustled up the stairs to his own room, feeling the excitement course through him. Investigating a murder and the gig coming up afterwards with Beth, where she'd soon be dying to hear all about Dakar. It was going to be a good couple of days.

He stepped around the various mounds of clothes on the floor, dumped there until common decency got sufficiently outraged to demand he do a wash. They were only half piles at the moment, though, nothing for common decency to get worked up about. There were various tea mugs scattered around the surfaces as well, next to the bed, on the chest of drawers, but he ignored these as well.

He walked over to his cupboard, taking off his tie. He chucked it venomously onto the bed and undid the top button of his shirt. Then he began searching for something he could wear that was exactly as informal as Dakar's style, but extremely distant from what Dakar was actually wearing.

He had just fished out a pair of smart-ish jeans when his memory treacherously brought up Sudgeon's words about how he'd be representing the firm. Knowing his luck, someone would give Sudgeon, or worse, Green, a detailed description of his casual sartorial style. And then he'd be for it. And wouldn't Green love throwing the words 'representative of the firm' at him?

He turned sadly and walked over to the bed, picking up the tie where he'd dropped it. He began putting it back on, but then stopped. Well, it might not be much, but he would go open-necked. Very new Tory. Couldn't criticise him if their own sad-sack politicians were doing the same, now could they?

Stewart went to throw the tie back down onto the bed, but stopped once again. He might need a tie at some point. Like if he had to go back into work.

He looked down at this small object of torture, his mind pulling in two different directions. Eventually he stuffed it into an inside pocked of his suit jacket.

Just in case. Couldn't hurt.

Chapter 11

Stewart's breath swirled around him in the air. The wind was getting up, getting underneath his long coat and making him shiver. Light clouds had appeared in the sky, the vanguard of the army of dark clouds coming to assert winter's dominion during the coming months. He stepped back further into the doorway, a makeshift shelter from the wind, and ate the last bite of a huge sandwich he'd quickly put together for lunch.

Dakar pulled up after he'd been standing there for a couple of minutes, right on time. Stewart stared at his car. It was a tiny grey thing, more like a trainer than a car. He took off his substantial coat, and quickly got in, nodding to Dakar's customary greeting. The car moved off silently into the Edinburgh traffic, Dakar concentrating on the road.

"Well, this is a nice set of wheels. Yours, is it?"

Dakar paused. "Thank you, my brother. It does not belong to me. I lease it from a company which specialises in electric cars, and I store it outside the office."

"You're hiring? I would have thought the books you wrote must have brought in enough cash to buy a car."

Stewart thought he caught a glimpse of a smile. "I own as little as possible, my brother. If I need something, I will borrow it with money and treat it as a gift."

Stewart nodded dubiously at this. His mind, the legal knowledge so tirelessly drilled in across years of dull lectures and problems, automatically told him that if you gave money in return for getting the use of something moveable, that was pretty much the exact definition of hiring.

There was silence in the car for a few minutes as Dakar drove.

"You decided not to change?" Dakar's tone seemed innocent. Maybe the tinge of mischief Stewart thought he heard was just in his head.

Stewart took a breath. He'd prepared an answer to this question as he stood waiting for Dakar to arrive. He was representing the firm. So he had to wear a suit. He hadn't realised at the time he'd indicated his desire to get changed, but had realised before he got changed and thus had decided not to.

Nice and smooth, no cause for embarrassment.

"Eh, no. Well, you know. I'm representing the firm. So, yeah."

Dakar kept his eyes on the road and said nothing.

"And well, also … Well, Mr Green, he seemed a bit, you know, a bit, intense, about me being professional. I mean, that comment about notes and a report, well, I'm ready this time, and I kind of thought the suit would, well, match. With taking notes, and reports. Professional. I mean, I think it looks more professional." Stewart blurted the words out before he trailed off.

In the name of the wee man, Scott.

Pause. "Yes. I felt Mr Green's intensity as well."

Stewart braced for more, but Dakar remained silent. As the seconds passed, Stewart felt the tension leave him as it appeared Dakar would not be following up with any kind of insult, as Stewart had braced himself for. Young Scottish malehood was basically constant sparring. Whenever anyone opened themselves up by saying something stupid, everyone else laid in mercilessly. Sarcasm, imitations in stupid voices, constant jokes. And that was just your brothers and mates.

Fortunately Dakar seemed to have been absent on the day at school where they taught you how to be male.

Stewart settled into silence as Dakar drove. He'd had a shufti at where Colinton was, to the south-west, but before the bypass. He knew it wouldn't take too long to get there.

He thought again about tomorrow night, telling Beth that he was working with Dakar again and seeing her reaction. Maybe, this time, he could even convince Dakar to speak with her for one of the one-hour slots he did for the rich and famous. As a favour. She'd love him forever for that one.

Stewart settled down happily as they passed over The Meadows and onto Bruntsfield place, heading for Holy Corner, where the church architecture still dominated, the buildings remaining even after the Church's influence had long waned. They took a right, heading down Colinton Road, a way that Stewart was unfamiliar with.

The traffic grew lighter as the surroundings themselves slowly melted from city into suburb, and the sky itself seemed to lighten, as if the clouds were trapped by buildings in the centre of Edinburgh. Rows of sandstone tenements gave way to semi-detached homes which in turn gave way to free-standing bungalows, sports grounds and parks becoming more and more frequent as Dakar drove.

"It used to be an old mill town, Colinton." Stewart jerked out of his seat as Dakar spoke.

"Eh, is that right, is it?" Stewart looked around at the buildings as they passed them.

Pause. "Yes. The Water of Leith provided them with their power. At one point, in the 18th century, one of the mills provided the special paper to the Bank of Scotland, to print their notes. They're all gone now, of course."

Stewart looked at him, unsure of what to say.

"I used to work here, when I first became a police officer. More often in Oxgangs, at the three high-rises that used to be there. Allermuir, Caerketton and Capelaw. But I was also in Colinton quite a lot. Or passed through it, perhaps that is the better term. There was not much need for the police."

Stewart nodded. High-rises. The ones in the Gorbals in Glasgow had been pretty godawful before they were brought down, by all accounts. Plus, of course, well, *Trainspotting*. It hadn't necessarily been high-rises, but the style was probably the same.

"Right, yeah. Awful places, eh?"

Pause. "When they were first built, they were the future. A village in the sky. And they were very modern at the time. But slowly families moved out, and no-one else moved in, and so over the years they became darker places, certainly. Lonely places. Although the sense of community in a high-rise was a powerful force."

Stewart nodded again, dubiously.

"We had to make our own entertainment. Getting onto the tops of the lifts, going up and down. And climb down the outside of the building, jumping from landing to landing."

Stewart looked back at the skyline, now bereft of the high-rises, with some respect. Insane certainly, but there had to be bravery mixed in there too. Something caught his attention in what Dakar had said.

"We?"

Pause. "I grew up in a high-rise, in Glasgow. Plean Street, out in Yoker, before I moved to Cumbernauld." Dakar paused for a second – or was it hesitation? – before he continued. "Colinton has always been rich, or certainly richer than its cousin, Oxgangs. I didn't realise at the time, but that always bothered me, I think. How two places could be so close to each other, and yet so unequal."

Stewart waited for Dakar to continue, but instead the man pulled over onto the side of the pavement. They were in a well-kept street in Colinton, outside an impressive house, dark solid stone across two stories. A small wall with a row of high bushes behind it obscured the lower house from the road.

A driveway was off to one side, leading up to a garage, but a tree on one side of the driveway leaned down over it, its branches obscuring much of the garage from the road. Next to the driveway entrance was a small break in the wall with two steps leading towards the house.

They both got out, into the cold air, and Dakar headed for the gap. They followed a path of paving slabs to the front door through a small, well-kept garden, the grass in the middle ringed by an earthen square where flowers continued to live, awaiting their fate as winter approached. Dakar knocked sharply, and a few moments later a short, slim women stood in front of them.

She had large round glasses, with brown hair cut short in a bob. She was dressed smartly, open-collar pastel shirt with white, oriental-style trousers and no shoes. A light scarf was wrapped around her neck, one end forward over her shoulder, the other trailing down her back. Woven bracelets decorated both of her wrists.

"Yes?" Her eyes had narrowed as she took in their appearance. One hand gripped the doorframe tightly.

Pause. "Good evening. We are looking for Sarah-Anne Mannings."

"Yes, that's me. What can I do for you?" The words were spoken with as much warmth as the air around them.

Dakar smiled. "My name is Sebastian Dakar. This is Stewart Scott. We have been asked to investigate the murder of your husband, Daniel."

"And who asked you to do that?"

Stewart looked at Dakar, Mannings' last words ringing in his ears.

But Dakar was already answering. "Technically, it is a firm called SSM. But truth be told—"

"Right, so it's Tom then." The woman looked at Dakar for a second in silence, then over at Stewart. She had a calculating look in her eye. Stewart held his breath, involuntarily. After a few more seconds of silence, she sniffed. "I suppose you'd better come in."

Chapter 12

"Tea? Coffee?"

Sarah-Anne had ushered them down a long hall into a big, open-plan area that combined a kitchen and a living room, with a kitchen worktop separating the two. The living room extended further around the corner, to the back of the house, with some comfy chairs, a sofa and a large TV. A couple of French windows ran along the back wall, showing a small patio of white paving slabs and a good-sized back garden.

The room, as if in keeping with the woman's appearance, was clean yet disordered, with magazines spread out on various tables and chairs and flowers dotted around the place. There were numerous bookshelves, the books spilling out of them. They seemed mainly to be about ancient cultures from around the world. There was one on ancient Norse mythology, a couple regarding Celtic cultural practices and even one about the Native Americans. There was an easel in a corner of the living room, with the beginnings of a star on it.

But there was something annoying Stewart about the room, something putting him on edge. He cast a glance around again. He just couldn't put his finger on what ... And then it came to him. The tick-tock of the clock on the wall was extremely, extremely irritating.

They sat at the kitchen counter in a couple of high chairs, on the dining room side. Sarah-Anne faced them over the worktop. "It's mainly instant I've got, coffee-wise, although I can brew up a fresh pot of coffee if you don't mind waiting." She pointed to a small metal coffee pot.

"Nothing for me, thank you, my sister," Dakar said.

"I'm not your sister."

Pause. "Not biologically, certainly."

She looked at him a moment longer, and then over at Stewart. "And you?"

"I'd take a cup of tea, if that's all right."

She nodded at this return to normality, turning to the tea cupboard. "What kind?"

Stewart gulped. He didn't drink real tea, only the fake, made-up stuff that had pictures of berries on the box and gushed on about infusions. He hated asking for it. He still remembered the first time he'd asked for one of those at a mate's flat. His reputation had barely survived the following few minutes.

"Eh, any kind of mint tea or berry tea would be great." She turned back to him, holding a flowers of the forest tea in one hand. He nodded gratefully and she flicked on the kettle.

"Now, I suppose you want to ask me some questions about Daniel and what happened that night." Her words remained blunt, her tone one of duty rather than pleasure. Stewart got his notepad out of his satchel.

Pause. "Yes, my sister. I am full of sorrow for your loss. Are you well enough to speak to us?"

Sarah-Anne exhaled and gave him a small smile, the first time her expression showed any kind of warmth. "Yes, thanks."

Pause, nod. "Forgive me, but before we start ... These books." Dakar indicated some of the titles Stewart had been looking at. "Yours?"

Sarah-Anne's expression became suspicious, but eventually she answered. "Yes. I've always been fascinated by ancient cultures. Things like putting a coin on each eye of a dead person so they can pay the ferryman. And why people believed in stories like that."

Stewart stumbled over that sentence, but made sure he got it down. Definitely one for the report for Sudgeon and Green. Assuming he sent a report to Sudgeon and Green. Still needed to work that one out.

"I too am interested in ancient cultures. I believe they have a lot to teach us."

Sarah-Anne relaxed a little as she nodded her assent.

Pause. "Before we begin to speak about what happened that night, can we please see the cellar where the body was found?"

"If you want. It's down there."

Sarah-Anne headed back out through the kitchen door, Dakar and Stewart getting up to follow her. She walked a few paces to a small door in the hallway cut into the wood, nestled under the staircase. She opened it, revealing a landing that turned ninety degrees down a flight of steps into darkness. The air that came out had a musty, cold quality to it.

She reached inside and pulled a cord, illuminating a few bald bulbs at the side of the stairs and then a couple in the cellar itself. The light cast was harsh, almost electric.

The Price to Pay

She took a deep breath. "Daniel's body was found at the bottom of the stairs."

Dakar looked towards the bottom of the stairs. "Do you mind, my sister, if we go down?"

"You're on your own. I haven't been back down there since that night."

Dakar nodded, then walked down without any seeming concern, his normal stroll.

Stewart could feel his heart begin to beat faster as he looked at the cold, shadowy steps down to where Daniel's body had been found, brutally murdered. He didn't believe in ghosts. At least not in the full light of day. Stewart gulped, and headed down after Dakar, trying to emulate his laidback style.

The other man had reached the bottom and was looking around. The cellar was not large, and the already small space was cut down further by the wooden wine holders around each wall, the bottles quiet and still in their ranks, as if paying homage to the dead.

Dakar crouched down by the foot of the stairs, where the wood was stained red in patches. Stewart stood beside him, staring at the large stain Dakar was crouching beside. There were other, smaller patches here and there. Dakar reached his hand out, almost brushing them, one after another.

Pause. "The knife he was stabbed with. Where was it?"

"Lying beside him." Sarah-Anne's tone mirrored the light in the cellar, devoid of warmth or energy. In spite of the small space, there were still shadows everywhere amongst the cold, grey concrete, deepened rather than dispersed by the unforgiving light.

Pause. "And he was stabbed more than once?"

There was hesitation from the top of the stairs, flowing down towards them. Stewart felt himself tense. "Well, yes. The police said he was stabbed in the chest and stomach. But I suppose Tom didn't tell you it all."

Dakar and Stewart turned to look up at her.

"One of his wrists had been slit."

Chapter 13

"A wrist had been slit, my sister?"

They were back at the kitchen table, Stewart gripping the warm mug of tea with both hands. All the little fears and doubts that had sprouted in the bleakness of the cellar had been driven off by the warmth of the kitchen. The tick-tock of the clock felt positively welcoming now.

Sarah-Anne nodded. "Slit and bandaged. But when they found the body, the bandage had been taken off."

Pause, a long pause. Stewart could see Dakar turning it over in his mind. "So at some point that night someone slit Daniel's wrist, and then bandaged it, and then the bandage was taken off?"

Sarah-Anne nodded. "Yes. And all of it after dinner. I would have noticed if he'd had the injury or the bandage before that."

Pause. "Where was the bandage found?"

"Beside the slit wrist. Someone had just cut it off."

Pause. "And you have no idea why, or where, or when this happened?"

She shook her head.

Pause, nod. "Perhaps we can now see the bedroom where he was attacked?"

She hesitated, staring at Dakar for a few seconds. Then she took a mobile phone out, and made a call. She spoke tersely after a few seconds.

"Hi, Tom. Did you … Oh, you did. What are their names? Yes, Dakar. And you can't remember the other one, but he's young and is a trainee at your office. Okay. I …" She paused, then took the phone away from her ear and looked at it, exhaling loudly through her nose. "Oh yes, lovely talking to you too."

Sarah-Anne slid the phone into a pocket, and looked back at Dakar and Stewart. Stewart smiled shortly, his face sliding back into a grimace.

He'd seen him that morning. That bloody morning! How bloody hard was it to remember someone's na—

"Daniel's bedroom. Yes, I'll show you." Sarah-Anne spoke abruptly, interrupting Stewart's thoughts. She stood and, without looking back,

The Price to Pay

headed out of the kitchen to the stairs. Stewart scrambled up to follow her, Dakar arising more slowly.

They walked up the stairs in silence, leading onto a small landing with five doors. They were a uniform varnished brown, in contrast to the white walls and creamy carpet. As Sarah-Anne walked over to one of the doors, she pointed to others. "Spare room," she said, pointing to the one furthest from the steps, "bathroom, guest bedroom and," she pointed to a smaller door nearest to the top of the stairs, "closet." She arrived at the door she had not yet introduced. "This was Daniel's bedroom. I haven't been in since the police left."

Pause. "You have not entered since the police left that night?"

She shook her head. "I've been in the en suite, but cleaning that was enough for me. I've moved into that bedroom, our guest room. Funnily enough, once someone's been murdered in a house, you get a lot fewer visitors." Sarah-Anne's expression remained grim even at these last words.

Pause. "The police have carried out all their tests in the master bedroom?"

"They told me that they were finished with it and I could go back in if I wanted to."

Pause, nod. Stewart's mind whirred in the Dakar pause. Why she was still in the house at all … Dakar asked the question almost as Stewart thought of it.

"You are not moving out?"

"I want to move out of here as soon as possible. But when I spoke to the estate agent she said we'd have to knock fifty thousand off the asking price because of what happened. Apparently people get spooked by these kinds of things. Ridiculous."

Pause. "You do not believe in ghosts or spirits, my sister?"

Stewart saw Sarah-Anne's jaw muscles tense. "Just because I believe ancient cultures have something to teach us, Mr Dakar, doesn't mean I believe in all the spiritual nonsense they contain."

Pause. Dakar either didn't notice or didn't mind the tension. "We heard Russell and Charles were put to bed early. Were they in the guest bedroom?"

Sarah-Anne nodded.

Pause. "May we see that after we have finished in this bedroom?"

"No, Mr Dakar, you cannot."

Stewart, having already begun to walk towards the master bedroom, faltered in his step. He turned back to Sarah-Anne. She'd crossed her arms and widened her feet, her face set in a scowl.

"I think I'm being accommodating enough. My husband was murdered, the police seem completely unable to find out who did it, I've had journalists at my door and now a couple of amateur detectives. You can see Daniel's bedroom, yes. But the guest bedroom is my bedroom, and you can't just waltz in." She was breathing deeply by the time she'd finished.

A long pause from Dakar. Then he nodded. "Of course, my sister. I am grateful you are entertaining us at all. I don't believe we will be long in Daniel's bedroom."

She stared at him for a second longer, then turned and disappeared down the stairs. Dakar opened the door to the bedroom. Stewart was immediately hit by a metallic taste in the stale air.

Dakar walked in, careful to step around the few red discolouration spots that stood out against the carpet, which was the same cream colour as the landing. He put on a pair of transparent gloves as he moved, bending to examine the faded blood splatters.

Stewart walked in after him, looking around the spacious room. The double bed to his left was an ornate wooden structure, with a towering wardrobe just beyond it. Another solid bit of a wood, in the shape of a make-up desk, was directly in front of him. Opposite the door there was a large window. It was in two halves, the top fixed but the bottom part able to slide up and down.

The room felt grim to him. Investigating a murder had sounded exciting. He'd seen those American cop shows, where for some unexplained reason the crime scene technicians investigated the crime rather than the detectives. Those guys had flashbacks and theories all exploding in their heads as soon as they looked at a crime scene.

Stewart didn't. They just looked like stains to him. He'd have thought it was red wine if he hadn't known better.

After examining the stains for a minute or so, Dakar stood and walked over to the window. Stewart reluctantly walked over to join him, avoiding the red patches.

The view was over the large garden. It was the typical suburban style, a stone wall separating it from gardens on each sides. It was mainly grass, although various flowers and shrubs were growing around the boundary, sheltered behind the wall. Near to the house the garden met patio, two metres of white paving slabs that ran along the back of the house.

Stewart had had a very similar garden growing up back in Glasgow, minus the plants around the edge. Or maybe there had been plants, but once he and his pals began using the garden as a football pitch and the walls as goals, the plants died off pretty quickly.

Dakar slid the window up with some difficulty and stuck his head out. He put a hand up, beckoning, and Stewart obligingly stuck his head out. The wall had decorative brickwork, bricks slightly sticking out in uniform places, every half metre or so, from the window down to the ground.

Stewart's grandparent's house had had something similar. As a child, he'd loved climbing up and down it. As an adult, he felt it was an invitation to burglary.

After a few moments, Dakar pulled his head back inside and looked over the rest of the room. He examined the desk, the bed and the wardrobe, first from the outside and then opened the drawers. Stewart didn't see what was in them, but apparently Dakar was satisfied.

The man turned and strolled over to the en suite door. The lock was broken, the wood around it splintered. Dakar pushed it and it opened. It contained a shower, sink and toilet, all a sparkling white. There was another door which led directly to the corridor.

Dakar took off his gloves, and put them back in his pocket.

"Shall we go back downstairs and speak with Sarah-Anne, my brother?"

Stewart looked at him, then looked around the en suite one more time. He hadn't seen much more than he'd been expecting, but then again, maybe that was normal. He nodded.

They left the room, but Dakar paused on the landing, examining the floor. Stewart did the same, although he didn't know what he was looking for. It was all the same creamy white carpet they'd had in the bedroom, unbroken by any other colour.

"Eh, Dakar, are you looking at anything in particular right now?"

Pause, shake of the head. "I'm checking to see if something isn't here, my brother."

Stewart re-ran that sentence in his head, then looked around. There didn't seem to be anything obviously missing.

"Eh, something that isn't here?"

Pause. "Yes. Bloodstains."

Chapter 14

"How long had you and Daniel been sleeping in different rooms?"

"Excuse me?" Sarah-Anne pulled away from Dakar, pulling herself upright, eyebrows raised.

They were back in the kitchen. Stewart once again had a warm mug of tea, Sarah-Anne having filled it up for him. He'd have to watch out, otherwise he'd be in the toilet all day.

He and Dakar sat on one side of the kitchen bar, while Sarah-Anne stood on the other. With the warm tea, it felt more like a chat rather than an interview about a murder. But Stewart had his notebook out, pen at the ready.

Pause. "I asked—"

"Who says we were sleeping in different beds?"

Pause. "You referred to the room as Daniel's bedroom, my sister. And if you haven't gone back in since the night he died, when the police finished, then the things you need to live must have already been in another room."

She waited for a few seconds, then shrugged. "Yes. Well. We had been sleeping apart for a few months." She sighed, looking down and twisting her wedding ring around her finger.

Pause. "How long had you and Daniel been married?" Dakar spoke gently.

"It would have been ten years in a few months."

Pause. "How did you meet?"

"In Glasgow. On a march against nuclear subs on the Clyde." A smile crept onto her face as she spoke.

Pause. "You have a daughter called Sandra?"

The smile seemed to harden now, as her eyes narrowed. "Yes. But that was before I met Daniel. Sandra's father is an American guy called Chad. Was. He's dead now." Her eyes drifted for a second as she spoke. "I was very young at the time, only eighteen. We carried on for about half a year, then I broke it off. Six months later Sandra came along. Chad never met her. Too afraid to, the stupid oaf."

Pause. "How did Chad die?"

"In a street scuffle with fascists, over in the US. About eight years ago." She smiled ruefully. "You live by the sword, you die by the sword. Although he was shot." She took off her glasses and began rubbing them with the scarf which trailed down her neck.

Pause, nod. "I am sorry for any pain you carry, my sister."

She looked at him, eyes narrowing in a reaction Stewart had seen Dakar get many times when people were trying to work out if he was being genuine.

"You do not get on well with Tom?"

The glasses were replaced, the eyes remaining narrow. "He always disliked me. He felt that Daniel married down. To be fair to Tom, if you care about those kinds of things, then he did. A well-educated private school boy marrying a daft young hippy. But Daniel didn't think like Tom."

Pause. "How did Daniel think?"

The skin on her forehead became taut as she frowned, the eyebrows pulling it down as they furrowed together. "He used to know what was important in life. But since he changed ..." She drifted off.

"Changed?"

"Oh yes. Daniel ended up quite far away from the man I married, in the end."

Pause. "What do you mean?"

She waited for a few moments, looking up at the ceiling, before eventually speaking.

"I don't know. It began about a year ago. At first, I thought it was just a mid-life crisis. He became more morose, quieter. He wouldn't talk to me. He bought stupid, expensive things, like a Jaguar classic car. I mean, the thing broke down all the time because it was so old, and spare parts were astronomical in price. He would take it out at weekends partying, like he was eighteen or something." She shook her head. "Recently, it became a lot worse."

She took off her glasses, rubbing them subconsciously as she thought. She put them back on before she spoke.

"The moroseness and irritation suddenly changed to anger. He became much needier as well, constantly craving attention and showing off, all these kinds of things."

Pause. "And you have no idea what caused this change, or why it got worse?"

"I have my suspicions as to how it began. But he refused to talk about it."

Pause. "What do you suspect?"

She smiled, but it didn't reach her eyes. "My suspicions, Mr Dakar, are my suspicions. I haven't told them to anyone else. The man I married didn't deserve speculation when he was alive, and he still doesn't now he's dead."

Pause. "They may be relevant as to why he was murdered, my sister."

"They're not." The answer was brusque.

Pause, nod. Stewart shifted uncomfortably in his seat, but the expression on Dakar's face remained amiable. "How old was Daniel?"

"Thirty-four."

Pause. "And you, my sister?"

"Thirty-six."

A long pause. Dakar seemed to be calculating, looking off into a corner of the room. At length he spoke again. "How often did Daniel go out at the weekends?"

"Maybe about once a month when it all started. He tried to hide it at first. But over the last few months it happened more and more, and he didn't seem to care that I knew. At first I asked him about it, where he was, but he just told me to stop nagging him. So eventually I did. Then sometimes, from nothing, he would boast about the crazy things he had been doing, like snorting cocaine and all sorts. Just trying to get attention, of course."

Pause. "But this only occurred at the weekends?

"Yes. Well, normally. During the last month or so, he headed out at night during the week a couple of times. That was different. I didn't smell any drink from him, for one. I was in bed by the time he got back, but I think it was about midnight."

Pause. "Which nights did he head out?"

She hesitated. "I don't remember the first time exactly. It was a few weeks ago. The second time though ..." She took a deep breath. "It was three days before his birthday."

Pause, nod. "And you had no idea where he went?"

"None. By that point we weren't sharing much."

Pause. "My sister, is there any possibility Daniel was having an affair?"

Stewart, scribbling away, held his breath as he looked up at the woman.

She took off her glasses, and rubbed the lenses for a second or two, before putting them back on and giving a smile full of sorrow. "The thought had occurred to me. And he'd certainly begun paying a lot of attention to other woman over the last year. Maybe he was, I don't know."

Pause, nod. "How did Tom react to Daniel's change?"

She sighed. "Tom loved it, of course. He's not a bad man, Mr Dakar. Daniel abandoned him, or at least that's how he saw it, and then his wife died. But then Daniel, the one he'd lost to the daft hippy woman, became just like him, practically overnight. Oh yes, Tom loved Daniel after the change. He thought he had got his son back."

Dakar sat back, and there was silence in the room for a few seconds, broken only by the sound of Stewart's pen racing across paper. Eventually Dakar came forward again. "How did Daniel and Sandra get on?"

Sarah-Anne smiled, and her face seemed to become lighter. "Very well. Sometimes I thought Daniel only married me because of her. She adored him. She took to him straight away, you know. She was only six when I introduced Daniel to her. I was so nervous. But she just smiled, and he laughed, and it was like they were father and daughter."

Her eyes drifted as she clutched her cup of tea more tightly, the earthy smell of Rooibos playing in Stewart's nose. "But she was distraught when she found out that Chad hadn't wanted to know her. It took her a couple of years to get over it all. Daniel was very good to her during that time, very patient with her, with the tantrums and hatred."

Pause. "And after he changed?"

"Sandra was seventeen by that point. She didn't really speak much to me or Daniel. I don't think she noticed Daniel change, to be honest. And then she moved out in the middle of August, for university. She actually moved into Daniel's flat. He rented it to her cheaply."

Long pause. "Where did she get the money to rent the flat?"

"She helped out at Daniel's dentist practice sometimes. They have a secretary, Dennis, Eleanor's husband, but I don't think he's very good." She took a deep breath. "Jane …" Sarah-Anne's eyes became hooded and her expression seemed to set on her face, her lips disappearing as they squeezed together, "… began working there last summer. But there were times when Jane couldn't make it, and Sandra, or even Russell, Sandra's boyfriend, would fill in."

Pause. "And Jane and Russell were also here the night Daniel was murdered?"

Sarah-Anne looked at Dakar, a stillness around her like the calm before a storm. "Oh yes. I invited Sandra and Russell, of course. But if I could turn back time, Mr Dakar, I would have made sure that Jane never came near this place."

Chapter 15

Sarah-Anne turned away abruptly to find something else at the counter. Stewart sat in the lengthening silence, looking first at Dakar and then at Sarah-Anne's back.

Pause. "Why would you want Jane to stay away?"

"Because of what she did with Daniel." Sarah-Anne turned back around. She hadn't found whatever she'd been looking for.

Pause. "And what was that?"

"Flirted like a little siren."

Pause, a long pause. "Perhaps we can start at the beginning here, my sister. Have you known Jane a long time?"

"She's like a daughter to me, Mr Dakar. Or at least she was until a couple of weeks ago."

Pause. "A daughter?"

Sarah-Anne sniffed. "Jane's mother died when she was very young, and her father threw himself into his work. She was an only child. I couldn't stand by and see her abandoned, so I spent as much time with her as I could, and tried to bring her up as my own. Sandra is an only child too, so I thought it might help them both. Like each would have a sister. I thought I had done a good job but ..." Her tone turned poisonous, "... it seems I didn't."

Pause. "What do you mean?"

"We all got on so well when they were growing up. To be honest, the only time it became an issue would be if Sandra and Jane fought over something, Sandra would sometimes snipe at Jane that she wasn't really her sister. But Daniel and I came down heavily on that. We were one family. It all sorted itself out as they got older, of course."

Dakar nodded, and waited, silently. Sarah-Anne took a deep breath, her expression pained.

"But then two weeks before his birthday, I found out Daniel had been going round to the flat, to see Jane on her own. She denied it all, of course. But then that night, the night Daniel died ... It was awful. So shabby, so clear. The siren! No, the succubus!" Sarah-Anne spat the antiquated words out with a particular venom.

Pause. "Are you sure this is what Jane was doing?"

"Judge for yourself, Mr Dakar. Look at what she was wearing that night."

Sarah-Anne dug into purse that was sitting on the kitchen worktop and pulled out a smartphone. She keyed through it, and then held up a photograph, turning the phone lengthways so that it maximised on the screen.

Stewart looked at the photo of the assembled guests. At one end he recognised Charles and Tom, Charles in particular looking happy with himself. He was wearing a smart-casual suit, while Tom was in one of his kaleidoscopically colourful cord suits, looking cheery.

"This is Daniel?"

Dakar pointed to a younger man, who Tom had his arm around. Sarah-Anne nodded. He was sharp-looking, tall and slim, hair jet-black with a sort of goatee thing going on, the younger cousin of his father's monstrous beard. He was wearing a truly horrific suit, a light turquoise colour. His eyes were wide and wild, almost crazy, like he had too much energy and it was overflowing out of him.

A man and woman stood off to one side. Even in the frozen shot of the photograph they looked stiff, their shoulders raised and pulled in, mouths pulled out at the edges not out of happiness but rather out of obligation. The man, short, balding and fat, was wearing what looked like a cheap variant of a Christmas jumper, with brown cords. The woman was tall and broad, with a hawk-like nose. She wore a long, dark green dress.

"Eleanor and Dennis." Sarah-Anne supplied the names as Dakar and Stewart looked at the different people.

Dakar pointed at another woman, who was standing next to Sarah-Anne. "Martina Donaldson." Her tone became harder, more business-like.

Martina stood looking darkly at the camera, her face tilted down slightly, thoughts masked behind a smile that didn't touch the rest of her face. Stewart couldn't tell how old she was, as she was blessed with the olive complexion that seemed to bestow eternal youth, and dark black hair that hung down her back. She was wearing long, loose trousers, a billowing shirt and a scarf draped loosely but exactly around her shoulders and neck.

Sarah-Anne herself stood in the middle, wearing a long dress that was patterned in different shades of deep red, with matching, elbow-length red

The Price to Pay

gloves. She seemed somehow alone, her husband away with his father and her daughter on the far side with her friends. There seemed to Stewart a kind of nobility about the way she was standing, erect and haughty.

There was then a blond guy, probably about Stewart's age. He was a bit taller than Stewart was. He had on jeans and a khaki shirt, the sleeves rolled up, and the kind of ruddy face that said he'd spent a substantial amount of time outside.

"That's Russell. Sandra's boyfriend."

Finally, there were two younger women, arms around each other. Stewart didn't require the familial resemblance to say which one was Sandra and which was Jane. Sandra was wearing smart jeans and a jumper, grey and blue. Jane, on the other hand, was wearing a lot of make-up, with a short, tight, black skirt, and a red shirt that had quite a few buttons opened. A black bra strap could be seen as one of her shoulders was exposed.

"I don't need to point out who Jane is, do I?" Sarah-Anne asked rhetorically, taking the phone back. "The dress invitation was smart-casual, not show off everything you've got. I thought what I was wearing was quite nice, but I was nothing compared to Jane. Plus of course I had to wear an apron most of the night." She muttered it towards the end.

Pause. "The suit Daniel was wearing …"

"Oh God, I know. I wouldn't have let that kind of monstrosity in the house. But Tom brought it with him, that night, as a present. Daniel loved it, I think mostly because he saw the look on my face when he put it on. He refused to take it off, no matter how ridiculous he looked."

Pause. "You had no other one like it?"

"Mr Dakar, I may not be the most fashionable woman in the world, but I do have some standards. There was nothing else remotely like it in the house."

Dakar moved his finger over to Charles. "You didn't know Charles before that evening?"

She shook her head.

Pause. "How then did he come to be invited?"

"Daniel invited him. I had no idea he was coming. But fortunately there was enough food for everyone."

Pause. "I thought it was surprise birthday."

"It was meant to be. But Daniel found out. I imagine Jane told him, after Sandra told her."

Dakar stared at the assembled people. "Who took the photograph?"

"Craig, Martina's son. He said he didn't like being in photographs." Sarah-Anne put her phone down again.

Pause. "When was this taken?"

Just after our wonderful dinner. Oh yes. It was fantastic." Stewart looked up in surprise, only to see Sarah-Anne sit back, her arms folded, lips vanished as they squeezed together. "Daniel couldn't keep his eyes off Jane, and she was looking pretty slavishly over at him. As the night went on, he just got louder and louder, talking and carrying on. Stupid man."

Pause. "And after dinner, there was a drinking game?"

"Yes. We went to the living room after dinner, and then the children went back through to the dining room. They got uproariously drunk. Or rather, Russell and Charles did, trying to show off. And we eventually had to carry them up to the guest bedroom."

Pause. "Daniel did not try to follow, to speak with Jane?"

A smile came over her face, but it was laced with contempt. "No. As soon as Jane had gone, Martina went to speak to him. She's another one who doesn't mind using her looks, Mr Dakar, to get her way."

Pause, nod. "Do you know what they discussed?"

She shook her head. "They were all whispers. Martina did look a bit upset afterwards, but she refused to tell me what it was about. Daniel looked quite happy though." Sarah-Anne pulled herself upright, her expression one of a person grudgingly conceding a point. "I did think that was a bit odd. That's why I asked."

Pause. "Did Daniel speak to anyone else?"

"Almost everyone, except for me, of course. Charles and Tom. Well, before Charles went to try and drink himself to death. Dennis was hanging around him as well. And when it was time to go outside for the fireworks, Eleanor was speaking to him. That also looked intense."

Pause. "Do you know what Daniel and Eleanor spoke about?"

"I was only his wife, Mr Dakar. It wasn't my place, I'm sure."

Pause, nod. "And then the fireworks show?"

"Yes. We all went outside. Tom was very full of himself, stoating around. I'm not all that interested in fireworks, to be honest, and I've had a lot on my mind recently, so I was just sort of daydreaming. And then Jane and Tom had some kind of fight about something, and then Jane began shouting and pointing at the window. And then I saw Daniel."

Pause. "Everyone was outside?"

Sarah-Anne shrugged. "I think so. I've thought hard about it many times. Everyone except Russell and Charles, of course. People were going in and out all the time before that, though. I put the beers, wines and spirits at the back door as well as any spare glasses I had, so they didn't have to, but ... People were still in and out, presumably to use the toilet."

Pause. Stewart took a moment to shake out his hand, the muscles cramping. It felt like his pen was on fire. "You didn't see Daniel go inside?"

She shook her head. "If I'd known what was going to happen, I would have been watching everyone. But as it was ... I was just thinking about other things, until I saw Daniel at the window."

Dakar leaned forward. "What did you actually see?"

"Daniel. He had his back to the window. He began banging on it, but then he disappeared, and there was some kind of crash."

Pause. "He began banging with his back to the window?"

"Yes."

Pause. "And what happened then?"

"Daniel disappeared. Then Jane began running for the door, and everyone charged up, en masse."

Pause. "You did not charge up?"

She sighed, and looked down. "No. Daniel had changed. Some of the things he'd said over the last month ..." She shrugged. "I thought it was a joke, not real. So I walked rather than ran." She closed her eyes, scrunching them up tight.

Pause. "Were you not concerned about Daniel?"

A deep breath, before she looked up. Her eyes were red-tinged. "Not really, Mr Dakar, not then. I felt more ..." Sarah-Anne looked around, as if searching the room for the right word, "... weary. World weary. You have to understand that Daniel had changed a lot, and was capable of doing pretty much anything, including some kind of sick joke on the kind of night when I had gone to the effort of organising a nice birthday for him. Especially on that kind of night."

Pause, nod. "Did you become concerned when you heard everyone else shouting?"

She shook her head. "No. Even when they shouted about blood, I still thought it was a joke. Later, when I saw the knife, I thought maybe something had happened."

Pause. "Where was the knife when you came in?"

"On the floor, amongst the other things. I don't think anyone touched it."

Pause, nod. "What did you see when you first arrived?"

"By the time I got there, Jane shouting about Charles and Russell being dead, of all things. I thought she was trying to create a distraction, to let Daniel get out or something. So instead of going in I ducked into the closet, watching the stairs, to see if Daniel tried to slip past." She shook her head, lips pursed.

Pause. "But you did not see Daniel?"

She shook her head. "No. But I saw Dennis go upstairs."

Pause. "You saw Dennis go up the stairs? When?"

"Just after Jane began shouting and screaming about Charles and Russell. He ran into the guest bedroom, where Jane was still having hysterics. At that point I went into Daniel's bedroom. That's when I saw the knife."

Pause. "Do you know if Dennis was upstairs before you?"

"No. I certainly didn't see him downstairs when I came up, and I'm sure I was last. Tom was still labouring up the stairs when I got to the bottom."

Pause. "Could he have been hiding downstairs?"

She shrugged. "It's possible. I didn't check the other rooms when I went upstairs."

Pause. "And when you came upstairs, did you lose sight of the stairs at any point?"

She shook her head. "No. I was watching them for Daniel."

Pause. "When you went into the bedroom, was the window closed?"

"Yes."

Pause, nod. "Was there much blood in the en suite?"

She nodded. "That's the strange thing. Well, one of the strange things. We saw him at the window, and the crash was just afterwards. But there wasn't much blood in the bedroom. There was much more in the en suite."

A long pause now, Dakar's eyes glinting in the light. "Is it possible Daniel could have slipped out the en suite onto the landing and hidden until later, and then slipped away?"

"No. I mean, I don't know about what others saw, but the door between the en suite and the upstairs landing has a bolt on it, on the inside. It was bolted. At least when I saw it."

Pause. "Was the en suite always locked?"

"No, hardly ever. That was the strange thing. There's only one key, and it was missing. The police found it in Daniel's pocket, on the body."

Pause, nod. "And I understand that afterwards you searched the entire second floor?"

Sarah-Anne nodded. "That's right. Well, if the body wasn't in that room, then it must have been nearby. It couldn't have gotten down the stairs. So we searched the entire upstairs floor, systematically this time, and didn't find anything. No blood, much less a body."

Pause. "And what then?"

Sarah-Anne's eyes narrowed, her lips becoming invisible. "Jane decided to announce to everyone that Daniel had told her he had been planning a big surprise for later that night." She ended in a shrug of frustration. "People thought the banging on the window might be it, some kind of joke he was playing on us all."

Pause. "We heard that you took Jane into the en suite after this?"

She nodded, and closed her eyes for a few seconds. She opened them again with a deep exhalation. "There is a limit, Mr Dakar. It was one thing for this to be done privately. But publicly was something else. I took her in there and demanded to know what was going on. I told her I wasn't angry, but that I didn't want any games."

Pause. "And her response?"

"She denied it all, of course. Began accusing me of things, like paranoia and jealousy."

Long pause, nod. "And then people left?"

"Yes. Sandra went off to the pub in case Daniel was down there having a good time. She took Jane and Craig with her. Eleanor and Dennis left too. Martina and Tom stayed. I don't know why Martina hung around. I'd asked Tom if he wanted another drink, because I wanted to try and speak to him about Daniel, about this latest escapade. And then Tom went down for another bottle of red, and ... he found the body."

Sarah-Anne took a deep breath and closed her eyes. She fingered her wedding ring again, her mouth forming a grimace as her mind recalled unwanted memories.

Pause. "I am full of sorrow for your loss, my sister."

Sarah-Anne nodded, trying out a smile as she wiped water away from her eyes.

Pause. "Why did Tom go down the stairs?"

She swallowed. "He wanted more wine. I didn't really fancy another drink after what had happened. Daniel was lying at the bottom of those stairs, the man I married … dead and gone. Tom had a fit when he saw him. We called an ambulance for him."

Dakar sat back, the stool creaking softly as his weight shifted over the top of it. "Over the last few months, was there anywhere Daniel went in the house, to be on his own?"

Sarah-Anne laughed bleakly. "Yes, there was. He used to go to the study when he needed time to himself. But more recently he went to the garage. He set up a little office there, made it into a little fortress. He kept the door locked all the time, and he kept the only key."

Pause. "And have you been in there since he left?"

"Not by myself. I showed the police where it was though."

Pause. "May we see it?"

She shrugged. "Of course. The police had a quick look at it, but didn't find anything. They thought Daniel might have removed whatever was important. Or, of course, whoever murdered him had."

Chapter 16

There was dust everywhere. Everywhere. Stewart looked at his suit, which had inevitably become a dust-magnet. Yet another dry-cleaning fast-approaching, then.

They stood in the garage. It was lit by a single lightbulb hanging from the middle of the low ceiling. Although 'lit' was a strong word, the pale light not penetrating much of the musty darkness. The air felt heavy and had a stale smell, too long in the same place without access to the outside world.

Most of the garage was taken up with stuff. And most of the stuff was unreachable because more stuff was piled in front of it. Old children's games, boxes of clothing, what looked like bits and pieces of a table tennis table, random bits of camping equipment, some weights, bits of a barbecue, shoes and other, unidentifiable stuff, all set to live there for the rest of its days.

A narrow corridor had been made to one corner where a stout old chair had been pulled up to a small wooden table, the wood planed and varnished. An electric heater stood beside it. Dakar had begun examining the set-up, and Stewart, after scribbling down a quick description of the garage, joined him.

The table itself was disappointingly clean, only a blank pad of paper and a few pens on top. The two far corners of the table were fast against one of the garage corners. A little bit of the nearside edge of the table was blocked off by a metallic shelf that ran along the garage wall. Dakar began looking at the shelves on either side, peering into them to see what was there.

Stewart crouched to look at the pad, using the light of his mobile and angling his head to see whether there were any indents in the paper from someone writing on the sheet on top of it. Nothing, of course.

Then he squatted down and looked under the table. There was an old filing cabinet there, painted a horrible off-white greenish colour, where the paint hadn't yet flecked off to reveal the rust. Stewart recognised the type from all those films made in the eighties. He reached for the first drawer but stopped when Dakar spoke.

"My brother." The voice was calm but had an urgency in it that made Stewart stop as his hand went to curl around the handle. Stewart looked over his shoulder, where Dakar was holding out a pair of disposable gloves towards him. He was nodding towards the filing cabinet.

"A good idea. But use these. Just in case the police decide to come back and look again."

Stewart nodded slowly, and pulled his hand back, remembering his experience with the wine bottle at Hanover House. No need for the cops to be looking for his fingerprints again. He took the gloves from Dakar and put them on, enjoying the snapping noise they made.

He turned back and pulled at the first handle, a thrill of excitement going through him. The drawer made a nasty noise as it came out, the metal parts sticking together. In it, there were a few pads and pencils, some pens, and other assorted stationery.

The next drawer down, making a far nastier noise than the first, revealed folders, all of them empty, standing upright in the filing system. They looked like they hadn't been touched in the last few years. The third drawer, the last one, was so completely stuck that Stewart could only open it a few inches. The light of his mobile phone showed nothing but dust.

Stewart closed the last drawer disappointedly. He opened the top one again, and had a look through the supplies there, but there was nothing he could see that caught his attention. He opened the first and second drawers all the way out, touching their backs, but he only felt the expected thin metallic sheet.

He closed it all and stood back up again. The thrill of excitement was only a memory now.

Dakar was leaning past the table, looking at the end of one of the shelves that ended beside the table.

"There is a hook here, screwed into the shelf. Recently, I believe." Stewart leaned over the desk next to Dakar, looking at the side of the shelf. There was indeed a small metal hook there, shiny next to the dull metal of the shelf. It was out of sight if you were standing at the desk.

Stewart leaned back as Dakar sat himself down in the chair. It gave an ominous creak. "The hook is, I believe, for a key."

Stewart nodded. Technically you could probably hang a coat from it as well, but if it was for your coat, it was in an odd place. You'd need to take it off, reach all the way around, and even then the coat would probably spill onto the top of the desk.

The Price to Pay

But Dakar was now reaching down to the filing cabinet, locking it in order to be able to pull out the key. He didn't really have to move to reach around to the hook and put the key on it, just shift his weight slightly. He brought the key back, examining it closely.

"Weird that the drawers scrape out, but the key turns so easily."

Pause. "Yes. And he locked the door, and ensured he had the only key. And yet he would leave his filing cabinet unlocked, with the key in there."

Stewart looked at Dakar, then back down at the filing cabinet. He crouched all the way down, to the underside of the filing cabinet. Craning his neck, he saw it had been raised, and stood on four small wheels.

The excitement coursed through him, twice as strong. He grasped the handle of the top drawer again, and pulled. The drawer itself didn't open, as it was locked, but the entire filing cabinet ran all the way out smoothly. There was an open-top compartment tacked on to the back.

Dakar smiled, and slowly reached around the shelf and hooked the key onto the hook. "Bravo." He looked at the revealed cavity. "Would you care to do the honours?"

Stewart nodded. It felt like he had electricity in his veins rather than blood. He reached down and pulled out a heavy black camera bag. He put it on the table while he looked back into the compartment. The removal of the camera bag had revealed a couple of big brown manila envelopes, A4 size. He pulled them out as well, placing them on the desk.

Dakar reached into the main compartment of the camera bag and withdrew an expensive-looking camera. He placed it on the desk, and also took out three lenses, one of them huge.

Stewart picked up the first envelope, before stopping as a part of his brain suddenly broke through his excitement and flooded his mind with doubt.

This was probably a police crime scene, or whatever they called it. Looking into the envelope might constitute interference in an ongoing investigation – a murder investigation, to boot. Maybe even opening the filing cabinet hadn't been allowed.

Hanover House welled up in his memory again, with an image of DC Lemkin accusing him of tampering with a crime scene. Well, maybe not accusing, maybe that was too strong a word. Trying to put the wind up him, that was probably a better way of saying it. But still. It had been scary enough, even if that hadn't been the way he'd retold it to his mates.

Stewart looked at the envelope in his hand.

"Eh, am I allowed to open this?"

Dakar paused. "Yes."

Stewart nodded once, waiting for some kind of further explanation from Dakar, or at least reassurance, but none seemed forthcoming. He took a deep breath.

Right then. Sod it.

He opened the envelope, and pulled out one small square piece of paper. It was some kind of form, with a bit of handwriting on it. He held it up for Dakar, who examined it.

"A prescription form. For Zopiclone. Signed by Eleanor, although the handwriting is difficult to read."

Stewart looked at the form again before he put it back in the envelope, placing it on the desk. He picked up the other envelope. It felt heavier. He felt the excitement building in him.

There were a number of photographs. He looked at the first couple, then took out the stack and put them on the table, where he spread them out. There were around twenty in total, each with a date and time stamp. Stewart recognised the background as Hotel Black. It was a posh new hotel, futuristic-themed, although in a robotic, computer kind of way rather than a spaceship kind of way. He'd never been inside, but he heard that the staff whizzed around on fake hover boards, wearing helmets.

The first few, stamped 15.9.17 at ten at night, showed a man hanging around outside a building. He was short and stocky, his muscular frame clear through the jacket he was wearing. He had short hair, almost like a military buzz cut.

The first three photos showed the guy outside, standing on the large, impressive steps of the hotel. The next six or seven of them showed a woman approaching, although only from behind, so all Stewart could see was that she had big curly blonde hair, high heels and was wearing some kind of business suit. They weren't the clearest photos, and in one a passing car obscured the entire scene.

The photos showed the man and woman hugging, kissing and then entering the hotel, hand in hand. Then the photos seemed to begin again, stamped 27.9.17, again at ten at night. They showed the same man hanging around outside the hotel, in different clothes. Again the approach of the woman, again with big curly blonde hair, wearing a suit, with heels. Again the embrace, and the entrance.

Stewart stood back from the photos, while Dakar examined them for a few seconds more. Eventually Dakar straightened up as well.

"Daniel was spying on someone." Stewart couldn't keep the excitement from his voice.

Pause. "It appears so." Dakar looked over at the compartment. "There is another sheet in there, I believe."

Stewart looked in and saw another sheet, lying full against the side. He pulled it out, and laid it on the table beside the photographs.

It was plain, with a few bits of scribbled writing. The first was '*15/9: GD at hotel with ?? Stayed there at least two hours. Unclear*', and then a few lines down, '*18/9, met MD. CD followed. Thug*'. Below this was '*27/9: GD at hotel, with ?? (same ?? as before?) Stayed there at least three hours. Overnight??*'

Pause. Dakar looked around at him, ghost of a smile on his face. "I suggest we go inside and ask Sarah-Anne if she knows anything about the prescription form or the photographs. And we should also try to identify the hotel in question."

"Eh, I think I know which hotel it is." Stewart spoke hesitatingly, because he was lying. He didn't think, he knew. He was 100% certain. "I'm pretty sure it's that fancy new one near Tollcross. The futuristic one. I think it's called Hotel Black, or something like that. I recognise it from the stairs. Can't think of any other hotel in the city that has these type of stairs. Maybe the big guys out in the countryside, Gleneagles or whatever."

Stewart re-ran that last sentence in his head. He had never actually seen Gleneagles hotel, but it stood to reason that it would have to have big, impressive stairs.

Pause. "Thank you, my brother. That makes things easier." Dakar tidied the photographs before he slid everything back into the envelope, notation page on top. Dakar picked up the bag, but as he did so, they both heard a noise. Dakar stopped, then reached inside the various pockets, finally coming out with a small, flat, black device that had a screen.

"What's that?"

Pause. Dakar turned it over once. "I believe it's the base unit for a GPS tracker."

"So Daniel was tracking whoever he was spying on as well?"

Pause. Dakar opened the envelope and put his finger on the guy in the photo. "I should not be surprised if the other part of this device is in the car belonging to whoever this man is."

Euan B. Pollock

Chapter 17

"Did Daniel take these?"

They were once more at the high chairs at the counter in the kitchen, Sarah-Anne looking at the photographs. Dakar had taken the envelope inside and spread a few of the photographs out in front of her.

Pause. "We believe so. Did he have an interest in photography?"

She shook her head. "Not that I knew of."

Pause. "We also found a GPS tracker device. Did you know Daniel had one of them?"

"He had GPS in the garage? But he had one in his car, as well."

Pause. "A GPS tracker, my sister," Dakar repeated, emphasising the word 'tracker'. "It is something that is used to track the movements of someone else."

"Oh. No, I didn't know he had one of them."

Pause. "What about the people in the photographs?"

She studied them again. "Well, they're a bit blurry," she said eventually, straightening back up. "I suppose Daniel was just learning how to be a spy when he took these?" She had her eyebrows raised.

Dakar just smiled back.

She put a finger on a picture. "I recognise him."

Stewart sat up immediately, looking at Dakar, his pen hovering over his pad. But the guy looked infuriatingly calm, taking his pause before he asked the obvious question.

"Who do you believe the man in the photograph is?"

"Graham Donaldson. Martina Donaldson's husband, Craig's dad. He runs a business, landscape gardening, focusing upon sustainability and permaculture."

Stewart looked up at this last word, eyebrows furrowed. Sarah-Anne caught his expression. "You know, the cultivation of land and animals in accordance with nature. So that anything you take out of the system is put back in, and it all works in balance. It's truly excellent work. Very much like the philosophy of the Native Americans. Before Caucasian Europeans committed genocide against them, of course."

Stewart nodded once dubiously, then wrote the word 'permaculture' down, along with all the other information, even the genocide part.

"What about the woman in the photograph?"

"I don't know who she is."

Dakar paused for longer than usual, studying the photographs again. "Did Daniel and Graham know each other at all?"

"They had met each other a few times, mainly because Craig and Sandra went to the same school. That was it, though, so far as I know."

Pause. "And Graham Donaldson was not here the evening that Daniel was murdered?"

"He wasn't invited, but he was here all right."

Stewart's tongue poked out as he struggled to get that one down.

Pause. "He came into your house uninvited?"

She shook her head. "After everything had happened, we phoned an ambulance for Tom and the police about Daniel. Well, the police found Graham sitting in his car across the street. Apparently trying to stay hidden."

Dakar's eyes tightened slightly. "Did you see anyone enter the garage the night Daniel was murdered?"

Sarah-Anne shook her head. "No. Well, the front part was always down. It's not been open in so long that it's rusted shut. So the only entry now is the side door, the one you used. But it would have been locked. Daniel always locked it, and he kept the only key with him. I mean, I was in and out of the house getting drinks for people, so it's possible something happened and I missed it, but I doubt it."

Pause. "The murderer could have taken the key from Daniel when he murdered him?"

Sarah-Anne paused in turn. "Yes, I suppose he could have. But his keys were in a pocket on the body when it was found though. So then the murderer would have had to have put it back."

Pause. "My sister, you say you didn't invite Graham Donaldson. Yet you invited Martina and Craig."

"Yes, I invited them. Well, to be honest, Martina pretty much invited herself. She knew it was Daniel's birthday. And she brought Craig along to see Sandra, although I don't think they've seen much of each other since Sandra went to uni."

Pause. "Why then not invite Graham?"

The Price to Pay

"Martina asked me not to. I know they've been having marital problems recently. Maybe Martina found out Graham was having this affair." She indicated the photographs.

Pause. Long pause. Dakar spoke more slowly than usual. "So Daniel was following Graham, taking photographs of him, and Graham was seemingly staking out your and Daniel's house?"

Sarah-Anne shrugged, and nodded. "That's the way it se— ... Martina!" Sarah-Anne's tone exploded. "Oh, that woman! She must have found out that Graham was having an affair! And then asked Daniel to follow him for her, and take the photographs. And ..."

She put a finger on the dates on the photographs, up in the corner. "Yes. This must be where Daniel was, those nights when he disappeared during the week. I think the dates are about right."

Pause. "Martina knew Daniel well enough to ask him to spy for her?"

"Apparently. That must have been why she wanted to come here that night!" Sarah-Anne's tone grew stronger and grimmer. She looked up at the ceiling, eyes seeing something other than the white paint.

Pause. "Is there any way Graham could have got into your house unnoticed during the evening? When you were out at the fireworks, for example?"

Sarah-Anne hesitated for a moment, then shook her head. "None. The front door self-locks, and there's a bolt on it that I always use. It was bolted when people began leaving, and I bolted it behind everyone. And there's no way to get directly into the back of the house. There's a wall between the garage and the house, so there's no passageway."

Pause. "If someone were inside and wanted to open the door, would that be possible? If they had no keys?"

"You mean that maybe Graham did get into the house around the back and then needed to get out? Yes. You can just open the door from the inside, and the bolt can be opened too. You couldn't re-bolt it though, once you left."

Pause. Dakar produced the prescription form. "We also found this. A prescription form. For Zopiclone. Do you know anything about it?"

She shook her head. "That's the same drug I'm being prescribed. I've had it for a few months, for stress, from my GP. But it's not one of mine. Not her signature."

Pause, long pause this time. Finally a nod. "Do you have an address for Martina and Graham? We should like to speak to them if possible."

Sarah-Anne hesitated for a second, then shrugged. "I have Graham. I do the accounts for his business." She pulled out her phone again, scrolled through her contacts and then showed them one for a Graham Donaldson. It had a work address, and a home address, the first in Loanhead, the second in Oxgangs. Dakar passed it to Stewart, who copied it down.

Pause. "Thank you, my sister. I would like to speak to your daughter as well about what took place that night as well. May I have her contact details?"

Sarah-Anne hesitated for a moment. "Sandra's coming through for brunch on Friday morning, if it can wait until then?"

Pause. "I should prefer to speak to her sooner, my sister."

Another second of hesitation, then Sarah-Anne nodded. She wrote down a number. "This is her mobile number. She's practically surgically attached to that phone, so you should have no problem getting a hold of her. She lives towards the West End, in Arlington Street. Not far from the motorway."

Pause, nod. "I would like to keep the photographs in the meantime, as well as the GPS tracker. I will return them to you once this is over. Is that acceptable?"

"You can take it all as far as I'm concerned. I don't need any more reminders of what Daniel became."

Pause, nod. "Thank you, my sister. I am grateful."

Stewart was already looking up from his notes by the time Dakar looked around at him, his mind triggered by Dakar's words and tone. He opened his mouth, then paused, and closed it again. He looked at Dakar for a second, looked down at the table with his eyebrows furrowed, then back up, expression clear.

"Nothing from me," he said. He passed Sarah-Anne's mobile phone back.

"My sister, was Daniel good friends with Charles?"

Sarah-Anne gave a short laugh. "Oh, Daniel liked Charles well enough. In his lucid moments he would tell me he always went to find Charles when he went out. He said Charles made the nights much more fun."

Stewart scribbled this down, even although privately he doubted Charles would make any night more fun.

Pause. "And did Charles like Daniel?"

Sarah-Anne looked back at Dakar in silence for a few seconds. Then eventually she shrugged, with the ghost of a smile. "You'd have to ask

The Price to Pay

Charles that, Mr Dakar. I know Daniel always wanted Charles there when he went out."

Long pause. "Did Charles and Daniel seem close that night?"

"Not at all." The strange smile still played around her lips.

Pause. "Did you put out an extra place for Charles at dinner? Once he arrived?"

Sarah-Anne hesitated, the smile dropping. "Yes. Yes, I must have. I didn't know he was coming."

Long pause, eventually a nod. "My sister, there is one further thing I should like to check upstairs, in Daniel's bedroom. Would you mind?"

"Go ahead." She waved in the general direction of the stairs. Dakar nodded, went to tidy up the photographs, but Stewart had got there first, ordering them and sliding them back into the brown envelope. He put it, and his notepad, into his bag. Dakar nodded, and they went back up and into Daniel's bedroom.

Wordlessly, to Stewart's horror, Dakar opened the window and then clambered out, resting his feet on the brickwork, facing back into the room. He had to hold on to the window ledge to stop himself falling. Stewart's eyes opened wider and wider as Dakar reached up with one hand, and then a second, to try and close the window. He got it down some way, but eventually had to give up. Dakar climbed back in and closed the window behind him.

"Impossible to close from the outside."

Stewart nodded, as if Dakar's actions were the most normal in the world. Dakar turned and walked out of the room, Stewart coming after him. He slid his notepad out, updating his notes as he hurried after Dakar.

Sarah-Anne was waiting for them at the front door. Dakar did his heart-nod thing, and Stewart and Dakar walked out of the house. Stewart shivered as they walked to the car, the air cold after the warmth inside.

Dakar stopped at the gate, and turned to look at the house. Stewart followed his gaze, up to the second floor, to the sloping roof which had a couple of skylights in it.

"I believe those two skylights would be a part of the guest bedroom. The only windows, in fact."

Stewart looked at them. If Daniel's bedroom had looked out over the garden, and the guest bedroom was opposite ... He calculated, then nodded.

Dakar stared at them for a few more seconds, unheeding of the cold, then took a deep breath, exhaling slowly. "Skylights," he murmured, to himself. Then he turned and walked out past the gate, to the car.

Stewart slid gratefully back into the small car, where some residual heat remained. Dakar pulled out a mobile phone. Instead of the black brick that Stewart had seen him with at Hanover House, it was a top-of-the-range smartphone.

"Will you excuse me, my brother?"

Stewart nodded, still studying Dakar's phone. "No worries."

He watched as Dakar began typing, his fingers flying at an impressive speed, given his age, over the keys. The man paused, re-reading what he had written, and then touched the screen one more time. Then he put the phone back in its cover, and slipped it into his pocket.

"Never expected to see you with a fancy smartphone."

Dakar smiled. "I purchased it a few weeks after we worked together."

Dakar started up the car, the almost silent engine taking them away from Sarah-Anne's house. Stewart got out his notes, and checked the time. *'Five thirty. Left Sarah-Anne Mannings's home. And heading to...'*

Stewart hesitated. They had the Donaldson's contact details, and Sandra's. But Graham Donaldson had been found outside on the night Daniel was murdered. Plus it seemed he'd been having an affair that was being documented by Daniel. So the Donaldsons, then, and the affair. And Dakar always wanted to go to the scene of the crime.

"Dakar?"

Pause. "My brother?"

"We're going to the hotel next, is that right?"

Pause. "Indeed. Then I think we should have a chat with Graham and Martina Donaldson, about his presence there that evening and about these photographs. What do you think?"

Stewart nodded, scribbling it down. Going to see the hotel and then the Donaldsons sounded good, in that it sounded logical. But it just didn't sound very pleasant:

'Hullo Mr and Mrs Jones, nice to meet you. Mr Jones, why were you hanging around outside a house where someone was murdered? Oh, and Mrs Jones, did you know he's having an affair? Look, we've even got some nice photos. And by the way, the dead guy was the one taking the photos of your husband having it off ...'

Might not make a wonderful first impression.

Then again, it would look good in the report. And that was important. Stewart shifted uncomfortably. Green, and those horrible glittering eyes. If he sent the report to Green. If. The image shifted to Manning, and that large beard, raspy, deep voice.

Stewart realised Dakar was waiting for an answer. He felt his cheeks begin to burn, but a fierceness surged through him, a demand sent from his brain to kill the fire in his face. If Dakar could have his pause time, then he could have his inner monologue time.

He cleared his throat. "Eh, aye. Sounds good. So, eh, you know where Hotel Black is then, do you?"

Pause. "I checked the address on my phone. I believe I know the street."

Stewart nodded. As he put his notepad back in his bag, he saw the envelope with the photographs.

"And we're giving these to the police?" He pulled the envelope half-out of the bag so Dakar could see what he was referring to. He would like to be there when Dakar handed them over. A fine feather in their cap.

Pause. "Not right now."

Stewart raised his eyebrows, his mouth opening. "But, eh, I mean, it is a murder investigation and everything …" Silence. "We'll be handing them over at some point, won't we?"

Pause. "At some point. Probably."

Stewart stared at him, but Dakar, eyes now back on the road, didn't seem inclined to talk any further.

Chapter 18

Dakar pulled the car over on a street, not far from Tollcross, on the side of the Cameo cinema. He got out of the car, Stewart reluctantly following. It was hard to be sure, but Stewart could swear that the air felt even colder. The clouds over the centre of Edinburgh darkened the whole city, nightfall come early in spite of the fact that sunset was still an hour away.

Dakar was looking over at the hotel, lit up on the other side of the street. He held up one of the photographs, Stewart peering over his shoulder. The picture was almost identical.

"We must be standing almost exactly where he was parked."

Pause. "Yes."

Stewart nodded, and quickly slid his notepad out, scribbling the confirmation down about Hotel Black.

"So, how are we going to investigate if Graham Donaldson was ever in the hotel? A smash-and-grab? Or maybe I can cause a distraction, and you can get on the computer or something?" Stewart couldn't keep the excitement out of his voice as he slid the notebook away and eyed their target, the hotel looking plump with potential.

Dakar looked at him curiously. "They are both strategies that might work, my brother. But I think I have an easier one."

Dakar walked over to the hotel, Stewart heading across the street after him. They entered the hotel, into a large, spacious lobby. A long reception desk dominated the wall opposite the entrance, while futuristically shaped chairs and sofas were scattered around, seemingly at random. Stewart saw that the person behind the desk was indeed wearing some kind of robotic helmet, although it looked a bit crap, like a cheap toy.

Whoever was responsible for the aroma clearly hadn't got the memo though. The place smelled, incongruously, of fresh wildflowers, although there wasn't a fresh flower in sight. Dakar took it in for a few seconds, then wordlessly turned and headed back out. He didn't stop, crossing over the road and heading towards the car. Stewart, a frown on his face, had to run to catch up.

The Price to Pay

As he walked, Dakar pulled out his phone again. He walked past the car onto a part of the street that was largely sheltered by an overhang from a nearby building. He dialled a number, and put the phone on speaker.

A voice answered after a ring or two. "All right, Dakar?" It was a throaty voice, a Glaswegian accent that had smoked too many cigarettes and had too much booze both last night and for a lot of nights previously.

"Good evening, my brother. My thanks for agreeing to do this."

"Aye, no bother, big man. Piece of pish, so it was. These swanky hotels spend all their money on looking good. None on security!" The rough voice made a noise that sounded like it was choking, although it could have been a laugh.

Pause. "Have you managed to access the guest list?"

"Oh aye. Two second job. What's the name you're after?"

Pause. "Graham Donaldson. Graham with an 'h'."

There was a sound of typing on the other end of the line. "Right, aye, got him. Been there three times. Give us a wee second now, I'll have a wee shufti." There was a pause for a few moments. "Right. You still there, big man?"

Pause. "Yes, my brother. Still here."

"Right. Eh, tenth of September, fifteenth of September and twenty-seventh of September."

Pause. "Was he there on his own?"

"Eh, aye, from what I can see. Haud on ... Naw, aye, reservation just for him, like. Double room though. But sure all the big hotels give you double rooms now, trying to make a wee bit extra." The throaty laugh again.

Pause. "And nothing since then?"

"No according to this, naw."

Pause. "Thank you once again, my brother. I'm grateful."

"No bother, big man. What goes around comes around, know what I mean?"

Pause. "Indeed."

"Aye. Right, catch you. I'm away for ma tea."

Pause. "Bon appetit."

"Whit?"

Pause. "Eat well, my brother."

"Aye, cheers. Cheerio now."

The line went dead. Stewart watched as Dakar slipped his phone back into its cover, then into his pocket.

Stewart couldn't really keep the disappointment off his face. In his heart of hearts, he hadn't really been expecting any kind of dramatic snatch-and-grab chat, but had thought it would have been something a bit more exciting than making a phone call hanging around on the street, trying to not to look too shifty.

Stewart pulled his coat tighter around him, the draining of excitement replaced by a bodily reminder of the chill in the air. "Who was that?"

Pause. "A man I have known for a long time."

"Right, aye." Stewart stopped, hoping Dakar would say more, but nothing further came. "And, eh, he spends his days getting into hotels' computer systems, does he then?"

Pause. "He primarily sends out phishing emails to subsidiaries of multinational companies, trying to trick people into giving up their passwords. He does do the occasional amount of work for security firms. I believe he is contracted to try and break into their systems, in essence as a test run. But I think he mainly makes his money from illegal activities."

Stewart realised his mouth was hanging open.

There was not a shadow of difference in Dakar's tone. "Shall we go to the Donaldson's house?"

Stewart shut his mouth, although he couldn't take his eyes off Dakar. "Eh, sounds good, aye."

They got back into Dakar's car, and pulled out onto the road. There was silence for a few moments as Stewart waited for Dakar to say something, even to acknowledge that what had happened wasn't something normal. Nothing came. ...

"Eh, so, that guy, you've known him a long time?" Stewart tried to keep his tone neutral. Dakar looked entirely unconcerned about what he'd just done.

Pause. "I arrested him four times while I worked as a police office. The first time I arrested him was the first time I met him. That was nine years ago."

Stewart caught himself with the open mouth again. He shut it firmly.

No more gaping, Scott. C'mon now.

"And, eh, now he works for you?"

Pause. "I would not phrase it that way. He occasionally does me favours, such as the one you just heard. He's extremely proficient. Of the eight times he has been arrested on charges related to cyber-crime, he was only convicted once, and that was for a lesser charge."

Stewart paused, digesting this. They were driving back out of the city again towards Morningside, the optimistically named Bruntsfield Links off to the left. Stewart had always thought there was some grand golf course somewhere in Edinburgh when people talked about the Bruntsfield Links. He hadn't realised they meant the wee pitch and putt area next to The Meadows.

"Right, right. And so, eh, I guess you do favours for him in return?"

Pause. "Yes."

"Right."

They drove on in silence for a while, up past Holy Corner, the churches rearing up on the left and right as they drove past, straight down Morningside Road this time.

"Eh, what kind of favours do you do for him, then?"

A slightly longer pause. "He is a troubled young man, in many ways, and had a difficult upbringing. He is fighting his inner battle, and I try to help him."

"Eh, right. But, eh, if he's doing this phishing stuff, it maybe doesn't sound like he's really trying to clean himself up all that much?"

Pause. "He has only been convicted of electronic crimes once. He has been convicted of violence, particularly with racial aggravations, on several occasions. It is the latter with which I help him."

"Right. Aye. No, that's not good, that sort of stuff. Eh, and the phishing stuff? You just leave that alone, do you?"

Pause. "We have never spoken about his efforts to try to obtain money illicitly from large multinational companies and their shareholders."

"Right, aye. I see. Okay." Stewart nodded. There was something in Dakar's tone at the end there. Or rather, there wasn't. His tone was exactly the same. But the lack of change was significant, Stewart was sure of it. He didn't know how, though. In fact, he wasn't really sure what had just happened.

Stewart grabbed his notepad in the silence, and began to write down what had occurred. Then he'd re-read it, and crossed out the part about how they had found out that Graham Donaldson had booked the rooms, firmly enough that it was no longer legible.

Stewart put his notepad away. He stole a glance at Dakar, but the guy's eyes were fixed on the road. Stewart shifted uncomfortably.

"You don't think there's any issues over privacy, or anything like that, getting a random hacker to pull someone's name from a computer?" Stewart said it suddenly, almost in spite of himself, looking straight ahead.

Pause. "No."

Stewart nodded, unhappily. "Why did we go to the hotel at all then? Why couldn't you just phone the guy and ask him from the car?"

Pause. "I wanted to see the lobby for myself."

"Why? What's so important about the lobby?"

Pause. "Perhaps nothing. Perhaps a lot. I find that it's good to visit places and see them for yourself." Dakar's gentle tone did not change in spite of Stewart's increasing irritation.

He took out his pad again, and noted that Dakar had wanted to see the lobby. Then he sat back, looking out of the window. His mind couldn't settle on any one thing, instead going back again and again to Dakar talking to the throaty voice over the phone.

The journey didn't take much longer, Dakar only having to take the right past the park to come straight into Oxgangs. They pulled up in a nice street, more towards the Colinton side of Oxgangs.

Stewart checked his watch. It was just past six thirty. The sun would be setting at the moment, unseen by the thick, angry cloud that now ranged from horizon to horizon, unbroken and unbreakable.

Stewart pulled his coat lapels up around his neck as he looked at the house they had parked outside. It looked almost like a bungalow with another, slightly smaller, bungalow plopped on top of it, standing in a row of similar but non-identical houses.

Dakar and Stewart headed up to the porch, opening the light plastic door and passing inside. It was ever so slightly warmer now they were out of the wind. Dakar knocked on the front door, a once-bright, now slightly marred shade of green. Stewart looked at Dakar, then at the door. He took a deep breath.

It was time. They were investigating a murder, and had already found an affair. Plus Donaldson had been found outside by the police. And he'd looked like quite a brutal guy. The door was potentially going to be opened by a man who was most certainly an adulterer and quite possibly a murderer.

Stewart gulped. Another deep breath as he heard the sound of footsteps inside.

Right. Forget about Dakar and his criminal associates.

Stewart scowled and screwed his eyes up. No fear. No weakness. That was key. A hard man expression. He was ready. Ready for however tough this guy was, however many bloody tattoos or whatever he had. Ready.

The door opened, and Stewart found himself glaring into Martina Donaldson's red-tinged eyes.

Chapter 19

Stewart's expression froze on his mortified face as Martina stared back at him, eyes wide in alarm.

"Good evening. Are you Martina Donaldson?" Dakar's kind voice cut across the two of them.

The woman lost her fearful expression a little as she tore her gaze away from Stewart towards Dakar, but still looked anxious.

"Yes. But I don't have time to talk about religion." The words tumbled out of her. She looked back at Stewart. "And I'm not buying anything ...?"

Stewart looked over at Dakar. He hadn't realised before, but given what they were wearing, they were a bit of an odd couple.

Dakar smiled, a warm, encouraging smile. Stewart could feel his face was hot, his cheeks burning with the familiar fire as he also tried a smile.

"My name is Sebastian Dakar. This is my associate, Stewart Scott. We're investigating the murder of Daniel Mannings."

Martina's lips pulled taut. "Are you journalists?"

Pause. "No, we are not. I used to be a police officer, and am now a private investigator. My associate is a lawyer at the firm that hired me. We have just spoken to Sarah-Anne."

Stewart had been nodding, but hesitated at that last part. It was kind of true, in that he was training to be lawyer, but mostly, or actually exclusively, not true, because he wasn't a lawyer.

"Sorry, I can't help you. I already told the police everything I know." She began to close the door.

"But the police didn't know everything we know, my sister. For example, that your husband Graham stayed in a hotel three times over the last month, and that there is photographic evidence of who he met there."

Martina froze in the act of shutting the door, her eyes widening with eyebrows raised. She took a deep breath. Her deep hazel eyes had a curious mix of hope and fear in them.

"The photos? Of Graham? You have them?"

Pause. Dakar's head tilted slightly forward. "Indeed."

"Where did you find them?"

Pause. "At Daniel's house. Amongst his possessions."

Stewart held his breath again. The moment seemed to stretch out, the half-open door neither opening nor closing. Stewart could see the struggle in her mind playing out in her eyes, flickers of doubt, hope and caution colliding like stars. Eventually, slowly, the door opened again.

"Come in." She turned, and began to walk back into the house, with Stewart and Dakar following her into the house, down a short hall into an open plan kitchen and living area, similar to the Mannings's place although a little smaller.

Martina sat down at a kitchen table, a rectangular thing of metal and plastic sitting squarely in the middle of the kitchen. There was an open laptop and a cup which had held coffee sitting beside a half-peeled orange.

Stewart and Dakar also sat down at the table. Now Stewart could see her properly, it was clear she was the woman in the photograph. She looked like she was Italian, or at least from somewhere down near the Mediterranean, with dark curly hair and her deep hazelnut eyes. She was dressed simply, in a pairs of jeans and a loose jumper, her dark hair braided in a single thick braid.

"We are not interrupting?"

She shook her head. "I work as a freelance translator, so I can work at any time." She closed the laptop lid.

"My sister, the photographs we have appear to show Graham with a woman." The woman looked back at him, her eyes growing misty once again. Stewart pulled the envelope out of his satchel and gave it to her.

She drew out one or two photographs and looked at them, briefly tracing her fingertips over Graham's image. "Graham ..." she murmured. Then she replaced them, handing the envelope back to Stewart. There was a smile on her face, but it was bittersweet, shot through with lines of sadness.

"I am full of sorrow, my sister. Although I believe what these photos show may already be known to you."

"I found out about a month ago, maybe more." She shrugged, and indicated her surroundings. "I have been thinking a lot about life."

Pause. "How long have you been married?"

She sighed. "Fifteen years. Can you imagine? Fifteen years. Thrown away for, poof. I don't know what."

Pause. "You are not from here, my sister?"

She shook her head. "I grew up in Spain, the north of Spain. But we moved to Scotland when I was eight, for my father's work. I don't think I've ever been able to fully get the accent." She smiled tightly.

Pause. "How did you know Daniel Mannings?"

"We went to primary school together in Glasgow, only for a few years. I went back to Spain after that for high school, but we got back in contact when I returned to Edinburgh with Graham. We were never the best of friends, but we met up for a drink sometimes. And then the children came along, Craig and Sandra, at the same time. They went to the same school, so I saw Daniel and Sarah-Anne more then."

Pause. "And you have seen him more recently?"

"Yes."

Pause, thoughtful nod. "You asked Daniel to follow Graham and take photographs of him?"

She sighed. "Yes. Graham, he had booked hotel rooms on his debit card. I put a GPS tracker in his car, and gave the base to Daniel, and asked Daniel to go to this hotel to see if anyone came for Graham. And Daniel did, and he told me he got photographs of a blonde, pale woman."

Martina smiled, but it was a dark one, her face flushed with red. "Men! Honestly. They always want what they don't have, no? I am dark – dark hair, dark eyes – and so he goes for some blonde woman. I asked him the colour of the eyes, when I confronted him. Blue, of course. Of course!"

She had grown quite animated as she spoke, her hands and arms swinging up and making various gestures accentuating her words.

"Where is your husband now?"

She shrugged, her breathing a little harder. "Probably at work. He always worked hard, very hard."

Pause. "His work is in Loanhead?"

"Yes. His office is there."

Pause. "Does he still live here?"

Martina looked at Dakar as if he had grown horns. "After what he did? Of course not."

Pause. "Can you tell us where he is living now?"

"Yes. I have the address written down somewhere." Martina got up, and began scrabbling around on one of the worktops. "You think Graham has something to do with Daniel's murder?"

Pause. "It certainly appears as a possibility."

"I can promise you this, my husband is not a violent man. Graham had a difficult childhood, let's say, but I shared a home with him for twenty-two years, and raised a child with him, and never a word of violence. Certainly no actions. And that's coming from someone who hates him!"

Pause. "Has he ever been in trouble with the police?"

Martina stopped scrabbling around for a second, and stood quietly. Then she began looking again as she spoke, more calmly. "Yes. He even spent some time in jail. When he was younger, he used to fight a lot. With everyone. He came to northern Spain after jail, looking to start a new life, I think. That's where we met."

She finally located a post-it, and turned back to them.

"Once he found out he was to be a father ... We were both young. But his determination to become a ... real, yes, real man got stronger. He began work as a gardener and builder. He kept working, and now, now he owns the business. He loves being outside. Even here." She gestured outside the window, a sceptical look crossing her face at the last two words.

Stewart felt a protest growing at this criticism of his land, but as his eyes followed her gesture, the protest died. The only appropriate word for the weather was 'minging'. Or possibly 'godawful'. To argue would be the epitome of defending the indefensible. ...

"He wouldn't even marry me until he was sure he could provide for his family. And now he provides for many of society's lost."

Pause. "What do you mean, the lost?"

"He only employs people with criminal records. To give them a second chance."

Stewart took the post-it note as Martina proffered it, and began copying the address. Graham was now also apparently living in Loanhead, as well as working there. Stewart didn't know Loanhead, but he knew it was near the big Ikea, just on the other side of the bypass.

Stewart heard the front door open and close again. There were a couple of quiet dull thuds as shoes hit the floor, and then a kind of shuffling that grew louder. A young man came into the kitchen, taking his coat off. He looked up as the three of them looked back at him.

He was a short guy, but solidly built. He had a tattoo around one arm, but Stewart could only see the bottom of it. Some kind of circle and lines, along one bicep. The sides of his head were shaved, and he had cropped hair on top, like an army cut or something.

Martina spoke first. "This is my son Craig."

Stewart wished he had his hard-man expression on now, but it was too late. The guy looked back at Dakar and Stewart with unabashed hostility. When he spoke, his tone was just as threatening.

"Who the hell are these guys?"

Chapter 20

"Craig!" The woman spoke sharply, following up with a torrent of Spanish.

Craig continued staring at Dakar and Stewart, like a Rottweiler in the moments before it attacks. As his mother continued his glare wavered, until eventually he snapped his head around to look at her.

Craig replied in his own stream of Spanish, as loud and as direct as his mother's. The two sounded like they would come to blows. Both began gesturing as the indecipherable argument went on, Craig's gestures encompassing Dakar and Stewart. After a minute or so, there was some kind of lull in the hostilities and Craig turned abruptly to Dakar and Stewart.

"Either of you speak Spanish?" His accent was thick Scottish, completely different to how it sounded when he spoke Spanish.

Stewart shook his head, and looked over at Dakar. He half-expected him to say that he was fluent in every language in the world, but the guy just sat there, shaking his head as well.

"What are you doing here?" Craig's eyes were like slits, glaring at them both, eyes shooting back and forth between them. The hostility in his tone had been suspended, at least, although it had been replaced with a heavy dose of suspicion.

Stewart looked over at Dakar.

Please, in the name of the wee man, don't do the pause thing. And, God save us, don't smile.

Dakar paused. And then smiled. "We are investigating the murder of Daniel Mannings, my brother. You were both there ..."

"What did you call me?" Craig glowered at him. His shirt lifted ever so slightly as his shoulders tensed. He took a step towards Dakar.

Dakar paused again. Stewart stared at him, feeling frozen in place. Dakar didn't seem to be aware of the tension, even although someone in a bloody coma would have a hard time missing it.

"My brother."

"I'm not your brother, pal." The words were shot back, accompanied by a step closer.

Pause. "Perhaps not in flesh and blood. Rather as a bond of our common humanity."

Craig's jaw muscles clenched. Stewart could see the calculation in his head, wondering whether Dakar was taking the piss. If he thought he was then ... yes ... Craig took a step closer, one step away from Dakar now. Both of his hands had clenched into fists, and his head had lowered, coming down closer to his shoulders, his eyes fixed on Dakar.

Oh well, that was that. Dakar was going to get mauled by some stupid young psycho, and Stewart would probably get the shite kicked out of him as well for the dual crimes of being in vaguely the same space and breathing.

Craig opened his mouth, but it was Martina's voice that cut across the room.

"Craig!" Craig glared at Dakar for a second longer, then his eyes flicked to his mother. "This is my house." Her tone was low but vicious, a whip cracking in the silence of the room.

Craig looked at her a second longer, then the eyes moved back to Dakar. Craig smiled, but the anger in his eyes remained. He stayed where he was, one step from Dakar. "It was dad's house too. Until recently."

"We can talk later."

"Not in front of your fancy new guests, that it?"

"Craig!"

Craig relaxed his shoulders back, his head coming back up as he took a step back. His tone became conversational, almost friendly as he addressed Stewart and Dakar. "She always tries to be so proper with new people. Pretending she's such a proper person herself."

"Craig!" The warning in the tone changed, the urgency giving way to fear.

Craig turned to his mother, indicating Dakar and Stewart with a thumb. "The old boy looks about your type, but I didn't think you liked the younger ..."

"Go to your room!" Martina screamed, rushing over to him. She screamed a torrent of Spanish in his face, throwing her arms around. At first he kept the sneer on his face, but then as the torrent continued, his eyebrows came together, the head coming down again like a hunter. He began shouting back in English, the Spanish words from Martina in between.

"Me? Oh, I'm the bloody problem, am I?" ... "You're just as bad as dad, but somehow he's the one that gets—" ... "Fine. Right, aye. Right!" Craig turned and marched out of the room. Stewart heard the footsteps stomp up the stairs a moment later.

Martina had her back to them, facing the direction Craig had retreated, and stood in a silence that rang around the room after the shouting. Stewart saw her hands go up to her face. Eventually she turned around.

She smiled, a smile that didn't quite make it to her red-rimmed eyes. "Sorry about that. It's been a hard time recently. And he didn't take it very well when I filed for divorce against his father."

Stewart looked over at Dakar. He felt overflowing with energy, the adrenaline pumping through him. Dakar looked gently concerned at most. The fact that he'd come within a gnat's eyeblink of getting leathered by an out-of-control psychotic young brick shithouse didn't seem to have fazed him.

"You have filed for divorce against Graham?" Dakar asked as Martina sat back down.

"Yes." The energy was drained from her voice.

Pause. "When will the divorce take place?"

"When the court decides that the man you love and trust betraying you over and over is a good ground for divorce." She spoke flatly, staring at the tabletop, like she'd had this conversation before. "The papers have been served on Graham, but we still have to find the other person. His mistress. Graham won't say who she is. So we have to wait."

Pause, nod. "Craig seems to be under the impression that you are, or were, also having an affair, my sister?"

Martina shot up from the table, weight forward on fists that had turned white as they pressed down on the surface.

"Mr Dakar," she spat the words, "I have loved and been faithful to one man for the last 15 years. Even now – even now – when I have the chance, I have chosen to remain faithful. In spite of what he has done."

Stewart rocked back in the face of this verbal assault, but Dakar remained unchanged.

"Does Craig then have any grounds for his beliefs?"

"No! Craig is a stupid child."

Pause. "Did Craig once follow Daniel? When you met him?"

She looked back at him, steadily, but didn't speak for a moment or two. She rocked back and forth, her weight transferring from knuckles to finger joints. Eventually she sighed and sat down, the wind once again coming out of her sails.

"One time, Craig saw Daniel, here. He came back early from work. Daniel was here, just in the kitchen, telling me about how he had seen Graham, and that he had photographs. Craig, he jumped to his conclusions. Daniel later told me that Craig followed him from the house, and threatened him."

Pause, nod. "Did Craig speak to Daniel on the night Daniel was murdered?"

"No! No. I told him to keep his distance, and so he did." She sighed again. Her face had turned pale, the very act of breathing seeming to cause her some effort. She put one hand to her forehead. "I feel very tired, Mr Dakar. I don't want to talk any further."

Pause. "Very well, my sister. I think I am beginning to understand what you are going through."

Martina looked up at him again, but it was a weary gaze, without the energy to light the fire of outrage. "You think you understand when the person you love – have loved for most of your life – betrays you? Betrays everything you've built together?"

Pause. "My wife had an affair that lasted nine months."

Stewart stopped writing, and looked up cautiously.

"Are you still together with her?"

Pause. "No. But we stayed together for a few years after we had worked through the fallout of the affair. It was not that that led to the break in our relationship, at least not directly."

"What then?"

Pause. "I changed my viewpoint on many things in life, including love. I believe she found that I no longer met her expectations of what I should be for her."

"Had you stopped loving her?"

Pause. "If anything, I loved, and love, her all the more."

Martina looked at Dakar, but said nothing. Stewart shifted uncomfortably at the feeling of pure rawness in the room.

"May we speak about the night Daniel died?" His voice was quiet, his head bowed ever so slightly.

Martina looked at him for a few seconds, then nodded.

The Price to Pay

Chapter 21

"You arrived at the house with Craig?"

"Yes. Most of the others were already there."

Pause. "How was Daniel during dinner?"

"Daniel? Fine. He was at the other end of the table. He seemed to be having fun talking to Tom. Just laughing a lot, very loudly."

Pause. "What happened after dinner?"

"We went to the living room, and had more wine and conversation. I don't really remember much. The younger people went back to the dining room after a while to have some kind of drinking game, that I remember. Two of the boys had to be carried upstairs. Thankfully not Craig. He wasn't drinking."

Martina crossed herself, eyes going skyward for a second.

"Then we went outside to see the fireworks. And then we saw Daniel at the window, and we all ran upstairs."

Pause. "The two boys being carried upstairs. Did you see them?"

"Yes."

Pause, Dakar leaning in. "You are sure they were drunk?"

She shrugged. "They could not really walk. Or talk."

Pause. He leaned back out again. "You spoke with Daniel after dinner?"

"Yes. After the children left. The girl Jane ... She seemed quite interested in Daniel. Poor Sarah-Anne. She'd tried hard, with a nice dress, but she ended up wearing an apron for most of the night." Martina shrugged again. "Once Jane was gone, I spoke to Daniel about getting the photographs. He said he would give them to me later, when the divorce process started properly."

Pause. "How much did you pay Daniel for the photographs?"

"I didn't."

A slightly longer pause. Stewart's pen flew across his notepad. "He did not charge you anything?"

"He said we would agree a price later." She put a hand to her forehead again, but drew it away after a second, and took a deep breath. "But he told me he had them, ready. That he had two sets, very clear."

Dakar nodded, eyes glinting. Long pause. "Is there any way Graham could have found out about the photographs?"

Martina shook her head firmly. "No. He had no contact with Daniel, and I didn't tell him."

Pause. "And this is all you spoke about?"

"Yes. But ..." She bit her bottom lip. "There was something odd."

Pause. "My sister?"

"At one point, Daniel saw I didn't have any wine. He called Dennis over and told him to go and get me a glass of red wine. And Dennis did it! Without saying anything. Then when he came back, Daniel told him he wanted wine as well, so Dennis went and got another glass for Daniel. Like a *camarero*, or something. A waiter."

Pause. "Do you know why Dennis did that?"

She shrugged. "I don't know. After Dennis came back with Daniel's wine, I turned away. I do not need to see the humiliation."

Long pause, Dakar's eyes fixed on her. Eventually he nodded. "When you went out for the fireworks, was everyone there?"

"Yes. Except those boys."

Pause, nod. "And when was the last time you saw Daniel before the window?"

"I saw him going back into the house, during the fireworks. But people were coming in and out, so I didn't think much of it. Apart from the fact that he winked at me when he entered."

Pause. "Did you see anyone go in after him?"

"Yes, Dennis. He went in a minute later. But he came back quite quickly."

Pause. "What about Jane?"

She shook her head.

Pause. "And after Daniel went inside?"

"The fireworks went on. At some point, Jane let a couple of crackers off. No. Bangers, yes? Yes. Bangers. Tom began shouting at her, and she began shouting back, but then she began pointing at the window, and everyone looked there."

Pause. "Aside the two drunk men, was anyone still inside when you saw Daniel appear at the window?"

Martina shook her head again, more firmly this time. "No. Everyone was outside."

Pause. "Including Dennis?"

"Yes. He had gone back over to his wife Eleanor, I remember." Martina shrugged. "I don't really like fireworks, so I was watching people instead."

Pause. "How long passed between Daniel going in and him appearing at the window?"

"A few minutes, perhaps? I'm not sure exactly. Not long though."

Pause. "Did you see Daniel's face at the window?"

Martina shook her head. "No. He was looking away when I saw him, at whoever was in the room with him."

Pause. "How did you know it was him?"

"I could still recognise him. And he was wearing that horrible jacket."

Pause. "And you rushed straight for Daniel's bedroom?"

Martina hesitated, and her tone became wary. "Yes. Well, everyone began to run towards the house, so I also ran. Jane and I were the first there."

Pause. "And you knew where the bedroom was?"

"Yes, I've been there before." Martina reddened as Stewart looked up. "I mean, I'd had a tour of the house previously. By Daniel. And Sarah-Anne. Together."

Pause. "What did you find when you got there?"

"The door was closed, so I opened it. Well, I tried. Someone had put a doorstop behind it, so it took a little while for us both to push through it. Then Jane squeezed through, and I went after her. She was screaming as soon as she got in. There was a little blood on the carpet. And there was a knife, covered in blood, lying among other things on the ground."

Pause. "But Jane took away the doorstop?"

"No, I did. She ran over to the window where the blood was. Well, the blood we could see. There was some at the en suite door as well, but I couldn't see that at first because the bed was in the way."

Pause. "Was the window open or closed?"

She bit her lip, eyes cast to the ceiling. They came back down to Dakar after a few moments. "Closed, I think. But you should ask Jane. She went there first."

Pause. "What did you do?"

"I remember I stood in the bedroom for a while. In a ... daze? Yes, that is the word. Jane ran over to the en suite, screaming about blood, but the door was locked. The rest came in behind me. Sandra, the poor girl, she looked like she was going to be sick. Jane called Craig, and he went over and broke the door down. And there was a lot more blood in there."

Pause. "And what next?"

"I remember Jane began shouting about the two men, Russell and Charles. She and Sandra rushed off there, and Craig went after them, so I followed. It was all surreal. Jane was hysterical, shouting they were dead, as if some mass murderer had been there. But they were just drunk. Then we all came back into the bedroom."

Pause. "Who was there when you managed to get into the room?"

"I'm not sure. It was all quite shocking. Jane and Sandra, yes. And Craig, he broke down the en suite door. Eleanor I remember too, standing over the knife. "

Pause. "Do you remember if Dennis was there?"

She hesitated, then spoke slowly. "I think so. Well, I remember him in the guest bedroom when I was checking Russell and Charles."

Pause. "And Daniel's bedroom? When you first arrived?"

She shook her head. "I don't remember. I don't know."

"And Tom and Sarah-Anne? Did you see them?"

"Tom arrived. He looked half-dead from the stairs, but he began searching the room. Under the bed. Sarah-Anne was there when I came back from the guest bedroom, standing by the window."

Pause. "What happened next?"

"Sarah-Anne organised a search. Poor woman. She looked so ... tired. Like she had no energy left. I remember she looked so ... so noble, yes, this is the word, amongst all the mess. Even holding the apron in one hand. So tired, but still so noble."

Pause, nod. "And Dennis was there at that point?"

"Yes. Everyone was in the master bedroom, I remember."

Pause. "In the guest bedroom, were the two men sleeping?"

"Yes. Sandra had tried to wake Russell, but said she couldn't. I tried too, but it was impossible. They were both ... You couldn't wake them. I even tried some tests I learned. With the nails and the eyes."

Pause. "The nails and the eyes?"

She nodded. "If you press a pencil or a pen on the nail ... bottom? Bed? The part at the bottom of the nail. It is very sore. If you are awake, you cannot stay still. And the same with the eye. There is a thing, a hole, or not a hole, but a ... Impression? Just above the eye. If you press on it, it is also very painful." Stewart frowned as he kept writing.

Pause. "And you did these both to Charles and Russell?"

"Yes. They did not respond, neither one."

Pause, nod. "Did you search downstairs?"

She shook her head. "Nobody looked there. No-one even suggested it, because we all knew that no-one could have ... done it. We were there so fast."

Pause. "No-one could have done what?"

"Carried a body down the stairs."

Pause. "After the search did not find anything, what happened then?"

"People calmed down. Once we saw Daniel's body wasn't there, they began to talk of other things that could have happened. The young girl, Jane, she said that Daniel told her he was planning a surprise for later."

Pause. "How did Sarah-Anne react?"

Martina raised her eyebrows. "She stayed calm, but it was a cold calm, if you know what I want to say? She took Jane into the en suite and asked everyone else to go downstairs. They came down a few minutes later. They both looked very angry."

Pause. "The dentist and her husband left shortly after that, is that correct?"

"Yes, that's right. They didn't want to stay. The children left too. Sandra volunteered to go and see if Daniel was in a nearby bar. And they all went, the children."

Pause. "Why did you not leave as well?"

Martina looked down at the table, her fingers playing with stray pieces of orange peel. "Well, I don't know exactly. There was a bit of wine in my glass, and I wanted to speak with Sarah-Anne. To explain. About why I'd been back in contact with Daniel, why I was there that night ... I thought she might have the wrong idea."

She fell silent, ripping apart a piece of orange peel before she looked up suddenly. "*A ver*, I'm in the middle of divorce proceedings, and Daniel will be a main witness for me. Was. Would have been. It is good that you found these photographs. Without them, it is more difficult. But I didn't know whether Daniel had told Sarah-Anne any of this. I just wanted to explain to Sarah-Anne that there was nothing ... that had happened between Daniel and me."

In the long pause that followed, Stewart shook out his hand. He scribbled three words in the margin: '*Learn*'. '*Bloody*'. '*Shorthand*'.

"Tom found the body?"

"Yes, poor man. We'd run out of wine. Sarah-Anne went outside to get some more, but there wasn't any. I was going to go to the cellar and get another bottle but Tom offered to go instead. Then we heard a shout, and Tom staggering back towards the kitchen. He collapsed when he reached the counter."

Pause. "What did you do?"

"I phoned an ambulance. Sarah-Anne got Tom into a seat, and then went to look in the cellar. She had to sit down as well afterwards."

Pause. "Tom did not say what was there?"

"Tom could hardly speak. I think he could hardly breathe. His face was purple, a horrible purple. It was awful. I thought he was going to die."

She paused, and took a deep breath.

"Sarah-Anne told me what was down there, that she thought it was Daniel. I went and saw. It was dark, but there was clearly a body down there, lying all ... how can I say? Wrong. All wrong. The arms out. I could see his face as well, looking at the ceiling. It was horrible."

Pause. "Did you see any blood?"

"Yes. There was blood on the steps. All the way down."

Pause. "Was the body still bleeding?"

Martina's eyebrows furrowed and she looked down at the tabletop. She looked up after a moment's thought. "I didn't look at it so closely."

Nod. "And then?"

"I went back to sit down as well, but then we weren't sure about Tom. So we tried to make sure he was doing okay. Sarah-Anne called the police from her mobile at some point as well. The ambulance came after a few minutes. They're really quite amazing in this country. I had to go with Tom to the hospital, so that Sarah-Anne could stay and deal with the police. He was in some kind of shock though, and didn't wake up at all. And after an hour or two, I left."

Pause. "How did you get home?"

"I got a taxi."

Pause, nod. A long pause. "Graham was found outside in a car."

She sighed. "Yes. Poor Graham. He also took it hard when I said it was over. He's been following me since then. Not like a stalker. Just offering to drive me home, this kind of thing. But he didn't do it, Mr Dakar. That's clear."

Pause. "What makes you say that?"

"There was no way he could have got into the house in the first place. The front door was bolted. Sarah-Anne had to open it for the ambulance crew. And then he'd have had to murder Daniel and get him downstairs without any of us seeing him. And then he'd have had to get back out of the house again."

Pause, nod. "Have you spoken to him since then?"

"Of course! He's the father of my child. I went to see him in the police station the next day. He had to stay there for the night. I told him he was an idiot for following me. Normally he argues with me, but that day, he agreed." She smiled, tinged with weariness.

Pause. "He was let go?"

"Yes. They asked if I wanted a stalking charge. I said of course not. The last thing he needs is more police in his life."

Pause. Dakar turned to Stewart, but Stewart was ready this time. He was getting better at distinguishing between pauses where Dakar was going to talk, pauses where Dakar had finished and pauses where Dakar was waiting for something else to happen. This was one of the latter.

"Nothing from me." He tried to keep the self-satisfaction out of his voice at this, the second time he'd called it right.

"Do you mind if we speak to Craig as well?"

Stewart's smug smile evaporated instantaneously, eyebrows shooting up and eyes widening as he looked incredulously over at Dakar. Talking to young Mr McNutjob, on his own turf, was clearly cruising for a bruising. At the very least.

Martina laughed, then stopped when Dakar's expression didn't change. "Seriously?"

Dakar nodded once.

Eventually she shrugged. "It's your life, Mr Dakar. Perhaps your young friend here can drag you out."

Dakar just kept smiling, maybe even a little more. "If need be."

"His room is at the top of the stairs, to the right."

Dakar got up to leave, Stewart following his example, slowly, eyes petrified with images of what was to come. Dakar stood for a second longer.

"Ah, my sister, two more things. Did you, or Craig or Graham, know Charles before that evening?"

She looked doubtful, and shook her head. "I didn't. The others, not so far as I know."

Pause, nod. "And Graham's business. Is it financially healthy?"

Martina's looked at him, eyes narrow. "It most certainly is, Mr Dakar. My husband works very hard."

Pause. "Thank you for everything, my sister. I hope there will be no blood that requires cleaning up after we speak with your son."

"*Suerte.*"

Chapter 22

Both of them went to the bathroom before they went to Craig's lair. Somehow, Stewart didn't think it was coincidence.

They reached the landing, and turned to the door. Stewart gulped, and got out his notepad again. He held it like a shield in front of him, albeit a small, paper, useless shield. His eyes moved between Dakar's face and the door, back and forward, waiting for the moment of no return.

Dakar knocked on Craig's door, two gentle raps.

"What?" The response came immediately from inside, the words direct, smashing through the thickness of the door and into Stewart's brain.

Dakar pushed the door open, and Stewart followed him in. The walls were painted white, but covered untidily with dark posters of bands and films, painting them black again. The windows were covered by posters as well, the light outside only getting in through chinks. A dark blue carpet contributed to the feeling of claustrophobia, turning the room into a small place.

Stewart could smell sweat and staleness, mingled with old food and bad-smelling clothes. Craig was lying out on the bed, unchanged. A laptop was open in front of him, blaring out music. Stewart recognised the tune, deep drums pounding behind words that were half chant, half song.

For one second, Craig's eyes blanked as they encountered Dakar and Stewart. Then they narrowed, a scowl coming onto his face.

"What the hell do you think you're doing here?" His teeth were bared after he spoke.

Dakar paused. Craig scrambled up into a sitting position.

"We would like to ask you some questions." Dakar spoke calmly into the urgency of the music.

"And why would I answer any questions of yours?" Craig closed the laptop case, the music abruptly stopping. Any lingering uncertainty in his tone had been replaced by a muscular hostility.

The silence was louder than any drumbeat as Dakar paused. "We are trying to find out who murdered Daniel Mannings."

"Bucky for you, mate."

Pause. "You are not interested in a murder that took place in a house when you were there?"

"No."

Pause. "You did not like Daniel Mannings?"

"No shit, Sherlock."

Pause. "My brother ..."

"I'm not your bloody brother." The words fired directly at Dakar as Craig stood up, his head coming down into the hunting position once again.

Pause. Dakar didn't turn a hair, or at least that's the way it seemed to Stewart. "You saw Daniel banging on the window?"

"I told the police."

Pause. "I should like to hear it as well."

Craig threw his stocky shoulders back. "I could just throw you out. Both of you." His eyes swept around to encompass Stewart, his paper shield useless in the face of such powerful enmity.

Stewart eyed the door. It was a few feet away. Slamming it in Craig's face would give them a few extra seconds to escape, of course. Except it wouldn't, because real life didn't work like it did in Hollywood.

Bloody Hollywood.

Pause. "My brother, your father is the only one without an alibi at the moment Daniel was killed."

Craig only hesitated for a split-second, but it was there nevertheless. "So that means he did it?"

Pause. "I don't know."

"He didn't."

"Then help me find who did."

Craig rocked backwards at Dakar's words, a firmness to them that was far harder than Craig's aggression. Craig managed a glare back, but after a second or two he sat back down on the bed.

"Yeah, I saw the guy banging on the window. He was just hitting it randomly with his fist, looking at something inside the room."

Pause. "Did you see his face?"

Craig shook his head. "Nut."

Pause. "How many times did he bang the window?"

"Twice, maybe. Then he disappeared. Everyone went upstairs, so I jogged up after them."

Pause. "What happened when you ran upstairs?"

"Mum and Jane were there, but there was a bit of queue outside. There was something up with the door, or something. Jane had managed to get inside just as I got there. Mum squeezed through after her, and then got the door open. We had to close it again, to let her get the doorstop out the way. Anyway, after that, mum kind of froze, 'cause there was a knife and blood on the carpet. Jane was going mental looking for Daniel, and pretty soon everyone was going mental. And then it turned out to be some kind of joke. Daniel had told Jane that he was going to give her a special surprise later, or something. So everyone gave up."

Pause. "You broke down the door to the en suite?"

"Yeah. We all got up there, and people began looking around for Daniel. Mum was just staring at the blood and Jane ... Jane was going crazy. Proper loco. She was at the door to the en suite, screaming about how it was locked. She was trying to knock it down herself, and then began shouting at me. So I went over and knocked it down for her."

Pause. "But no Daniel?"

"Nut. Plenty of blood though. Much more than in the bedroom."

Pause. "Did you go to the room where Charles and Russell were sleeping?"

"Yeah. Jane ran through there, after the en suite, and began shouting they were dead, so I went through as well. We all did, pretty much. They were fine though. Just totally out of it. Mum did that nail thing to them, and she said they were definitely out of it."

Pause. "And after the search, you went to the pub?"

"Yeah. Sandra suggested it. She said we'd go and have a look for Daniel, but I think she figured out that Jane wasn't exactly the flavour of the month with her mum. They had a wee chat, her mum and Jane, and Jane wasn't too happy when they came back downstairs."

Pause. "How was Sandra's mum looking?"

"Like she was going to kill Jane. I stuck by Jane once she came downstairs. Just in case anyone went for her. Well, if Sandra's mum went for her. Then we headed down the local sharpish."

Pause. "Jane did not leave your sight after that?"

He shook his head. "Nut. I've seen a couple of catfights before, and they're vicious. Female of the species, and all that."

Pause. "Did Jane talk to anyone else?"

"Nah. We left pretty much straight off. Well, Sarah-Anne came over to her and gave her her bag, and told her to get out. And that was that."

Pause. "She did not pick up anything else outside?"

Craig's eyebrows knitted together. "Outside? Nut."

Pause. "Did you see anyone pick up anything from the front garden?"

"The front garden?" Craig's head withdrew slightly, his gaze lingering on Dakar as if Dakar wasn't quite right in the head. "Nut."

Pause. "Who all went to the pub?"

"Me, Sandra and Jane. Russell and that nob of a legal guy were both totally out of it."

Stewart wrote '*nob of a legal guy [Charles Robbin]*' especially carefully. Something to quote in the report, that one. In spite of Craig's hostility, Stewart felt himself warming to him a little.

Pause. "What happened when you went to the pub?"

Craig shrugged. "We had some drinks. Water for me. I had an early start the next day. Or at least I thought I did. Nice overtime work, but it got cancelled the next morning. We'd only been there half an hour when Sandra got a phone call from her mum to say they'd found Daniel. We went back, and the police show was in town. My mum had gone off to the hospital by the time we got back, so I cadged a lift back here with the police."

Pause. "How did you get to the local?"

"We walked. It's only five minutes."

Pause. "And when you were outside during the fireworks show, did you notice if anyone went inside the house?"

Craig shook his head. "Nut. I was watching the fireworks. Quite impressive really. The old boy had done a good job. He lost it when Jane let off a couple of bangers though. Thought he was going to go for her, but then everyone was looking over at the window where Daniel was."

Pause. "Did you see anyone go downstairs or come upstairs while you were looking for Daniel?"

He shook his head. "I was too busy watching Jane go mental, then breaking down doors for her."

Pause. "Do you remember who was in the main bedroom when you went to break down the door to the en suite?"

Craig looked dubious for a second, then shook his head. "Too busy watching Jane."

Pause, nod. "Where did you get your tattoo?"

Craig's eyebrows pulled together, forehead furrowed at this sudden change in subject. He glanced involuntarily down at his arm, where

Stewart had seen the half-tattoo earlier. Craig's sleeve had ridden up now, and Stewart could see the whole thing. It looked like an 'A', surrounded by a circle which the ends of the 'A' pushed through.

Stewart studied it. He'd seen it before, somewhere. A poster for a film, maybe? The one with Natalie Portman with a shaved head and the guy who'd been Agent Smith in *The Matrix*.

"Why do you care?" Craig interrupted Stewart's thoughts, although his words were aimed at Dakar. His tone reassumed the hostility it had had when he'd first encountered Stewart and Dakar. He tugged his sleeve back down.

Pause. "I support what it stands for."

Craig's eyes narrowed, but eventually he nodded again. "Local chapter, here in Edinburgh."

Pause, nod. "You believe your mother was having an affair with Daniel Mannings?"

Craig's eyebrows pulled together once again. "Of course she was. Secret little meetings. In this house. This bloody house! Dad's barely left the bed, and she's already getting someone else in." Stewart watched as Craig's fists curled tight again, his expression becoming uglier.

Stewart looked over at the door. So near, and yet so far.

Pause. "You never saw anything explicit?"

"She's too bloody smart for that. I caught them once though, here. Came home early from work. They were chatting away happily together, oh yes. Very friendly with each other."

Pause. "Was that the day you followed Daniel from here?"

Craig drew himself up, throwing his shoulders back. "Yeah, I followed him. I had a nice wee chat with him. He tried to act the hard man, but he was shiteing himself. You can always tell with these bawbag types." A proud tone appeared in his voice. "Anyhow, I told him to stay away from my mum."

Pause. "Did he agree?"

Craig laughed, a low, throaty unpleasant sound. "He told me he was going to phone the police. Ha. Arsehole."

Pause. "Your father was outside the night Daniel died. Do you have any idea why?"

"He's been trying to show mum how much he loves her. Same thing that night."

Pause. "He has done similar things previously?"

"Aye. Quite often, to be honest. He's really trying. But mum's being a complete cow to him."

Pause. "Did you know your father was outside?"

"Nut. Otherwise I'd have told him to come down the pub!"

Pause. Stewart caught it, was ready when Dakar looked at him. He went to shake his head, but hesitated. Maybe he should ask something, after all. Show that he was part of the team with Dakar, not just trailing around as a note-taker. That would show Green. Although of course he'd never hear about it. Still, the principle of the thing.

"Eh, Craig," Stewart studied his notes. The panic welled up in his mind as he realised that he had now started and couldn't not finish. "Did you, eh, well. Yes. Eh. Actually, did you speak to Daniel at all that evening?"

There. That was a proper question. Right grammar and everything.

The guy looked back at him, with no little hostility, but eventually shook his head. "No. Mum asked me not to. I knew that if I went to have a word, I'd end up having plenty of words. No need to have a square-go." Craig hesitated. "But I heard him talk all right. Such a …" He trailed off, a dark look on his face.

Stewart looked at Craig, then over at Dakar. Dakar nodded at him.

Stewart turned back to Craig. "Eh, what do you mean that you heard him talk?"

"Daniel was talking to that legal guy, just after dinner. Both of them were killing themselves laughing about how good-looking some women were. And do you know which women Daniel was talking about? Jane, and Sandra. I mean … I can understand Jane. She was giving him the eye all night. But his own step-daughter! I mean, Christ's sake." Craig muttered the last words, shaking his head.

Stewart nodded, slowly, and wrote that down. He looked over at Dakar again, but the guy didn't look like he was going to intervene anytime soon, instead sitting with the gentle smile on his face.

"Right, aye. And did you hear him say anything else?"

Craig shook his head. "Nut. I just caught that part. I didn't want to listen to any more. Russell began talking to the legal guy, and they ended up having a drinking game, so I went to have a look. They both needed carrying upstairs. The girls took Russell. I carried nobhead. Might have bumped his head a couple of times on the way up. Pure accident, of course." Craig snorted with satisfaction.

"Okay, thanks for that." Stewart began making his notes.

"My brother, when you carried Charles and Russell upstairs, did they seem drunk to you?"

"Oh aye. Both of them were totally out of it. They were practically both asleep already. Couldn't walk or nothing."

Pause. "One last thing. What were you wearing that night?"

Craig frowned again. "Eh, jeans and a t-shirt. And I had my puffer jacket with me." He pointed over at a jacket hanging on the back of the door, a dark blue colour.

Nod, pause. "What colour were your jeans and t-shirt?"

"Why the f—" He began, but stopped. "Blue jeans. A black t-shirt. And white Nike trainers, while we're at it."

Pause. "Thank you for your time, my brother." Dakar stood up.

"My paw didn't do this."

Dakar looked at Craig steadily for a second, put his hand on his heart, gave his head nod and turned and left. Stewart looked at Craig, who looked back at him. He tried to give a smile, but it came out as a grimace.

When the door finally closed behind him, he realised he was sweating. He wiped it away. They hadn't been assaulted, that was the main thing.

As they trailed down the steps, Stewart looked at his notes. Only one question mark.

"Eh, Dakar?"

"My brother?"

"Eh, what was that thing about the tattoo?"

Dakar looked at Stewart for a second. "The tattoo is an anarchist one. It seems Craig is a member of the local chapter here."

Anarchist! Images loomed in Stewart's mind. Masked people, shouting and screaming, throwing Molotov cocktails and the like at riot police. Protesting at big economic events. And the 'A', of course, was the symbol of anarchism.

Stewart nodded. Violence and Craig. Made sense.

They reached the bottom of the stairs, but instead of heading out, Dakar turned and walked back to the kitchen. Stewart followed him automatically.

Martina was still sitting at the table, staring in front of her. She looked up as they came in, and smiled weakly.

"You survived. Congratulations."

Pause. "Thank you, my sister. I have one more question for you. Did you know your husband was outside the night that Daniel died?"

Martina hesitated, looking torn. "Yes, I did. He phoned me to tell me, and sent me a couple of messages. Telling me he would give me a lift home. He always tried to make it sound normal, like we were still together." She sighed.

Pause. "Can we see your phone?"

"The police took it. To see the messages for themselves."

Pause. "But you had no intention of going home with him?"

Martina shook her head vigorously.

Pause. "Did you tell him that? During the phone call, or in a reply to a message?"

Martina looked at Dakar steadily for a second, then shook her head. "I just ignored him. Isn't that the best way?"

Pause. "Thank you, my sister. I hope we meet again soon."

Martina nodded, uncertainly, and stood up, showing them to the door. But Stewart stopped on the threshold, and turned to her.

"Eh, Martina?"

She raised her eyebrows, her head turning slightly to the side. "Yes?"

"How do you know that stuff about nails and eyes, to see if people are awake?"

She pulled her scarf around herself. "It is quite incredible, the things we learn, when we go out and experience life."

Stewart nodded, thanked her and then turned away. He and Dakar walked towards the car, the darkness wrapping itself around them after the door closed behind them. Stewart shivered, and not solely due to the cold.

They got into the car, Stewart noting they'd left the house at seven thirty. Their destination was ... He realised he didn't know. He turned to Dakar, but then stopped before he spoke, his brain working it out. He spoke with a sinking feeling.

"Dakar?"

Dakar turned again, still smiling. "My brother?"

"We're going to try and find Graham Donaldson, aren't we?" His tone was resigned.

Pause, smile. "I think he would be the most logical person to interview next."

Stewart updated his notes fatalistically.

"Do you think he's as mental as his son?"

Pause. "He will be as he is. Guessing in advance won't change him one way or the other."

Stewart nodded, and sat back. What Dakar had said was true, of course. But when you had just squeaked away from the son of Satan, and someone said you were off to see their dad, not worrying about it was easier said than done.

Chapter 23

They drove over to the Loanhead address. It was a short drive, no more than 20 minutes along the bypass, the lights of Dakar's car piercing the darkness. Stewart knew the hilltops of the Pentland Hills dominated the horizon to the south-west, the darkness hiding them at the moment, but that was about it. While he knew inner Edinburgh quite well, around The Meadows, the Old Town, and down into parts of the New Town, out here was terra incognita for him.

The house they stopped in front of was a little cottage, set back from the road. It stood sadly, paint flecking off windows with dirty glass. For some reason it reminded Stewart of an abandoned puppy. A small path led to a blue door through a garden abandoned to nature, the long grass threatening to take back what was once its own. Dakar pressed the bell, producing a buzzing noise. No response. Dakar buzzed again, three or four times.

After a lack of further response, he turned to Stewart. "I doubt Graham will be at his work at this time. I suggest we end here for the evening."

Stewart nodded again as he checked his watch. It was eight now, and his stomach was reminding him he hadn't eaten since the sandwich just after he'd got changed. He pulled his coat tighter around him as the wind blew, whatever heat the earth had managed to get during the day whisked away by the jealous air.

The final thing he had to do was write up his report, and fire it off to Sudgeon and Green, then he could put his feet up. He looked at Dakar. He should probably include his thoughts. To show the thoroughness of his work.

"Eh, so, I wouldn't mind picking your brain on how we're going so far. What we've learned today, that kind of thing." They headed back out of garden, Stewart trying not to get the sheaves of grass on his long coat.

Dakar stopped outside the car in spite of the air being absolutely Baltic, standing in his creamy white coat. As Stewart waited in the silence, his stomach rumbled so loudly that he automatically clutched it. He looked at Dakar, his face going red. The man smiled.

"I'm happy to discuss my thoughts, my brother, and to hear yours. But why don't we do it at my room? I have some warm food there. You are most welcome to share."

Stewart hesitated. He was pretty knackered, and his brain was already looking forward to going home and collapsing on the sofa. On the other hand, free food was not to be scoffed at. The current state of his supplies was pitiful, consisting of cornflakes, milk teetering on the edge of the use-by date, bread that had fallen off that edge some time ago, ham, butter and, of course, the ubiquitous tomato sauce.

Beth came to his mind as she so often did, without warning. He knew how she'd react once he told her he'd had dinner with Dakar, in Dakar's place. The gig tomorrow night was looking better and better.

"Eh, aye, sounds good. Sorry, I mean yes. Yes, let's do that."

Dakar nodded, and the two got into the car. It pulled smoothly away, silently, from the kerb, heading back for central Edinburgh. They cut back along the bypass before heading up towards Morningside, the other side of Oxgangs this time, and past the Edinburgh Royal. Dakar pulled up outside the building where he gave his classes.

He plugged the car into one of the electric charging posts before turning and walking up the stairs. Stewart followed him up, the wind whipping around him. It was really getting up now, carrying with it a penetrating cold. An old key opened the old, heavy door, and they went inside. The lights in the reception came on as they went in.

Stewart had forgotten, of course, that Dakar lived in the same place where he gave his classes. He'd been here once before, when he had first met Dakar before they'd gone down to Hanover House. He'd been pretty shocked to have seen a small room at the back which seemed to be not only Dakar's office but also his bedroom.

Stewart looked around the reception. Some places looked really different at night, when they were empty. His old law school, for example. A big old place, built of pale red sandstone blocks, the interior dotted with statues and painting. Grand during the day, when there were people around. But Stewart had been studying in the library late once, on his own, and on his way out his brain had suddenly decided it was just like one of those old mansions that zombie movies were set in. By the time he finished the two-minute walk out the place, he hadn't met another soul and was convinced zombie dogs were hammering through the halls to eat him.

The Price to Pay

But Dakar's place wasn't like that. The reception was the same, simple place it had been in the daylight. The walls remained blue fading into green and back again, soothing in their minimalism. A polished wooden floor had oriental-style rugs at regular intervals, muted lighting along the floor.

Stewart saw the various types of seats strewn around the reception area he remembered, ranging from a bean bag to an austere, hard-backed chair, looking like a disapproving grandfather among grandchildren. The wee fat golden Buddha guy was also still there, in his alcove, having a great old time just being alive.

Dakar led the way back to his room. They walked across the wooden floor where the yoga classes were held, Dakar's loafers making little noise while Stewart's shoes click-bloody-clacked all the way. No lights came on this time, but emergency lights allowed them to see their way. They were more eerie though, throwing a green pallor around the place. The skylight was pure black, the angry clouds directly overhead and blocking out any moon or starlight.

Stewart shook his head. There was nothing to worry about here, inside Dakar's own fortress. He got his notes out from the bag instead and began thinking about what to include in the report. He'd had to filter stuff out, of course, but he was pretty sure he'd got everything important. He began looking at what to remove. The anarchist tattoo. That could probably go. Although Craig being inclined towards violence might be important.

Dakar opened the door, one hand turning on the lights, before he froze. Stewart, immediately behind him but with his head down looking at his notes, bumped straight into Dakar's back, like some crap imitation of the Marx brothers.

Stewart looked up, frowning, but his face cleared as he looked at Dakar. He was staring across the room, an unprecedented expression of disbelief on his face. Stewart followed his gaze, and saw another man sitting on one of the chairs in the room.

The sitting man was tapping out a beat on one palm with a pencil he held with the fingers of his other hand. He looked up slowly, smiling like he'd been expecting them. His face was triumphant as he slowly rose to his feet.

"Well now, Sebbie, my old mate. How are you going?"

Chapter 24

Dakar was like a statue, eyes wide, nostrils flared. Even his hand, used to flick on the light switch, remained outstretched, as if he'd forgotten about it.

The man waiting for them, thumped the pencil a few more times into his other hand. "Ba-da-boom." He smiled broadly. "Guns 'n' Roses. Can't beat the classics, can you?"

He took a step towards them, and threw his arms open.

"C'mon, Seb. Aren't you pleased to see me again? Been a long time, eh?" One of his arms came forward as he held out a hand. Dakar, his expression like he was witnessing the impossible taking place, reached out his own hand slowly. He shook the man's hand as if it was some kind of alien object.

"And won't you introduce me to your friend here?" The man looked at Stewart now, and as their eyes met, Stewart felt the hair on his neck creep up as tens of thousands of years of genetic instinct came into play.

"This is my friend, Stewart Scott." Dakar spoke slowly, still examining the other guy, as if he might disappear any moment. "My brother."

The man went to say something, but stopped at Dakar's last words. "Ah, c'mon now, Seb. Don't peddle this 'brother' crap with me. I know you, remember."

There was a pause, but not like the normal Dakar pauses. Dakar spoke as if he were saying a chant. "You are my brother."

The guy laughed a laugh devoid of any humour. "Aye, right, Seb. You might fool the young boys like him ..." the man nodded at Stewart, "... but I know you too well."

The man turned to Stewart. "Frank McPherson." He held out his hand. Stewart's eyes darted to Dakar for a second, but the guy looked lost. Stewart slowly reached out and took Frank's hand. The man shook it roughly.

"Why are you here, Frank?" Dakar asked him, still curious, still disbelieving, looking like he wanted to pinch himself to make sure he was awake.

"Sebbie, Sebbie! Where are your manners? No 'how are you?' No 'where have you been for the last ten years?' Aren't you happy to see me again?" The tone was light-hearted and yet wrong in some way, some off-note in it that Stewart couldn't quite identify.

Then the familiarity of the expression hit him. The man had the look of the Glasgow psycho, the guy who would be laughing with someone, for all the world their biggest pal, then glassing them a second later for some imaginary slight no-one else knew about.

Dakar opened his mouth, but it was like he was having difficulty with his words. "How are you, my brother?" The words stuttered out, as if it was Dakar's first time speaking.

"That's better! But shouldn't we sit down first, Seb? I mean, that's only polite, isn't it?" The man went and sat back down where he was, and turned to look at them. There was a flicker, just a flicker, of anger in his eyes when he saw they were both still standing, but it was gone in an instant. "Come, come, join me! No need to stand on ceremony."

Dakar walked slowly over, sitting down on the only other seat. He was blinking rapidly, like he was catching up to reality. Frank looked at Stewart. "Ah, I didn't expect Sebbie here to have company. You'll just have to stand, friend."

Frank smiled at Dakar. "That's better, much better. We're all old friends now."

Stewart looked at him, the man himself now, rather than just his eyes. He had been quite a thin guy once, but he now had a big gut from drinking too many beers, giving him the same shape as a thin, pregnant woman. He was quite short too, almost in spite of his big manner. A sallow face testified to an unhealthiness. His hands twitched irregularly, fingers pulsing unevenly.

He was wearing an old, pretty beat-up suit and shirt, no tie, and had a hat on with what looked like a small notepad tucked into a dark brown band that went around it. As Stewart looked at it, the man reached up a hand and touched it, with the same kind of religiosity that people used when crossing themselves.

"I keep it to remind me. We all have to use computers and all that crap these days, but real reporters know that to get the truth, you have to get out there, pound the streets, speak to people, get it from the horse's mouth. That's the only way you can tell who's lying and who isn't. Just like police work, eh, Sebbie? That's what you used to tell me."

The man turned back to Dakar, but the only noise was Dakar's breathing, coming in shallow waves.

"You asked me how I was, didn't you, Sebbie? Wasn't that your question?"

Dakar sat silently, but eventually nodded once. His expression was still that of a man trying to catch up with current events. The man smirked at him, and gave a little laugh. Then he leaned suddenly towards Dakar, the smirk dropping, and Stewart saw the psycho appear in his eyes. "How do you think I am, Sebbie, after you left me to hang?"

There was silence in the room after the man spoke, his hard, urgent tone slowly fading. Dakar leaned away from the guy's intensity.

"My brother, I know ..."

"You don't!" The man screamed it. "You don't know! And I'm not your brother!" He lifted one hand and prodded Dakar's chest across the desk. "You don't know." He wiped away the flecks of spittle that had appeared at the side of his mouth.

Dakar put up his hands placatingly, but the other man took no notice. Instead Frank leaned back and took a deep breath, his glare fixed on Dakar.

"Let me tell you. Let me, tell you." He put an emphasis on the word 'me', his finger indicating first himself, and then Dakar. "After you left, after I got hung out to bloody well dry, I got fired. Straight off. Professional misconduct, Dakar, professional bloody misconduct. My editor said without a word from you, he'd no choice. I couldn't get a job for love nor money, Dakar. Even the goddam *Raker* wouldn't take me on. The bloody *Raker*, for Christ's sake!"

Frank paused, his wild breathing the only sound. His eyes were fixed on Dakar with an intensity that was painful.

"And I tried. Oh yes. Hit all the local pubs, so I did. Got a couple of good stories, proper stories, as well. And not a soul would take them. Papers wouldn't touch them if my name was on the by-line. No chance. And then Gemma, she told me she'd had enough. Spending too much on drinking, not bringing in any money. Apparently I wasn't the man she'd married anymore."

The man stopped again, his breath intake insufficient to keep up with the sheer strength of his words. Stewart leaned away. He could practically feel Frank's anger, radiating out like waves.

"I am full of sorrow for you, my brother." But Dakar's tone sounded careful rather than kind.

"Aw, cheers buddy. Cheers old pal. Well, I'll be on my way then, shall I?" Frank's eyes flashed with fire and brimstone. "No, Sebbie. See, I'm back now. Been in rehab, all that crap. Back on the streets. No more boozing. No more 'one for the road'."

"I am happy to hear that, my brother." Dakar interrupted, but his tone was awkward, like an actor trying to perform a role beyond his skill.

"Stop with your bloody chat! Just stop it!" The man screamed the words at Dakar. He wiped away some more flecks, settling himself down again with a deep breath. "But I'm happy you're happy, Sebbie. I am. Really. That's great. See, you're going to help me. You're going to help me get back to where I was."

Dakar opened his mouth to say something, but then closed it again.

The man turned abruptly to Stewart in the silence. "He ever talk about me?"

Stewart cautiously shook his head.

Frank snorted. "Should have known. I used to be the eyes and ears of this town, lad. I knew everyone who was worth knowing, could find out whatever, and everyone, every man and his dog, owed me favours. But that's all gone now. Thanks to him." He thumbed towards Dakar, before he turned to him. "But you're going to help get me back to that place, my old pal."

Dakar hesitated. "If it is money you want, I can—"

"I don't want your charity." The psycho came into full view for a second, in the man's tone, in his eyes, in everything. He bared his teeth, before the lips rolled back down. "No. See, I want stories. Crime stories. And you're going to give them to me. Just like old times." The man flicked his eyes over to Stewart again. "He never told you about how we used to work together either?"

Stewart, his eyes following from one man to the other, shook his head mutely.

"Thick as thieves, we were, down the pub. Sebbie would feed me little bits of info about his cases, juicy stories, and I'd write them up. And I helped him a few times, finding stuff out. Once or twice I even ran a false story for him, to try and flush out a real scumbag."

Stewart looked over at Dakar. His eyes were fixed on Frank, and Stewart could see the wildness behind them, the peace disturbed.

"I am no longer in the police." Dakar's breathing had grown shallower still.

"Oh I know, Sebbie." The man reached over and patted one of Dakar's hands. Dakar flinched at the touch. "I know. I've read your books, you see. I know all about you and Grace, her affair, falling apart, the working with monks. I know. I saw you never mentioned your own sleeping around in there, Dakar. I guess there probably wasn't space?"

Dakar bowed his head in the face of Frank's triumphant smile.

"But, see, I have a few friends left in the industry, people that didn't duck and run for cover when it all went to shite. And one of them told me about a suicide that turned out to be a murder that he wrote up for a local rag. Down in the borders. And do you know what he found when he talked to some of the people involved?"

Dakar looked back up, his breathing becoming deeper.

"They all told him about someone called Sebastian Dakar, some Zen guy, who solved the whole thing. Some of them were very nice about you, actually. And I thought, oh-ho. O-bloody-ho. Very interesting." The man rolled out his 'r' for longer than normal, drawing the last word out.

The man smiled with glee as Dakar nodded once.

"See, you're not the only detective! So yeah, you're not in the police anymore, Sebbie, that's true. But you're still out there mixing it up with the bad boys. Even if you are some sort of PI, or something. Meaning, you can still help me out with stories."

Stewart looked at Dakar. He opened his mouth, but Frank held up a hand.

"And it seems to me, Sebbie, seems to me, that maybe you've got something new already, eh? Otherwise, why is this one here, all dressed up in a fancy suit, with some kind of report?" The man scratched his nose casually as he spoke, but his eyes flickered between Dakar and Stewart quickly.

Stewart looked down at his notes, held uselessly in one hand, then over at Dakar. But Dakar was still looking at Frank. Stewart could feel his cheeks heating up. He looked back over at Frank, whose eyes had lit up. He tapped his nose once, and winked at Stewart.

"Knew it. I can smell these things, my boy. You're going to tell me how it was done, once you work it out, Sebbie. All the details."

Dakar took a deep breath. "And if I don't?" His tone was heavy, under tight control.

The man's face turned angry, the psychotic gleam rekindling behind his eyes. "You owe me, Sebbie. You bloody well owe me. Never gave your name up to the public, did I? Never fingered you as my source, eh? I kept my mouth shut for you. You owe me. You absolute bastard." The man's voice was trembling now, and his entire face seemed to be shivering. His fingers twitched violently.

"I know." Dakar's tone was curt, the acknowledgment of an ugly fact. "But it can't go back to the way it used to be. I tried before, Frank. I tried to make it better. But you wouldn't let me."

Frank practically snarled over at him. "Oh yes, I remember. Seb and his bloody wonderful teachings. Two months after I'd lost Gemma, you stupid bastard. Two months after I'd lost her. And you turned up, you and your bloody wisdom. 'Don't worry', 'be happy', 'make your suffering useful' … It was a bunch of crap back then, Seb, just like it is now. I don't care how many books you've sold."

Dakar nodded once. "It was the wrong time then, Frank, I know that now, but it cannot be—"

But Frank interrupted him, with a low, vicious voice. "I know things about you, Sebbie. Things you've done. Bad things. Things that'll take this new life of yours away. Forever."

Dakar looked up now, and he was tense, tense in a new way. Tense, like an animal.

The man's voice became a whisper. "You remember, don't you? Billy Cronop? Oh yes, you remember. The coppers were naughty boys that day, Sebbie. Very naughty boys. If all that were to come out, well. There would be a wee spot of bother, wouldn't there?"

The man trailed off. Dakar's eyes were narrowing again, as Frank looked murderously at him.

"And that's all quite beside the fact there'd be a pissed-off murderer on the street looking for some revenge. Remember, Sebbie, Crudup didn't target the man himself. And Jamie and Sam? They would make some good revenge now, wouldn't they?"

Stewart looked at Dakar. He'd never seen his eyes like this before. His face, normally so open and peaceful, was contorting, shadows appearing as lines spread out across his face. Stewart caught a movement, and looked down in amazement to see Dakar's hands forming into fists.

"We've all got to atone for our sins, Sebbie. The Good Lord tells us so. And if you don't want to pay the price, maybe Jamie and Sam'll pay it for you?"

Dakar remained silent, but Stewart could see his jaw lock in place, the muscles clamping down so hard that hollows appeared in the cheeks of his thin face.

"Tick tock, Sebbie, my old mate. I need a story, and you've bloody well got one. Here's my number." The man took a card out of his old suit coat, and put it down on the desk. "Give me a call, or a text. When it breaks, or when you work it out, whenever. I'll be waiting. In the meantime ... Remember Billy Cronop, and Jamie and Sam."

The man walked over to the door. Stewart looked at Dakar, swallowing loudly, but Dakar was staring at the journalist with an anger Stewart had never seen before.

Frank turned back. "I'll see myself out. Don't be a stranger, Sebbie." The man smiled at Dakar, gloating in the face of his hostility, then he looked at Stewart. "You as well. My new chum. Stewart Scott. Stewart Scott." Frank rolled Stewart's name around his tongue. "Good name. I'll remember it."

Stewart froze. Frank laughed and disappeared out of the small room. They heard him whistling as he left, his shoes sounding out his path across the wooden floor.

The silence blanketed them for a full minute before Stewart eventually looked at Dakar. The man was staring at the door, a glassy look on his face, like his expression had been fused in place. Stewart sat in the silence for a while longer, awkwardly twisting his notes in his hands. Eventually he broke it.

"Eh, you all right?"

Dakar remained silent, still looking at the door, as if he hadn't heard.

"Eh, right. Tell you what. Why don't I head off as well? If everything's all right." Stewart hesitated. "Well, as all right as it can be."

Stewart waited, but no response came. Dakar didn't even look like he was on the planet at the moment.

"And, eh, for tomorrow ...?"

Silence, broken only by Dakar's hand scrabbling on the desk, his eyes still fixed on the door. Eventually he located his phone, and held it up. "I'll be in touch." His voice was low and throaty, and his eyes never left the door, the last spot Frank had been standing.

Chapter 25

Stewart woke up when his alarm went off. Seven forty-five. But he was working with Dakar this morning, so there was no need to get up and rush into work. And he'd sent the report last night, as instructed, overcoming the issue of both sending and not sending reports by sending a technical version of the report to Green and Sudgeon, and a fatter, more comprehensive one to Mannings. It would be enough of a fudge to get him past Mannings' rage, he was sure.

He hit the snooze button, a feeling of contentment spreading through him.

It felt like he'd only just closed his eyes when his alarm went off again, this time showing eight fifteen. Stewart turned it off, and prepared himself mentally for the effort of getting out of bed. He glanced out the window, where it looked lighter. The clouds from the night must have moved on. The sky was being lit up by the rising sun, wisps of white cloud being painted reds and oranges.

Stewart stretched his arms and legs for a second or two, then collapsed into a small ball again. He slowly sat up. Time to get back to investigating a murder with Dakar.

Dakar. Christ.

The events of the night before flooded back into his head, images of Dakar's frozen face and Frank's manic grin. Stewart grabbed his phone, checked it. Nothing from Dakar. He went to message him, but then stopped. Eight fifteen. He put his phone down, and instead grabbed his jogging trousers.

Stewart could just about see the start of The Meadows from his bedroom window, where Melville Drive began to head over to Tollcross. The trees, their leaves a cascade of browns, reds and yellows, were being whipped by the wind, the branches dancing around like puppets played by a demented puppet master. In spite of the sunlight, Stewart felt a shiver pass through him.

Stewart went downstairs. Saz was in the kitchen. She also looked like she was just up, in her PJs and hair all tangled. Not the hair that the women in the adverts had, but genuinely tangled, with bits sticking out everywhere.

"Morning." It was more of a grunt than a word. She was crunching through some cereals.

Stewart grabbed down some cornflakes. "How's it going?"

"Yeah, not bad. Got pleading diets this morning. Guess how many cases are going through court."

Stewart hesitated. People only ever asked you to guess if the number was either really high or really low. And ever since the start of her second year, when she'd got her robe and gone into court, Saz had been bringing back stories about how overloaded the court system was. So a high number, then. Problem was, he had no idea how many were normally in there.

"Eh, 28?"

Saz smiled triumphantly. "92 … 92 bloody cases. Insanity."

Stewart tried to look suitably impressed, in spite of his complete ignorance over how hard, or easy, the court was. "Heavy."

Saz nodded, taking another spoonful of cereal. "Shouldn't you be jamming toast in your mouth and getting ready to run to work? You know, so you can be there early and pretend to your bosses that you're working really hard?"

"I work my arse off, my public sector friend. But it just so happens that today, I'm on a totally different assignment, and so I don't need to go to the office."

"Oh yeah? What's that?"

"Actually, it's a criminal investigation." He said it grandly.

Saz frowned, mouth full of cereal again. She swallowed. "Criminal? Shouldn't the police be doing that?"

"They did. But they didn't figure it out, so we're taking a look now too." His chest swelled.

"Do the police know you're doing it?"

Stewart opened his mouth, then closed it again. He shrugged. Saz's frown grew stronger.

"Stewart, you might be interfering with an ongoing investigation. That's serious stuff."

He crossed his arms. "Well, the cops have already investigated. They've spoken to everyone we've spoken to. We're just trailing along behind them, looking at what they've already looked at."

He stopped there, the photographs looming into his mind, his question to Dakar about whether he was allowed to open the envelope alongside the memory.

Saz swallowed the cereals she was crunching. "What crime are you investigating?"

"Eh ... Can't really say, sorry. Firm gave me all kinds of warnings not to."

"Jesus, Stewart, some of the places you find yourself ..."

He grinned, relief running through him.

Saz finished her cereal, and washed up her plate. "Okay. Well, anyway. I hope it goes well. I need to head off, and start marking up these cases before they go into court. Not that it really matters anyway. Admin are so overworked that they can barely even cite the witnesses you need." Saz headed back up the stairs, Stewart nodding wisely in his complete ignorance.

He kept on eating, pulling out his phone. Twenty-five past eight. Still nothing from Dakar. He would give Dakar five more minutes and then phone him, and find out what was happening.

He wondered when he should start billing from. Now, probably. Except, well, this job was from Tom Mannings. He would know all the nonsense that went into the six-minute billing. Still, better make a note of it just in case.

Stewart typed into his phone that he was reviewing the report from the day before, starting at eight thirty. There. Evidence, if Green or Sudgeon demanded it, of what he was up to.

A couple of minutes later the stairs squeaked.

"Forget something?" Stewart shouted over his shoulder.

There was no reply, but a kind of frozen silence rolled back towards him. Stewart twisted around in the seat.

Beth was standing just outside in the hall, in her pyjamas, hair tangled. She had a confused expression on her face, eyes screwed up as the light invaded her pupils. "What are you still doing here?"

"Eh, well, I'm still working with, eh, that new client. And they start a bit later in the day. So I don't need to go into work. At least not yet. So just taking it easy." For some reason the song *What a Wonderful World* came to his mind, the throaty voice of Louis Armstrong reverberating around his head.

She nodded, her confused expression giving way to one of pain as she made her way into the kitchen. Stewart recognised that particular look, having seen it a fair few times in the mirror. He took another spoonful of cornflakes.

"Late night last night, was it?"

She looked over at him, eyes remaining half shut against the watery light coming in through the windows. She nodded once, dimly, and cast her eyes back down at the breakfast she was preparing.

Stewart wandered over, hands in pockets. "Was it worth it?"

She looked around at him, her eyes widening in shock. Stewart took a step back, and held his hands up. "The hangover," he clarified. "Was it worth the hangover?"

She stared at him for a second or two, and then shook her head slowly. "No, Stewart, it wasn't worth it." Stewart found himself frowning as Beth looked back down. He'd had bad hangovers before, but he couldn't remember being in this much pain. Anguish, even.

"No, I guess it never is, the morning after." He stopped. She was still looking down. "Eh, you all right?"

Beth looked up at him for a few seconds, like she was almost about to burst into tears, then turned and looked back down at the cereal. Her breathing was short and sharp. Stewart waited for a few more awkward seconds, then nodded helplessly and turned and wandered back over to the living room table, past the breakfast bar.

"Stewart?"

Stewart turned around. Beth was looking at him, her eyebrows raised in the middle causing worry lines to settle on her forehead, her eyes large, like a puppy.

"Aye?"

Beth hesitated, her mouth open. Eventually she spoke, almost a whisper. "You're still coming to the Oak tonight, aren't you?"

Stewart nodded happily. "Looking forward to hearing live one of these singer-songwriters you're always raving about."

Beth swallowed again, her voice louder this time. "And you're not going into work? At all?"

"Nope. Not going into work. I'll be with Dak ... David, again." Stewart's eyes opened a bit wider as he almost uttered Dakar's name, but Beth didn't seem to notice.

She nodded once, wincing at the effort it cost her. "Okay. Tonight, then. We can speak then." Beth turned back to her cereal preparation without waiting for him to respond, having finally managed to pour the milk into the bowl. Then she took her bowl and spoon, walked out of the kitchen and up the stairs without looking at him again.

Stewart watched her leave, eyebrows furrowed as she disappeared. Well, at least she hadn't caught his almost giving the game away about Dakar. After work he would head to the office party, do his hobnobbing, and then meet Beth. Ideal.

He picked up his phone. One missed call, Dakar's number.

His phone had been on silent, the way he always kept it. The ringtones annoyed him, and there was nothing quite as exhausting as getting the thrill of hearing a message and then the comedown of reading some inane chat or, even worse, some message a company had fired you in a pathetic effort to get you to buy something.

Stewart rang back, and Dakar instantly picked up.

"Sorry I missed your call," Stewart said immediately. "Eh … Yeah."

"Good morning, my brother. How are you today?" It was undeniably Dakar, but the strain in his voice was now accompanied by fatigue.

"I'm good, thanks. Eh … Yourself?" Stewart spoke the question cautiously.

There was silence on the line, and what sounded like a deep breath. "I've been better."

"Right. Yeah. Okay."

"I think we should go back to Graham Donaldson's house today, to try and speak with him. I'll pick you up at nine outside your front door." Dakar's tone was flat.

Stewart hesitated himself now. "Right-oh. I'll see you down there."

"Okay." The phone went dead. Stewart looked at it. Well, Dakar might not sound good, but at least he was still operating. That was something.

He looked at the time. Twenty-five to nine. Plenty of time to grab a shower, get dressed and get out. Dancer. He loved lazy mornings.

There was a commotion on the stairs, and Stewart saw Saz flying out.

"See you. Have a good one."

"Aye, you too," Stewart replied. He headed upstairs, pausing for a second as he passed Beth's room. There was a stillness there, an absence of noise and activity rather than mere silence. Stewart shrugged and headed on to his own room, grabbing his towel and heading for the bathroom.

Chapter 26

"How are you? My brother?"

Stewart sat in Dakar's car, staring out the window. The cold Scottish morning, it turned out, was not much different to the cold Scottish night, except you could see better. Far better, in fact. The clouds were marching across the sky, true, but they hadn't taken over yet, and sunlight was brilliantly attacking the dark stone buildings of Edinburgh, making them glow.

He turned to look at Dakar. They'd exchanged greetings, but then Dakar had driven in silence. Stewart had watched him carefully but apart from checking his wing and rear view mirrors quite a bit, he seemed generally okay.

"Eh, aye, grand. And you?"

"I'm fine." A flat tone, devoid of the warmth and kindness Stewart had begun to take for granted.

Stewart nodded. He'd never expected to hear Dakar play the Scottish male game where, no matter how terrible life was, the only acceptable answer to someone asking after you was 'fine'. But here they were.

The drive out to Graham Donaldson's house was uneventful, the rush hour traffic largely dispersed by the time they got out there. But after trudging up to the front door in a wind that swept through the overgrown grass in waves and eddies, there was once again no answer. They retreated back to the warmth of the car.

"His business isn't far. We'll go there and find him." Dakar's first words since claiming he was fine.

Stewart nodded again, even although Dakar hadn't been asking his opinion. Dakar's expression as he drove was a faraway one, and every now and again, Stewart would see his eyes narrow further and hands harden around the wheel, a physical response to whatever thought had just passed through his head.

They headed out to Loanhead again, turning past the Ikea and, following a maze of small roads, pulled up outside a white building. It was a bungalow, a normal door on the left and a garage door on the right. There was a van parked outside, marked with the livery of Donaldson's business, Donaldson's Living Landscapes.

Dakar headed for the door without saying a word, and Stewart could see a light on in there through the windows. Stewart steeled himself again. This time. This time, he knew that not only was Graham Donaldson cheating on his wife and alibi-less for the brutal murder of Daniel Mannings, he also knew that the guy had done jail time for a violent crime.

Stewart gulped. Christ.

A muscular, short man answered the door. He had short hair, and seemed quite young, only a few years older than Stewart. He was wearing black combat trousers and a black t-shirt with the white lettering of the firm. One arm was entirely covered in tattoos, while the other was unmarked, giving an odd kind of asymmetry.

"Can I help you?" he asked gruffly. His mouth was set as if he felt he had enough on his plate already, and his eyes were red, like he'd had a late night the night before.

"We're looking for Graham Donaldson. Do you know where he is?" Dakar's expression was equally irritated and tired, two men who didn't want to be there or talking to each other.

"Graham? Naw, sorry, I don't. If it's work you're looking to have done though, c'mon in and I'll take your details." The man turned and walked back into the office before Dakar or Stewart could reply.

They followed him into one big open room. It was poshly decorated, with stands spread out through the room displaying photographs of garden landscapes, and one model of a big field with stone terraces with small trees.

The guy headed off to a desk on the right, sitting down, motioning for Dakar and Stewart to sit on the opposite side. He pulled out a notepad and pen, his attempt at a smile coming over more as a tired grimace.

"So, what kind of thing are you looking for then? We do anything up to half a hectare, just us. Above that, we'll need to look at bringing in partners, but we've got a number of subcontractors we trust."

"We're not looking for you to do any work for us."

The guy looked up from his notepad and pen. "What are you here for then?"

Pause, deep breath. "We're here to discuss the finances of the business. It's why we were looking for Graham."

The guy sat back, and threw the pen down on the notepad. "Bloody vultures, you bank guys are. Look, we've said we'll get back to you on the restructuring loan. But you need to give us more time."

"The bank's worried it won't get its money back."

The man glared at Dakar, and therefore didn't clock Stewart's mouth hanging open as he also looked at Dakar.

Dakar leaned forward into the man's hostility. "We're here to help. But we need to find out more about the business."

A snort. "What, our PowerPoint presentation wasn't good enough?"

"We just got this case. Look, we're the good guys. We're on your side."

"There are no good guys at the bank."

Dakar looked at him, then sighed, shaking his head. "If that's your attitude, there's no point wasting our time." He turned to Stewart, who'd managed to reassemble his expression into something approaching professional. "Let's go."

Dakar got up and turned to walk out the door, Stewart aping his movements while desperately trying to keep his expression blank. He counted the steps to the door. One, two, three, four, Dakar was at the door now, five, he was turning the handle …

"Hey. Hey! Jesus, mate, all right. All right. But I can't go through everything again. I don't have the information to hand."

Dakar turned around slowly, letting the door handle go. He looked at the guy in the chair, then over at Stewart. Stewart looked back, ignorant of what Dakar wanted him to say and terrified that whatever he did could break the pretence. After another couple of seconds, Dakar turned and walked back to the desk.

"Just tell us what you can." Dakar sat back down. Stewart did the same, cautiously, studying Dakar with an attempted nonchalance as he looked for cues.

"We're a small permaculture company. We don't pull in massive amounts. But like Graham was saying, this is a growth area."

"I know about permaculture, and I'm with you, it is a growth area. A lot of talk about the environment just now, a lot of people ready to part with their money for the sake of their conscience. But what makes you different to the other firms? Bigger firms?" Stewart couldn't believe the assurance in Dakar's tone.

"We've been doing it a long time, so we're trusted. And we know our stuff, about the basics. We find a water tank under the house, we stick it on a hill so you're using gravity, not fighting it. We plant certain types of plants together because they grow better. We stick yellow and purple together to attract insects. We use the edges, the zones, and we've got a lot of templates in place that we can tailor to individual needs. We're much better than the big guys. They're beginners." The guy leaned across the desk, his voice gaining in enthusiasm the more he spoke.

Yellow and purple together ... Stewart managed to keep up, but not by much. Pretty sure that Green and Sudgeon wouldn't give a rat's arse for this stuff, but he would stick it in the report anyway. They had wanted details, and come hell or high water, Stewart was going to provide them. Along with a very detailed six-minute billing breakdown.

"You guys have clearly been doing well enough for a while. What changed?"

The guy shrugged as he sat back into his chair, a gesture of frustration rather than ignorance. "Big companies moving into this area. Look, it was really niche for a long time. Other companies were all about landscaping for profit, and if that meant busting up nature, fine. If Madame Smith wanted a big bloody fountain that wasted water 24 hours a day, that was no issue so long as she could pay."

The guy pronounced 'Madame' in the French way, although his thick Scottish accent ruined the effect.

"We were a small firm, working with the few people conscious of the problems back then. Now, everyone's doing it, with the new environmentalist wave. And so we're getting squeezed. Big businesses copy what we do, or they seem to, anyway, but do it at a loss at the moment so they can push us out the market. Then they can raise prices later, once all the small competitors are gone."

The guy paused, his mouth turning down as he looked sourly at Dakar.

"And now Graham is getting his arse kicked by guys like you because these arseholes are coming in and undercutting him."

"I've also heard your firm have a specific employment policy?"

The man sneered. "Going to hold that against us as well, are you?"

"I don't have time for pointless questions." Dakar's voice was hard and flat.

The guy reached up and rubbed his jaw for a second, then brought his hand back down. "Yeah, we do. We employ ex-cons. Only ex-cons. Give them a way to get back into society. Graham always says his old gaffer took a gamble on him, and he's willing to do the same for others."

"Any issues so far?"

"Like what, mass murder?"

Stewart saw Dakar's jaw muscles clamp together, and his head tilt down.

"No, no problems." The guy spoke hastily in the face of Dakar's displeasure. "A bit of thieving here and there, but we're careful about that. The biggest problem is truancy. Graham doesn't give too many extra chances out, but he makes sure everyone understands that right from the off."

"What was your last annual turnover in a healthy year?"

There was a pause from the guy now. Stewart looked up. The guy was looking really suspiciously at Dakar now.

"In the good old days, say ten years back, we normally, after all was said and done, turned over about 30 grand a year, after tax. Now, we're that far in the red regularly. Did you seriously not look at our presentation? Surely you know our business numbers? That's what you guys are all about."

"Presentations are one thing. Getting out and meeting people, getting it from the horse's mouth, that's where the real story is. That's the only way you can tell who's lying and who isn't." Dakar's tone grew grimmer as he said the words, and an image of Frank welled up in Stewart's mind.

Dakar stood up abruptly. "Thanks for your time, Mr ...?"

"Morrison."

Dakar nodded as they shook hands. "I'll be in touch." He turned and strode out of the small office. Stewart followed him out, hurriedly packing his notepad back into his satchel.

"Eh, Dakar?"

The man didn't break stride.

"Did you just, eh, lie to that guy to get information? About the bank, and everything?"

Dakar didn't look around at him, and walked swiftly over to the car. "I didn't say a word of a lie. If he drew some wrong conclusions, it's not my job to correct him."

Chapter 27

They sat back in the car, slowly getting warm again. Stewart looked down at his notes.

So Graham's business was in financial trouble, and pretty serious trouble by the sounds of things. But … He flipped back his notes. Yes, Martina had said it was 'in good health'. Stewart circled the notation. Maybe Graham had lied to her about that as well.

He looked at Dakar, but the man was in his own world, staring out into the world but seeing nothing. Stewart checked the time. Ten in the morning. The sun was being defeated as the new set of dark clouds moved slowly but inevitably across the sky, squeezing the sunlight out. It was an impressive sight, nature on earth temporarily defeating the power of a star.

"So, what do you think? Dentist and her husband next?"

Dakar's faraway expression didn't change, but he replied straight away. "It's time to pay a visit to Sandra, Jane and Russell. I want to know more about that drinking game." Dakar turned to him. "And I need to test something else."

Stewart nodded, turning down to his notes, as much to get away from Dakar's intensity as to write. Going to see Sandra meant a trip to Glasgow. The office party loomed into his head, Sudgeon's words and face accompanying it. Stewart surreptitiously set an alarm for ten to six on his phone.

Dakar, meanwhile, had taken out his smartphone and was typing in a number. It answered after a couple of rings.

"Good morning. My name is Sebastian Dakar. I'm investigating the murder of your stepfather, Daniel Mannings. I'd like to speak to you about it."

Stewart couldn't hear what the other person said, but the suspicion in the voice was clear.

"No, I'm not a journalist. Tom Mannings asked me to look into it. We already met your mother, Sarah-Anne, yesterday. She gave us your contact details. You can check with her if you want."

The voice on the other end again. Sounded a bit less wary.

"Yes, we would come through there. In fact, we're planning to head through to Glasgow now. Perhaps we could meet in a café near Arlington Street?"

Stewart strained to hear what the voice on the other end of the line was saying, but unless he actually put his face next to Dakar's, it wasn't really possible.

"Yes, Whisky sounds fine. We'll meet you there." Dakar took his phone away from his ear. "We're meeting them at twelve thirty on Woodlands Road. A pub called Whisky."

Stewart made his note. He actually knew the pub Whisky, on Woodlands Road, pretty much just opposite the Old School House and the Stand comedy club. When he'd been growing up, Stewart had always gone to the Garage. But as he'd grown older he had crossed the M8 and spent more time out towards the West End, getting drunk in a more sophisticated and expensive way. Both Whisky the pub and whisky the drink had been a part of that, before he'd ended up fully in the West End, at places like the Oran Mór and down Ashton Lane, before going to clubs like Viper, the last showing that his sophistication was only skin deep.

The car pulled smoothly away, heading for the bypass. Stewart settled down, looking out the window himself. He always enjoyed heading back to Mother Glasgow.

They were soon at the bypass, the Pentland Hills now visible in the remains of the sunlight. Cultivated fields next to the bypass led up to bare rolling hilltops, darker and lighter patches delineating heather and grass.

Stewart looked over at Dakar. The guy seemed quite focused, eyes staring out the window.

"Eh, Dakar?"

"Yes?" No pause this time. His tone was a wary one.

"Eh, I hope you don't mind, but eh, well, after what happened last night … Eh, well, I was kind of wondering, but who was that guy Frank?"

Dakar kept looking at the road as they left the bypass and got onto the M8. His voice was hard when he spoke. "Frank McPherson used to be a crime reporter, for the *Daily Reporter*, back when it was a print journal."

"Ah, right. And, eh, you knew him, then, did you?"

"Yes. What he said was correct. We often worked closely together, and drinking together. We were quite good friends, in the end. And I did ask him for a number of favours, including running false stories to try and get someone to break cover, and he almost always did them for me."

"Right, okay. And what happened to him?"

Dakar's face hardened further, the hands gripping the steering wheel until his knuckles went white. "He …" Dakar stopped. His eyes flicked over at Stewart, a hard look, before they went back to the road again. There was a pregnant pause, one of someone trying to work out how best to say what was on their mind.

"There was a murder. A brutal one. A teenage girl, 19 years old, raped and dumped out in a wood. I was the DI in charge, and I was sure her uncle had done it. He just … well, he ticked every box for me. No alibi at the time. Relations between him and his niece not that good, but some contact. He was a loner, oddball. He'd always had a special liking for the niece, according to the family. She disappeared in an area near to where he lived."

Dakar paused again, a deep breath before continuing.

"Frank wrote a number of stories about the murder, all of them about this uncle, based on information I fed him. They were pretty sensationalist. A number of other journalists jumped on the story as well. And under this avalanche of stories, the uncle was harassed by almost everyone."

Dakar paused again, overtaking a car on the bypass before pulling back in. Stewart looked down at the speedometer. Yesterday, Dakar had driven at least five miles under the speed limit. Now he was breaking it by ten. It sounded like the little electric motor was at full pelt.

"He lost his job as a lecturer, people threw stuff at him in the street, he got animal shit put through his front letterbox … The court of public opinion can move quickly once a verdict had been reached." Dakar's tone was dark as he trailed off.

Dakar paused, another deep breath. "And then we, the police, found out another person, an ex-boyfriend, had committed the murder. Confronted him with DNA evidence, and he confessed to it. Nailed-on case. The uncle sued Frank and his newspaper, and was awarded hundreds of thousands of pounds in damages. You heard what happened next, to him. I … I was going through a bad time. Personally. I had just found out about my wife, and it was like my mind was … broken. I didn't help him. I should have, but I didn't. By the time I had sorted myself out, it was too late. He'd been crucified."

A silence descended on the car, the only noise the air passing by them as they sped along the dual carriageway. Stewart watched as they passed the Livingston turn-off, and then went past the odd pyramid structures,

Scotland's own small version of the Ancient Egyptian structures, just smaller, covered in grass and with sheep grazing on them.

Stewart turned back to Dakar, and took a deep breath. You were as well hung for a sheep as for a lamb.

"Eh, and didn't Frank mention something else as well? Some gangster or other people, who might be after you? Or the cops?"

Dakar nodded, his expression unflinching hard. "A man called Billy Cronop. He murdered two small children who were playing in a playground in Glasgow. He did it because one of the children was the only son of another gangster. Billy Cronop's gang wanted revenge, and so they went after his boy. He was seven. The other child was killed because …" Dakar shrugged. "Because she was in the way, I suppose. She was eight."

Dakar paused, heaved in a large breath, his hands twisting back and forth over the wheel, like they were trying to wring water from the black plastic. "Billy Cronop was convicted and sentenced to 24 years in jail. That was just over ten years ago. My last major case."

Dakar looked like he was carrying a millstone around his neck, his shoulders hunched up around his neck, head low, staring forward. Stewart opened his mouth to ask more, but something about the way Dakar's shoulders moved, his head lowering further, stopped him.

Instead Stewart turned away and pulled his phone out, its back angled towards Dakar. He went away from the BBC website, his default page, and typed the name Billy Cronop into a search engine. A lot of hits came up, so he narrowed it down by adding the words 'murder' and '24 years'. That got him the story he wanted, on the BBC ironically, of Billy Cronop's conviction.

And there it was, in black and white. A double murder, Crudup shooting one child in revenge for some gangland murder, with the other one being hit and killed by one of the stray bullets, in the very city they were racing towards. Neither set of parents had commented, understandably, but when Stewart got to the end, there were some words from Detective Inspector Sebastian Dakar:

'There is no sentence that can undo the carnage that Billy Cronop has wreaked on these families. At the very least, justice has been done and a cold-hearted killer has been put behind bars for a very long time.'

Stewart re-read the words, then scoured the article again. There wasn't any kind of controversy, no loose ends that hadn't been tied up. No mention of any gangsters called Jamie or Sam either. The rest of the story concerned itself with the gangland scene in Glasgow. Stewart went back to search engine, and read some other accounts of the trial. None of them mentioned any controversy, no potential miscarriage of justice.

He went back to the search engine again, this time typing in '*Sebastian Dakar*'. He immediately got about 36 million hits. The first page was all about Dakar since he'd become a Zen guru, with mainly book reviews plus some interview appearances on TV and radio.

He added the words '*detective inspector*' and put the whole thing in quotation marks. A lot of older stories crowded his screen, all crime stories, where Dakar was giving interviews. He clicked through a few of them. Mainly murders, but also some big drugs cases. One or two kidnappings. They were fascinating, the backgrounds drawing Stewart in.

He was halfway through an extortion case when Dakar spoke.

"Stewart?"

"Aye? Eh, yes?" Stewart hurriedly closed the internet page, looking up at Dakar.

"We're here."

Stewart looked around. True enough, they were now back in Mother Glasgow, sitting idling on one of the streets just off Woodlands Road.

Stewart put his phone away. The Billy Cronop case would have to wait. Time to investigate the murder of Daniel Mannings again.

Chapter 28

Stewart gripped the table edge. Yup, absolutely solid, made of heavy wood. If Dakar went off the deep end, at least he'd have some trouble ripping the place up.

They were sitting at a table in Whisky. Stewart far preferred pubs to bars, and Whisky was certainly the former. Everything was more solid than its bar equivalent, from the furniture right through to the food and drink. Wooden tables that looked like they could withstand the nuclear apocalypse, 'pub grub' that put a bowling ball in your stomach and drinks called things like 'heavy' because they were basically a meal in a pint glass.

Bars, on the other hand, were more lightweight and fancy. Tables in weird shapes and sizes, the only food finger food and expensive drinks with odd names that came in tall glasses and small measures. Stewart always felt bars were wrong in Scotland. They belonged in places like New York, but not here. The Scottish psyche was born of terrible weather and fights for survival. Pubs reflected that. Bars did not.

Whisky was most certainly a pub pub, one of the newer variants that maintained the solid furnishings and refreshments while cleaning the place up and letting some light in, so it seemed a place you might actually want to be rather than be driven into by depression and loneliness. The wooden chairs had decorated cushions, and the wooded fixtures looked like they'd been freshened up too. The smoking ban had helped too, of course, removing the blanket of smoke that normally provided a low ceiling, at the same time upping Scotland's general life expectancy by at least a few years.

Stewart was feeling the solidness of the table with a certain amount of relief because when they had first come in Dakar had paused for a few seconds, then plunged back out the door again. He re-entered a few moments later, swept a gaze around the place with narrowed eyes, and only then gone over to one of the wooden tables, Stewart following him tamely over.

The Price to Pay

The pub was almost entirely empty, minus two or three old men sitting at the bar, slowly supping their drinks/meals. They looked suspiciously at Dakar and Stewart, particularly after Dakar's display, but Stewart ignored them. The old days of walking into a pub and facing down the locals had now disappeared, in big cities at least. They were the ones who were living in the past.

Stewart's stomach had been letting him know that it had been a while since breakfast, and it was with great pleasure he ordered fish and chips with mushy peas. Combined with plenty of tartare sauce and some ketchup, it was basically the meal of champions. Dakar asked for water, and after a second's hesitation, Stewart asked for some too.

Stewart eyed Dakar nervously. The guy was pretty preoccupied with something. Stewart pulled out his notes and checked his watch. Just before half twelve. "So, we'll talk to Sandra first and then maybe try and find Jane and Russell?"

But Dakar was standing up, looking over at the door. "It looks like we can kill three birds with one stone. I'd guess that's her. And she's brought company."

Stewart looked over at the entrance, recognising Sandra as the girl who had walked in. She had long blonde hair, which fell to her shoulder blades, and a pale face. She seemed quite tall, maybe as tall as Stewart, but combined with her thinness, it made her look gangly. She was wearing a big coat, a headband that looked like it was straight out of the Sixties and sparkly jeans.

Two more people came in behind her. The first was Russell, who looked neat. He was clean-shaved, his blond hair combed over in a way that made you think of cricket and private schools. He was wearing dark blue jeans, the sensible kind that your mother would buy for you. On top he had a zip-up jacket, the thin but warm kind used for hiking.

Jane was the shortest of the three, slim with a pixie-like face. Her features were accentuated by shoulder-length dark hair that fell down and framed her face, and some powerful red lipstick. She had a black coat on, that came down to the top of her legs. Below that, she was wearing a tight pair of jeans, also dark. This was finished off with a pair of black slip-on shoes.

This group all headed towards them as soon as they saw them. Stewart stood up as well.

"Good afternoon. My name is Sebastian Dakar, and this is my colleague, Stewart Scott." Dakar had got back his neutral tone, even if he couldn't quite mask the weariness. He even managed his hand-on-the-heart thing, although it was mechanical rather than flowing.

Stewart stuck out a hand, and got a shake from each of them. Jane really went for it, trying to crush his fingers, the shock of it hitting him as much as the pain. He kept his expression neutral, as if he hadn't felt anything at all.

"I'm Sandra Mannings. This is Russell, my boyfriend. And this is Jane, my flatmate."

"Good to meet you all. Thanks for coming to speak to us. Please." Dakar indicated the seats at the table. Stewart nodded at them in general, shaking off the pain in his fingers as surreptitiously as he could.

They sat down, taking off their coats. Sandra had on a green jumper, while Jane was wearing a Franz Ferdinand t-shirt underneath, a woman in black and white shouting out the band's name in colourful words.

"Mum told me Tom had hired you. If we can help find out who killed my father …" Sandra spoke earnestly, staring at them with large eyes.

"We all wanted to come, to support Sandra." Russell broke in. He had his hand protectively around Sandra's waist.

Dakar paused. It might even have been a Zen pause, although Stewart knew that was probably wishful thinking. "I am sorry about what happened."

Sandra nodded, slowly. "It's been a hard couple of weeks. But why did Tom ask you to look into this?"

"He doesn't think the police will find the person who murdered your stepfather."

"My father, Mr Dakar. Even if we weren't related biologically." Sandra spoke fiercely. "And Tom thinks you two will?" Stewart pulled himself more erect at her disbelieving tone.

"So it seems."

The food arrived, and the three others ordered their drinks. Stewart began to tuck in, his stomach dancing in anticipation of the sustenance arriving.

"You've been together for a long time then?" Dakar looked between Russell and Sandra.

Sandra nodded. "About two years, now."

"How did you all meet?"

"We all went to school together."

Dakar turned to Jane. "I heard you spent quite a bit of time with Sarah-Anne when you were growing up."

Jane sat back in her chair. "Yeah. My mum died when I was two. Sarah-Anne sort of looked after me."

"And you got on well?"

"She was like more of a daughter than I was." Sandra threw a look over at Jane as she interrupted, but it was full of old humour. For a second, Stewart saw a flash of Sarah-Anne in her. The look got the glimpse of a smile from Jane, although it quickly disappeared behind her bored expression.

"Yeah. Well, up until a couple of weeks back. We had a bit of a blow-up then. Daniel had come round to the flat, and I think she got the wrong idea. She thought there was something between us."

"Was there?"

Jane's nose wrinkled as if she had smelled something terrible. "Who the hell do you think you are, asking something like that?"

"I'm the man investigating the murder of a man you're alleged to have slept with. That's who I am."

"You're also a man I don't have to talk to if I don't want." Jane put her hands palm down on the table, leaning forward over them.

"Jane, come on. He's trying to help. And if he can work out what happened to dad, I mean … Just, let's talk to him." Sandra held out her hands, palm down, towards Jane, who was still glowering over at Dakar.

There was a pause for a few seconds, then Jane nodded once, curtly. Sandra smiled, then turned back to Dakar.

"But Mr Dakar, that really is a ridiculous question. My dad was like a dad to Jane too. He treated her just like he treated me."

"So of course there was nothing between us. It was insane, actually, how she changed. Sarah-Anne, I mean. One minute we were fine, the next thing she's accusing me of being a … succubus. I mean, Jesus Christ. Who even knows that word? Although it doesn't help she was already nuts."

Sandra threw her a harsh look, but Jane just shrugged in the face of it. Stewart got the impression this was a conversation they'd had before.

"And before that, you and Sarah-Anne were close?" Dakar aimed his question at Jane.

"Pretty much. Well, you know. Mothers and daughters do argue. But yeah, it was all fine. Before she went totally off the deep end."

Dakar turned back to Sandra. "Daniel owned the flat you lived in, is that right?"

"Yes. I moved in because he gave me a discount. Family. He gave it to Jane as well."

"And Daniel came to the flat?"

"Only a few times since we moved in, about six weeks ago. The first was just to help us move stuff upstairs. A couple more times after that."

Stewart finished his food, but before he could begin to appreciate the satisfied feeling, part of his brain that his stomach had been holding hostage finally managed to get free and scream at him that he should be taking notes. He grabbed up his pen and flipped the notepad open.

"Why?"

"Just to chat with us. We even had a few drinks together the first time. It was quite cool, actually."

"And that's the only thing that happened a couple of weeks back as well." Jane broke in, her voice heavy with anger. "Daniel came over. He was looking for all of us, just to have a drink and a laugh. But Sandra and Russell were out. And Sarah-Anne heard that Daniel had been over and I was the only one there, and went off the deep end. Absolutely mental."

"Ah." Dakar let the noise escape, accompanied by a deep nod.

"We came back just as dad was leaving." Sandra chimed in. "We didn't actually get to talk to him, he was just getting in the car. But it wasn't late or anything, and he couldn't have been drunk as he was driving. Jane was on the phone when we got back. Everything was perfectly normal, I mean. Just like all the other times. I don't think it was fair of mum to lose the plot at Jane just because she was the only one home when Daniel came around one time."

"She still invited you to Daniel's party though?" Dakar looked at Jane.

"I told her I was coming anyway. It wouldn't have been right for Sandra and Russell to go and not me."

"Did either of you notice any change in Daniel in the months before he died?"

"No, not really. Well, I mean, we began having some drinks together. But we've both recently turned eighteen, and we're going to university. I mean, isn't that what fathers do? Dad began to treat us more as women rather than girls. But I think that's normal."

Jane, who had shaken her head to Dakar's question, nodded in assent to what Sandra said. "Yup. That's definitely true."

"You knew Daniel as well?" Dakar aimed at Russell.

"Yes. I met him properly when we began going out. And then I helped out at his surgery every now and again."

"Right, yes. All three of you worked at the surgery?"

"I worked there for a couple of years, and Sandra or Russell would cover for me whenever I couldn't make it, or didn't fancy working." Jane spoke.

"And you stopped working there when you moved to Glasgow?"

The three looked at each other, before Jane turned back to Dakar.

"You haven't talked to Eleanor yet?"

Dakar's face became guarded, his eyes going between the three of them. He shook his head.

"We stopped working there because we were accused of theft."

Chapter 29

"Theft of what?"

"Eleanor said that some prescription sheets were being stolen. And she blamed us. She said one of us was doing it."

"They thought it was me, though." Russell broke in. "Apparently it only happened when I had been working." He made quotation marks in the air when he said the word 'apparently'.

"Did she ever accuse you?"

"Not directly. She called Sandra, Jane and I into a room, and said that the day before she'd put a prescription sheet down, and today it was gone. We didn't say anything, and then she ordered us all out. Said she would speak to Sandra's dad."

"And were any of you stealing prescriptions sheets?"

"Of course not!" Sandra shot back. "They weren't being stolen at all."

Dakar frowned. "What do you mean?"

"She was losing them and then blaming others for it. It was ridiculous."

"Why do you think that?"

"Well, it wasn't any of us, was it?"

"It never went any further?"

"No. We were all going to stop working there anyway, because we were coming through to Glasgow. And so we left them to Dennis and his incompetence."

Dakar leaned back in his seat. "Yes. I've heard Dennis wasn't the best secretary?"

"That's the understatement of the century. He had no idea about spreadsheets, or schedules, or …" Russell threw his hands up in frustration.

"About computers." Jane took up the narrative. "Electrical devices. He could barely switch on a computer. When I first arrived, I sorted it all out in a couple of weeks. We could do things in one hour that took him a whole day." She snorted. "I've heard they're going to take a new secretary on, actually. Because Dennis can't cope on his own, now we've left."

Dakar leaned in closer now, and brought his hands forward onto the table. He clasped them one in a fist and put the other one over the top, resting his chin on both. "That night. The three of you came to the party together?"

"Yeah." Sandra answered.

"Did any of you help Sarah-Anne put out a new place for Charles when he came?"

They all looked blankly back at him. "What?"

"When Charles arrived, did any of you help Sarah-Anne put out a place for him?"

"That was all set up already." Sandra answered.

"But you got there before Charles?"

Sandra shrugged. "Yeah. Why?"

Dakar nodded. "How was dinner?"

Sandra looked at the other two, then back to Dakar. "Nice. Daniel seemed a bit flat when we first arrived, but he picked up later."

"When did he pick up?"

"Towards the end of the dinner. Once the wine began to flow, he began talking more, getting a bit louder."

"Did any of you speak with Daniel in the lounge after dinner?"

"I did. Just went to say hello." Jane spoke, a lazy smile on her face. She didn't look like she'd been paying too much attention up until then, head down, intent on tracing her finger over the logo on a beermat. She didn't look up when she spoke.

"Was that when he told you about his big surprise?"

Jane laughed lightly. She kept her head down, still tracing the beer mat. "Yes. He told me he had guessed he was getting a surprise birthday party, but was sure it'd be boring. So he'd planned a big surprise for later."

"Did he give you any details about what it might be?"

Jane shook her head, eyes still on the beer mat.

Dakar frowned ever so slightly towards Jane in the silence that followed, but then turned back to the other two. "Tell me about the drinking game."

"A stupid thing." Russell spoke, running one hand through his hair, his hand rubbing his neck as it came down.

Pause. "Was it your idea?"

"It wasn't anyone's idea really. Charles and I were arguing about politics, and as he was losing like all conservatives do, he began bragging about how much he could put away. Well, I was a bit far gone by that point, and next thing I knew, we were sitting opposite each other back in the dining room, drinking beer and shots."

"What were you drinking?"

"Vodka. Straight. And the imported beer that Charles had brought with him. I told him not to." Jane now, looking mockingly over at Russell for a second.

"Yes. You and Sandra both thought it was a stupid idea." He smiled ruefully. "I think I remember up to shot five. After that …" Russell's face twisted, and he made a kind of shrug with his head. "Curtains."

"Who was supplying the drinks?"

Sandra raised a finger. "We brought the bottles through with us. One vodka, and Charles's beer bottle. Elephant beer, in a great big champagne bottle. Silly boys."

"We just kept pouring and pouring. The glasses were never empty." Russell said. His eyes were downcast, his voice miserable.

"Have you had that reaction before? A blackout?"

"Yes, sometimes. My memory is the first thing to go when I drink, I'm afraid. It was one hell of a hangover as well."

"Do you remember the fireworks show?"

Russell shook his head. "Next thing I remember is being woken up by a policeman wanting to ask me some questions. Difficult to handle with a raging hangover. Even took some blood from me. Probably more booze in there than blood."

Dakar turned back to Jane. "I understand you also brought some fireworks to the show?"

Jane laughed, shortly, looking up now from her beermat. "Oh yes. Last time I try and bring a gift to that house. I let off two bangers, nice sparkly things, just trying to join in, and Tom almost took my head off. Apparently I was spoiling his show. I didn't really get a chance to respond. That's when …"

Jane turned to Sandra. The other girl nodded at her, and looked down. Jane reached over and squeezed her arm, although her eyes were on Dakar. "When Daniel began banging on the window."

"Did either of you see Daniel going into the house?"

Jane shook her head, but Sandra nodded. "I saw dad go in. He was looking pretty happy. Quite excited, really."

"Did either of you see anyone else going into the house?"

Jane shook her head again, made a *tsk* sound and looked back down at the beer mat. But Sandra nodded again. "I saw Dennis going in as well."

"Did you see Dennis coming out?"

Sandra shook her head. "But he must have. I remember I was just in front of him when we ran into the house."

"What about Martina? Or Craig?"

"The Donaldsons?" Sandra looked doubtful, then shook her head. Jane shook her head as well. "Craig was standing next to me most of the time. Martina, I don't know, but she always seemed to be outside whenever I looked over at the door."

"And was anyone still inside when Daniel appeared at the window?"

Sandra shook her head. "I'm pretty sure everyone was there. Once we got upstairs and saw the blood, everyone began thinking about who could have been in the room with dad. But we were all pretty sure everyone had been outside."

"Except Russell and Charles," Dakar noted. Stewart looked up from his scribbling at Russell. The guy shifted uncomfortably.

Sandra spoke, her tone flat. "I couldn't wake either of them, Mr Dakar. Martina tried too. And neither could the police, and they were there pretty soon afterwards."

Dakar nodded. He leaned forward a little, addressing Sandra. "What did you actually see at the window?"

"Dad. Banging. A couple of times. Then a crash after he disappeared."

"Did either of you see Daniel's face?"

Both Jane and Sandra shook their heads. "No."

Dakar seemed to be turning something over in his mind, but he eventually nodded. "And what did you do then?"

"We all rushed upstairs." Sandra took up the narrative again. "But there was no body. Just … blood, the knife and mess." Sandra began whispering, leaning in close, her tone still one of confusion, like what had happened couldn't be real.

Dakar turned to Jane. "You were one of the first ones there, with Martina?"

"Yeah. We got there at pretty much the same time."

"What did you do once you got upstairs?"

"Ran into the room, looking for Daniel. The door was jammed by some kind of doorstop. I managed to get it open enough to squeeze through. And once I was in, I saw the blood at the window so I ran over there. But I couldn't see anything outside, or down on the patio. And then I turned around, and saw the blood at the en suite door. Leading to the en suite door, like a trail. So I ran over there, but the door was locked."

"And you shouted at Craig?"

"I couldn't break it down, could I? I tried, plenty." She looked irritated. "And the guy was just standing there, being useless."

"And why did you run through to Charles and Russell?"

She shrugged. "I panicked. Blood everywhere like that, you know, in the bathroom too. So I ran through. Then neither of them was moving, and I thought they'd been murdered too. Like some kind of horror film. So I began screaming." She shivered slightly.

"When you got into the bedroom, the window ... Closed or open?"

"Closed."

"Are you sure?"

"Sure. I remember looking out into the garden to see if Daniel was there."

"And?"

She shook her head.

"You remember who else was there when you were running around?"

"Sandra, of course. And Martina, she was just wandering around the room. Craig was leaning against the door, until I got his bloody arse in gear. After we'd broken down the en suite door, I caught a glimpse of Sarah-Anne standing at the top of the stairs for a second, glaring at me. Like some snooty queen or something." Sandra threw her a pained look, but Jane just shrugged.

"This was before you went to check on Russell and Charles?"

She nodded.

"And Dennis and Eleanor?"

"Eleanor was there. She was just looking at the knife, in horror. Dennis ... I don't know. I saw him later on. But I can't remember if he was there at first."

"And what about Tom?"

"Oh, he was there too. He basically collapsed onto the bed when he saw the blood and all, and stayed there until we organised the search."

"Do you have anything to add?" Dakar turned to Sandra.

"Not really. I came in just as Jane was getting to the en suite door. I was feeling pretty sick, to be honest. I've never liked the sight of blood, and there was a smell of it there as well. Craig broke the door down and there was even more. When Jane ran off and began shouting about Russell and Charles, I stumbled through to the guest bedroom behind her. But dad wasn't there, and Russell and Charles seemed fine, so we all came back through to the main bedroom. Mum was there, and we searched the upstairs properly. But we didn't find ... anything, then."

"And the people? You remember the same things?"

"Martina, Craig and Eleanor I remember. And Dennis too, I do remember him in the main bedroom. And Tom coming in and falling onto the bed. He was seriously out of breath. I felt horrible when I was running up the stairs, like something awful had happened, and he ... he gave me bad vibes that night. He always does. He's a bit creepy."

Dakar looked at Sandra, and cocked his head to the side, gazing at her before his eyes drifted off to a spot on the wall. Stewart watched as Dakar's hands came together and began sliding over each other, like he was washing them or something.

The silence lasted a few seconds before Dakar broke it, looking at Jane. "And then you decided to tell everyone about the joke Daniel had mentioned?"

Jane looked uneasy again. "Yeah. I mean, the blood and the knife ... I'm pretty sure that wasn't part of it. I got freaked out by that. So after the search, when we didn't find anything, I thought I'd better say something."

"And Sarah-Anne wasn't pleased when you told everyone what Daniel had said to you."

Jane looked down sourly. "Someone else who tried to take my head off."

"What did you talk about, when she took you into the en suite?"

Jane threw up her hands. "What you'd expect. A wild claim that Daniel and I were an item somehow, and some promise that we could all live in harmony if I just owned up to it. It was insane. I left as soon as I could."

"That's when we thought that maybe dad was at the pub, laughing at all of us. So I volunteered to go and look there. And take Jane with me." Sandra chimed back in.

"You all went to the pub?"

"Yes. We thought maybe the blood was fake, and that messing up the bedroom was part of his big surprise. To scare everyone. Plus, well, everyone needed a drink. But then mum phoned, and ..." Sandra broke off, heaving a deep breath. Her eyes began to redden. Russell pulled her close.

"We all came back to the house. It was like pandemonium, flashing lights everywhere. Tom had been taken to hospital. And the police were crawling all over the house. They took our statements, and then took us back through to Glasgow."

Dakar looked at Sandra and Jane, his eyes narrowed. "When you were up there, after the banging at the window, did you see anyone go downstairs? Or come upstairs?"

They both shook their heads. "There was so much running around and panic, I didn't really notice anything. I was too busy looking for Daniel." Jane answered.

"Did any of you know Charles before that evening?"

The three looked at each other, then shook their heads.

Dakar sat back, and looked over at Stewart expectantly.

Stewart looked at his notes. He put one hand up to cover his mouth as he studied them, then brought his hand away. He looked back up, shaking his head almost with frustration. "Nothing from me."

Dakar nodded, and stood up slowly, turning back to the three as he did so. He took his coat from the back of the chair as he spoke. "Thank you for your time." He said the words mechanically, as if he'd said them a million times before.

The other three stood up as well, and began pulling on their coats too.

"You're leaving as well?"

The three nodded. "Only came out to meet you, Mr Dakar. That was all." It was Jane who spoke, sounding cheerful.

Dakar looked at her for a moment, the look of an elephant deciding it was too much effort to try and squash an annoying fly. He went over to the bar, where he paid before turning to head out.

Stewart grabbed his coat and bag, sliding the notepad and pen inside before he also headed for the door. They stepped outside into the cold Scottish afternoon. Slivers of rain were beginning to come down, a matinee performance for the true rain that would arrive shortly.

He looked over at Dakar. "So, eh, what do you think?"

"Someone is lying to us."

Chapter 30

Dakar began walking up Woodlands Road, towards where the car was parked. Stewart followed him, looking back over his shoulder. The other three were heading in the same direction, albeit a bit more slowly, their heads down. Stewart cast a glance at his watch. One thirty. The sky wasn't as dark as it had been in Edinburgh, the clouds not quite as menacing.

Stewart looked around again when he heard a woman begin shouting. "Sandra. Sandra!"

Sarah-Anne crossed the street towards Sandra, Jane and Russell. She didn't notice Stewart and Dakar some thirty metres further up the street.

"Why is she here?" The words carried plainly across to Stewart from Sarah-Anne. It was equally plain that while the words were addressed to Sandra, Sarah-Anne was looking at Jane.

"Mum—"

"Sarah-Anne—"

Both Sandra and Russell began speaking at the same time.

"I wasn't asking you, young man! Sandra, how can you still be friends with her? After what she's done?"

"Mum, for God's sake—"

"She humiliated me! In front of everyone!"

Jane broke in. "M— ... Sarah-Anne, there was nothing ..."

"You! You keep quiet, girl. You've done enough damage to the family."

"But—"

"As soon as I get control of that flat, you'll be out on your ear, child. I just hope to all the gods you don't get involved with any more married men."

"I never did anything with Daniel!"

"Don't lie! My husband wouldn't have bothered with you if he wasn't getting something in return. I knew him that well!"

"I swear—"

"Silence!" Sarah-Anne practically screamed the word at her. A number of other people on Woodlands Road had stopped and were watching.

"No! No I won't be silent! You don't know anything ..." Jane roared back at Sarah-Anne.

"I know bloody well enough, young lady! Sandra, I just don't understand how you can still be friends with her."

Sandra sighed, and spoke in a low tone, low enough that Stewart couldn't hear her. Her shoulders were slumped, the humiliation of mother and best friend screaming at each other in public weighing her down.

Stewart practically jumped as Dakar suddenly began walking back towards the group. He hurried after him.

"No I won't stop! Do you realise what she did? Do you know how much I put up with to stay with your dad, to work on our marriage? There was still a chance. And then I find that Jane, who I took in when ..."

Sarah-Anne trailed off as she caught sight of Dakar walking towards the group.

"Mr Dakar! Ah. Hello. And Mr ... Mr, eh ..." Sarah-Anne blushed, and so did Stewart as she struggled to remember his name.

"Scott." It was Jane who said it, her tone sullen, eyes turned away to the side.

"Mr Scott, yes." Sarah-Anne sounded relieved, but she didn't look over at the rescuer who she had so recently been lambasting.

Dakar nodded to her.

"Ah, we were just, eh, having a chat." Sarah-Anne looked around the other three, who were all looking down or away. The shame hung heavily in the air. "About the flat arrangements." Her tone was lame.

"So I heard. What are you doing through in Glasgow?"

"In Glasgow? Oh, I just came through to see Sandra. I wanted to take her out to lunch. To discuss the flat arrangements, you know. As I said."

There was a strained silence, broken by Dakar. "Can I speak to you for a minute?" He addressed Sarah-Anne.

"Yes, of course. Sandra, wait for me here. Then we can go to a café or something."

Dakar wandered a few steps down the road, Stewart right behind him. Sarah-Anne followed them a few moments later. Stewart looked back at the group of three. Sandra was muttering in a low voice to Jane and Russell, who turned to leave. Russell had to hurry to keep up with Jane, who was striding away.

"You think Jane was carrying on an affair with Daniel before he died?"

Sarah-Anne nodded vigorously. "I'm sure, Mr Dakar."

"You're getting all that from the fact that Daniel visited the flat once when she was on her own and she was giving him some looks on the night he died?"

"She says it was once." Sarah-Anne spoke viciously. "But I'm sure Daniel went to the flat many times. When Sandra and Russell were out. To see Jane. Only Jane. And ..." she took a deep breath, "... he spoke about her sometimes." Stewart's eyebrows shot up. "Her and Martina. Whenever he really wanted to hurt me, Mr Dakar, he would begin talking about the way other women looked or dressed, and compare me to them. He used Jane and Martina mainly."

A grimace appeared on Dakar's face, pulling the skin taut across his cheekbones. "I see."

"Yes, well. It didn't work most of the time. I just told myself that this was the monster speaking, as it were. Not the man I married. At some point he would be himself again, and then he would apologise, and cry, and tell me how sorry he was about what he'd said."

"Most of the time?"

Sarah-Anne gave him a tight smile, her eyes becoming glassy as the water sprang into them. "We're all human, Mr Dakar."

"I hope you can forgive Jane for anything she's done." Stewart looked over at Dakar in surprise, the words a strange counterpoint to his bleak tone and severe expression.

Sarah-Anne snorted. "I hardly think she deserves it, Mr Dakar."

"The forgiveness isn't for her. It's for you."

Sarah-Anne gave him an odd look, then nodded slowly. "One thing I forgot to mention to you when we spoke before."

"What's that?"

"Someone had been in the study. Downstairs. It wasn't ransacked, exactly, but I noticed things had been moved since when I'd gone in earlier that evening. I was doing a quick clean of the house. A couple of drawers were lying open. Daniel could have done it, I suppose, but he was hardly ever in there over the last few months. I only saw it once the police arrived. It doesn't seem all that relevant, because it can't have anything to do with the murder, but, well, anyway. I thought I'd mention it."

"Anything missing?"

"Not that I know of. I mean, it's possible. But I don't think Daniel kept anything in there anymore."

"Okay. Thanks for that."

"Goodbye, Mr Dakar. Goodbye, Mr Scott." She said Stewart's name gratefully. Then she walked off and collected Sandra, the younger woman remonstrating to her mother but keeping her voice low.

Stewart looked over at Dakar, who watched the two women for a moment longer before turning to Stewart.

"Pretty mental, eh?"

Dakar's face was inscrutable. He nodded once, but that was it.

Chapter 31

Stewart sat in the car, feeling worried. Very worried.

As they had made their way back to the car, Dakar had checked his phone. He had looked up with a wild look on his face, nostrils flared, swift breathing, like an animal being hunted. He looked frantically up and down the street, his eyes jumping between people.

They sat in the car now, but it had taken a few minutes before Dakar had given up on whatever he was looking for. The man remained silent. He looked around once again, then pulled away slowly from the kerb.

They got back on the M8 quickly, but neither the tension nor the silence in the car left. Dakar began driving faster and slower, seemingly randomly, overtaking a car one second and then immediately moving into the inside lane and slowing down.

Once they got past the Cathedral turn-off, Dakar's driving evened out. For ten minutes they drove normally towards Edinburgh, the massive five- or six-lane road slowly dwindling until it hit two lanes after the Carlisle turn-off. Stewart began to relax again as they passed the Harthill services.

Then Dakar suddenly twisted the steering wheel so that they took a slip road, even although they had been almost passed it on the highway, swerving so hard that Stewart was pushed to one side of the car.

They reached a roundabout, Dakar twisting the wheel again as they screeched around, and then raced off into some wee village, Stewart missing the sign telling him what village it was as he hung on for dear life.

They raced up one little street, and then took a left at a roundabout, before Dakar had immediately done a U-turn so they had been back at the roundabout again.

Dakar raced back onto the roundabout, going straight through it, and then sharply turned left, right and one final left before he glided into a small space, and turned off the engine. The car fell silent, a complete stillness suddenly imposed, broken only by the sound of Stewart's heavy breathing.

Stewart looked over at Dakar in the sudden silence. The guy was searching the rear view and wing mirrors with an animal intensity, his eyes flicking madly between them.

Stewart breathed out. One hand had gripped the seat belt tightly during the manoeuvres, while the other had automatically found the little grip above the door. He was holding on so hard it took a second or two to loosen his fingers. He looked over at Dakar, whose eyes were still darting between mirrors. Stewart cautiously twisted himself slightly so he could see behind them in the wing mirror next to him. There was nothing there.

They sat in silence for a few minutes as Dakar maintained his vigil. Stewart slowly, cautiously, relaxed from his status of highest alert, taking deeper breaths as the immediate possibility of a life-ending accident receded.

The minutes ticked by slowly as Stewart sat, watching Dakar. After what seemed like an eternity, Dakar spoke.

"We're going."

Stewart nodded once. Dakar's tone hadn't invited discussion.

The car took off once again, no sound as it started up and pulled away. They drove back to the roundabout, but then went through two more villages before Dakar pulled back onto the motorway and they continued back to Edinburgh.

Dakar seemed to have calmed down again, his driving within the range of sanity once again. In spite of the apparent return to normality, Stewart gripped his seatbelt tightly before he spoke.

"So, eh, what was all that about?"

But Dakar just grimaced, and shook his head. The car fell back into silence, Dakar focusing on the road. Stewart turned and looked out of the window as the Scottish countryside whipped by. He had planned to get the rest of the information about the Billy Cronop story, what it was that Frank was holding over Dakar's head, but there was no chance of that now.

He slid out his notepad instead, making sure he could read his own handwriting and correcting a few things. He wrote some notes about the argument between Sarah-Anne and Jane, and checked his watch. It was three.

"Eh, Dakar, where are we off to now?" He thought he knew the answer already, but he didn't fancy being presumptuous.

"To see the dentist couple. I made an appointment at four for us." Dakar spoke flatly, still staring into his mirrors, the hunted expression in his eyes.

Stewart opened his mouth to ask more, then shut it again. He wrote down what Dakar had said, then went back to looking out of the window as the scenery whipped by.

The Price to Pay

Chapter 32

The car pulled up to a handsome building in Morningside, one of those sandstone types that people built back in the day with money made from the exploitation of other countries. Coats of arms of long-forgotten people had been carved into the wall, faded now, merging into the brickwork they once stood out against.

Stewart could smell the rain in the air, tasted that particular wind that presages a storm coming. He hurried after Dakar past a solid wooden door into a large corridor. The dental practice was on the second floor. A receptionist stood behind the desk as they entered. She was looking through some documents, but glanced up and smiled at them when they came in.

Stewart immediately found himself putting his hand up to his hair, pretending to be running his hand through it while desperately trying to pat it down. He also took a quick glance down his front, checking the suit was in order, before he looked back up at the woman.

She was short, but to Stewart seemingly perfectly formed. She had a beautiful face, a small, cute nose accompanied by two large brown eyes. Her skin was darker than Stewart's, clearly Pakistani or Indian ancestry a couple of generations back. Dark brown hair was tied back in a ponytail.

She was wearing a navy suit with a white shirt. Stewart found his eyes drawn to the open collar. Somewhere in the back of his head it struck him as a bit off for a dental receptionist to be dressed that way – normally they had the white coat on, didn't they? – but the thought came and went.

She put the documents to one side, and cocked her head as she looked at them. "Are you here to see a dentist?"

Even her voice seemed lovely, the words flowing into Stewart's ears and lighting up his brain.

"Yes. Mrs Lawson. We have an appointment." Dakar was studying the woman, his eyes narrowed.

"Are you patients?"

Dakar shook his head.

"Then what are you doing here?"

"We're investigating a crime. And we think Mrs Lawson can help us."

The woman smiled at them, a small smile full of secrets.

"But the police investigate crimes. And you're not the police, are you?"

Dakar smiled in turn, the smile an adult gives when a child thinks they're being clever. "No, my sister. We're not the police."

She waited for further information, but Dakar just looked back at her, the two staring at each other. Eventually she broke the silence.

"What did you say your names were? And I'll go and have a word with my colleagues."

"I didn't. But this is Stewart Scott. I'm Sebastian Dakar."

Stewart smiled at her as well, but the woman's eyes had opened wide when Dakar said his name.

"You're Sebastian Dakar?" Dakar nodded once. He didn't seem surprised by this reaction.

"Let me go and speak with my colleagues. In the other room. Would you mind taking a seat here? I won't be more than five minutes." She sounded excited, and Stewart's smile drooped away. He was already a bit-player in this particular story.

Dakar nodded, took a seat. Stewart did the same, walking slowly over to a chair and lowering himself into it with a sigh.

People forgetting his name and feeling invisible around attractive women whenever they found out who Dakar was ... Another day in the life.

The woman disappeared through a room behind the reception door. Stewart cast around the waiting room, looking at the bright glossy magazines that littered the tables, although none of them seemed appealing. Then he looked up at Dakar. The guy had lost the intense look he'd had in the car, his shoulders back. He was even leaning back a little into the seat.

"Eh, Dakar?"

"Yes?"

"Eh, I was wondering, if you didn't mind of course, but well, I had a wee look at the Billy Cronop thing ..."

Silence. Dakar put one hand on top of the other together, then moved one over the other, the wringing action Stewart had seen him do when they'd been talking to Sandra, Jane and Russell.

"Well, I was just wondering ... It all looked above board to me, you know. I read about it online. Didn't look like there were any loose ends or big shakes the defence had at trial, anything that even sniffed of something fishy. So, eh, what was Frank talking about? About someone doing something bad?"

Silence. But it was a silence where Dakar was thinking what to say, not the one where he had nothing to say. He spoke after a few seconds.

"After the conviction, I went out with some people to celebrate. Frank was there as well, and it ended up just him and me. I told him, after a lot of drinking, that some of the evidence that had been found in Billy Cronop's house, evidence tying him directly to the scene of the crime, hadn't been there before the police arrived."

Stewart nodded automatically. Then he stopped nodding as he realised what Dakar was saying.

"The cops planted something?"

"That's what I told him." Dakar's voice was flat, conveying unpleasant but necessary news.

"Christ. Right."

There was a silence in the room, a heavy one as Stewart looked at Dakar. The man put one hand to his forehead, and began rubbing it.

"If an accusation were to be made, that evidence had been planted, it would lead to a review of the case, of course. And if that accusation were to be found to be true, then Billy Cronop would almost undoubtedly be set free."

"Right."

"And, of course, the police officer who allegedly moved the evidence would also most likely be put in jail."

Stewart nodded, his eyes staring at the floor in a mirror image of Dakar. Christ, this bag of shite was just getting heavier and heavier.

"Who was the officer?"

"Me."

Stewart sat back, his head hitting the tall seat as if he'd been punched. He gazed at Dakar, silence falling like thick snow and weighing everything down for a minute or two. Dakar kept on looking at the floor. He'd stopped rubbing his forehead. Now he was just holding it.

"And who are Jamie and Sam? Frank said to remember Jamie and Sam, that they'd have revenge too. Are they gangster friends of this guy Crudup? Or from another case?" Stewart leaned forward.

Dakar put his hands together in his lap as he looked at Stewart. He sat very still. "Jamie and Sam are my daughters. Frank was reminding me that

Billy Cronop went to jail not because he'd killed the person he hated directly, but rather their child."

Stewart fell back again, his head smacking the back of the tall seat once more.

"And, eh, well ... What you told Frank. About planting the evidence. Is it true?"

Dakar leaned back now, and exhaled deeply. He opened his mouth.

"Well, gentlemen, sorry that took me so long. I've just had a little chat with my colleagues, and we'd all like to speak with you together."

Stewart looked round. The woman had reappeared at the doorway.

Dakar stood up, Stewart hurriedly following suit. The torture in Dakar's eyes was gone, the narrow, focused determination retaking its place.

"I take it your colleagues don't want to speak with us here?"

The woman smiled, her eyes glinting in the light. "Oh, you are a sharp one, after all. I wasn't sure to believe it, in spite of the stories."

Stewart looked between the woman and Dakar, his eyebrows pulling together as he frowned. He slid his notepad out of his bag. He didn't know what was happening, but he should at least write it down.

"You didn't answer my question."

The woman smiled, or at least the ends of her mouth turned up.

"No, they don't want to speak to you here. They want to speak to you over at Torphichen."

Stewart stuck his tongue out as he wrote it all down. He'd never heard of Torphichen.

"Eh sorry, how do you spell that?" Stewart broke in. "Is it another location for the dental practice?"

"No. That would be the police station."

Stewart looked back up again, his pen freezing mid-word. The woman put her head to one side as she looked back, eyebrows raised in what might have passed for sympathy.

"The police station?"

"Yes."

Dakar turned to Stewart. "She's a police officer. CID, I'd guess, given what she's wearing and that the Daniel Mannings investigation is a murder one. From after my time, though, so I'm presuming just a DC."

The upturned ends of the mouth again. "DC Safdar. Pleased to meet you both."

Stewart gaped at her.

"Why are they at the police station? Witness statements must have already been taken from both of them." Dakar's hands came up in front of him, open, long fingers outstretched. His face wore a confused expression.

The woman smiled in triumph, waved a finger at Dakar. "No, no, Mr Dakar. I'm not to answer your questions."

Dakar smiled, and dropped his hands. "This colleague of yours, the one giving the orders. DI Thomas?"

"The very same."

"We're under arrest then?"

Stewart rotated his gaping expression towards Dakar.

But the woman shook her head, her lips pouting in mock-sadness. "First thing I asked. But apparently not. I've to make it very clear you are not under arrest."

Stewart managed to get his mouth shut, feeling his heart pounding.

"Then why should we come?"

The woman shrugged as Stewart looked at Dakar with an appalled expression anew. "It's your choice. DI Thomas told me that it would be to your benefit. You might even get a chance to chat to the dentist and her kept man if you're very lucky."

Dakar was nodding until the last words, when he frowned. "Kept man? Dennis? He worked here as the secretary, didn't he?"

She nodded as she went to gather the documents on the desk. "The usual story with the successful professional employing their young pretty other half, but with the genders flipped. And taking out the young and pretty part."

Dakar snorted, a smile on his face. "Daniel couldn't have been a happy bunny over that."

"No, I gather he wasn't. And as he was doing the lion's share of the work, well …" She shrugged again.

"So actually Daniel was keeping Dennis, not Eleanor."

The woman nodded, amused look on her face as she gathered up the documents. "It's no wonder he was a bit pissed off."

"I can't believe Eleanor wasn't making enough to keep her own man. As a full-time dentist, surely she could?"

"No, they could only do it because Daniel was bringing in so much. If …" The woman finished putting the documents in the file and trailed off. She whipped round to Dakar, fire burning bright in her eyes.

Stewart looked at Dakar, who stood looking back at her with large eyes, his hands and arms out in front of him in a gesture of innocence. It reminded Stewart of football players who had just crunched into someone, taking both legs and entirely missing the ball, then standing up with protestations of innocence as the referee stormed over.

'I hardly touched him, ref'. Aye right.

"No more info." The woman spoke curtly as she snatched up the documents and put them under one arm. She marched past them, towards the exit.

"My apologies. I forgot you weren't allowed to share."

Stewart hadn't thought the woman could look angrier, but somehow she managed.

"I'm also reconsidering my instructions not to arrest you. Let's go."

Chapter 33

The police station at Torphichen wasn't what Stewart had been expecting. He'd never seen the inside of a police station, but he'd imagined a place with hustle and bustle, cops continually bringing in cynical, wearied-looking criminals in cuffs to a soundtrack of anguished howls from those already inside and the rattle of prison bars.

Instead it was a quiet place, like any other public sector office, the only difference being the preponderance of police information posters around the place. In an odd way, the placid, soulless atmosphere was worse than the hectic scene he'd imagined, like a hell being run by bureaucrats.

They'd followed DC Safdar in Dakar's car, the cop and her male partner leading the way. He was a youngish guy, an eagerness in his eyes that betrayed his inexperience, and all too evident compared to the hooded eyes of DC Safdar. Stewart hadn't caught his name, not that he'd tried very hard. They had driven into the parking lot, left the car and walked up a ramp to a back door.

They followed DC Safdar down a couple of corridors before she turned into a room, Dakar and Stewart following her in. The male cop had headed off somewhere else with the bag of documents seized from the dentist place, clutching it as if it were precious booty.

The room they entered was small and bare, concrete walls with blue and white lines running around them. The only distinguishing feature was a large piece of blackened glass. DC Safdar and Dakar took up a position in front of it, Stewart hurriedly joining them.

Through the glass, Stewart could see the back of two heads, one blond and one slightly darker. He recognised them immediately as belonging to DC Lemkin and DI Thomas, two cops who he would forever remember after they'd threatened to arrest him for tampering with evidence at Hanover House. DC Lemkin was leaning over a bit of paper, scribbling notes down.

Opposite them sat Eleanor, the same awkwardness about in her real life that he'd seen in the photograph. She truly was a bear of a woman. Her lips were slim, though, pressed together, and she had oddly skinny fingers splayed out on the table in front of her. She reminded Stewart of many of the teachers he'd had in primary school, giant women who had towered above him.

Her face was twisted into a position of outrage as she looked at some sheets of paper in front of her.

DC Safdar leaned over. "They only took them in about ten minutes before you two turned up, so we shouldn't have ..." she began, but then they all heard Eleanor's voice.

"Are you accusing me?" The words came through loud and clear in their spying place.

"Certainly not, Mrs Lawson. You're not a suspect. I haven't even asked any questions about Daniel's murder yet. I'm just wondering if we've somehow misinterpreted these emails." DI Thomas responded, his voice sounding blasé, bored even. His hand gestured out to the sheets of paper between them.

"Daniel had become a difficult person to work with."

"We know, Eleanor. We know. You're not the first person to tell us about Daniel's personality. We believe you. But you understand, of course, DI Thomas, he has to follow up all lines of enquiry. It's his job." DC Lemkin's tone came through now as he stopped writing for a second, leaning out across the table, one hand outstretched as if he were going to take Eleanor's hand in his.

Mrs Lawson settled back a little in her seat. "Well, then. I mean, yes. These emails are genuine, if that's what you're asking."

"Mrs Lawson, Daniel brought in about two-thirds of your business, didn't he?" DI Thomas again, his voice straightforward, reasonable.

Mrs Lawson shrugged, her thin lips thinner than before. "Yes. That's in the accounts. I never tried to hide that." DC Lemkin began scribbling again.

"In fact, if Daniel were to leave, then you might struggle to stay afloat, financially speaking. That's what the accounts show as well. All those outgoings, Dennis's wages, renting those nice rooms in Morningside—"

"We would have been fine."

"Sure? Because that's what Daniel was threatening to do, wasn't it? He was threatening to leave the practice, taking his clients with him."

"Like I said, Daniel had become difficult to work with."

"And like I said, there's no other interpretation of these emails, is there?"

"Should I have my solicitor here?"

DI Thomas sucked in his cheeks with an intake of breath. "That's a big step, Mrs Lawson. Getting a solicitor. How long can we hold someone before we have to charge them, DC Lemkin?"

"Twelve hours, sir." DC Lemkin spoke in a resigned voice. "But there's really no need for that, Eleanor. I think DI Thomas just has a few more questions, and then you can go home."

She looked at him, slightly suspiciously, then back at DI Thomas. "Just a few more," the other policeman echoed, holding his hands up in a surrendering motion, but he had a smile on his face.

Stewart suddenly caught a sound, and looked around in his own room. Dakar was whispering to DC Safdar, an appalled expression growing on her face as the words continued.

"No, I won't!" she replied, also whispering, but fiercely enough to carry across to Stewart.

Dakar whispered something again, and DC Safdar took a deep breath. "Fine!" she whispered again, angrily. She took some paper from Dakar's hand, glared at him, glared at Stewart, and then turned and marched out of the room.

Stewart watched her go, a miserable expression on his face. Why was it that when women loved Dakar, it was like he was invisible, but as soon as Dakar got into shite, it splattered all over him as well? Stewart looked accusingly over at Dakar, but the man was looking back through the window. He looked like he was enjoying himself.

They heard the tap on the door, and saw DC Safdar go in. She gave DI Thomas two pieces of paper.

"Sorry, sir. I'm told it is very urgent. It's from the one I radioed in about."

Stewart could now see DI Thomas's face in profile, and his expression was very still. He turned and studied the glass, before he turned back to DC Safdar. "Thank you, DC Safdar."

The woman turned and left. DI Thomas looked at one piece of paper, a square, then placed it face down on the table. Then he read whatever Dakar had written on the second piece of paper. He turned again to the darkened glass, an unreadable expression on his face, and scrunched up the bit of paper and let it fall to the ground. Then he turned back to Mrs Lawson.

DC Safdar had arrived back just in time for the scrunching and dropping of paper. She turned unsympathetically to Dakar.

"Told you."

Dakar gave her a knowing smile.

"Why didn't you volunteer these emails, Mrs Lawson?"

"They weren't relevant."

"Your business partner, who brings in the majority of the money to your practice, threatens to leave, then turns up dead, and you think it's not relevant?"

"That's right." The conviction in Eleanor's tone wavered as she replied.

"You argued with Daniel in the lounge, is that right?"

"We had a discussion, yes. I told you. I was trying to convince Daniel to promise to stay, to stop these childish threats of leaving. I also asked him again to stop bullying Dennis at work. Honestly, he was awful to poor Dennis."

"Did you talk about the prescription sheets that had gone missing?"

Eleanor's face drew a blank. "The prescription sheets?"

"The ones you claimed were being stolen?"

"Yes, yes, I remember them. But no, we didn't talk about them. No more have gone missing, not since those children left."

"Was there any possibility Daniel was stealing them?"

"Daniel? But he had his own prescription pad. He wouldn't need to. Not unless …" Eleanor's mouth made an 'O' at this new line of thought. "You think he took them? But why?"

"You didn't discuss them with Daniel then?"

She shook her head, mutely.

"One more thing, just to remind myself. Did you see Daniel's face at the window?"

"Yes, yes I did. I told you already. I was looking around, because fireworks don't interest me that much, and saw him at the window. He was looking out, almost like he was waiting for something. Then he turned away, and began banging, and Jane began screaming."

"And according to you, after you rushed upstairs, Dennis was with you the entire time?"

"Yes. I've told you that. I'm sure he never left my side."

"Yes. Well. We'll perhaps come back to that in the future."

She stared at him archly. "You should go back to that Jane girl in the future," she said, her tone spiteful for the last few words. "She was staring at Daniel all night, like … like she was on heat or something! And I told you already that Daniel had been saying things to her at work, also saying how nice she looked. There was definitely something between those two."

DI Thomas sat back. "We're pursuing all lines of enquiry, thank you." He nodded over at DC Lemkin. "Well, thanks for your help. Like I said at the start, I'm sorry we had to ask you a second round of questions. You can go now."

Mrs Lawson looked at each of them, nodded eventually. "And Dennis as well?"

DC Lemkin was nodding. The woman stood and was halfway to the door, DC Lemkin escorting her, when DI Thomas cleared his throat.

"Actually, I need to ask him one or two more questions. Something that just came up."

"For goodness sake! Will this never end?" she demanded, her composed expression quivering.

"Sorry about this, Eleanor. I'm sure it won't be more than a minute or two." DC Lemkin was aiming for the butter-wouldn't-melt tone, but Eleanor didn't even bother looking at him, instead glaring at DI Thomas.

She turned abruptly and left the room, DC Lemkin heading out after her, his frame filling the doorway to the point where his cropped blond hair almost skiffed the wood at the top. DI Thomas got up and began to walk slowly towards the window.

"I know you're there, Dakar. You and your bloody notes. I haven't missed them." His eyes widened, and his head went side to side as his glare slid around. Stewart realised with a shock that the window was only one-way, and DI Thomas couldn't see them.

DI Thomas glared for a moment longer, then turned and went back to his seat. A few moments later, DC Lemkin reappeared, a small, balding man following him. Stewart recognised him as Dennis.

"I must protest," the man spluttered as DC Lemkin brought him in. "You told me earlier that I—"

"Sit down," DI Thomas practically barked at him. The man complied, sullenly. DC Lemkin retook his seat, getting a fresh sheet of paper in front of him.

"Mr Lawson, I need to ask you something else. You went downstairs at one point, didn't you, when everyone else was upstairs?"

Dennis looked appalled. "No, I did not!" he said. "I was upstairs with everyone else the whole time after we saw Daniel at the window. This is harassment!"

"There is a witness—"

"I've already told you, I didn't go downstairs. Eleanor will vouch for me. I don't know who this witness is, or what their problem is. Is it Tom? I bet it's Tom. He's always had it in for me. Listen, I didn't go downstairs after we went up to see what had happened to Daniel. Not until we'd finished searching the second floor, and everyone went downstairs."

DI Thomas held up the bit of paper he'd placed down on the table. "Mr Lawson, are you sure you didn't go downstairs, perhaps to Daniel Mannings' study?"

The man froze in his seat, eyes slowly widening. The only audible sound in the room was his breathing. "I want a lawyer."

DI Thomas sat back. "Don't think that's necessary just yet, Mr Lawson. I just want an answer to one question. Did you hide downstairs while everyone rushed up, or did you go upstairs and then come back down?"

Dennis' eyes slipped from DI Thomas to DC Lemkin and back again as he licked his lips. His eyes slid over to the door.

"Just answer that one question, and we'll release you, I promise. We know you were downstairs."

Another lick of the lips. "After I went upstairs." The words came out in a low croak. "I went up, then when everyone else went through to the guest bedroom, I ran back down. I didn't go into the study though. I got to the door, then that girl Jane began shouting about other people being dead, and I chickened out. Ran back upstairs. That's it. I swear it."

"And you went downstairs for this?" DI Thomas waved the bit of paper.

"Yes." Dennis spoke in a rasping voice.

DI Thomas leaned back in his chair, staring at Dennis, head cocked to one side. Eventually he leaned forward again.

"We're not holding you. You can go. For now."

"Can I ... Will you ..." Dennis looked helplessly at the piece of paper.

"Forging prescription pads is a serious offence, Mr Lawson. Saying that, we're looking for a murderer. If you didn't murder Daniel Mannings, then I suppose you don't have to worry about this. Just don't do it again."

Dennis almost collapsed with relief, DC Lemkin having to take him by the arm and help escort him out. DI Thomas scratched his nose for a few seconds before he also got up and exited the room.

Stewart subconsciously began to crouch back as soon as DI Thomas disappeared from sight. He took a step closer to Dakar as the door to their own room opened. DI Thomas was shorter than DC Lemkin and far less aggressively muscular, neat hair combed off to the right with a side parting, but as he stood silhouetted in the doorway he seemed like a massive, towering giant.

"You two. Outside. Now."

Chapter 34

Stewart scurried past DI Thomas out of the door. DC Lemkin stood waiting, not exactly releasing balloons or popping champagne corks at seeing them again.

"This way," DC Lemkin grunted, turning and heading along the corridor. Stewart followed him, then paused, looking over his shoulder. Dakar was strolling along, DI Thomas marching firmly behind him. DC Safdar had, disappointingly, disappeared.

They ended up outside, back in the parking lot. DI Thomas stopped and looked at them both, lighting up a cigarette as he did so.

"You two." He said it flatly, the tone leaden. He took a deep draw, and blew out the smoke to one side.

Stewart nodded, tried a smile. No response from either cop.

"You bloody two. Like a nightmare I can't get rid of." The same tone, a leaden monotonous black that matched the dark clouds overhead. DI Thomas took the cigarette out, tapped the ash and watched it drift down to the ground. "C'mon," he said suddenly, the moment the ash hit the ground. He began walking away from the police station, out past the barrier.

Stewart hesitated for a second, then saw DC Lemkin standing watching him, daring him to disobey. Stewart quickly hurried down the steps after DI Thomas.

DI Thomas stopped at a car parked on the street, and told Stewart and Dakar to hop in. They got in, taking the back seat, while DC Lemkin got into the driver's street and DI Thomas took the passenger seat.

"The local," was all DI Thomas said, opening his window and blowing smoke out.

It was a short ride, over across The Meadows, deserted now as everyone and their dog prepared for the dreich assault that was about to hit the land. They passed Edinburgh Uni, the buildings like merciless judges as they passed.

The car came to a halt. DC Lemkin and DI Thomas got out, opening the doors for Stewart and Dakar. Stewart went to thank them, then remembered they'd been in a police car and it was almost certain that you couldn't open the doors from the inside. He thanked them anyway, expressions about it costing nothing jumping into his mind.

They were on a street just off Clerk Street, only about ten minutes' walk from Stewart's flat, directly outside a pub called The Bothie. It had always seemed a pretty ordinary pub to him. He'd passed it several times in his comings and goings, in fact, and at no point had he ever guessed that it was some kind of secret police torture chamber.

The sun hadn't quite set, but it was on its way down, the short days becoming shorter. The wind had picked up, whistling along the Edinburgh streets, stealing any heat that had remained. The smell of rain in the air was getting stronger. Stewart cast his eyes upwards. Impossible though it was, the clouds seemed somehow closer, as if they were coming down on the city from above.

DI Thomas didn't wait for the rest of them, instead heading in, the others coming along behind. There hadn't been much light outside but even so, Stewart's eyes took a minute to adjust to the gloom of the bar. It was a pub, much like Whisky, except it hadn't got around to cleaning up its act yet. The barman was wiping the bar when they entered, not so much cleaning as spreading the dirt more evenly.

"You. What'll you have?" DI Thomas stood at the bar, looking at Stewart.

Stewart froze. He'd have to have a beer. DI Thomas already had a pint of what looked like heavy plonked in front of him. But on the other hand, he couldn't have a beer. He was working. What happened if Green or Sudgeon materialised in here, demanding to know what he was doing? Granted, the chances of Sudgeon and Green coming in here were approximately the same as the survival expectancy of a snowball trying to tap dance its way past the denizens of hell, but still.

DI Thomas was looking at him. The barman was looking at him. Christ, it felt like every person in the bar was looking at him, eyes in all the dark corners leering in his direction. Couldn't have a pint. Too much. Couldn't have a soft drink. Too little. Maybe a shandy? Half beer, half soft drink? Stewart began to sweat. Right, yes, a shandy. But maybe that was still too much.

The barman began to look really bored now, even annoyed, sunken eyes seeming to sink deeper as he stared at Stewart …

"Half a shandy please!"

The words tumbled out without a space between them, one long sound, his voice echoing around the bar. If everyone in the bar hadn't been looking at him before, they definitely were now. Stewart felt his face light up.

"Shandy? Half?" The barman had one of those particularly masculine voices, a deep, Scottish voice which sounded like he gargled pebbles each morning to roughen up his throat. He wasn't even attempting to mask his contempt.

Stewart nodded, mutely. The barman turned to look at DC Lemkin and Dakar, standing behind Stewart.

"Pint, half orange, half lemonade?" DC Lemkin nodded once. He didn't look embarrassed at all. "And what about you?"

"Water, my brother."

The barman gave Dakar an odd look, but turned to get the drinks. DI Thomas relocated them to the corner booth, which stood on its own, and faced the door. Stewart and Dakar sat down opposite him, Lemkin arriving a second later with the other drinks. Stewart could feel his face begin to cool again.

DI Thomas took a deep pull of his heavy, supping the cold dark liquid before he sat back and smacked his lips. He said nothing, instead taking a deep sigh of heavenly satisfaction. He looked skywards for a few seconds before his eyes came back down.

"Normally I wouldn't drink on the job, not any more. New regulations and all that shit. But when I see it's you two – you bloody two – that are investigating this … Needs must, when the De'il drives." He took a second deep pull on the pint, smacking his lips again.

He leaned forward. "Baffled, Seb. That's what the papers are saying I am. Baffled. I'll show them though. I'm close. It'll come. And then I'll show them baffled." DI Thomas spoke with a certain warm promise in his tone.

"Good of you to ask Dennis that question for me. The answer narrows down the list of liars quite a bit."

DI Thomas scowled. "It wasn't a bloody favour. Think I would let you anywhere near an interview in an ongoing murder investigation if it was up to me? No bloody chance."

Another deep pull from the pint, his tongue wiping away the white foam left behind. It was a heady mix that reached Stewart's nose, dark chocolate of the heavy, the fizzy lightness of orange mixed with lemonade and the lemony smell of his own shandy, all mixing with the dark, deep bouquet of the bar .

"I'm under orders. The powers that be. Apparently the dead boy's father is an old pal of the chief. I've to give you a look at some evidence. No statements, though. Privacy concerns. The autopsy reports." DI Thomas paused, another pull, wiping stuff away again. "Apparently once you're dead, no-one really gives a shite."

Chapter 35

Stewart looked on, astonished, as Lemkin wordlessly produced a file.

He spread out photographs on the table in front of them. Stewart glanced at them, and found he couldn't pull his eyes away. He'd seen Daniel in life in a photograph, and now he was getting treated to him in death. The photographs showed the stairs down to the cellar, plus the cellar itself, this time complete with body. Stewart began to get his notepad out.

"No notes!" DI Thomas growled the words at him.

Stewart slid his notepad back into his bag. DI Thomas glared at him for a second longer, Stewart focusing on his bag, before the man turned back to Dakar.

"Body was at the bottom of the stairs. This is it in situ. The dark patches on the stairs and floor are blood. DNA tests show it belonged to the deceased."

Stewart stared at the bizarre photographs. There Daniel lay, eyes closed, facing out, arms and legs splayed out. There was blood coming out of his mouth, and dark stains on the front of his shirt. It was horrible but fascinating at the same time.

"The blood in the bedroom and the en suite. Was it Daniel's?"

"Aye. All of the blood, upstairs and downstairs, all his."

"Bugger. That makes life harder. And the knife?"

"His blood as well. No fingerprints."

Dakar nodded without looking up. "Defensive wounds?"

"None. No bruising or cuts to the arms or hands, not even any of that handy DNA they always find under fingernails in all that CSI malarkey. Absolutely diddly-squat. Some bruising on the torso though, back and front."

"And this is the suit jacket we've heard so much about?" Dakar pointed at the body.

DI Thomas picked up a different photograph and handed it over, the suit jacket on its own, body-less. It truly was hideous.

"What about the stuff everyone else was wearing?"

DI Thomas nodded, and picked up some more photographs. He gave them over. Stewart watched as Dakar studied each set of clothing, recognising each one from the photographs. Martina's was first: the trousers, shirt and scarf. Russell and Charles came next: smart-casual and then a suit. Then Sarah-Anne's: the red dress, this time with gloves, and an apron, a pure, spotless, innocent white. Sandra and Janes' outfits followed, then Stewart recognised Craig's description of his stuff. There was a final set, jeans, a t-shirt and a jumper.

"Whose are these?" Dakar fingered the photograph.

"Donaldson's. The elder. We seized them when we found them in the car."

"Anything on any of them?"

"Not a drop of anything suspicious anywhere. On anything."

Dakar sat back, then nodded. "How did he die?"

DI Thomas nodded to DC Lemkin, who cleared the first set of photographs and replaced them with a second. Stewart looked eagerly at them, then looked even more eagerly away from them. He'd never seen a post-mortem before. Having had a glimpse of one, he didn't really fancy ever seeing one again.

After a deep breath, Stewart forced himself to take a second look at them. He managed one more glance, then turned quickly away again.

It was Daniel's body, on one of those thin metallic tables they used to cut people up, with drains for the blood. There were some big wounds in his chest. The body was a kind of pale grey, and in various parts of the photo bits were open, before being sown shut in later photos. The face looked peaceful enough, although Stewart felt sure there would be an expression of pain at what was happening down below.

It was as he was looking away from the photos, taking a deep breath, that the words came quietly in his ear.

"Do you know, they take a circular saw and open up your skull? Then they take your brain out, and slice it up, bit by bit?"

Stewart looked around in shock. DC Lemkin had leaned over the table towards him and was whispering the words softly in his ear.

"Don't ever die in a suspicious or unexplained way in Scotland. Otherwise ..." DC Lemkin indicated the photographs, Stewart straining to hear him, before the cop suddenly made a loud, high-pitched whining noise, like a saw. Stewart jerked back away from him. DC Lemkin leaned back with a satisfied look on his face.

The Price to Pay

"He died …" DI Thomas stared at DC Lemkin before turning to Dakar, "… from four stab wounds to the chest and abdomen, which caused massive blood loss. Mainly internal bleeding." DI Thomas pointed to one of the photographs, which showed the wounds on the dead man's chest. "Although—"

"What?"

"Turns out the boy was going to be shaking hands with death pretty soon anyway. When they opened up his head, they found a tumour in his brain. In the frontal lobe." He looked down at some notes, a frown on his face. "The experts tell me it involves loss of social inhibitions, personality change, and a lack of realisation of the above. Basically you go bad, and don't know you're out of order. His wife did say he was acting a bit weird recently. Six to eight months he had left, untreated, and no guarantees it could be sorted even if they did catch it."

Dakar sat back, the wood creaking as his back weighed against the booth. "And he didn't know he had it?"

DI Thomas shook his head. "Apparently these things aren't caught unless someone notices that he's been acting strangely and they get someone in to have a look."

"How long had it been there?"

"The pathologist guessed it might have started growing a couple of months ago. So whoever our murderer is, they probably didn't have to go to the trouble. Daniel was on his way out." DI Thomas tapped the photographs as he spoke.

Dakar sat for a few seconds, then nodded to himself. He turned his attention back to the photographs in front of him.

"Was there much blood on the cellar floor?"

"There were some pools there, yes. Our pathologists think Daniel might still have been alive, even if only barely, when the murderer got him into the cellar. Or it could be because our murderer saw fit to slit Daniel's wrist as well."

"Yes," Dakar said, still looking at the photos. "Then bandage it, then cut it off again. Do we have any ideas about that?"

"You're not a copper anymore." DC Lemkin's words were like a missile, shot directly at Dakar. Stewart'd almost forgotten DC Lemkin was there.

Dakar looked at DC Lemkin, who looked steadily back. There was a few seconds of silence, before DI Thomas spoke. "Boy makes a good point, Seb. No more 'we'."

Dakar turned back to DI Thomas, but nodded himself after a few seconds, almost sadly. He turned his attention back to the photographs.

"And there was a knife found down in the cellar as well?"

"Yup. Same thing. A pretty bog standard kitchen knife, wiped clean of prints. There's a block of them, standing in plain view in the kitchen. Would have taken a second to swipe one for upstairs or downstairs. Or both."

Dakar nodded, and sat back again. DC Lemkin began sweeping the photographs away.

"I can tell you about the bloodwork as well. We did some on the boys sleeping it off in the guestroom. Russell Fletcher and Charles Robbin. Both of them were pretty adamant in their statements that they'd had blackouts that night, and worse-than-normal hangovers."

DI Thomas paused, his eyebrows raised as he waited for the guess to come.

"Drugged?"

DI Thomas pointed one finger out at Dakar with one hand, while a finger from the other hand went to his nose. "Oh, that's a bingo! They both had roughly the same amount. Zopiclone. When mixed with alcohol, it puts you into a deep sleep within an hour. Enough to knock them both out. It's no wonder they both had a tough morning."

Dakar nodded, a long pause following. His expression was that of someone having a nice walk who had just found an ugly brick wall in their path.

"Dennis?"

"Nice trick with that." DI Thomas said it grudgingly. "Looks like it might have been Mr Eleanor who was swiping the prescription forms after all."

"Someone's got to have something heavy on you to make you come like a dog when whistled and play as your personal waiter. Daniel must have caught him red-handed one day and kept the thing to blackmail him."

DI Thomas nodded. "Could be. But he wasn't the only one with access. Both Martina Donaldson and Sarah-Anne Mannings had been prescribed a drug containing Zopiclone for stress, a few months back. And, of course, Eleanor Lawson can prescribe whatever she wants. Although, at the end of the day, you can get this stuff on the streets."

Pause, nod. Stewart realised these weren't the Dakar pauses. These were a policeman's pauses.

"Oh, one more thing from the bloodwork. Daniel Mannings had cocaine in his system. And, it turns out, so did Charles Robbin."

Chapter 36

"Charles and Daniel had cocaine in their systems?"

"Aye."

"Daniel picked up during the dinner, a few folk said."

DI Thomas nodded again. "Probably off to the toilet for a quick line, make everything more fun."

Dakar nodded, leaned back. He looked like he was seeing infinity in a random bit of wall, his expression one where the brain is working so hard it's stopped processing external stimulations. The hands came over and slowly, slowly, slipped over one another. Stewart's mind raced as soon as he heard Charles mentioned. An associate doing cocaine wasn't necessarily the biggest news story in the world, but the cops having evidence of it jumped it up the gossip chain significantly. Plus doing it with a partner's son …

Dakar was back in the present. "When you looked in the guest room … Did you find any booze in there or drugs in there, anything like that?"

DI Thomas shook his head. "Nada. And we asked all the guests as well. The girls swore they didn't have any booze or drugs with them. Plus Sarah-Anne Mannings said that the guest bedroom wasn't exactly the place she'd keep the spare drinks and drugs cabinet."

"That one verbatim?"

"You should have heard the tone she said it in."

Pause, a calculating expression on Dakar's face. "And the boys didn't have any on them when they went upstairs?"

"Sandra actually checked the boys' pockets before they went in to make sure they didn't. She said that she'd once put Russell to bed when he seemed pretty far gone, only to find that he'd woken up and got stuck back in a few hours later. So she wanted to make sure."

A glint of light had appeared on Dakar's face. "Dennis heading downstairs …"

"Aye. Dennis. He might have been ransacking the place and met Daniel when the guy was trying to slip out, I suppose. A quick fight, a stabbing. But it would have had to have been very quick. He was back upstairs within a couple of minutes. Plenty of folk put him in the guest bedroom. And no blood on him."

Dakar paused, looking up to the sky, his hands coming up and doing the hand-washing gesture for a second or two. "Yes. But Dennis followed Daniel inside the house when he first went in ...?"

DI Thomas looked at him sourly. Dakar met his look evenly.

"Look, you can tell me his explanation, or I can go and ask him. And when he asks why I'm there bothering him, I'll be sure to let him know the exact reason so he can complain to the chief."

The sour look turned sourer, but it was accompanied by a grudging shrug. "He first claimed he wanted to talk to him about his threats to leave the business, but I'd guess he really went in to see about that form. Says he went in, couldn't find him in the kitchen, waited a minute or two to see if he was in the bathroom, and when he didn't come back, went back outside."

"What about Daniel's face? Did he see it at the window?"

DI Thomas shook his head.

Dakar leaned back. "Do we believe him?"

"No more 'we', Seb." The two men looked at each other in silence for a moment. "Anyway, that's where we are just now. So if Tom Mannings asks, you can tell him we've cooperated fully with you and shared everything we're allowed to."

Dakar held out a hand across the table, palm down as DI Thomas and DC Lemkin went to get up. Both men stopped.

"There's something else you have, Malky. Something you're not telling me. You weren't all that excited about Dennis. You've got someone else in the frame."

"There's plenty else, Seb. All I have to give you is the autopsy stuff, and bloodwork. Nothing more. I've already helped you out by telling you what Dennis told us."

Dakar paused, a pregnant pause, his head cocked to the side. DI Thomas turned his head, so he was looking at them almost sideways, his eyes on Dakar. "And there's something you're not telling me."

"We can always trade."

"You've got to be bloody joking."

"We found some photos at Mannings's house that your boys and girls missed."

DI Thomas looked down at him, and Stewart could see the anger in his eyes. Eventually he sat back down, Lemkin beside him, both leaning forward onto the wooden table, which creaked ominously under their combined weight.

"This had better be worth it."

Dakar turned and began rooting around in his own bag. DI Thomas's eyes turned to Stewart, his jaw clenched tight. Stewart put his hands up, and shot his eyes towards Dakar. DI Thomas grudgingly slid his look back over to Dakar.

Dakar pulled out the brown envelope. He pulled out the photographs and laid them across the table. DI Thomas and DC Lemkin studied them.

"Donaldson," DC Lemkin said, his finger landing on the image of Graham Donaldson standing on the steps of the hotel.

"Outside Hotel Black, if I make no mistake," DI Thomas agreed. He looked back up at Dakar. "What's this all about?"

"The desk in Mannings' garage slides out. That's where these were, and the prescription pad. And there was a piece of paper with dates and initials on it." Dakar pulled out the sheet of paper with the writing on it.

DI Thomas glared at Dakar for a second, while DC Lemkin devoured the information on the last sheet Dakar had produced. He looked down at the photo again.

"That blonde isn't his wife."

Dakar nodded.

"An affair, then?"

"That is the way it seems."

"So ..." DI Thomas sat back. He spoke slowly, eyes distant, but his face cleared and, of all things, a smile appeared. "Donaldson is playing away from home, on at least a few occasions according to these photographs. Daniel somehow gets wind of it ..." His eyes narrowed as he said these last words.

"Martina asked Daniel to follow Graham, and to take photographs."

DI Thomas slammed his hand down on the table, the thunderclap of noise making Stewart jump. "I knew it! We've bloody got him! He finds out Daniel has been following him, getting evidence of the affair. She divorces him, and is going to use the photos in court. And so bye-bye Daniel. I knew it. I bloody knew it was Donaldson!" DI Thomas had turned to DC Lemkin, fist clenched in triumph.

Dakar leaned forward now. "What else have you got, Malky? We both know him being found outside on the night isn't enough. Even with motive."

DI Thomas looked at him, slight smile. "He's also the only one not accounted for when Daniel gets attacked in the house. And he's got form for these kinds of things. He's been done for minor assault and BoPs plenty of times." DI Thomas turned to Stewart. "That's a breach of the peace to you." He turned back to Dakar. "Assault to severe injury landed him inside."

"A long time back though."

"Leopards don't change their spots, Dakar. What was it you always said? 'Past behaviour is the best predictor of future performance', something like that?"

"Still nowhere near enough. Not even for the fiscal, much less a jury."

DI Thomas leaned in. "If only you knew, Seb. It's bloody well the answer." His smile was one of vicious pleasure as Dakar looked blankly back.

DC Lemkin shifted in his seat. "Malky, didn't you say you weren't going to—"

DI Thomas cut him off with one raised hand, but he kept looking at Dakar. "In the spirit of giving, Tommy boy. And schooling our famous Zen boy here. Donaldson was found with a burner phone on him. Only one message, capital letters, sent that night: 'Front door open. Everyone at fireworks.' A second burner phone had been dumped in the kitchen bin."

Stewart's eyes opened wide as DI Thomas spoke, the man's glee evident. Dakar still had on his poker face.

"Traces on the second one?"

DI Thomas shook his head, a dismissive look on his face. "None, but it doesn't matter. We know who it was. Probably can't nail him, unless one of them spills, but we've got a clear path for Donaldson into the house, and therefore to Daniel. And while we don't have any of Dennis's fingerprints in the study—"

Dakar's eyebrows shot up. "You don't have one from Donaldson?"

DI Thomas just smiled. "More than one. He was inside that house, Seb. That very night."

Chapter 37

DI Thomas let the pause linger, a smile on his lips.

"How do you know they're from that night?" Dakar asked it guardedly, like a boxer behind his gloves as the blows rained down.

"Sarah-Anne cleaned the whole place before the party, including the study. So it couldn't have been before. And we got some nice clear ones from all those nice clean surfaces."

Dakar looked back into the face of DI Thomas' smile, with nothing left to say.

"You can find out with the rest at the press conference. Lemkin, get the nearest uniforms to go and arrest Donaldson."

The younger detective nodded and slid quickly out of the booth. DI Thomas sat back, satisfied, then looked down at the table. His smile slowly slipped from his face.

"When did you find these photographs?" His eyes shot between them.

"Yesterday morning."

"Yesterday morning?" DI Thomas leaned forward, burly forearms on the table. "For Christ's sake, Dakar, there's a whole murder room set up! As soon as you found these, you should have been on the blower to me."

"I wanted to ask Donaldson about them myself."

"That's bloody well obstructing the course of justice! You should have brought them straight to us!"

"We both know not giving information to the police is not a crime."

"You always said it ought to be."

"I've changed."

"Could've fooled me." DI Thomas spat the last words at him.

DC Lemkin slid back in, his eyes locked on Stewart and Dakar as he heard DI Thomas' irate tone.

"They've had these photos since yesterday morning."

"Yesterday morning?" DC Lemkin's outrage imitated that of DI Thomas.

Stewart looked down. He knew they should have given them to the police earlier. Knew it.

"I wanted to speak to Graham Donaldson about them." Dakar sounded calm in the face of the outrage.

"You were going to show the prime suspect some of the main evidence against him before we'd even had a chance to see it?" DI Thomas shook his head, while DC Lemkin's face mutated into an expression of disgust. "You're not a bloody copper anymore, Dakar. Stop acting like one."

If the blow hit, Dakar didn't show it. "We found them. If we hadn't got involved, they'd still be sitting in that garage."

"Don't give us it, Dakar. You might have found them this time, but we'd have got them eventually. Once Martina told us that Daniel had been taking pictures for her, we'd have found them." DI Thomas turned to DC Lemkin. "Lemkin, we'll want to be speaking to Martina again, find out why she didn't tell us she'd employed Daniel to follow her husband."

Lemkin nodded, and pulled out his notebook.

DI Thomas put the photographs away, back in the brown envelope, and gave them over to Lemkin. "We'll be needing your statements again. Full chain of custody reporting for these. Bloody hell, Seb."

There was the sound of a phone ringing, and DI Thomas pulled out his mobile.

"Yes, DC Safdar?"

The image of DC Safdar came into Stewart's mind as there was some speaking on the other end. He felt a little bit happier.

"What? And no-one has any idea where?" DI Thomas' urgent tone pulled Stewart out of his daydream. "And his house?" A few short words, a clearly annoyed tone. "Yes, all right. I know you're not an idiot. Post a couple of uniforms on both locations, and make sure everyone is on the lookout. Right. Bye."

DI Thomas hung up. "One more thing to tick off against Donaldson. The boy's done a runner. Left work, didn't say where he was going, just took off. No-one at his house, either. What do you think now, Zen man?"

Dakar just shook his head, but his lips were pulled back in a grimace.

"Ha!" DI Thomas slapped the table again. "So things are now going against the great Dakar, eh? Well, I always said—"

But someone interrupted him, a man approaching the table. A man sporting a worn-out suit, with a ridiculous hat on his head. In the hat was a small, old, notepad. And on his face was a manic grin.

"So, this is where you're all hiding!"

Chapter 38

Stewart stared at Frank McPherson for what seemed an eternity, his mouth open. He snapped back into the land of the conscious when DI Thomas' words cut across him.

"What the hell are you doing here?" DI Thomas' tone was pure irritation, but Frank's grin didn't waver.

"Nice to see you too, Malky! Been a long time. I'm with Dakar now. I had a chat with him the other night. If he gives me stories, I'll keep schtum about all the terrible shite I know about him."

DI Thomas and DC Lemkin stared at Frank for a second longer, then swept down to Dakar in an almost synchronised manner. But Dakar was still staring at Frank, his expression once again disbelieving.

"Is that true?" DI Thomas's tone sounded dangerous to Stewart, his nostrils flared like a wolf about to leap.

Dakar shook his head mutely, his eyes never leaving Frank. He looked like he was seeing the impossible, like Frank was some kind of ghost.

"Come, come, Sebbie my old sweetfruit. You brought me here. From Glasgow, over to the dentist's place, and then to the police station. Then I came here. I've been watching from the bar the entire time." Frank's voice struggled to contain his glee.

"What the hell are you playing at, Dakar? Christ, you don't just bring in any old journalist, you bring in Frank bloody McPherson ..." DI Thomas spoke in a low, harsh tone, but even he looked taken aback when Dakar turned and shot him a venomous look in turn.

"I didn't bring him!" Dakar's hissed whisper cut across the room.

Frank looked pleased with himself. He took his notepad out of the band running around his hat and opened it, a pencil in his other hand at the ready. "So, Detective Inspector, any comment on how the Mannings' murder inquiry is going? How about a look at some of those photographs you've all been gaping at? That post-mortem set looked interesting and—"

"You're not making any friends here, Frank." DI Thomas cut him off.

"Friends? Friends?" The journalist practically spat the word when he said it the second time, notepad and pencil falling to his side. "I know all about friends, Malky. And I know all about leaving people to burn. So. Give me a nice comment, and I'll leave you alone." A smile reappeared. "For now."

DI Thomas put his elbow on the table and rubbed his forehead with one hand. "There's nothing to tell, Frank."

Frank laughed shortly, a laugh without any humour. "Think I came down with the last rain? Post-mortem photos being pulled out by you, other photos being pulled out by Dakar here, your wee messenger boy running out urgently …" DC Lemkin looked like he fancied taking a swing at Frank, but the journalist ignored his murderous expression. "You've got something, Malky."

DI Thomas kept rubbing his head. "Fine. Okay. We've got someone in mind. Enough to charge them. We haven't got them yet, but once we do, I'll let you know. Enough?"

Frank looked at him for a second longer. He sniffed once. "Why don't you give me the name as well?"

DI Thomas's look darkened. "No names, Frank. Not yet. Didn't work out all that well last time, remember?"

Frank's eyes gleamed bright for a second, but the daft grin soon reasserted itself. "Guy or girl? And someone who was there that night?"

But DI Thomas just shook his head. "That's all for now. Like I said, once we've got them, you'll be the first to know. I'll even hold off from letting the rest of the pack in on the secret for half an hour."

"Half an hour? What the hell am I meant to do with half an hour? I need at least six hours."

DI Thomas's eyebrows shot up as an amused smiled appeared on his face.

"You have been out of the game for a while, Frank. You're talking about old deadlines – paper deadlines. In this digital world, anything new gets snapped up and ripped apart within ten minutes. Believe me, after your story appears on a website, it'll be two minutes before the first phone calls come in. Thirty seconds, even."

Frank looked at him searchingly. Eventually he shrugged. "Okay. One more thing you've got to tell me though." His smile grew manic.

"What's that?"

"What are these two doing here?" He indicated Dakar and Stewart. "Cops can't do without the help of Sebastian Dakar? Calling him in on all your murder investigations, are you?"

DI Thomas shook his head irritably. "No."

"Is he a suspect then? That would make a great headline, Malky. 'Murder! Former DI turned PI a suspect in a brutal stabbing.' Please. C'mon."

DI Thomas shook his head irritably again, swinging it with some force this time. "No, he's not a suspect. Neither is this one." He indicated Stewart.

"Helping you with your inquiries?"

"Tempted as I am to drag his name down," DI Thomas said, "no."

"Then what?"

"Then nothing."

Frank's lips made a pout. "You're not giving me a lot to go on here, Malky. You know what that means. Speculation."

"I've given you plenty, Frank. You can't just show up here and get all the good stuff straight away. That's not the way it works."

Frank shut the notebook, replacing it in his hat. "No, I can't, can I? Well, I'll see what I can do. You know what editors are like these days though. Drama, action, speculation. Most of the news is made up of speculation nowadays. Facts don't just garner the same attention they used to."

"Just keep it straight, Frank and I'll give you a bell once we've brought the person in. All right?"

Frank looked at him for a second, then pulled out a card. "All right then. Mess with me on this, and I'll mess with you right back, good and proper. All of you." His manic grin was on full beam.

DI Thomas nodded as he sighed, and took the card out of his hand. He rubbed his forehead one more time before he turned to his colleague. "Why don't you see Mr McPherson here out, Tommy? Make sure he leaves, eh?"

DC Lemkin nodded and got up, towering over the journalist.

"My, my, now you're a very big glass of water, aren't you?" Frank had to crane his neck to catch DC Lemkin's eye.

"I wouldn't try him." DI Thomas' voice came flatly from behind the colossus. DC Lemkin's murderous face turned a darker shade of purple at his inability to intimidate Frank.

Frank stuck his head around DC Lemkin's torso and winked at DI Thomas. "Thanks for the hospitality boys. I'm looking forward to hearing from you soon!" Frank gave a big wave as he turned and left, DC Lemkin stalking behind him.

In the awful silence Frank left behind him, DI Thomas slowly turned back to Dakar. "What the hell was that, Seb?" He spoke in a measured tone, but it was the calm before the storm, when the world seems to stop, holding its breath.

The silence lengthened. Dakar's eyes had followed Frank all the way out of the bar, and now they looked at the door, like they were frozen.

"I said—"

"I didn't bring him here."

"Is this why you've been running around interviewing everyone? More publicity for the almighty Zen master? For God's sake!" He kept his voice down, but the anger made it tremble. Stewart carefully put down his half shandy glass, the amber liquid sloshing against the sides of the glass as if it too wanted to escape.

Silence. Dakar turned slowly to DI Thomas, an ugly look on his face. "I didn't bring him here."

"You might owe him, but I bloody don't. If any of what I told you – any of it – gets into his story, it's all over for you. Understand me?"

"I didn't bring him here!" Dakar slammed both hands down on the table. Stewart leaned away as others in the bar looked over at the noise, but DI Thomas didn't flinch.

"You'd better not have. I had a big enough mess to clean up after you disappeared, Dakar. I'm not cleaning up anymore."

Dakar sat silently, glaring back at him. DC Lemkin had returned, and stood next to the table, a silent golem waiting for its orders.

"Get the hell out of here. We're done. We'll get chain of custody statements from you later. Lemkin, escort these two out as well. Get them the hell away from me."

Lemkin nodded, as if he'd been waiting for this. "Let's go."

Stewart immediately grabbed his coat and satchel and began to slide out, praying that Dakar would do the same. He stood up, and squeezed past DC Lemkin. The cop barely looked at him, his stare focusing mainly on Dakar. The man was still in a glaring competition with DI Thomas, both of them breathing heavily.

Slowly, almost painfully, Dakar stood up. He looked at Lemkin for a second, then back at DI Thomas. "I didn't bring him here." He repeated the words in a low tone, shaking his head ever so slightly as he spoke. Then he turned to follow Stewart out.

DI Thomas leaned forward suddenly, hissing words as if he were firing bullets. "No more investigating from you, Dakar, or your little pup there. I hear anything more, and I'll bring you both in, the full rigmarole. Remember, they don't like ex-cops in Bar-L."

But he was speaking to the man's back. Dakar just kept on walking.

Chapter 39

"I didn't bring Frank there."

Dakar spoke in a hard tone, his eyes fixed on Stewart as the drops of rain began to fall around them.

They stood outside the police station, the walk back cold and silent. Now they were standing next to his car, the cold, dark night close around them, the wind stronger than it was before. Dakar's clothes looked odd on this new personality, ill-fitting where before they had seemed natural.

Stewart swallowed, and nodded once. He looked at the ground, unable to meet Dakar's eyes.

Dakar took a deep breath, and gestured for Stewart to get in the car. He didn't start the car once they were inside though, instead sitting, grasping the steering wheel tightly and staring out into the darkness as if some answer was out there, somewhere in the shadows.

The silence continued for a few minutes. Stewart looked around at Dakar, but the guy hadn't changed his position, not one iota. Stewart felt like some crappy forgotten ornament.

Stewart looked back out of the window, arms hanging uselessly down by his side. Suddenly his phone began to make a noise. Frowning, he pulled it out. An alarm. Set for ten to six. For the office party.

Christ. Stewart looked round at Dakar again, urgently this time. The man hadn't reacted to Stewart's phone sound. Actually, Dakar didn't look too good. But then, what was Stewart meant to do? It didn't really look like Dakar was ready to share his troubles. Was he meant to just hang around him all night, on the off-chance he might say something? And, of course, at the end of the day, he worked with Dakar once in a blue moon. He worked in the firm every day.

"Eh, Dakar?"

Dakar looked around. Stewart leaned away from him ever so slightly, gulping.

"You all right?"

Dakar continued looking at him for a second, then turned back to stare into the shadows again.

"Eh, thing is, I've got that office party tonight. I thought that as we seem to be finished for the day ... Well, it's actually starting about now. I'm sorry to bail and all that ... I know it's maybe not the best time. Thing is, eh, is there any chance ..." He trailed off as Dakar looked back around at him, his expression set, eyes shielded behind whatever mental defences he had erected.

"I'll drop you at your flat." The words came out in a tone as dark as the night around them.

"Okay. Eh, thanks. And is there anything I can, you know, well, do?"

Dakar pushed the ignition button instead of answering, and the car pulled away with its normal lack of noise. Stewart glanced over at Dakar once or twice, but the guy was staring at the road, expression unchanging. He wanted to say something, but finally gave up, turning instead to look out of the windscreen at the miserable weather outside.

Spots of rain were coming down more and more heavily. Dakar didn't bother with the windscreen wipers, and the world outside became more and more fractured as they drove along.

Stewart shifted in his seat. His mind raced to find a way to square the circle, both not ditching Dakar while also making the office party in time to show face. But he couldn't do both. And it seemed like he couldn't really help Dakar. And if he didn't make the office party ... well, it would be a serious black mark on his record, majorly denting his hopes of getting a job at the end of the year. Especially as Sudgeon had pointedly reminded him recently about it.

He checked his watch again, surreptitiously, as the car pulled up outside the flat. Six. He'd have to do the report as well, of course. That would take a bit of time too. Or maybe it was over now, now the police had decided it was Donaldson?

The car had stopped, but Dakar was still looking forward, out into the night.

"Eh, I guess that's it for the Mannings case, if the police have worked that it was Donaldson? I guess it sort of makes sense, what with the affair and all."

Dakar closed his eyes.

"Shame we didn't find him first, I suppose. If only that GPS Martina used on him was still active!"

The steering wheel creaked as Dakar's knuckles whitened around it. Stewart looked at the thin, long fingers.

"Right, yeah. I mean, it's a tough case. Was a tough case." Stewart paused for a moment, wetting his lips. "Just, about the case, I'll be needing to write that report for today, and I was wondering—"

"Jesus Christ! You and your bloody reports! A man died here! Stabbed! Don't you care about who actually murdered him? Or you only worried about what the partners will think if you haven't crossed every bloody 't'?"

Stewart sat stunned as Dakar shouted the words from half a metre away.

"Eh—"

Dakar rounded on him. "You and bloody Malky. How stupid are you? Makes sense? Makes bloody sense? Tell me then, why did he fight Daniel in his bedroom, with a window into the garden where everyone could see? And then why dump the body in the cellar? And how did he magic it down there? And why, why the hell, in the name of all that's holy, after managing to pull off this crime, did he sit around in his car and wait to be collared? Makes sense? Jesus!" Dakar whipped back around to face forward.

Silence expanded out into the car, the only sound the raindrops outside thumping down. Stewart looked down into the floor, a hollow feeling in his stomach that felt like it was sucking in all his organs.

"No, yeah. Guess you're right. Sorry." Stewart eventually broke the silence, his voice barely strong enough to be heard over the rain.

"Aaaah!" Dakar exclaimed with frustration, hit the steering wheel with the butt of both of his hands, once, hard. He blew out a big bit of air. Then he put one hand to his temple, rubbing it as if he was trying to go through the skin to the skull. "Something here isn't right!" He practically shouted the last word. "It's there. It's all there!"

Dakar slowly lowered his head until it was almost touching the steering wheel, his face a mask of agony.

Stewart looked at the bowed head for a moment, his lips two bitter lines across his face. Then he got out into the rain that bit into his face, and the wind that pierced to his bones, and closed the door behind him.

Chapter 40

Stewart stood looking at himself in the mirror in his bedroom. He'd typed up his report mechanically, a technical recounting of everything they'd done that day, cutting bits here and there without any conscious thought. In the end he hadn't included the part about the police issuing an arrest warrant for Donaldson. He didn't know why not.

The concern of who to send it to didn't even register with him. The report went to Sudgeon and Green, and then an identical copy went in a separate email to Tom Mannings.

The only thing in his head since the moment he'd left the car had been Dakar's words, bouncing around, echoing and pulsating every time they crashed off one side of his brain heading for the other. How stupid was he? Very, in the end. To think he could just rock in and solve it, something that the police couldn't work out. Yes. Really bloody stupid.

He had a blue suit on. Smart-casual, those had been the instruction for the office party. Normally this would be a tough choice, his mind calculating what others might think about what he was wearing. But now he couldn't bring himself to care about any of that. All of his thoughts felt dull, and dense, and uninteresting, floating in his head like big, heavy old rusted super tankers in a gloomy grey sea where nothing lived.

He caught a taxi to the office, waiting under the eaves of his building until the taxi arrived, out of the worst of the storm that was breaking. Breaking it was, though, the rain coming down like machine gun fire. He'd have to get a taxi to the Oak as well, if he didn't want to turn up looking like a drowned rat.

Dakar's car was gone when he came out of the house, and he stood staring at where it had been until the taxi arrived. The journey was a silent one, Stewart staring out the window at nothing. The Meadows flashed past, as did Lothian Road and Princes Street, but Stewart could have been looking out into utter darkness for all he saw.

He checked his watch as he walked into his firm's building. Seven. A few of the high heid yins would be left, so at least he could show face. Then they could pretend that he'd made the effort to 'network' and

The Price to Pay

everyone could pretend to believe he cared about his career. And then he could go home, ditch the suit and head out with Beth to the Oak for this gig.

At least that was something to look forward to, a small ray of light in a dark, cold day. He really didn't fancy talking about working with Dakar at that exact moment, but hell, good music, a beer or two and some facetime with Beth would cheer him up. And he could always lie about how it was going with Dakar.

He walked into the boardroom where the party was taking place. It was up on the partners' floor, a place Stewart normally went once in a blue moon, although now he was here for the second time in two days. He felt no excitement, or fear, or boredom, or anything. He felt nothing, in fact, just going through the motions until he could go somewhere else.

It was a massively long room, where on normal days a large, faux-oak polished table sat in the centre with chairs on those little roller wheels around the edge. A place where serious people – mainly old, white-haired men – could discuss serious business. Today was no normal day though. Today was a day the partners were letting their hair down, such as they had left. The padded seats had been removed, presumably by the secretaries. The table, pushed to one wall, was now serving as the bar and buffet, holding the very best food and drink from the local posh supermarket.

There was a large gaggle of people there when Stewart arrived, a hum of noise in the air accompanied by a scent of perfume, aftershave and ambition. Partners, associates, secretaries, trainees, paralegals … Stewart tallied the groups as he looked around. That was basically the ranking order too. Stewart had heard things about what happened to the paralegals. Screaming, shouting, a bin being emptied over someone's desk. Bad times.

He could see Green and Sudgeon off to one side with a small gaggle around them, so at least they would be easily avoided. Stewart studied the rest of the crowd. On the plus side, few, if any, would want to talk to him. On the down side, a number of them would probably awkwardly try to do so, taking pity on a trainee who they presumed must be desperate to get a job.

He shook his head. He'd get some food, and then head off. At least he could say he'd been there, and it wouldn't be a lie. That would do.

Stewart made it halfway to the table when he heard his name.

"Scott."

Charles Robbin stood behind him, staring at him with his gimlet eyes. He was wearing a very smart three-piece suit, a handkerchief poking out of a breast pocket. The get-up made him look like he had walked out of the 19th century, or was a member of the modern-day Tory party. He had a glass of white wine, but it looked untouched. He was leaning away from Stewart as he spoke, as if to be seen with him was the social equivalent of contracting the Black Death.

"Hi, Charles." He spoke without even his normal politeness.

Robbin didn't waste any time, taking Stewart's arm and steering him towards a quieter part of the room.

"How's the investigation going?" His tone was light, but his eyes bored into Stewart like a drill going into the earth.

Stewart thought back to Dakar shouting at him in the car, claiming the only person without an iron-cast alibi couldn't have done it.

"Fine."

Charles nodded, silently. Normally, Stewart would have expected some comment on his flat, irritated tone of voice. But today Charles was the worried one.

"Listen. Erm. Terrible things, these investigations. Throw up all kinds of spurious, irrelevant details. Things that never need to see the light of day. Do you know what I mean?"

The word 'cocaine' floated through Stewart's head, in big white crumbly letters.

"Yes. Yes, I know exactly what you mean."

Charles squinted at him. "Good. Good man. Listen. I'm sure it won't, but if anything did come up about me, or anything I might have …" Charles paused suddenly. "Ah, done, I'd be very much in your debt if you could make sure it didn't become known in the firm. Too many damned rumours around this place already. Ha."

Stewart looked back at him, nodding slowly, waiting for this awful conversation to be over.

"And I would be very happy to acknowledge that debt. I can be a useful man to know." Now his voice was weightier, the words coming slowly. Charles stared into his eyes, presumably waiting for a light of understanding.

Stewart pulled his shoulders back, suddenly aware of how tense they were.

"So, ah, has anything come up yet? About me?" Charles tried to keep his voice neutral as he cast his eyes down to his wine glass, before they suddenly shot back up.

Stewart looked at Charles for a few seconds. A part of his brain knew that, normally, this would have him on edge. To tell about the cocaine, not to tell ... To have Charles in his corner. Did he want that? For the job later, perhaps. But perhaps not.

But now, now, all he cared about was this conversation being over.

He shook his head.

Charles smiled with relief. "Good man. Let me know if anything does. Only me. I'll be sure to make it worth your while." He turned and walked away, leaving Stewart on his own.

Stewart headed towards the buffet table, deliberately aiming for people he didn't know, sliding around the outside of groups, and avoiding eye contact. Within seconds he was there. He grabbed a paper plate, and was just reaching out for some kind of sweet chilli wrap when he heard a voice behind him.

"Hi, Stewart."

He automatically turned around, hand unconsciously retracting before his stomach could intervene. Jennifer was smiling, holding a large glass of red in front of her in both hands, although she seemed smaller than she usually did, like the weight of this occasion was pressing down on her.

"Jennifer!" Stewart felt a jolt go through him, like his brain had just been kicked back into life. He blinked a couple of times. "Hi. How's it going?"

"Good thanks, yeah. Just, you know, here."

"Yeah." He took a deep breath, and managed a smile. "Chatting with the rich and famous?"

She smiled a little wider. "Oh, I don't know. These occasions always feel a bit awkward."

"A bit like the zoo, right?"

"A zoo?"

"Yeah. I mean, you, me, Michelle, Hamish and a bunch of others at the bottom of the food chain, we're all competing for attention, like the animals. Doing tricks in our cages. The partners are the tourists, wandering around to see if there's anything interesting. And then those of us they like, they give their attention to. Maybe even take us home."

She gave a small laugh. "Yes, maybe." She took a gulp of her drink, and right on cue, into the silence, Stewart's stomach rumbled ominously, furious at its frustrated expectations.

"Oh, I've stopped you from eating. I'm so sorry."

Stewart went to reply, empty paper plate in his hand, but in the end just nodded and turned to the table. He gratefully loaded up a couple of wraps and some bits of hard bread with paté on top, biting into one of the wraps as he turned back to her. Thankfully it didn't go everywhere, as it was prone to do.

Maybe the big man upstairs was ready to turn around this day for him.

"I sometimes think, when I get really hungry, that my stomach starts eating itself."

Stewart looked at Jennifer as he chewed, Jennifer's cheeks slowly turning pink in the silence. He swallowed.

"Yeah. Could be, I suppose."

"I meant that I used to think that. When I was little. When my stomach made noises." She spoke urgently.

"Right, aye. Of course." Stewart saw her cheeks turn red.

"Did you know I used to think that cars moved because of the gas shooting out the exhausts? I thought that's what pushed them forward." Jennifer giggled, her embarrassment spreading into a smile, the red in her cheeks fading.

"Really?"

"Oh yeah. Until I was about eight or something. Then I had an argument about it with my brother. He tried everything to convince me, talking about buses, and then big trucks, saying they were too heavy to push with gas. But even with the trucks, I was sure that's how they worked. The exhaust points backwards at some point, so that must be how they move forwards."

"So what changed your mind?"

"He asked me how cars reversed." She laughed, the red now entirely disappeared.

"Oh yes, I see how that could be a problem."

Stewart nodded. "The mental equivalent of a pile of bricks landing on your head." There was a beer on the table, invitingly within reach and it had been a long day. He reached over and grabbed it, with a twist top. He untwisted it with relish, practically tearing the thing off, and took a swig.

"So, can you tell us what you're working on yet, or are you still going to be all cloak and dagger again?" Her tone was playful.

Stewart smiled grimly. He looked over at Sudgeon and Green – far, distant people – then back at Jennifer, right next to him.

"Do you remember a few months back I went to watch that guy Sebastian Dakar working? Investigating a suicide? It was down in the Borders."

Jennifer nodded as she took a sip.

"Well, I'm basically doing another investigation with him. I can't say what it's about though, sorry." Stewart paused as Dakar's face flashed through his mind again, the words echoing in his head. "Although we might be finished."

She nodded. "Might be? You don't sound very certain."

Stewart shook his head bleakly. "No. I'm not. It's just ..." He shook his head. "It's just that the police think it's one guy, and Dakar doesn't, and I don't have a clue who it was, and I don't know how it's going to end. It's all gone a bit wrong."

"Well, tomorrow's a new day. Maybe there'll be light at the end of the tunnel."

Stewart nodded. Yeah, could be. Just might be an oncoming train.

Chapter 41

"Pinky swear, was it?" Michelle asked, laughing raucously at her own joke. She had put away quite a few wines before she had arrived, a dynamo of energy regarding work gossip. It hadn't taken long for Stewart's mission to come up, and he'd explained in the same way as he had with Jennifer.

"Or boy scouts?" Jennifer joined in, Michelle laughing twice as hard.

"Everyone's a comedian tonight, aren't they?" Stewart smiled, but it was tinged with sadness. He was on beer three, but the small bottles weren't really sufficient to carry him off in a warm haze. He tried to banish the memory of Dakar shouting in the small car, surrounded by the cold, dark night, as he stood bathed in the bright lights of the firm office, awash in the legal small talk, but it remained stubbornly there.

"Ah," Michelle said, wiping her eyes. "At least you get to work with the partners though. Most of them don't know our names."

"If it's any consolation, Mannings didn't even know I worked for the firm when I went to see him. Dakar had to tell him. And yeah, Sudgeon says hello sometimes, but Green just glares at me. The other partners don't know I exist. Hardly like they ever call me in for a social chat. I'm no Hamish." He paused. "They don't even say hello to you guys?"

"None of the partners say hello to us. Ever," Michelle answered.

Stewart glanced around the room. It had cleared out since he'd been talking with Jennifer and Michelle, but there were still a few high heid yins left. Sudgeon and Green were in a little knot with a few other men. Charles was one of them. Stewart could see that Hamish was there too. Of course he was. Stewart felt a sour taste in his mouth.

He turned back to Jennifer and Michelle, who were talking about something or other, but his thoughts again centred on Dakar. Where would he have gone? And the answer welled up in Stewart's mind, an image of Dakar's cramped, dark, lonely room. Stewart remembered the look Dakar had given him when Stewart had asked to go to the office party. It might be dark in his room, but it wouldn't be as dark as Dakar's mind.

And he was here, seriously considering going over to have conversation with people he disliked in the hope that they'd pay him more than the minimum wage so he could keep on doing the same stuff, year after year. He looked back at Michelle and Jennifer, and put his beer down on the table. It wasn't that far to Dakar's place, after all.

"Right, I'm—"

A booming voice cut across the room. "Scott! Scott!"

Stewart looked around. Sudgeon, unbelievably, was calling his name. The man made a 'come here' gesture with one hand, almost impatiently.

Stewart looked back around incredulously at the girls, who were both staring back at him. Jennifer had cocked her head to one side. Stewart could see the amusement in their eyes.

"Didn't he say something about social chats a second ago? I can't quite remember ..." Jennifer turned to Michelle inquiringly.

Stewart put up his hands. "Look, hold on a wee second. This is the first time—"

"Scott!"

Stewart stopped, closed his eyes and put a hand up to his face, his back to the group of men so they couldn't see. "In the name of the wee man—"

"Time for you to go and join your boy's club, 'Scott'. For one of those nice social chats. Enjoy." Jennifer and Michelle turned away. Stewart looked at them for a second, looked over at the door, then clenched his teeth. He grabbed his beer, turned and walked over.

"Can't have you standing the whole night talking to women, now, can we, Scott?" Sudgeon said, his face painted with a welcoming smile and red cheeks. "Particularly not trainees."

"Eh, no, sir."

Sudgeon was holding a glass of red wine, as were all the other men. Stewart cradled his beer with an odd feeling of defiance. There were seven of them in total. Sudgeon and Green, Charles, three guys Stewart didn't know other than that they were senior associates, and of course Hamish. Hamish looked particularly unamused that Stewart was now the centre of attention.

"Sir? No 'sirs' just now, Scott. How's it going with Dakar? I do hope he's not infecting you with his ludicrous utopian ideals! Ha ha ha."

Dakar's face again loomed in his mind, the anger in the car. As soon as he could wriggle free of this ... Beth and the Oak could wait. She'd understand. "Safe to say he's not, Mr Sudgeon. I would—"

"Good man! Last thing we need. That report of yours makes for amusing reading. Excellent to go to sleep with, eh?"

"But a little less irrelevant detail, like the sartorial style of the victim or the nature of permaculture, would be appreciated." Green cut in, his normally bright eyes dull. Stewart smiled with a grim pride.

"You know Hamish wanted to work with Dakar? Didn't you, Hamish?" Sudgeon turned towards the other trainee with an amused smile. Hamish's sullen look became further tainted, his cheeks going red.

"Dakar turned him down flat! Ha ha. Said he wanted to work with you."

Stewart looked at Hamish, but the guy was looking at the floor. No wonder, then, Hamish had looked so annoyed that morning. Wasn't used to having Stewart picked above him. But there was no flash of schadenfreude. Instead he felt an odd feeling of solidarity, as if he and Hamish were fighting dogs, being provoked to lash out at one another for the amusement of the crowd.

"I think it might be time for me to go home!" Sudgeon boomed. There were gentle murmurs of protest from the senior associates. "No, no, I'm not young anymore. Not like you chaps!"

Sudgeon looked between Hamish and Stewart. "The rest of them are taken, like me, but I bet you two will be heading out tonight, painting the town red. Probably find some lucky young ladies to take home as well, eh?"

Stewart's eyebrows came together as he frowned. Hamish was recovering his smile, although the rejection of Dakar had clearly left its mark.

"In my prime, many moons ago, I used to get through three or four a week, you know." Sudgeon spoke as if conveying an important secret. "And that was back in traditional times, when young ladies truly were ladies. From what I read in the newspapers now, that's probably conservative for you young guns!"

Sudgeon looked between them, but after a moment he cocked an eye towards Hamish.

"Eh, Hamish? You're a smart young buck. You'll be fighting the ladies off with a stick tonight, no?"

"Oh, I won't be heading out tonight."

"Oh?" Sudgeon sounded not only alarmed but annoyed, a frown coming over his face. Stewart understood why. Hamish wasn't playing along. Even if he wasn't heading out, he should still be lying and say that he was to let Sudgeon revel in his topic.

But there was something in that, something dangerous, because Hamish was a master player of this particular game. Stewart could smell it. Hamish was smiling properly now, a nasty little smile. Stewart shifted uncomfortably. He could probably finish his drink and then head off to check on Dakar. Sudgeon wouldn't be happy, but Sudgeon's contentment was low on the priority list now.

"I was out last night, Mr Sudgeon, and picked up a lovely young lady then. A few drinks, and then back to my place, and we were up all night. Up all night." He repeated the words slowly. "I'm exhausted. It's a wonder I made it into work."

Sudgeon guffawed, clapping Hamish on the back. Stewart looked around the rest of the group. Charles and two of the senior associates were also smiling as if they were genuinely enjoying this, but the other one had a look of tepid enthusiasm at best. Green was smiling metallically, as if he was touching something hugely unpleasant.

"Oh yes, young women these days! I bet she had you scrambling all around the bed, eh?" There was a gleam in Sudgeon's eye now.

Stewart looked away. In the name of the wee man. Nothing to do but sit there and listen to this shite. Well. At least he had his beer. He could focus on that, and escape as soon as possible.

"Oh yes. All round the bed, all kinds of different positions. And the noises she made! Incredible. I thought the neighbours would complain!"

"Ha! Desirous of more, was she?"

"Oh yes. Quite a bit more." Stewart snuck a look at Hamish. Funnily enough, he was looking at Stewart, not at Sudgeon.

"What I would do for a fit young woman who wanted to have plenty of exercise in the bedroom! Ha ha! And will you be seeing this young lady again, or are you moving on to sow your seeds more widely?"

Stewart stared fiercely at his bottle, fighting the overwhelming impulse to shake his head.

"Oh, I don't know. I wouldn't mind another go." Hamish spoke almost modestly.

"Ha ha! Quite right! Keep going until you're bored. And does this young nymph have a name?"

"Yes. Stewart knows her, actually." Stewart looked up with a jolt from his beer, and saw Hamish still staring at him, his finger on the trigger. "He lives with her. Her name's Beth."

Chapter 42

Stewart felt like he was underwater, with everything moving slowly. He could see fine, but all he could hear was muffled noises, mouths opening and closing, seemingly laughing – laughing? – all to the soundtrack of the dull beats of blood pumping through his ears.

Sudgeon was saying something, looking at him, although he couldn't make out the words. It looked like it might be quite important. He listened harder.

"Well, Scott? Sounds like this young woman is quite a tempting mare! I suppose you've also had your way with her, eh?" Stewart almost stepped away from the loud, booming voice as if it had physically struck him.

Hamish was laughing. Sudgeon was laughing. Everyone was laughing, in fact, all around the circle. Stewart saw big rows of gaping teeth everywhere. It was like the world had gone mad.

Stewart opened his mouth to respond, with no idea what was going to come out, but Sudgeon saved him the trouble. He clapped him on the shoulder in a way that he probably thought was hearty.

"Ha, good man! Of course you have! And you, Hamish, you should most certainly see her again. If she can make a young stallion like you exhausted, she must be quite a creature! Perhaps not one to marry, of course, but good entertainment in the meantime."

Stewart, still feeling like he was in suspended reality, idly noted that Hamish had been a buck but was now a stallion. He wondering if Sudgeon had some kind of pecking order of sexual prowess in the animal kingdom. Lion, stag, stallion, buck? Something like that?

Hamish looked faux-modest for a second. "Oh, we'll see. I believe she had a rather good time as well, so I'm hopeful she'll be, shall we say, desirous of a second night."

Sudgeon almost spat out the slug of wine he'd just taken in delight, just barely managing to swallow it before he now clapped Hamish on the shoulder.

Sudgeon seemed to enjoy touching young men. The second thought floated in and out of Stewart's mind.

The Price to Pay

But he had an uncomfortable feeling now, like a stone in his shoe, but one that was underneath his skin, so wherever he placed his weight it irritated him, and it was getting worse, like the stone was getting bigger, or maybe there were more stones ...

It felt like someone threw ice-cold water in his face. Beth had slept with Hamish. She – Beth, his Beth – had got naked with this, this person. This morning. Of course. She'd been tired, grumpy, late. The sad look she'd had. The night before. She'd slept with him. With Hamish. Had sex. Been naked with him, and then slept with him, and then slept beside him. And woken up. Naked. Sex. With Hamish. Beth. With Hamish. And this morning. She'd known. She'd known.

Sudgeon was looking at him, waiting for a response. Stewart could feel the anger now, but it was steady in his mind, a hum, like some kind of focused white-hot energy. He felt like he could hear and see and smell and feel everything, perceive all that was happening around him.

"Sorry, sir?" Stewart spoke carefully.

"Ha, in a world of his own! Probably thinking about the last time he had the young filly to himself. Don't get jealous now, there's plenty to go round. Particularly when you're a good-looking young man with a spare bit of money. And you'll get that soon, Scott, no doubt. Don't worry."

Stewart felt hot, cold and full of energy simultaneously, like he could punch through the oak table with one blow. He looked at the gargantuan stupid windbag in front of him before his eyes slid over to Hamish, who was looking warily back at him. He focused on him for a moment, then turned back to Sudgeon.

"I'm not worried, Mr Sudgeon. And I've never had a similar experience to Hamish with Beth, sir. I consider her a good friend. I'm also happy to assure you that this guy ..." he indicated Hamish while keeping his eyes on Sudgeon, "... is not someone I am jealous of."

Sudgeon pulled himself upright, his expression becoming uncertain. Stewart could feel the new wariness in the rest of the group, the men all leaning back, drinks that had been held by their side now being held up universally across their chest. "I see. My dear boy, I hope you understand I didn't mean anything against your good friend. I speak purely out of admiration for a girl who is reportedly so young and attractive."

Bollocks to this for a game of soldiers. Bollocks. To. This.

Stewart smiled, a manic grin. "Of course, Mr Sudgeon, I fully understand." He turned to look around the group. The happy merriment was gone now, everyone watching him closely, as if they'd just found out the animal they'd brought into their house wasn't tame but savage. "I'll take my leave, gentlemen, and wish you all a most pleasant evening."

Stewart turned away from the group. He marched back over towards Jennifer and Michelle, who were still chatting. They looked up as he approached.

"Having a nice time with all your boyfriends over there?" It was Michelle who asked, but her smile disappeared when she saw Stewart's expression.

"Just came to say goodnight. And that I bloody hate macho bullshite. Really, really hate it. I'll see you guys later. Have a good one."

Stewart turned and strode out into the hall, not waiting for a response. He grabbed his long coat and headed down towards the service elevator. He was still flushing, hot and cold, practically bouncing on his feet.

She had slept with Hamish. With Hamish. Beth. The woman he adored. She had slept with him. The guy he loathed. She knew Stewart loathed him. Stewart had told her that. But she'd slept with him anyway. Hamish. Of all the people.

The thoughts flew through his mind, constantly recycled over and over again, his body stiff with anger and energy. The blood was pumping through his veins so intensely it was painful.

He was outside now. The storm was in full flow, the rain pelting down onto the concrete floor, smashing into Stewart's unprotected head as he stood in the darkness, clenching and unclenching his fists. Thunder boomed overhead.

He walked back to the flat, up Lothian Road and across the darkness of The Meadows, unheeding as the wind buffeted him and the rain poured down. Lightning flashed, showing trees swaying wildly and leaves being swept around as the wind treated The Meadows like its own personal playground. He found himself outside the door to the flat all too quickly, with the same thoughts, over and over.

Beth was sitting at the table in the living room, eating some kind of green leaves. He didn't know what it was. Didn't care. All that was important was the anger. It was in him, in a way he couldn't ever remember having before.

She looked up, saw him, and he knew that she knew that he knew.

"Where's Saz?"

Beth looked at him, mouth half-full of salad, fear in her eyes. She swallowed quickly. "Eh, she's out, I think. Went to the pub straight from work. Stewart, you're soaked! You need to—"

"Hamish?"

"What?" But her voice was trembling.

"Hamish?" He repeated, his voice the colour of steel.

She put her fork down, took a deep breath. "Stewart, I'm sorry. I—"

"Do you want to know how I found out? Your new man, Hamish, boasting to me and my work colleagues about how you kept him up all night, all the different positions, how you were crying out his name, begging for more. You couldn't even tell me this morning, eh? Before I walked in there?"

Beth sat there, seemingly stunned.

"Nothing to say?" Stewart spoke into the silence.

Beth's eyes began to tear up, but she swallowed, and there was anger in her face now, replacing the fear.

"I said, nothing to—"

"You know what, Stewart? You don't own me, okay? I'm not your girlfriend."

Stewart stared at her for a second, then nodded slowly.

"Okay. Yeah. You're right, I don't own you. And yeah, you're not my girlfriend. Perhaps not even my friend. So the next time one of your eight million shagging partners begins boasting about it to me and the rest of the world, you know what? I won't say you're a friend of mine. I'll just laugh along. Christ."

Beth glared at him, a mixture of tears and anger, although it looked like the tears were coming out on top.

"Actually, know what as well? I think I'm out. Don't need to be staying with folk who aren't friends of mine."

She wiped her eyes. "What do you mean?"

"I mean I'll get out the flat, go find a new place. And you can start bringing all the boys back here instead of staying over at their place. I don't want you to feel bad, you know."

Stewart could see the blows were landing, Beth recoiling at each sentence, but he didn't stop. He stood over her as she sat in the seat, the elation coursing through him as he channelled all his anger directly at her.

Stewart heard the sound of the door opening and closing, and Saz's voice shouting from the hallway. "Hellllllooooooooooooooo! Dearest flatmates of mine. Who's at home? I'm just dropping by for a quick pit-stop before I …"

Saz came around the corner. Stewart could smell the drunken fumes coming off her, but she sobered up pretty quickly.

"What's going on?"

Stewart kept looking at Beth when he responded, his voice hard, flat. "This one here'll tell you, no doubt. Her new boyfriend's told everyone else in the world. I'm heading off to bed. Long day today. Plenty to think about."

Beth glared at him through her tears as he turned around and walked past the astonished-looking Saz before he marched up the stairs and went into his bedroom.

Stewart didn't bother turning on the light. Instead he got his suit off, leaving it in a crumpled pile all of its own, and grabbed a towel. After he'd dried himself a bit, he got on a pair of comfortable trousers, thick socks and a fleecy sports hoodie.

He sat on the bed, looking emptily into the darkness. His mind was beginning to whirl now, the anger slowly dissipating as his focus and concentration frayed, unwound and then dissolved in a swirl of emotions.

Beth was right, of course. That was the godawful thing. He didn't own her, he didn't have any claim over what she did. But for Christ's sake. Even if they weren't any more than friends, they were still friends. Or had been, at least. She knew how much he loathed Hamish, and she certainly knew that he liked her.

And he had nowhere else to go, no-one else to talk to. He couldn't talk about it with his mates. It was barely allowed to show you were upset when it was your girlfriend who had done something like this, much less some girl you just fancied. As for his brothers, they had their own lives, their own families, and besides, this had never been something they'd discussed.

He felt a spot hit his hand, and for one second he thought his hair was still wet, still dripping. But then he realised it was his tears that were flowing. He bent his head and licked the wet patch like an animal licking its wound, tasting the salt.

He hadn't cried in ages. Couldn't remember the last time he'd cried because he was upset. Scottish males weren't allowed to do that. Anger, yes, but not upset, and certainly not tears.

There was a cautious knock at the door. "Stewart? You all right in there?" It was Saz's voice, as circumspect as her knock had been.

He hurriedly wiped his eyes. "All good, thanks." He forcibly kept his voice neutral, as if he didn't have a care in the world.

"Mind if I come in?" The door creaked open slightly, a sliver of light coming into the room.

"Actually, Saz, I'm a bit tired the now. Mind if we leave the chat until later?" Even he could hear the edge in his voice.

The door paused for a second, reminding Stewart oddly of the day before, an age ago, when he and Dakar, the best of pals, had been standing outside Martina Donaldson's door.

"No worries. But you are okay, right?"

"I'm fine. All good." The stock response was even more of a lie this time than it was all the other times.

"Okay. Listen, sleep well, hope everything's all right, and I'll catch up with you tomorrow, yeah?"

"Aye. Okay. No bother. Have a good one."

"Okay." The door closed again with a click, and Stewart was once again left alone, in the darkness.

He sat there for a long time, occasionally feeling the tears come down his face, or a huge surge of emotion well up in him, which exploded through him with some kind of whole body shiver. His mind whirled, the thoughts queueing up – from Beth, to Hamish, to home, to his family, to work, to Sudgeon, to Green, to Dakar – round and round and round and round.

At some point his phone lit up with a message. At first Stewart ignored it. There was no-one in the world he wanted to talk to right now. But after a few minutes his curiosity got the better of him, and he picked it up. Wiping his salty wet face with one hand, he brought the only light in the darkness up to his face. It was Dakar.

'*Graham Donaldson has just been arrested.*'

Chapter 43

Stewart was sitting in a barber's chair, looking at himself in the mirror, and Dakar was the barber, except he wasn't cutting his hair, he was taking out Stewart's brain and slicing it up, but Stewart wasn't feeling any pain, and they were having a nice chat, but then Dakar found a big stone in Stewart's brain, and was angry, holding it up, and shouting, more and more, louder and louder and louder ...

Stewart woke up with a shock. His alarm was going off beside him, screaming at the world that it was seven thirty. He rubbed his eyes.

Stewart sat upright as the memories came crashing back. The memory of Dakar's fury the previous night sent a cold shiver through him. And then Dakar being on his own. He'd meant to go and see him, hadn't he? But he hadn't. No, because ...

Stewart could feel the dread loom in his mind. Beth had slept with Hamish. It was true. And then he'd come back and absolutely unloaded on her. Stewart could almost feel his heart shrivel and harden, like skin around a scar wound, as he remembered standing over her so triumphantly, barking and snarling at her.

Stewart managed to get up and struggle his way through to the bathroom. He'd fallen asleep in the clothes he'd been wearing. After the warm water of the shower, he came downstairs slowly, dragging his feet. Beth was in the living room, reading a book at the table. He went to say something, anything, about something, anything, but nothing came out. Instead he ate breakfast no more than a metre away from her, with Beth not so much as looking at him.

It was as he was selecting a suit that he realised that he didn't know if he had to go into work. It was Friday, the third and last day of his assignment with Dakar. But the police had arrested Graham Donaldson for the crime, and so far as Stewart knew, they didn't have anything to show the police were wrong. Plus there was the small matter of Dakar being furious with him.

But he couldn't just sit around. His mind would torture him. He had to do something, even if it was read drafts of a bloody contract or whatever.

Maybe he could get the Raker file – his file – back. Plead for it with Sudgeon, promise never to desert again, beg. And then he could work on it and things like it forever, and ignore any more emotions he ever had.

Stewart put his suit on. He heard Saz singing in the shower on his way out, and shook his head in wonder. So cheerful. He tramped down the stairs and headed outside.

It was a cold day, a bit gusty, but the storm from the night before had blown itself out, the grey clouds that had replaced their darker cousins far less threatening. Stewart got a taxi, feeling sufficiently low that even walking to work was a bridge too far.

Stewart got into the office, and took off his coat and scarf. Michelle and Jennifer were there, but no Hamish.

Thank the big man for small mercies.

"How's it going?" Michelle looked up. "Didn't expect to see you until Monday."

"Aye, yeah. Me neither. But the thing with Dakar might be finished, I'm just waiting to hear. So I thought I'd better come in."

"You all right? You sound a bit flat."

"Ha, yeah. Tough night last night."

Michelle laughed. "Long night after the office party?"

Stewart paused as he considered the events of the previous night. "That's one way of putting it, aye."

He sat at his desk, starting his computer and checking his emails. Nada, or at least nada of interest. He began looking at his to-do list. Nothing pressing. He looked up at Michelle and Jennifer. "Eh, if I can help with anything, then just give me a shout. I don't have anything major on right now, since, well …" Stewart gestured a bit helplessly in Michelle's direction. "I'm not claiming anything back, or anything, just offering to help," he added hastily.

A mischievous smile came over Michelle's face. "Well, actually, a couple of days ago one of my so-called colleagues just dumped some crappy file all over my desk without so much as a by-your-leave. Maybe you could help with that?"

Stewart smiled with relief. "Some people are the worst."

"I know! This guy's definitely one of them."

Stewart smiled again, tired muscles creaking the sides of his mouth upwards, but it was a smile nonetheless.

Michelle waved a stapled document at him. "Here. I've been drafting a memo on the materiality of counter-offers. But I worked late on it last night, and I might have gone a bit off the deep end." Stewart got up and collected it from her, then headed back to his desk.

After a few seconds of looking at it, he muttered, "To think I entrusted my beautiful file into such hands ..." He glanced up, to see Michelle staring at him with her eyebrows raised. He gave her a quick wink, and another smile.

Ten minutes later, Stewart was halfway through the draft – good quality, he had to admit – when he heard the door open and close. He looked up to see Hamish walk in, a surly look on his face, like a kid who's just been told they're not allowed any more sweets.

Stewart began to scowl. Memories of Hamish boasting last night, as well as his thoughts about the night itself, took over his mind. He felt the righteous energy bubble up inside of him, the white-hot anger coursing through him once again.

He put his head down and gritted his teeth. It felt like his anger was boiling over, like he was going to explode. He gripped the draft tightly with both hands, trying to get back the narrative of what had been happening, when he slowly became aware that someone was standing in front of his desk.

Stewart looked up. Hamish was standing there, immediately in front of his desk, leaning forward on his knuckles, his face red.

"What the hell do you think you're playing at, you little prick, telling Beth what I said last night?"

Stewart looked at him for a second or two, and almost felt himself relax.

Ah right.

He let the stillness that enveloped the room settle for a good few seconds, and studied Hamish. The guy had his suit jacket off, and sleeves rolled up, burly forearms on full display. Stewart looked at his face. Sullen, angry, with a pinch of fat showing underneath one chin.

Stewart spoke quietly and carefully.

"Come again?"

"I said, what the hell do you think you're playing at, you little prick, telling Beth about what I said last night?"

Stewart put Michelle's draft down, and tidied the papers, squaring off all the edges. Then he stood up, and walked around the side of the desk.

Hamish turned to meet him as Stewart walked right up to him, eyeball to eyeball.

"What did you call me?"

Hamish turned redder. "Eh, I said ... I said, what the hell do you ..."

Stewart grabbed his the collar with both hands. "I didn't ask what you said. I asked what you called me?"

Hamish recoiled from the grip, an astonished expression on his face, and grasped Stewart's wrists, trying to dislodge them. "What the ... Get your hands ..."

Stewart leaned into him, and marched Hamish, off-balance, backwards until he reached the wall, Hamish's head knocking into it.

"What did you call me?" Stewart spoke deliberately, tightening his grip on his lapels and yanking Hamish's face towards him.

Hamish, still with hands on Stewart's wrists, yelped as Stewart pulled him closer. He struggled for a second longer, the fear shining brightly in his eyes. Stewart let him struggle for a second or two.

"One more time, Hamish, you disgusting, sad, piece of humanity. One more time." Stewart slowed his speech down, enunciating carefully. "What did you call me?"

There was less than ten centimetres between their eyes.

"I ... I called you ... I ... I ..."

Stewart waited, patiently. He'd never been in this position before, but something in his Glasgow DNA told him how this game was played. Either the other one maintained the insult, in which case it would be time to break out the duelling pistols. Or in this case, for Stewart to hit Hamish as hard as he could in the stomach. Or ...

"Nothing. I didn't call you anything." Hamish spoke, his breathing coming in short, wild gasps.

Stewart relaxed his grip, a happy smile appearing on his face. He let him go, and then straightened Hamish's lapels where he'd mangled them.

"No. No, I didn't think so." As Hamish relaxed, Stewart leaned in, his forehead gently touching Hamish's forehead, his lips twisting downwards. "Now, you pathetic little arse-kissing brown-noser, if I ever hear you talk about Beth, or any woman, that way again, I'll end you. I will bloody end you. You understand me?"

Hamish's eyes opened wide again before he slowly began sliding away from him, along the wall, nodding. Stewart smiled again, the psycho smile, before he turned and walked back to his seat, his back to Hamish. He slid back into his seat, and picked up Michelle's draft again.

"How dare you, Scott, you …" Hamish began, from the other side of the room.

Stewart shot up out of his chair, and began to stride determinedly over towards Hamish, but he needn't have bothered. Before he'd managed two steps, Hamish had disappeared out through the door, slamming it shut behind him.

Stewart stood in the middle of the room and looked at the door for a second, taking a deep breath in and out. The metaphorical spilling of blood over, the enemy vanquished, Stewart took a second deep breath, blowing his cheeks out as he exhaled.

He looked around the room. Michelle and Jennifer were both staring at him, frozen.

Shite.

"Eh … sorry about that. Just, eh, yeah … You know, sometimes …" he gestured with his arms in the vague direction of the door. "Eh …" He lapsed into silence.

Michelle and Jennifer remained rooted to their seats.

"Eh … Eh, yeah. Aye." Stewart nodded a couple of times, tried a smile that ended up as a grimace, and turned back to his desk.

He collapsed into the seat. So much for not being a Glasgow psycho. When push came to shove, that was exactly what he'd turned out to be. And now Jennifer and Michelle thought they shared an office with a bloodthirsty lunatic.

Just brilliant, Scott. Just bloody perfect. You absolute muppet.

His head was already down, but it bowed further under the deluge of self-flagellating thoughts. He grabbed the top of his head with both hands.

He heard a cough. He looked up, undoing his hands and lifting his head, to see Jennifer and Michelle standing in front of him. Jennifer put a hot cup of tea down in front of him.

Both their gazes were fixed on him, their faces set in a scowl.

"Eh, thanks?" Stewart said, looking at the tea.

"What was he saying about women?" Michelle's tone was as set as her face, like concrete.

"Who? Hamish? Oh, eh, last night, the group of guys, Sudgeon, Green and, eh, well, you know, you were there. Hamish was boasting to that lot

The Price to Pay

about sleeping with women. You know the kind of crap. This position, shouting my name, up all night, exhausted, et cetera."

"And who's Beth?"

"My flatmate. Works over at the Scottish Government." He paused, the anger stopping him saying more, but only a second. "Eh, a really nice person. I've no idea how she ended up with a toe-rag like Hamish. But yeah, she's cool. You'd both like her, I'm sure."

They nodded, before they turned back to their desks.

Stewart picked up the tea and smelled it. Lovely. Some kind of fruity thing. He took a sip. Bit hot, but in a minute or two, it would be ideal.

He looked at Michelle and Jennifer, both of them bent back to work, and felt the small shoot of guilt grow in his mind.

He knew.

He knew he was angry that Beth, specifically, had slept with Hamish, specifically. If Hamish had been boasting about some unknown girl, Stewart would probably have just listened, maybe thrown in a cheeky wee yawn, and then diplomatically left the group as soon as possible. And if Beth slept with some random guy, well, yes, it got to him, but nowhere near like last night.

Stewart's work phone began to ring.

He looked down at the name, then up at Michelle and Jennifer. Stewart smiled, but it was shot through with unpleasantness. "Sudgeon."

"Didn't take Hamish long," Jennifer said grimly.

Stewart nodded slowly at her, then turned to look at the phone, the name there, just like two days ago when he'd been summoned to begin work with Dakar. Except there was no promise now. Just fear.

He had to answer. And he'd have to keep playing the hard man. No story ever ended with the hero apologising to the bad guy and begging to keep his job after beating up his henchman.

Stewart took a deep breath and picked up the phone, but before he could say anything, Sudgeon's flat voice came down the line. "My office. Now."

The line went dead.

Stewart held the phone for a second longer, then put it back down again. His hand was trembling.

He stood up, putting his hands on the desk in front of him to help support his weight, the fingers quivering as he leaned down on them. "I've been summoned." He tried to think of a joke, but nothing came. He tried to flick a smile, a shaft of light to break the gloom, but nothing happened, his muscles unresponsive.

"Good luck," said Jennifer, her tone intense. Michelle tried to give him a smile, but it ended up more as a frown, her mind unable to disassociate from the reason for the summons.

Stewart walked to the mirror and checked his tie. His hands fell uselessly to his side after a moment. You might care about how you looked when you faced the firing squad, but the firing squad didn't give a toss what you looked like.

Chapter 44

Stewart trudged to Sudgeon's office, head down. The rich colours of the carpet and walls seemed dull to him now, the thickness of the carpet sucking more and more of his energy away. He felt a vibration in his pocket, and pulled out his phone. A text from Dakar: '*Good morning, my brother. Can you meet me downstairs in your office at twenty past nine?*'

Stewart stopped, and re-read the message. Then re-read it again. Then a third time through. He put his phone away, and continued to Sudgeon's office, his trudge becoming a walk, his head back up. Then he stopped after a few paces and pulled his phone out again. He read the message for a fourth time.

He opened a search engine, and searched for Daniel Mannings. There was a story there on some random news website he'd never heard of, posted that morning by a 'staffer', that the police were making progress in the hunt for the killer, and planned to arrest someone soon. It promised more details as soon as they became available.

He put the phone away again, and walked slowly on to Sudgeon's office, stopping outside the door. He pulled his phone out again to read the message. Fifth time. He checked his watch. It was a ten past nine.

He took a deep breath, and read the message from Dakar one last time. He breathed out slowly. Then eventually he began typing: '*Been summoned by Sudgeon. Just going in now. Will let you know when I am free.*'

He put his phone on silent and put it back in his pocket. Then he took one final deep breath, exhaled, and turned to Sudgeon's door.

He knocked and after a short, sharp 'Come!', walked inside. Sudgeon sat at his table, Green to his right. Hamish sat across from them, a gloating smile on his face as he looked over his shoulder at Stewart. Stewart looked back at Hamish stonily.

Bloody wee toerag.

"Sit down, Stewart." Sudgeon.

Stewart came and sat down, next to Hamish but as far away from him as possible.

Sudgeon leaned forward. His normal faux-cheery expression had been replaced by a stony one of his own. Stewart found himself wondering if the latter was as fake as the former.

"Stewart, Hamish informed us of your conduct this morning. I want to say to you that threatening or belittling one of your colleagues is absolutely unacceptable." Sudgeon flicked a few pieces of lint off the shoulder of his suit.

"Unacceptable," Green repeated. He was leaning back in his chair, hands clasped in front of him but down in his lap. He didn't bother looking at Stewart when he spoke.

"We are, in particular, concerned about the physical manhandling. That is entirely intolerable and cannot be repeated." Sudgeon spoke in a dull monotone, still inspecting the shoulder of his suit.

"Cannot be repeated," Green said, in the same diffident tone, looking up at the ceiling.

"Do you understand me?" Sudgeon again, his eyes back on Stewart now. But there was no intensity there, no effort at intimidation.

Stewart eyebrows knotted together as his eyes went between Sudgeon and Green. He nodded once, carefully, waiting for the trap to be sprung.

"Good. Hamish, that is all. You may go. Stewart, we want to speak to you further."

Stewart stayed seated while Hamish slowly stood, his gloating vanished, leaving wide eyes and an open mouth. He stood stock still for a second, then turned away from the desk.

"Hamish?" Sudgeon called.

Hamish turned around just a bit too quickly, breathing a little ragged, betraying his hope that something may yet happen. Stewart felt the adrenaline spike through him, his muscles tensing as he waited for what Sudgeon was going to say.

"Make sure you close the door firmly, there's a good chap." Sudgeon smiled at him then, a Judas smile.

Once the door was closed, extremely firmly, Sudgeon leaned in. There was a gleam in his eye. "Stewart, to express your feelings in the way you did is absolutely unacceptable. What is absolutely acceptable, and indeed encouraged, is the fire in the belly!"

Green leaned in as well now, head low, his eyes brightening. "It's what we've been missing from you. A bit of fight. A bit of stepping up to the plate and swinging hard, even if you miss."

The Price to Pay

Stewart nodded, slowly, trying to keep his face blank as his mind raced to catch up with just what the hell was happening. Stepping towards a plate and swinging. Didn't the Greeks use to smash plates after dinner?

"Hamish will do well here. You, on the other hand, always seemed a bit uncertain to us, like you never believed in yourself. But now, we see the fire! And we like it." Sudgeon's words were still somehow booming, even in a low voice.

Stewart nodded once again. He just about managed to keep his stony expression on.

"So, no more grabbing people, throwing them against the wall, or calling them ..." Sudgeon looked down at a piece of paper in front of him, "... a 'pathetic little arse-kissing brown-noser'. At least not when they can hear you. Understood?" He gave Stewart a wink.

Stewart nodded again. It seemed like the only thing to do. Sudgeon sat back in his chair, apparently satisfied.

"How's the investigation with Dakar going? I won't lie to you, Stewart. He asked for you after he turned down Hamish. But that kind of work won't advance your reputation with the firm one iota. If you want to get a job here next year, it may be wise to ensure that the work with Dakar is completed as soon as possible. Get back to the real nuts and bolts. Start billing again. I'll give you the Raker file back, and we'll get you into some even better files after that."

Stewart hesitated. Dakar's words and face loomed up in his mind, next to the text message that morning, all mixed together to make no sense whatsoever.

"It's fine, Mr Sudgeon. We'll finish today."

"Very well. But then you come back and start directing all that energy where it should be directed. Working for us."

Stewart nodded again, vigorously, and tried to replicate the look on Sudgeon's face. He had no idea if he succeeded, but Sudgeon and Green – and Green! – both smiled at him.

So miracles did happen.

"Capital! Let me know when you're finished with Dakar. I have a meeting on a new case for the firm at twelve, and I need someone to take minutes. If you can be here for that, you'll be the man for the job. And that would simply be the start of it. Thereafter we'll get you something meatier to get your teeth into. See what you're made of."

"Yes, Mr Sudgeon. You'll be the first to know." He stood and walked out of the room, feeling the stares of Green and Sudgeon on his back until he closed the door. His hands were trembling. He clenched them into fists, but they wouldn't stop shaking. Glaring at them, he headed back to the office.

Christ, who knew assaulting someone could be a career boost? Maybe he should murder someone? They'd give him a job for life ... Murder!

He hurriedly pulled out his phone. A text, from Dakar: *'No problem, my brother. I am downstairs, whenever you are ready.'*

Stewart stopped, again standing in the corridor, just looking at his phone, wavering in front of his face. He used his other hand to grab his wrist, trying to steady it. It was nine twenty-five. The morning had barely started, and he'd already faced down Hamish and confronted Green and Sudgeon. Next up was Dakar.

He put his other hand up to his temple and wiped down over his eyes, looking down, away, around, anywhere. Eventually he looked back at the phone: *'Am free now. Will grab stuff, and head down. Be there shortly.'*

He put his phone away again and walked back to his office, unheeding of those he passed. Michelle and Jennifer were still there, with Hamish now at his desk. Stewart felt the tension in the room as he came in.

He slowed his pace as he walked deliberately across to his desk. He nodded once at Jennifer and Michelle, reassurance that everything was okay. Once he reached his desk, he turned and looked at Hamish. He stared at him for a second, Hamish looking defiantly back. Then Stewart reached up one hand with two fingers raised, one finger pointing at either eye, then he turned and pointed the two fingers directly at Hamish.

I'm watching you, pal.

"Not nice when your haunders don't back you up, is it? When the big boys don't do your dirty work for you?"

Hamish's face became red, and his expression seemed to freeze on his face.

Stewart picked up his suit jacket, and walked back across the room, ignoring Hamish. He grabbed his long coat, scarf and his satchel before he turned to Michelle and Jennifer. With a flourish, he let the satchel fall into the correct position, down by one side.

"I'm heading out to work with Dakar again. Maybe see you later. Have a good one."

The Price to Pay

Michelle nodded at him, and Jennifer even gave him a little wave which he returned. Stewart didn't bother looking at Hamish as he walked out of the office, and took the lift to the ground floor.

Stewart took another deep breath as he walked around to the front lobby, still trying to stop the trembling in his hands. There was Dakar, resplendent in his grey checked trousers, brown loafers, white coat and bunnet.

Stewart could instantly perceive the difference though, in spite of the man wearing identical clothing to the night before. He had his calmness back though, somehow, a little island of simplicity in the middle of a sea of people coming in and out of the office, talking on phones, rushing around.

Dakar looked at him, pulled the hand-on-heart thing, with the little inclination of the head. Stewart stopped when they were a metre apart.

"My brother, I am full of sorrow at how I acted last night. I can only hope that you can forgive me."

Stewart hesitated, then shrugged. "Aye. Aye, of course." He muttered the words, but gave a nod.

Pause. "I gave into my fear, my brother. I gave into my fear, and became angry, and unleashed that upon you. I am sorry. We often treat those close to us in the worst way, my brother, but that was not what I intended."

Stewart looked back at him. "Don't worry about it."

Pause. "Do you remember, yesterday, just after we saw Sarah-Anne arguing with Jane in Glasgow?"

Stewart nodded, a frown on his face.

"I received a message from Frank just before we got into the car. It said that since we'd had a chat with the daughter of Daniel Mannings and her friends, and then bumped into his wife, he was guessing we were working on the investigation into Daniel Mannings' murder."

Stewart's eyebrows furrowed together. "Yesterday, just after we'd spoken to them? That's not possible. I mean, how did he know where we were?"

Pause. "The only thing I can think of is that he followed us. Or someone did, at his request."

Stewart rocked on his heels slightly, feeling like someone had just punched him in the face.

"And that's why you went mental with the driving."

Dakar nodded. "I was trying to lose whoever it was that was following us on the way back to Edinburgh."

"But Frank managed to find us in the pub?"

Pause. "I did not bring him." Dakar shrugged. "At least not consciously."

"Why didn't you just tell me this yesterday?"

Pause. "Yesterday was not a good day for me, my brother. But last night I stopped listening to my ego and instead went back to the self, and then I understood."

There was silence for a few seconds as Stewart digested that.

"I have also dealt with Frank's threat. I am no longer afraid."

Stewart hesitated. "How have you dealt with it, exactly? Have you spoken to Frank?"

Pause. He put one hand to the side of his head, touching the temple with two of his fingers. "I have dealt with it up here."

"Okay. Right. Well, glad to hear that. But, so, what now? The police have got Graham Donaldson. And I know you don't think he did it, but if it wasn't him, well, I still don't see how anyone else did it."

Dakar paused, nodded. "They'll hold Graham the twelve hours, and then charge him. We must act before he gets charged. Otherwise Malcolm will be in trouble."

"Malcolm?"

Pause. "DI Thomas. Malky."

Stewart nodded. Three names for the same person, but they all conjured up radically different images.

"Why would he be in trouble?"

Pause. "When you are in charge of a murder investigation with this much media attention, charging someone with all the fanfare of a press conference only for it all to fall apart can be fatal for your prospects. Particularly if you don't have any other suspects, but the murderer can only be one of a small number of people."

"Really? Okay. Hang on though. This is a guy who was threatening to put you in Bar-L – both of us, actually – if you kept on investigating. Why do you care if he messes up?"

Dakar exhaled a deep breath, softly. "He is my brother. And I owe him a great deal."

"So how long have we got?"

Pause. "Graham was arrested just after 11pm last night. I was informed about it immediately after it happened."

"DI Thomas told you that?"

The Price to Pay

Pause. Dakar gently shook his head. "They have scheduled a press conference for eleven to discuss what they are calling a major new development in the case. That gives us ... one hour and thirty minutes."

"And what will we do if we bump into the police and they ... talk to us?"

Pause. "We will talk back to them."

Stewart snorted. But Dakar just looked back at him with the simple look, like he wasn't joking.

Well, if Dakar was sure, then Stewart could be sure as well. Or at least he could plead ignorance. The judge would probably show him mercy, for being a total muppet. Probably.

"Okay. Where are we off to?"

Pause. "We have to speak with Charles."

"Charles? Right, okay. Yeah. I saw him last night, actually. He's still worried about what's happening."

As they walked back into the office in silence, the thought which had been trying to get Stewart's attention hit him between the eyes.

"I still don't see how convincing DI Thomas to give up on Donaldson is going to help him. I mean, he'll be left without a suspect then, won't he?"

Dakar paused, the two of them at the lift, and pushed the button. "I believe I already know who murdered Daniel Mannings."

Chapter 45

They stood in the lift. Stewart looked at Dakar in shocked silence. The guy just looked ahead, at the inside of the lift doors, neutral expression.

"You know who the murderer is?"

Pause. "I believe so."

"So you know how Daniel's body got downstairs?"

Pause. Dakar turned to Stewart. "That part was straightforward. It was much more difficult to work out who slit Daniel's wrist."

Dakar broke off as the lift doors opened, and two lawyers stood facing them, chatting away. Stewart knew them a little bit, but not much. One senior associate, one junior. They looked a little oddly at Dakar. The junior associate nodded slightly, to be fair, as the groups passed each other.

Dakar strode along the corridor, his usual stroll replaced under the pressures of time. Stewart waited for him to continue from where he'd stopped, but the man didn't say anything as they came to Charles's office. The door was slightly open. Dakar knocked on it.

"Come!" Charles's voice.

Dakar and Stewart stepped inside. Charles glanced at them, his eyes widening as he saw who it was. Gerald, his officemate, looked at them with a mixture of confusion and irritation.

"Who are you?" Gerald asked.

"Gerald, take a walk." Charles snapped it at him, but his eyes didn't leave Dakar and Stewart.

"What? Charles, this is my bloody office as—"

"Now, Gerald!" Charles turned on him with a snarl.

Gerald slowly got up, his eyes like slits as they slid from Dakar and Stewart to Charles. He grabbed his coat and scarf. "I'm going to grab a coffee. I'd ask you if you want something to eat, but it looks like you've got plenty of things on your plate at the moment." He spoke tartly, and slammed the door behind him.

Charles spoke as soon as the door was closed.

"I would appreciate a little warning next time you plan to visit." He glared at Stewart as he spoke. Stewart just looked back at him blandly, his emotional responses all worn out.

"I feel sorrow for your reaction, my brother." Dakar said it gently enough, but if he was feeling sorrowful, it didn't sound like there was a lot there.

Charles's lip curled up as he looked at the man. "What do you want, anyway?"

Pause. "To ask you some more questions about that evening."

"I already told you everything."

Pause. "I have some further questions for you."

"Look, I really don't have time." Charles indicated the paperwork in front of him.

"Neither do we, so I will come to the point. You brought the cocaine that you and Daniel later snorted that evening, didn't you? You were always the one who brought it?" Dakar's tone and expression never wavered.

Charles's expression froze for a second, his eyes bulging, and then a sickly, goblin smile spread across his face. He stood up, the smile expression fixed on his face like a Halloween mask.

"Ah, I see. Yes. Well, that changes matters. Please, sit down, sit down. Take a seat, yes." Charles walked rather quickly over to the door, opening it and glancing out into the corridor. Then he came back inside, closing the door firmly once again.

"Do any of the partners know?" He spoke urgently, all business.

Pause. "I have not told anyone. If they have learned from any other source, I do not know."

"Who else would have told them?" Charles rounded on Stewart. "Scott! I swear to God, if you've said anything, I mean anything—"

"I haven't told anyone." Stewart was surprised by how short his tone was in the face of Charles' outrage.

"The police may have informed them, my brother."

Charles looked at Dakar for a second, then he cast his eyes to the side, calculating. "The police. That's how you know about the cocaine?"

Dakar inclined his head.

"I see. I can't imagine the police will care all that much. They're looking for a murderer, after all. I'll give the officer a call though."

Pause. "You brought the cocaine, didn't you?"

Charles shrugged. "What makes you say that?"

Pause. Stewart surreptitiously took out his notepad and pen and began writing.

"My brother, I do not have a lot of time. In just over an hour, an innocent man will be charged with the murder of Daniel Mannings, and a friend of mine will make a career-ending mistake. You brought it, did you not?" Dakar's tone remained reasonable.

"What makes you think I brought it?"

Pause. A small sigh. "My brother, I am sorry to cause you such fear, but I have no time." He turned to Stewart. "Do you have Mr Sudgeon's office number? And I will inform Mr Mannings later about how Charles was supplying his son with cocaine."

Charles almost leapt out of his seat, his knuckles white as he gripped the arms of the chair. "Jesus Christ! Yes, yes, I brought it, every time. My god."

Dakar turned back to him. "He was blackmailing you, my brother? Threatening to tell his father that you snorted cocaine, unless you kept on supplying him with more."

Charles' eyes went back and forth between Stewart and Dakar, but eventually stopped on Dakar. "I should never have let him have some of my snow that first night." Charles' misery burst out of him after having been bottled up for so long.

Pause. "What time in the evening did you take it?"

"During dinner. Daniel gave me the sign, and we both went to the upstairs bathroom. A quick line later and we were both bouncing off the walls. Made the party miles better."

Dakar sat back at that, quiet for a second, nodding his head. He looked at Charles again. "Daniel spoke to you about Jane and Sandra that night, didn't he?"

"Yes. He was telling me how good they looked, and that if he wasn't Sandra's stepfather, he might … try it on."

"You disapproved?"

Charles drew back, his eyes wide. "Of course! The girl Jane I understand. She even seemed to be receptive to the idea, to be honest. But there is a line, for God's sake. Your own stepdaughter!"

"Did you say anything to Daniel, voice your disapproval?"

"Well, no. No. I mean, how could I? His house, and all that. No. I was very polite."

Long pause. Charles shifted uncomfortably in his seat.

Dakar smiled. "Thank you, my brother. I wish you well."

The sickly smile came back. "Same to you, I'm sure. Will I, ah, be hearing from you again?"

Pause. "Not from me personally, I don't believe." Dakar paused again. "From others, I could not say."

They walked out of his office, down to the lobby and went outside. The storm had not only blown itself out, but in its fury had ripped the sky free of clouds. It remained chilly, but in the sun, where they stood, it was almost warm.

"Dakar?"

Pause. "My brother?"

"Had you finished what you were going to say about Daniel's wrist?"

Pause. They approached the car. "Asking the wrong question is often the issue with mysteries. Like moths and candles. Everyone asked why moths wanted to fly into a fire and seemingly commit suicide. The wrong question. The right question was how moths navigated. Once it was realised that the moths mistook the flame for the moon, we realised the moths thought they were flying in a straight line by keeping their sun on one side. In fact they flew in a tighter and tighter circle, until they fell into the flame."

Stewart waited for more to come, but Dakar seemed to have finished speaking.

"And that relates to Mannings' murder how?"

"The key question, I find, concerns the slitting of Daniel's wrist. Once you know who slit his wrist, the rest falls into place."

They arrived at a car. It looked like Dakar's old one, still shaped like a trainer, but it was black rather than grey.

"New motor?"

Dakar smiled, nodded. "Yes."

"Something wrong with the old one, was there?"

Pause. "It had become tainted."

Stewart hesitated himself as Dakar slid into the car. Tainted. Ominous word. Dakar started the car, and pulled away from the kerb.

Stewart frowned as he thought about Daniel's slit wrist. It was important, no doubt, an aggravating piece of the puzzle. But the major one? The thread that unravelled everything? He stared out the windows as they headed up towards Princes Street, the Lothian Road end. The buildings flashed past, reflections of sunlight lighting up the Edinburgh streets.

He'd promised himself he'd do more than trail around behind Dakar this time. Now was the time. Who slit Daniel's wrist? Donaldson, of course. Although there didn't seem to be any reason. And Dakar was convinced it wasn't Donaldson. So forget him, for now. But no-one else could have done it. They were either outside or comatose. And if that was the case ...

"Dakar! Dakar, I know who slit Daniel's wrist! The only person who could have done it!"

Pause, a smile on Dakar's face. "Very good, my brother."

Stewart sat back, satisfied with himself. Nothing else was falling into place, true, but at least he had the first part. And he had the rest of the journey to think about it.

"So where are we off to now?" He checked his watch. Nine forty-five.

"The last post. And then we will see if we can't stop DI Thomas from bringing his career to an unfortunate end."

Chapter 46

They drove along in silence, heading back out towards the bypass, in the same direction they had driven over the last couple of days. Stewart looked out the window, running through all the things they'd learned. Nothing occurred to him.

Eventually, looking around, his eyes fell on Dakar's backpack sitting innocuously on the back seat, the only object in the otherwise tidy car.

"What's in the bag?"

Pause. "I had to do some shopping this morning, before I came to your firm."

Stewart nodded, waiting for more, but nothing came.

He wouldn't take the bait this time though. Instead, another question came to his mind. "Eh, Dakar, Sudgeon told me that Hamish offered to help you on this one, but you turned him down and asked for me. Is that right?"

Pause, long pause. "Yes, my brother."

"Why?"

"I'm not certain. Perhaps ..." Dakar looked over at him for a second. "Perhaps I see myself in you, when I was younger. And I'm interested, then, in how we work together."

Stewart looked back at him, at this odd Zen guy with his crazy dress sense, and nodded once. There didn't seem to be anything else to do.

Stewart began to recognise the route they were taking, down past Morningside and out towards the bypass again. The sunshine made this part of Edinburgh doubly attractive, the green spaces enjoying a last dose of sunshine before the long winter months. In no time at all they pulled up outside Sarah-Anne Mannings' house in Colinton.

The car stopped, and Dakar pulled out his phone. He began sending a text. Stewart couldn't help but see the words and the recipient. It was being sent to one Frank McPherson.

'*My brother, you will find what you are searching for...*'

Stewart stared in shock, but suddenly felt his own phone began to ring. He looked away guiltily, and fumbled it out of his pocket. He didn't recognise the number itself, but he recognised the type of number. His office.

"Stewart Scott."

"Stewart, my boy, it's Brian here."

"Hello, Mr Sudgeon." Sudgeon's booming tone, jovial on the surface, had an undercurrent of irritation, a nasty riptide.

"We've just had word from Tom. Apparently the police have arrested someone."

"Oh. Yes. Yes, that's right, Mr Sudgeon."

"Stewart, my boy, you don't sound very surprised to hear that."

"Eh, well, no, Mr Sudgeon. Dakar told me last night."

"Last night? Before the party?"

"Oh no, eh, no, Mr Sudgeon. After the party. And, eh—"

"But regardless, you knew this morning that someone had been arrested?"

"Eh, well, yes, Mr Sudgeon."

"And you didn't feel the need to mention it when we saw you?"

"Well, sir, we aren't sure that they've got the right person."

"Stewart! Come now, my boy! Even in this day and age, I presume they still have to have some form of evidence before they arrest someone?"

"Well, yes, sir, that's true, I suppose, yes. But it's maybe not quite as simple—"

"Stewart!" Sudgeon roared his name. "It seems perfectly simply. Someone was murdered. The police have made an arrest. Due process will follow."

"Yes, sir, Mr Sudgeon. I suppose you're right."

"Yes, I am. So we can expect you back at the office imminently?"

"Eh, well. Well ..." Stewart paused. Dakar had finished with his phone, and now sat and looked at him in silence.

Sudgeon, and Green, and Hamish, and Charles, and then Dakar the night before, and leaving him, and Dakar now, this morning. And Sudgeon's eyes again, always calculating. And ties. And suits.

"Stewart?"

"Yes, Mr Sudgeon, hello. I lost connection there for a moment. I understand what you're saying, sir. We just have a few loose ends to clean up, and then I will immediately return to the office. It should be before twelve. I hope that conforms to your expectations."

"Loose ends? Twelve? That's …" There was a pause … "almost two hours away! And the police have arrested someone! What possible—"

"Yes, sir. We've arrived at our destination. I will have my report ready for you, a final report, as soon as possible."

"Stewart, I—"

"Goodbye Mr Sudgeon, and thank you."

Stewart hung up the phone. He was sweating, the beads poking out his forehead.

He'd just hung up on Sudgeon. He'd just hung up on a partner in his firm. A partner. Sudgeon.

He was dead.

Sudgeon would kill him.

His phone jerked again in his hand, vibrating. The same office number again.

"Ready, my brother?"

Stewart's eyes were torn up and away from his phone, to look into Dakar's eyes. They were simple, yes, unmoving, but in that depth there was strength. A lot of strength.

Stewart looked down at this phone again. He took a deep breath, wiped his head free of sweat, then pressed the cancel button on the phone firmly. Then he put it on silent, just for good measure, and put it away.

"Ready."

Chapter 47

They stood in silence outside the door for about thirty seconds, waiting for a response to Dakar's knock. Stewart's legs began jogging as his mind screamed, running on pure adrenaline, replaying the moment over and over, each word Stewart had said, imagining Sudgeon's cold fury at a trainee brushing him off, the revenge he would take.

The door opened, interrupting his thoughts. Sarah-Anne Mannings stood in front of them, her normal clothes overlaid by an apron with the words 'Best Mum in the World' scrawled on it.

Her eyebrows rose as she looked at them. "Mr Dakar, Mr Scott. How can I help you?"

"My sister, Graham Donaldson has been arrested for the murder of your husband, Daniel."

"Graham's been arrested? Impossible. He couldn't have killed him."

"The police are convinced he did it. May we come in, my sister?"

She hesitated. "I've got guests right now …"

Pause. Dakar checked his watch. Stewart looked at his as well. Ten ten. Fifty minutes to go before the press conference.

"Yes, your brunch with Sandra. My sister, we have no time. I now know what happened that night. I must speak with you."

She paused for a second, eyes narrow, but then stepped back to allow them in. Dakar walked towards the kitchen, Stewart alongside him. As they emerged into the open area, Stewart saw that Russell, Sandra and Jane were seated around the living room table.

They had seemed quite relaxed when Stewart and Dakar first came around the corner, but the atmosphere almost immediately became a wary one.

"I am glad you are all here," Dakar said as Sarah-Anne came back into the room. "And I am glad that you seem to have forgiven Jane, my sister."

"I took your words on forgiveness to heart, Mr Dakar. I ended up inviting them all to brunch."

Dakar turned to the other three. "The police have arrested Craig's father Graham for killing Daniel."

Wary expressions became confused. "How did he do it?" Russell.

"I don't believe they know how it was done."

"Then why did they arrest Graham?" Sandra now.

"Because in spite of the fact that it was a seemingly impossible crime, it was done, and therefore someone did it."

There was a pause as everyone digested this, broken by Sarah-Anne. "All well and good, Mr Dakar. But what can we do about it?" She pottered over to the kitchen. It looked like she was in the middle of making some snacks.

"I've come to get a confession."

Chapter 48

Everyone in the room froze, looking at Dakar, including Stewart. After a second or two, in the deadly silence of the room, Sarah-Anne slowly rotated until she had Dakar in her sights.

"Excuse me?"

Pause. "I said that I've come to get a confession."

"And you think someone here is going to give you one?"

Pause. "Indeed."

"Mum, what's going on? What the hell is he talking about?" Sandra stood up.

"I don't know, darling." She crossed her arms, facing off against Dakar like a couple of chess champions across a board, awaiting his opening move.

Pause. "A man has been arrested, my sister, and will most probably face trial for the murder."

Sarah-Anne stiffened. "It couldn't possibly have been Graham. There was no way for him to murder Daniel – at any time – and get away unseen. And even if he could, how did he get the door bolted after he left?"

Pause. "They will say he had an accomplice."

Her forehead wrinkled, then smoothed again. "Craig, you mean?"

Pause, nod. "And they found Graham's fingerprints in Daniel's study."

Sarah-Anne's mouth fell open.

Pause. "The police can put him in the house. That night. And so you see, the case against him grows stronger. Strong enough, perhaps, to convict." Dakar pressed his advantage.

Sarah-Anne hesitated for a moment, then leaned forward on her toes, growing in height. "And the slit wrist, and the blood in the en suite? And Daniel being killed in the bedroom and the body ending up in the cellar?"

Pause, Dakar beaten back in his attack. "I do not know, my sister."

Sarah-Anne came back down onto her heels again, the redness in her face receding. "Well, there you are then."

Pause, a shrug. "Yet the police have to charge someone. Even if it fails in court, they can always pass that off as the vagary of a jury, justice undone by some of the more bloody-minded lay persons drafted in. But someone will face trial. And there is always the possibility, then, of a conviction."

Stewart looked around at the other three in the moment of silence that followed. Sandra's eyes were wide open, her lips pulled back somewhere between horror and fear. Russell had one arm around Sandra, his eyes shooting between Dakar and Stewart, pulling Sandra close at the same time. Jane's face was dark, her shoulders hunched. She was looking at the mug in front of her as if it might be some kind of weapon.

"And," Dakar continued, "if they decide it was not Graham Donaldson after all, they will look around for another suspect. Starting with Dennis, I would imagine."

Sarah-Anne relaxed, the lines in her face disappearing. "Dennis couldn't kill a mouse, much less Daniel." She waved her hand as if batting the accusation away.

Pause. "I tend to agree, my sister. Theft seems more his level of criminality. Theft of prescription sheets, for example."

There was a collective intake of breath from the three at the table.

"I knew it was that dickhead!" Russell declared. "I said it at the time."

Pause, a nod. "And blackmail provides a powerful motive. Daniel had a prescription sheet filled out by Dennis. I presume he caught him red-handed. And Dennis was downstairs, on his own, at a crucial point. You yourself told us that, my sister. I believe Dennis went to ransack the study for the sheet, but only got as far as the door before he lost his nerve and ran back upstairs. But if Daniel had somehow slipped past everyone, perhaps in the commotion of people running from room to room, he and Dennis may have met."

"And what? Dennis murders Daniel, throws him into the cellar and then waltzes back upstairs to chat to the rest of us? With blood all over him? No. Impossible." Sarah-Anne was more relaxed now as she saw Dakar's moves, a slight smile even finding its way onto her face.

Pause, nod, Dakar again beaten back in his efforts. "Then were I the police, I would start entertaining more exotic theories. For example, what if it were not Daniel at the window at all? What if someone were playing as him? Russell, for example."

Stewart saw Russell's face become a perfect 'o' of astonishment, his eyes widening as the impact of Dakar's words hit. Sandra looked around at him, then shrugged his arm away violently. Russell turned to look into her tightening eyes.

"He had nothing to do with this!" Sarah-Anne leapt to Russell's defence, the smile gone as Dakar made his move.

Pause. "He was in the house when Daniel appeared at the window. What could be easier than to dispose of Daniel earlier in the evening, perhaps when he first went inside, and then to take his place at the window and pretend to be Daniel? By the time everyone rushes upstairs, he is safely back in bed, snoring away."

"I look nothing like Daniel!" Russell cut in now, his voice unnaturally high in the face of the accusation.

Pause. "The turquoise jacket can mislead people. That is how most people identified Daniel, as he was facing the other way when they saw him. With the help of an accomplice, you could then slip the jacket in a bag, along with a wig. The accomplice could then spirit it downstairs and redress Daniel's body in the cellar."

"And the blood on the clothes? It's a messy business, stabbing someone." Sarah-Anne cut back in.

Dakar paused for a few seconds here, eyeing Sarah-Anne, then shrugged lightly. "A jumper worn and then also put into a bag, also spirited away by the accomplice. Dumped at their leisure, once the fuss over Daniel's disappearance had broken down."

Sarah-Anne glared at him, the silence elongating. But suddenly the tension flowed out of her, and she smiled, the smile of triumph. Her eyes sparkled.

"But you forget, Mr Dakar. Russell was drugged so heavily that he couldn't be woken. Everyone will testify that he wasn't faking sleep. Martina did the nail bed test, and the supra-orbital test. And ..." she held up her hand in excitement as Dakar moved to reply, "... there couldn't have been time for the drugs to kick in before the rest of us arrived, a couple of minutes later."

Her head tilted down as she challenged Dakar, her smile the one of a chess player in a commanding position. Stewart looked over at Dakar, feeling helpless. Every suspect thrown up so far thrown back, every method of committing the crime batted away.

But Dakar didn't seem concerned. In fact, in his face there was some kind of final acceptance. And, it came to Stewart, Dakar's look of regret might be because the game was over, rather than because he had lost.

"True, my sister. But tell me. How do you know Russell was drugged?"

Checkmate.

Chapter 49

"I ... I ..." Sarah-Anne began to flounder, her eyes shooting away from Dakar's gaze. Sandra stood up, her eyes wild, looking between her mother and Russell.

"Someone tell me what is going on. Right now." Her voice trembled as she spoke. Russell looked helplessly up at her, while Sarah-Anne gripped the table edge in front.

Dakar spoke, into the silence. "I will explain the how, my sister. We can then discuss the why."

Sandra turned on him, her savage expression slamming squarely up against Dakar's calm. In the face of her ragged breathing, Dakar began to speak.

"First, let me say Russell had nothing to do with it. It was your father Daniel who was banging on the window. But he was not being attacked. This was rather all part of a plan, to create his own disturbance at his surprise birthday party. First, he threw things on the ground. Slitting his wrist, he dropped some blood in the bedroom and let more spill out in the en suite. Then he bandaged his wrist up, ready to start his performance."

Stewart nodded as Dakar spoke. That Daniel was the only person who could have slit his wrist was logically inevitable when you knew everyone else was either outside or comatose.

Sandra had sunk back down into her chair as Dakar spoke, his measured tone the only sound in the hush of the room. Russell cautiously put his arm around her again.

"His preparations complete, he began his banging at the window. As everyone rushed upstairs, he climbed out of the window himself, closing it as far as he could, and then went to the cellar. He stood, I believe, at the top of the stairs, waiting for something."

Dakar took a deep breath. "It took me a long time to work out what happened here. That evening, far from being chaotic, as it appeared from the outside, was exquisitely planned. The timing was crucial, but it was carried out beautifully."

In the silence that followed, Dakar looked around at everyone present, until his eyes rested on Sarah-Anne.

"There was one thing you told us, my sister, that my mind kept returning to last night. I could not shake it. You told us that you saw Dennis go up the stairs. Go. Not come. It is a small thing, and yet ... If I am in my home, and someone is visiting, they come to my house. They do not go to my house, if I am there. And so, I began to think: what if you were not up the stairs, as you claimed, but down the stairs?"

"Really, Mr Dakar, I hardly think ..." But Sarah-Anne trailed off herself, her bluster forcing her to start but leaving her nowhere to go.

"Contrary to what you told us, my sister, you did not follow the others up. In truth, you hid downstairs and watched Daniel go into the cellar. You opened the door, and when Daniel turned around, you stabbed him through the chest four times."

Sarah-Anne took a deep breath. "I was upstairs with everyone else."

Pause. "Yes, my sister, you did go upstairs eventually. But, as I said, the timing here is critical. If I may, I will divide what took place into three events; everyone going into the master bedroom the first time, most people running through to the guest bedroom to see if Charles and Russell were still alive, and finally, everyone coming back to the master bedroom. You did appear, but only after everyone had convened in the master bedroom on a second occasion. Ample time for you to take a kitchen knife, hide, open the cellar door, stab Daniel and push him down the stairs."

Sarah-Anne was glaring at him, her hands now spread across the table point, the skin white to breaking point. She put two hands up in a questioning manner, her lips pursing. "And Daniel's blood? I stabbed him and then just ran around with blood all over me and hoped no-one would notice?" She spoke curtly.

"No, my sister. You walked. When you stabbed Daniel, you wore your apron, which took the brunt of the blood spatters. You were also wearing a dark red dress with long gloves. After murdering Daniel in the cellar, you took off your apron and gloves, folded the gloves inside the apron and, quite possibly with spots of Daniel's blood on your dress, walked upstairs to see everyone."

Stewart's jaw hit the floor, stunning him out even of his scribbling for a second.

Sarah-Anne's eyes narrowed, and she crossed her arms. "The police have the apron I wore, Mr Dakar, and they examined the dress and gloves. It was practically the first thing they did when they got there. If they had found something like you say, don't you think I would be in jail just now?"

Pause. "The police examined the apron you presented to them, not the one that you had been wearing. This is clear. The apron I saw in the police photos was spotless. Not just a lack a blood, a lack of anything. A lack of use. It was new." Sarah-Anne said nothing, but her mouth tightened, her lips disappearing. "And the police examined the dress you were wearing at the end of the night, not the beginning."

"This is all nonsense, Mr Dakar." There was a stillness about Sarah-Anne that Stewart hadn't seen before, as if she were waiting to decide between fight and flight. "You have no proof of any of this."

Pause. Dakar sighed, softly. "I am sorry to cause you such fear, my sister. But we have no time. An innocent man stands to be publicly accused. There was truly no blood on the clothes you wore at the end of the night or the apron you gave the police. But the apron, and clothes you changed out of," Dakar reached into his backpack, and pulled out two police evidence bags, one with a crumpled red material inside of it and the other with something white spattered with red, "have, I am as sure as I can be, blood on them."

Sarah-Anne's expression ossified instantly, as if the fossilisation process that normally took millions of years had happened in the blink of an eye. Stewart saw her eyes dart over towards the table where the other three were sitting, before they refocused on Dakar.

Dakar held up the bag. "If these had fallen out of a bin between here and the pub the younger people went to that night, it would be an oversight in an otherwise truly well-executed plan."

Sarah-Anne remained rooted to the spot, but another voice broke the silence.

"I saw Sarah-Anne upstairs." Jane spoke. She was staring at the mug, as if trying to shatter it with the force of her mind. Her hands were clenching it so tightly that the skin was white almost everywhere, the blood being forced out.

Pause. Dakar turned to meet this new challenge. "No, my sister, you did not."

Jane whipped her face round towards him. "I'm telling you I did."

Pause. "Yes, you are telling me you did. But we both know you are lying."

"I did it!" Stewart whirled back to Sarah-Anne, who was yelling the words. "I did it, Mr Dakar. Just like you said. I confess." She began to get her wild breathing under control as everyone in the room stared at her.

"Mum ..." Sandra said the word with a horrified expression.

"I'm sorry, my darling. I'm so sorry. I'll explain. I'll explain everything." She turned back to Dakar, her shoulders forward, hands out in supplication. She was practically falling forward over the breakfast bar as she spoke. "I did it. You're right. I'll tell the police. Graham will go free. Call them. Call them now. I'll say. Everything."

Pause. Dakar smiled, but it was filled with sorrow. "We must have the entire truth, my sister."

"You have it! You know it! I did it." Sarah-Anne repeated the words, her tone flooded with desperation. Stewart looked between the two, the maniacal intensity of Sarah-Anne against Dakar's implacable calm.

Pause. "You were helped, my sister."

"No! No, I wasn't. I didn't need any help." Dakar opened his mouth to speak, but Sarah-Anne cut him off, taking a step around the breakfast bar towards Dakar. "He was my husband! My responsibility!"

Pause, a shake of the head. "I am sorry. But hiding the truth now only serves more pain later."

Sarah-Anne stared at him, and she seemed to wilt away, like a flower being burned in a fire.

"Once I realised it was Daniel at the window, and he himself had gone downstairs, out of the window, there were two difficult questions. Who closed the window? It is impossible to close from the outside. One can close it most of the way, but not all. And secondly, what was in the cellar that Daniel wanted?"

"I did it on my own." Sarah-Anne mumbled the words, looking down at the ground, like she hadn't heard what Dakar had just said.

Pause. "You were helped by your daughter."

"No!"

Stewart's eyes almost fell out of his head as he turned to look at Sandra. But her appalled expression couldn't have been faked.

"Your adopted daughter."

Chapter 50

"No. She did nothing." Sarah-Anne bared her teeth as she spoke, her lips rolled back in a gesture deep in the DNA of every human as she looked back up at Dakar.

Dakar turned to look at Jane, who still gazed at her mug, still trying to shatter it under the combined pressure of her fingers and her mind. Then he turned back to Sarah-Anne. He spoke gently, almost sorrowfully.

"Another thing that has niggled at my mind throughout this whole investigation was that you didn't have to put out an extra chair for Charles. That meant you knew he was coming already, and so someone must have told you. Not Daniel, this I was sure of. It took me a long time to realise who. Jane seemed close to Daniel. And yet, up until recently, she was very close to you. And when I considered that maybe your fight wasn't as genuine as it appeared, then the entire night began to make sense."

Nothing stirred in the room. Dakar turned to look at the younger woman.

"Jane was the one who told Daniel of the surprise party. She proposed the idea that Daniel appear at the window to scare everyone, and suggested Daniel climb out of the window and wait for her in the cellar."

Jane's eyes didn't move from the mug in front of her.

"She set off the bangers which let Daniel know everyone was outside and that he could start his little charade at the window. She was also the one who got to the window in the bedroom first, and closed it firmly."

"The window was closed!" Sarah-Anne interrupted, but Dakar did not look away from Jane even as he addressed Sarah-Anne.

"No, my sister. Jane closed it all the way. That is why she rushed over there first. She also carried out her part of the plan to create a distraction, allowing you to slip upstairs, by shouting that Charles and Russell were dead."

Jane looked up at him, her eyes bloodshot, shoulders slumped, as if to say something, but then she looked back down at the mug again.

"And, as we have heard, Jane placed you upstairs with everyone else before everyone gathered in the main bedroom. But she was the only one."

Dakar indicated the two crumpled police bags he had put on the kitchen bar. "And, the end of your plan that night, she helped you change out of her dress and put on a new, identical dress, before taking and disposing of the dress, gloves and apron you were wearing that evening."

"No, Mr Dakar, that's not possible. I was with Jane the entire evening. I would have remembered any time she was helping my mum change clothes." Sandra spoke. Her voice was trembling, and her eyes moved back and forth between her mother and her adopted sister. She had to wipe away the beginning of tears in her eyes.

Pause. "Were you with them in the en suite, after the search failed to find Daniel's body?"

"No, I wasn't. But they were shouting at ea …" Sandra trailed off.

Dakar spoke. "The falling-out between your mother and your sister was always a pretence, concocted some time in advance of Daniel's birthday party. It continued afterwards, with the fake argument in Glasgow. To try and ensure that no-one would have the two of them working in conjunction."

Sandra looked at Dakar, then wildly around at Sarah-Anne and Jane. Sarah-Anne closed her eyes, while Jane just kept looking at her mug.

"In the en suite, your mother placed the bloodied dress, apron and gloves in a white bag and gave it to Jane. Jane then left the house as soon as possible, taking advantage of your thought of going to the pub to see if Daniel was there. Craig even told us that your mother gave Jane her bag and told her to get out. On the way there, Jane then dumped it in one of the bins."

Stewart looked at Jane and Sarah-Anne. The former still sat with the mug in her hands, but now she was turning it, over and over, between her fingers. The latter had bowed her head, eyes still closed, her weight pressing forward onto fists on the breakfast bar.

"Mum, is this true? But why? Why do this?" Sandra voice broke as she spoke, the tears running away from her eyes down and over her cheeks.

Sarah-Anne's eyes remained closed, but her face creased further, lines appearing on her forehead as if she was in physical pain. She was rocking gently, back and forth.

"I didn't want you to see him that way."

"What way?" Sandra cried.

"He had turned into something different, Sandra. He wasn't Daniel anymore. He wasn't your father."

"What do you mean?"

Sarah-Anne remained silent for a few moments, but then another voice cut in. Jane's voice trembled as she spoke.

"Sis ... sis, he had been saying things to me for a while. Comments about how good I was looking, and about what I was wearing. While I was still working in the dentist's surgery. At first I thought he was just joking, but he kept on. And it got worse." Jane exhaled after she spoke.

She straightened her shoulders and sat up, finally placing the mug down, then turned to face Sandra.

"I'm sorry, sis. I thought after we left the surgery it would stop. But whenever he came to the flat, he would say things when you couldn't hear, when you were out of the room. And then, two weeks ago, the time you saw him just leaving the flat, it was worse. He wanted ..." She took a deep breath. "He said I should do things for him." Her voice fell lower. "Sexual things."

Sandra's eyes were widening, her mouth gradually opening as if she was watching a horror film.

"And that night, the last time he was in the flat ..." Another deep breath. "He said that if I wouldn't do it for him, he would get you to do it for him. He thought that was hilarious. And so I ..." Jane gestured in Sarah-Anne's direction, "... I phoned mum for help."

Sandra rocked back in her chair, a dazed look coming into her eyes. Russell pulled her tightly towards him. But she pushed his arm away and turned to look at her mother.

"When Daniel came home, I confronted him with what he had done, telling him it was unacceptable, that his behaviour over the last months had been unacceptable." Sarah-Anne took up the narrative as Jane looked back down.

Sarah-Anne put one hand to her left shoulder, the tears now streaming down her face. "He hit me. Here. And that was the moment. The moment I knew what had to be done."

She wiped away the tears, sniffed as she breathed in deeply. "I had been thinking about divorce before that, but at that point, I knew. The man I loved was in there. But so was a monster. I stayed with him so long because I knew Daniel – the Daniel I loved – would be fighting it. But at that moment ... I knew he had lost. I had to kill the monster to save the man. Unfortunately the man couldn't survive the process."

Sarah-Anne took a deep breath, and turned to Sandra.

"I'm so sorry, Sandra. You'd already lost your biological father. I didn't want you to know what Daniel had become. I wanted you to remember him as the man he was. The wonderful man. Even if I'd divorced him, he would still have been able to see you and who knows what he might have done? And so I thought if he was murdered in a way where no-one could have done it ... You might never learn what he had become."

Silence settled on the kitchen, broken only by the sobs of Sandra, stifled as she leaned into Russell's shoulder.

"The change that began about a year ago ... A fertility test?" Dakar asked gently.

Sarah-Anne nodded. "You guessed then. Yes, I think so. We had been trying to have another child. He wouldn't tell me, like I said, but I'd had Sandra already, so I knew that it probably wasn't me. And whenever I brought it up, he would get very angry. From then on, it was like he had a mid-life crisis but on steroids. The partying, drinking, snorting cocaine, buying all kinds of expensive nonsense."

Sarah-Anne stopped for a moment, her expression hard, but then she smiled again.

"But he had his lucid moments, when the man I knew and loved reappeared. He told me about Charles, how he was blackmailing him, threatening to go to the police about the cocaine. And how he toyed with Eleanor, threatening to leave the business, and how he could command Dennis to do whatever he wanted. He was so ashamed of himself."

Dakar nodded, but remained silent.

"But the monster would always reappear." Sarah-Anne shook her head, her eyes drifting. "Always. And then, a few months ago, it became far worse. He began getting angry, shouting and screaming. His lucid moments disappeared. I don't know why. I don't know why it happened."

Pause. "Daniel had a brain tumour."

"A what?"

"A brain tumour. They found it post-mortem. It had been growing for a few months, they believe, coinciding with Daniel's worsening behaviour. It was in his frontal lobe."

She stood stock still as she stared at him, frozen in time. Even her tears seemed to hold on her cheeks.

"I am told these tumours can destroy a person's sense of etiquette, and moral decision making. I believe it is that which explains the more extreme

The Price to Pay

behaviour, towards the end. It was nothing you had done, and there was little Daniel could do. It was literally destroying his personality."

She began blinking more quickly, her eyes roving around the room but not seeing it, instead part of whatever mental calculation she was making.

"So in a way, it wasn't really Daniel at all ..."

Dakar nodded once, and looked down at the ground, his hands clasped in front of him.

"Could he have been treated?" There was a tremble in her voice now, a portent of the emotional reservoir held in check only by the shakiest of dams.

Pause. "They do not know, my sister. Even if it had been found, quite possibly not."

"Possibly not ..." she murmured, bloodshot eyes drifting away to the side, her thoughts trapped in her own private hell.

Silence enveloped the room, Stewart slowing down his scribbling on the pad to avoid making any sound. Dakar turned to Jane, Sarah-Anne looking like she was in her own private hell.

"Why did you decide to drug Charles and Russell?"

"When I told Daniel about the party, Daniel said he was going to invite Charles. Sarah-Anne had told me about Charles and Daniel doing drugs. I thought it would be good if someone was in the house when Daniel did the thing at the window, to try and confuse things a bit. And if he was drugged, I thought that would be fittingly ironic. So I took some of the Zopiclone that Sarah-Anne had, and used that. It seemed to fit the bill." Jane turned to Russell. "You, you idiot, got it by accident. It was in his beer. Then you started drinking the same stuff for the drinking game. I told you not to."

Russell managed a raising of the eyebrows in acknowledgement, looking like the rest of his energy had been sucked away.

Pause, nod. "And why was Daniel's bandage taken off?"

"Curiosity." Sarah-Anne smiled as she rejoined the conversation, but it was a gesture full of sorrow. "I hadn't been upstairs, and had no idea about the blood show Daniel had put on. Suddenly he had this bandage across his wrist that he hadn't had before. I ran down the stairs and cut it off quickly, just to see what had happened. Then I dropped the knife and headed upstairs. When I saw the blood, I realised what he had done."

She looked gaunt, her cheeks pale, but somehow noble as well, drawing herself up to her full height, like a French aristocrat about to meet the guillotine.

"Always a price to pay, eh, Mr Dakar?"

Pause. "Indeed, my sister. There is always a price, and someone has to pay. And it cannot be Graham Donaldson." Dakar spoke gently. He paused again, longer this time. "Not everyone needs to pay it, however."

Sarah-Anne looked at him for a second, before the light of understanding came into her eyes. She leaned forward, deliberately and slowly. "You would do that?"

Pause. "I would."

"What are you talking about?" Jane stood up, putting the mug firmly down on the table.

"Your mother murdered him, my sister, in the physical sense."

Sarah-Anne turned to Jane. "Yes. Yes, I did. He was my husband. This is my responsibility."

"Mum, we'll …" Jane began, but stopped under her stern look. Sarah-Anne's severity slowly melted away as she looked at her.

"You two will have to look after each other."

Jane looked over at Sandra, who sat huddled into Russell. Her face was white, her nose and eyes competing for how much liquid they could produce.

"She helped kill my father." Sandra sniffed as she pointed over at Jane.

Sarah-Anne lifted her hands and brought them down, face down, onto the surface. The thunderclap it produced made Stewart jolt in his seat.

"Your father was already dead, Sandra. He was already gone. I know it's hard, and you're getting all this at once, but that's the way it was. I killed a monster. A monster who wanted you to give him sexual favours." Sarah-Anne's voice was uncompromising, but softened as she continued. "I know you're upset, my darling. And we should have told you. Jane wanted to tell you, actually. It was my decision not to. I wanted you to remember Daniel as a good father. But everything Jane did, she did because I asked her to. And it's only right that I should pay for that. But only me."

Sandra looked at her in silence, her lips trembling.

"I need to know you will be there for your sister. Your sister, Sandra. The only one you've got. And you're the only one she has."

The tears were flowing now as Sandra looked around at Jane. Jane's own expression was a wretched one, fully exposed between the rock and the hard place where she found herself. After a few moments, Sandra turned and buried her head back into Russell's shoulder.

The Price to Pay

Sarah-Anne took a deep breath, then turned back to Dakar. He looked down at his watch, and Stewart did the same. Ten thirty-five. "A friend of mine will be here shortly. He will take down your confession."

"And what do I tell him?"

Pause. "Your confession."

Sarah-Anne hesitated. "But how was it done? Mechanically, I mean? If it was just me, how did I do it?"

Pause. Different though. No, hesitation. Dakar looked slightly confused, as if this thought had just occurred to him. "So long as you plead guilty, it won't be challenged in court."

"Yes, I understand that. But what do I tell your friend who is coming now?"

Hesitation again from Dakar. He put up one hand. "A moment, my sister."

But the moment stretched out into ten seconds, then twenty seconds, then thirty seconds as all eyes rested on Dakar. His forehead was creased as he looked at the ground, mouth slightly open, teeth together.

"Eh …?" Stewart raised his hand.

Everyone turned to him.

"I got an idea."

Chapter 51

The doorbell rang.

"My brother, could you go and let my friend in? He will undoubtedly be accompanied by some of his colleagues."

Stewart, the excitement coursing through him after he'd explained his idea and how it would all work, felt infected by a sour feeling. He'd forgotten all about Frank. It seemed very, very wrong now, to have him come in and taint the place with his presence. And also, well, it was ten forty. Not a lot of time to get in touch with DI Thomas and stop him from announcing the charges against Donaldson.

Stewart sighed heavily as he turned and tramped towards the front door.

Well, Dakar had his own price to pay. And at least the story Frank would put out would only snare Sarah-Anne. Jane would get away. And maybe, in the end, it was the right thing to put Frank back on track. Maybe. But then, maybe not. Maybe Dakar was just afraid.

Colleagues. Well, that meant a TV camera, maybe some more reporters. He hoped Frank wouldn't milk it. Just get his info, a shot or two, and then leave.

Stewart paused as he got to the front door, and took a deep breath. He had no idea what to do. Just Frank, smiling manically? A microphone shoved in his face with questions, a video camera behind it?

He had thought Dakar had got his Zen back today, that he'd found that peace he always seemed to have until Frank had appeared and upset it.

Guess you should never meet your heroes.

He yanked the front door open.

DI Thomas and DC Lemkin stood outside. Both of them looked furious, although DI Thomas's face contorted into a twisted smile when he saw Stewart.

"Ah, Stewart Scott," he said, his tone almost ironic in the face of Stewart's astonishment. "I should have known. You're under arrest for attempting to pervert the course of justice."

Chapter 52

Stewart looked at DI Thomas stupidly. DC Lemkin reached out and took his unresisting hands, cuffing them to front. Stewart looked down at his hands with the same stupid expression, then back up.

"You have the right to remain silent. Anything you do say can be used against you in a court of law." DI Thomas continued laconically. "You have the right to a solicitor …" he paused, and made a show of looking around, "… although it looks like you're the only one around here just now. And you have the right to have someone informed of your arrest. So we'll be sure to tell your mother."

Stewart continued to look at him blankly. It felt like his brain was juddering, like a CD player trying and failing to read a scratched CD.

"Where's Dakar?"

Stewart's brain eventually kicked back into gear. Saz floated into his mind. A drunken night out, and she'd kept telling him, no matter the situation, no matter how friendly the police sounded, if they ever asked you a question, anything, the answer was always …

"No comment?"

DI Thomas lunged forward and grabbed Stewart's shirt with one hand, pulling him close, the fury flowing out from him. Then he took a deep breath, let go, and put his hand on Stewart's shoulder instead, patting the wrinkles he'd made back out.

"Look, I don't have much time. Any time. I'm not here for you. These …" he tapped the handcuffs, "… are to make sure you don't run off. Now, where the hell is Dakar?"

Stewart looked at the irritation on the faces of the cops, and then turned back towards the hall. He tried to raise one arm, and ended up raising both of them, to point towards the kitchen. The cops barged past him without a further word, marching down the corridor.

Stewart looked back outside, but couldn't see anyone. He closed the door, and then headed back towards the kitchen, slowly, feeling each step as he did so. He cautiously tested the handcuffs. They were solid, all right. Real, proper handcuffs, bracelets of metal around his wrists.

Arrested. He'd been arrested. That was it, then. Done. He'd probably become homeless and end up begging on the streets. Or in prison, in one of those chain gangs. If they still existed.

Stewart stumbled into the kitchen just after DI Thomas and DC Lemkin.

"Good morning, Mrs Mannings. I'm sorry we're bothering you," DI Thomas said. "DC Lemkin, please arrest Dakar. Let's make sure they're finished with this investigation."

Stewart had never seen anyone look as satisfied in their work as DC Lemkin as he walked over to Dakar.

"Sebastian Dakar, you are under arrest for attempting to pervert the course of justice. Anything you say may be used against you in a court of law. You have the right to a solicitor, although …" Lemkin turned and looked at Stewart, a smile on his face, "… the only one present is also under arrest so it might take a while. And you have the right to have another person informed of your arrest."

"Cuff him." DI Thomas's tone was short and brutish.

Lemkin pulled out a pair of handcuffs. Dakar put his hands in front of him quite willingly, and DC Lemkin snapped the handcuffs on.

"Feel that, Dakar?" DI Thomas.

Dakar stayed silent, a gentle smile on his face. He looked generally happy with how the whole thing was going.

DI Thomas turned back to Sarah-Anne. "Don't worry, Mrs Mannings, Mr Dakar here – and Mr Scott – won't be bothering you again. We just came to pick them up personally, but we can't stay. I'm giving a press conference in twenty minutes. It'll be public shortly, so I may as well tell you now. We've got Graham Donaldson in custody for Daniel's murder."

"Graham Donaldson did not murder Daniel Mannings." Dakar spoke gently, but the words carried around the room.

DI Thomas sighed. "Come on, Dakar." He walked over to him.

"In fact, he had a strong motive to keep him alive."

"To keep him alive? When he'd found out that Daniel had taken photos of him having an affair to be used against him in court? Have you lost it, Dakar?" He turned to Sarah-Anne. "I'm sorry, Mrs Mannings. I don't know if you were aware, but Daniel was taking photographs of Graham Donaldson meeting another woman. In revealing circumstances, if I can put it that way."

"Graham Donaldson was not having an affair." Dakar's voice was gentle but insistent, as DI Thomas reached out and grabbed his arm.

The Price to Pay

"Yeah? What would you call a married man meeting another woman in a hotel clandestinely? Kissing her outside?" DI Thomas said it with a laugh. "C'mon, time to go."

"Graham's business was in trouble. It will soon go under, financially, and there will be a number of creditors making claims on Graham's personal assets. In order to forestall this, Graham and Martina concocted a sham affair, with Graham at fault, to engineer a divorce. That way, Martina could save half of the assets from the marriage."

DI Thomas hesitated, one hand gripping Dakar's arm.

"Of course. Big blonde hair, and those ridiculous heels." Sarah-Anne was smiling wanly.

"Indeed. The polar opposite of his wife, Martina. I was suspicious, I have to admit, when the photographs showed them meeting outside the hotel so publicly, when there was a large lobby they could have met in. Plus the woman was only ever seen from behind. Once I found out that Graham had booked the rooms under his own name, it seemed more and more like a set-up."

DI Thomas's eyes hardened as he looked at Dakar. Even with cuffed hands, Stewart had managed to slide his notebook out and then a pen, and was awkwardly but determinedly scribbling it all down as fast as he could, pad balancing on his knees.

Dakar turned to look at the man holding him. "And it means that Graham Donaldson not only had no motive to kill Daniel, he had a strong motive to keep him alive. Daniel was key to convincing the courts of the authenticity of the sham affair, and thereby saving at least some of their property from creditors."

DI Thomas shook his head, his fingers pressing tighter around Dakar's arm. "And what about the message, telling Donaldson the door was open? And his fingerprints all over the study?"

Pause. "Daniel refused to give the photographs to Martina, although he made sure she knew he had them. I presume he was going to blackmail her as well. The burner phone that you found dumped in the house belonged to Martina, not Craig. I don't think he knows anything about the sham nature of the affair. I imagine that Graham came inside when the fireworks began, after Martina sent him that message and ensured the door was unlocked. To look for the photographs. Graham may even have been in the house while Daniel carried out his game at the window."

"Or! Or Donaldson killed Daniel in the cellar, then went upstairs and played out the charade himself. Then he hides, and as everyone rushes into the bedroom, he slips downstairs. He puts the suit jacket back on the corpse and escapes out the front door. And his son bolts it behind him." DI Thomas spoke with the tone of a person who has what they believe is a really good idea.

Pause. "And if he had been seen? You will have to explain to the fiscal that Graham passed back through the house, presumably with Daniel's blood on him, having stabbed him multiple times."

A shrug. "It could have happened."

"Of course, you'll have to explain how Daniel's blood came to be in the bedroom."

DI Thomas's eyebrows furrowed at this.

"And, my brother, you will have to explain in court why he slit Daniel's wrist, decided to bandage it afterwards and then cut it off again."

DI Thomas's expression darkened.

"Then you will have to discuss why he decided to kill Daniel when he had a powerful motive for keeping him alive."

DI Thomas looked decidedly stormy now as Dakar continued in his gentle tone.

"And, of course, the killer question. Why, having murdered a man in his own house, managed to hide the body against strong odds, put on and then cut off a bandage, escaped, then cleaned himself up … why did he remain outside until the police arrived? Even after the police arrived? He could not have failed to see the police cars pull up, with sirens screaming. And yet he remained there until the police came out of the house and found him."

DI Thomas looked back at Dakar, his expression frozen in place. His eyes were wild though.

"You have not made it public yet, my brother? Any charges against Graham Donaldson?"

DI Thomas slowly shook his head. He checked his watch, Stewart automatically doing the same. Quarter to eleven.

Dakar nodded. "I suggest you do not."

DI Thomas looked at Dakar steadily for a long few seconds, the clock in the kitchen registering each passing second. He closed his eyes, then took a deep breath and let go of Dakar.

"Lemkin, radio HQ. Tell them to let Donaldson go." Lemkin went to protest, but without opening his eyes, DI Thomas held up a hand. "We can always re-arrest him and charge him later if we get more on him."

Lemkin's expression looked both like he was sucking a lemon and bloody furious about it. "And the press conference?"

DI Thomas kept his eyes shut, but one hand came up and began massaging his temple. "Cancel it. I don't fancy getting eaten alive. I'll get enough of that from the chief."

"I wouldn't cancel the press conference, my brother."

DI Thomas opened his eyes, glaring directly at Dakar, his jaw clenched so hard Stewart thought he could hear his teeth squeaking. He looked like he was about to hit him.

"You love knocking shit down, don't you? What the hell would I tell the press? 'Yes, we had a suspect, but we've just figured out now that actually he didn't do it. And no, now you mention it, we don't have another one'. For Christ's sake, Seb."

Dakar turned slowly to look at Sarah-Anne.

She took a deep breath. "I murdered my husband."

DI Thomas looked at her as if she'd just announced her true name was Laetitia and she was the queen of fairyland.

"Excuse me?"

"I murdered my husband." She repeated the words calmly, standing with her shoulders back, ready.

DI Thomas looked cautiously over at DC Lemkin, who was looking equally shocked. He nodded once, and the other officer hurriedly took his notepad out of his pocket.

DI Thomas looked around the rest of the room. His cautious look didn't last long. By the time it passed over Stewart and Dakar, he looked like he smelled a trap. His gaze came back to Sarah-Anne.

"Sarah-Anne Mannings, I'm arresting you as a suspect. You have the right to remain silent, and you have the right to legal counsel. You have the right to have a third party informed of your arrest. Would you like to exercise any of those rights?"

"No."

"Very well. Is there anything you'd like to tell me about the death of your husband Daniel Mannings?"

"Yes. I stabbed him."

"Why?"

Sarah-Anne took a deep breath. Stewart felt the excitement course back through him again, his eyes fixed on the woman. The litmus test.

"It was an accident. Daniel had disappeared at the window, and there was the knife, and blood everywhere. I was all shaken up. Later that night, after the children left, I went to get a bottle of wine from the cellar. I had my back turned, and someone grabbed me in the darkness, turned me around and began screaming in my face. I was carrying a knife and I just struck out, by instinct."

DI Thomas looked cautiously at her, scrutinising her face. "But how did Daniel get out of the bedroom?"

"He climbed out of the window, and then closed it, balancing on the bricks." Dakar interrupted gently. "And if someone had happened to stay in the garden in spite of all the drama and seen him then the joke would be ruined, but apart from that … no big deal." Dakar looked at Stewart. DI Thomas followed his gaze, his glare also landing on Stewart.

Stewart felt himself blush, but in spite of his glow, he still met DI Thomas's glare. Dakar had raised the same objection when Stewart first laid out his alternate version, and Stewart had given him the same answer, the same words. 'No big deal.'

DI Thomas's eyes narrowed as he looked back at Dakar. "You keep quiet." He turned back to Sarah-Anne, but she was nodding along.

"Yes, he must have climbed out of the window and then shut it behind him. There was no other way for anyone to get in or out of that room in the time it took us to get there. And then he must have gone to the cellar and waited for someone to come down, to scare them."

"Why were you carrying a knife?"

"I was chopping some more food in the kitchen, just some snacks, when I realised we needed some more wine. I forgot I was carrying it, and just headed down."

DI Thomas nodded slowly at this, the disbelief still clear in his face. "And what about the blood upstairs? If you stabbed him down there, how'd it get up there? And all the stuff on the floor?"

"I don't know for sure, but Daniel was a showman. Maybe he slit his wrist and dropped some blood around the place, before he bandaged it again? Same with the things on the floor. To make it look like a fight had taken place."

"And the bruising on his body, Mrs Mannings?" DI Thomas's eyes were like slits.

"I kicked out at the person who attacked me as well, Detective Inspector, even after they fell to the floor. I was terrified, just reacting. That's why I kept stabbing and kicking."

DI Thomas stared back at her, his eyes considering.

Sarah-Anne took another deep breath, but pressed on. "I had no idea who it was, or what, I just struck out blindly. It was only after I calmed down I realised it was Daniel. But by then he was already dead."

"And then?"

"I panicked. At first I tried to help him, pick him up from the back and drag him up the stairs. I got some way, but not all that far. But then I realised how it would look. So I dropped him, and his body rolled back down the stairs. I just left him there."

DI Thomas sniffed. If anything, the disbelief was growing on his face, not decreasing.

"We tested your dress and gloves for blood and didn't find any. You would have been covered with the stuff, if what you say is true."

"Yes, but fortunately, I had a second dress, identical to the first. I bought two because I wasn't sure which one fit better. I ran upstairs and got changed into the other one quickly and washed my face, then I hid the first one in the garden before Tom went to the cellar. I planned to discover the body myself, later, but he went down before me."

DI Thomas sniffed, and Stewart could see the workings in his eyes. But then they narrowed again. "Then, Mrs Mannings, would you care to explain why you took the bandage off Daniel's wrist?" There was a touch of triumph in his tone, as he posed his own killer question.

Sarah-Anne took a deep breath. There was silence in the air for a moment. "That's how souls escape from our bodies."

DI Thomas's eyebrows shot up and his eyes almost popped out of his head.

"Excuse me?"

Sarah-Anne made a show of gesturing to the books, her eyes again meeting Stewart's for a millisecond as she looked over towards the bookcase. "One of the ancient Celtic tribes believed that the soul escaped after death through the wrist. I wanted to make sure that my husband's soul also escaped."

DI Thomas looked at her, mouth slightly open, for a few seconds. Then he looked around at the books. Then back to Sarah-Anne.

Stewart smiled a secret smile as the silence in the room grew. Everyone else had protested this part of his proposed explanation, claiming it was too crazy. Stewart knew otherwise. It was the part that would seal the deal. Everyone secretly wanted to believe that murderers were different from them. And any kind of craziness would do.

DI Thomas nodded again slowly, as an accepting expression appeared on his face. He turned to look at Dakar, still a little stunned.

"My brother, this will be your collar. Right down to a confession. And you might take some pleasure in explaining to the press what the word 'baffled' truly means."

DI Thomas closed his mouth again. He stared at Dakar for a few seconds, then pointed to the corridor. "A word. Now." He headed out into the corridor, Dakar strolling after him in spite of his cuffed hands.

DC Lemkin came over to stand beside Stewart at the doorway, blocking the route into the corridor and shielding Dakar and DI Thomas from the view of those in the living room. He took up an at-ease stance, his hands behind his back. He didn't say anything. Stewart snuck a look up at him, but he was looking stonily over at the other four people in the room.

"They're not too tight, are they? The cuffs?" Lemkin continued looking straight ahead, speaking in a low voice that only Stewart could hear.

"Eh, the cuffs? No, no. Thanks. They're grand." Lemkin nodded, and settled back into silence.

Stewart heard the voices of DI Thomas and Dakar speaking down the hall.

"You're sure?"

There was silence behind him, and Stewart recognised the pregnancy of the Dakar pause in action. "Indeed, my brother."

"And Donaldson isn't involved? At all?"

Pause. "I believe not."

There was a pause, from DI Thomas this time, then a big exhalation. "Right."

The two men re-entered the room, Stewart and DC Lemkin stepping to one side. DI Thomas looked at Sarah-Anne, and nodded. "DC Lemkin."

Stewart watched DC Lemkin re-read Sarah-Anne her rights and charge her with the murder of her husband. As he went to escort her out, DI Thomas called wearily after him.

"Keys." DC Lemkin produced a small key and threw it to DI Thomas, who then leaned over and uncuffed Dakar. He then walked over to Stewart and took the cuffs off of his hands as well. Stewart rubbed his wrists.

"Thank you, my brother."

"Consider yourself unarrested." He glanced over his shoulder at Stewart. "You as well, Scott. As if it never happened."

Stewart let out a deep breath he hadn't realised he'd been holding. Thank the big man for small mercies.

Chapter 53

Stewart stood outside the house, beside Dakar. The police had taken statements from both of them, and had just left, taking Sarah-Anne with them. Jane stood beside them, watching the cars leave. Sandra and Russell were still in the kitchen, Sandra having refused to move.

"You couldn't just have left it, could you? Now we've lost our mother as well."

Pause. Dakar turned to meet Jane's livid look. "If we undertake an action, my sister, it is perhaps well to be ready to pay the price for it. Your mother has paid it for you. A brave woman."

"She didn't have to. You could have just not said anything."

Pause. "Perhaps, my sister."

Jane's voice quivered as she spoke, her accusation flung straight at Dakar. "This is your fault."

Pause. "I am full of sorrow that you feel that way, my sister."

"I'm not your sister."

She glared at Dakar for a second longer, then turned and stomped back into the house. Stewart watched her disappear before he and Dakar began heading for the car.

"Lucky you found that dress and apron in the bin, then. Might have been hard to convince her to confess otherwise."

Pause. "But I did not. The murder was eleven days ago, and the bins had been emptied by the time I got there. I bought the dress and apron when I was shopping this morning. I don't know if they were the same as the ones Sarah-Anne had, but it didn't matter. All that mattered was the colour."

Stewart stopped and gaped at him, open-mouthed. "You lied!"

Pause. Dakar stopped as well. "By omission, certainly."

"You said they had Daniel's blood on them!"

Pause. "I said I was as sure as I could be that they had blood on them, my brother. I never specified whose blood. And indeed they do. I visited a butcher shortly after buying them, and splattered some blood on myself."

"I … But … Are you allowed to do that?"

Dakar began walking again. "We make our own rules, my brother."

The Price to Pay

Stewart nodded. Well. In the name of the wee man. Dakar had been so calm throughout. Wouldn't fancy playing him at poker.

"And so Craig had nothing to do with it? I really thought that it was him who opened the front door for his dad. What with the anarchist tattoo and everything."

Pause, a shake of the head. "Anarchist philosophy is not a violent one, my brother. In fact, if true anarchists took power, society would probably be more organised than it is now. And, I believe, a lot fairer."

"Oh aye? Know a lot about anarchists, do you?"

"I am one."

Stewart stopped and gaped again, then had to hurry to catch up as Dakar kept on. But Dakar stopped next to his car as another car pulled up. It screamed to a halt, sufficiently sharply for the front of the car to dip and the back to rise slightly, and the driver rocketed out.

Stewart saw Frank get out the car and run around it towards them. He rocked back on his heels. He'd forgotten about the text message Dakar had sent, the whole idea of Frank shoved violently out of his head when the handcuffs encircled his wrists.

Frank looked feral. Deranged even, eyes bloodshot, spit at the side of his mouth.

"You bastard! You bastard, Sebbie! Forty bloody minutes to that address and back down again. I've been all over looking for you."

Dakar paused, and Stewart saw him take a deep breath. Stewart leaned ever so slightly away from him.

"My brother."

"My brother! I'll bloody my brother you! What the hell's your game, sending me on a wild goose chase to a monastery?"

Pause. "I believed you might find the peace you are seeking there."

Frank looked at Dakar like Dakar had just said he'd met Santa Claus walking down the street. "Come again?"

Pause. "I had believed you might find peace there, my brother."

"Peace? All I found was a big empty place that smelled of shite! I just passed the police cars leaving here. What the hell happened, Dakar? Tell me!"

Pause. Dakar shook his head. "I am full of sorrow, my brother, but I shall not do that."

Now Frank's expression changed, hardening. "You'll bloody well give me my story, Sebbie, or I'll file a different exclusive. This story or your bollocks. You can choose. And don't forget Mr Crudup and Jamie and Sam."

Dakar's eyes narrowed, but he took a deep breath. "I have made my decision, my brother. It is too late now."

Frank snorted, his eyes opening slightly wider. "You've got to be joking. You know what I'll publish. You remember that night, that drunken conversation? That's what I'll lead with, Sebbie. I'll back it up with every little thing you told me, but that'll be the headline. He'll get out, Sebbie. And he'll be pissed."

Pause. "I have made my decision, my brother. The police are holding a press conference in ten minutes, although I imagine it will be delayed by a little while. If you hurry, you might make it." Dakar's tone was firmer now where it had been gentle before.

Frank began nodding, his eyes glinting. "Right then. So it's done. You. You're for it. You're bloody well for it now. My brother." He jabbed a finger towards Dakar as he practically spat the last couple of words.

Frank spun round, and got back into his car. With an obscene gesture towards Dakar, his car roared away down the road, the same direction the police had gone. Stewart watched him go, and heard Dakar breathe out deeply through his nose.

After watching Frank leave, they sat in silence in the car. Eventually Dakar broke it.

"I understand how Frank found us yesterday. It was your comment about Martina putting a GPS in Graham's vehicle. Frank had put a GPS on my old vehicle. That's why I traded it in temporarily for this one."

"That's why you said the car was tainted, is it?"

Pause, nod. "Indeed."

Stewart sat in the silence. Normally an ex-journalist with a grudge swearing vengeance on Dakar, having been earlier thwarted in a technological effort to track him, would have got Stewart's heart racing. But now, now, he just felt worn-out, like he'd been through the wringer.

"Think he'll follow through on what he's threatening?"

Pause. "Quite possible. He is very angry."

"What will you do if he does?"

Pause. "We will see. There is a price to pay for all actions, mine included."

Stewart nodded. Well, it was over, then. Dakar had managed to sort it out again.

The Price to Pay

"Let us go back, my brother. It has been a long day."

The silence settled. Stewart checked his watch. Eleven thirty. He should be back in time for Sudgeon's meeting at twelve, to diligently take notes, and try to pretend to those present that, in the dangerous political waters of the office, he was a shark rather than a swimmer with armbands.

He watched the buildings flash past as the city seemed to grow more substantial around him, like flesh being added to a body as the buildings crowded out the green spaces until they were in entirely urban areas.

"Do you feel bad at all? I mean, about Jane? She's getting away with murder. Literally."

Pause. "No, my brother."

"Why?"

Pause, a slight shrug. "Given what happened, and who Daniel had become, perhaps Sarah-Anne and Jane did the right thing. But it would be intolerable for Graham Donaldson to be charged, possibly convicted, of this crime."

"Is that your choice to make?"

Pause. "It's a choice I had the power to make, and so therefore the responsibility to make. You, Sandra, Russell and Jane have all made the same choice."

"Any of us could tell the police what truly happened."

Pause. "True. That too is a choice you'll have to make, every single day of your life. You just have to decide what you think is right."

The silence settled again as Dakar slowly wound his way back to SSM. The day had given birth to the afternoon amidst some light clouds, the sun breaking through in patches, almost like it was trying to repair the ravages of the storm the night before.

Stewart looked out the window. Of course what Dakar said was true. And he'd come up with the story, the alternate story, as to how Sarah-Anne could have done it herself. So long as the cops didn't bother checking you could close the window from the outside, there weren't any holes in the theory. And did Jane really deserve to face a criminal justice system that was, according to Saz, more about getting through the business than actually achieving justice?

Stewart sighed, and looked back at Dakar. The guy didn't seem to be troubled by that question. But he'd made his choice, and seemed happy enough with it. Another thought hit him.

"Shame about the Donaldsons, though. I guess they'll go down pretty hard now, what with the business failing and their sham affair exposed."

Pause. "Graham Donaldson's business will not fail."

"What do you mean?"

Pause. "There is a foundation, the Redistribution Foundation, that supports certain projects throughout Scotland. Graham's business, being both environmentally sound and providing jobs for the ex-convicts, certainly qualifies. They decided today to give an annual grant to cover whatever shortcomings the business has, until it regains profitability. Thus, no debt, no failure."

Stewart's eyebrows furrowed. "How do you know this?"

Pause. "One day I will tell you where all my money goes, I think. Or perhaps I will show you."

Stewart looked around at Dakar, but the guy was focusing on the road. He turned and stared back out of the window, his brain too mangled with murders, and deception, and personality changes to pursue anything any further. The person he'd really like to discuss it with, of course, was Beth.

Stewart froze as her image rose in his mind. Beth. Next to the unwanted image of Hamish, grinning, boasting. He felt his expression sour, his shoulders slump, tiredness overwhelming him as the thoughts and images began to flow through his mind.

Hamish. And Beth. Lying naked, next to each other. But strangely, that part, that part didn't bother him anymore. The worst part, the part that made him want to curl up into the foetal position, was an image of Beth smiling, and laughing, and hugging Hamish, and have a joke with him as they cuddled, under the co—

"My brother?"

Stewart looked up with a jolt. "What?"

They were sitting at some traffic lights. Dakar was looking searchingly at him.

"Are you well, my brother?"

"What? Aye, fine." Stewart felt the tiredness flow through him again as the short adrenaline spike ebbed. "Well, you know. I've been better, let's say. But aye. Grand."

Dakar looked at him in silence, a gentle look, but it was enough for Stewart to crumble entirely.

"Well ... It's Beth. My flatmate. You know, the one who ... the one I spoke to you about. The other time. She ... she got together with a guy.

The Price to Pay

That guy at work. Hamish. I found out at the office party last night. Hamish was boasting about it. And then ..."

He took a deep breath.

"Then I went back to the flat and went mental at her. I mean really mental. Like, you think you had a go at me last night? Nothing compared to what I said to her. Nothing." Stewart could hear his voice quivering as he spoke, and his body shivered as well.

Dakar signalled the car to pull over, and drove into a parking space on the street. He killed the engine, and remained silent until Stewart spoke.

"Well, yeah, that's it, really. I mean, yeah, when I heard Hamish was boasting to the rest of the guys, and I came home, straight away afterwards, and ... Jesus. She was just there. And I just let fly, with everything I was feeling. I was so angry."

Stewart felt his face was wet. Christ. Crying. Again. Twice in two days. But bollocks to it. Too tired to care. And besides, it didn't matter. Not in front of Dakar.

"I am full of sorrow, my brother."

Stewart just nodded, looking down at his feet. A tear rolled down his nose and plunked onto the ground.

Normally, he knew, crying in front of any other male would ... Stewart kicked the thought out viciously. Who cared what he did normally?

"Aye, well, only myself to blame really, isn't there? I mean, she doesn't owe me anything. She can go and do whatever she wants with whoever she wants. Without the threat of a verbal doing from one of her flatmates who's stupidly in love with her."

Stewart kept looking down into the foot well as silence settled in the car, interrupted only by his own occasional sniff. He looked back up after a minute or so. Dakar's gentle expression hadn't changed.

"So what would you do now, if you were me?"

Pause. "Were I you, my brother, I would forgive myself, and then apologise to Beth."

"Forgive myself?"

Pause. "Indeed." Stewart shook his head at the absurdity of the suggestion.

"What do you mean?"

Pause. "My brother, to forgive another is a demanding task. To forgive oneself is harder still. For all the little mistakes we make, we have a choice. We can use them as a whip to beat ourselves, or we can forgive ourselves the things we have done to others. Many choose the former. But unless you forgive yourself for what you have done, then your life will be a hard one."

Stewart looked at him through the mist of tears, then turned away.

"And apologise to Beth?"

Dakar inclined his head.

Stewart nodded in turn. That was something he could do.

"And then what do I do?"

Pause. "It is all you can do. It is for her to decide whether to forgive."

"But what if she doesn't?"

Pause. "You cannot control the actions of others, and so there is no point concerning yourself with them. Apologise. There are few actions in the world that are truly unforgiveable. And have the strength to forgive yourself. You can do no more."

Stewart wiped his face. The tears were drying up now, the fear and pain coming back down to manageable levels. He nodded once again. There was something else he could do.

"You still doing your rich and famous one-hour gigs?" Stewart asked, still looking down.

Pause. "Yes."

"Want to do me a favour?"

Pause. "Tell me, my brother."

"Give one over to Beth, will you?"

Pause. "My brother—"

"Not for me, to try and impress her. I don't care about that. Just … She deserves it. I know she's not rich or famous, and neither am I, but … Just give her one hour. She's a good person, trying to improve herself. And you can help."

Pause. Long pause. "One day, my brother, you and I will talk more."

Stewart nodded wearily. "Okay. And Beth?"

Pause. "She has her hour."

Chapter 54

Stewart arrived at work, checking his watch as he flew past the secretaries to the lift, where he jammed his finger on the button. Ten to twelve. It seemed to take forever, Stewart alternating between bouncing up and down and trying to smooth his hair, tie and suit into place. In spite of knowing it was useless, he pressed the button a few times more.

Eventually it arrived, and he went up to his floor. He ran to his office and burst in.

Michelle and Jennifer looked up in surprise as Stewart hurried over to his desk.

"Hello," he called as he arrived at the desk. He dumped his bag and coat, and grabbed out his notepad and pen.

"Everything all right?" Michelle ventured.

"Aye, grand. Just got one thing I need to run and do, then I'll be back." He smiled quickly at them both and bundled back out of the office, high-tailing it towards Sudgeon's office. The lift again seemed determined to thwart him, but it arrived eventually and he took it up. Five to twelve.

He rushed over to Sudgeon's office, just as Sudgeon and Green were coming out.

"Mr Sudgeon!" Sudgeon turned and looked at him, his surprise quickly being replaced with mock-politeness. "Mr Sudgeon! Ah! I'm here." Stewart panted in between his words.

"Ah, Stewart. The prodigal son returns."

"Good of you to find the time to speak with us, Scott. We know you're very busy." Green's tone could have cut ice.

Stewart nodded, panting. "Yes. Eh, yes. I'm very sorry about earlier. Bad connection, and then—"

"Stewart, you were on the outskirts of Edinburgh, not outer Mongolia. Lying about a bad connection won't aid your cause."

Stewart froze as Sudgeon looked at him with all the warmth a tyrant has for a slave.

"Eh, well, the thing was that we had—"

But Sudgeon held up his hand. "Stewart, you will forgive me," he said, in a weighty tone, "but given your unreliable nature, I took the liberty of finding a replacement for you. Someone who can be trusted."

Hamish appeared from inside Sudgeon's office, armed with his own notepad and pen, right on cue. There was no gloat, though. He looked miserable.

"Eh, okay. Right. Eh, Mr Sudgeon, I just want to—"

But Sudgeon held up a hand again, cutting him off. "I don't really have time right now, Stewart. The meeting starts in five minutes, and I like to be on time for things." He paused, tilted his head down as he looked at Stewart. "I've assigned you the narratives for this month. As you know from last year, it may not be taxing, but it is a time-consuming job. I suggest you get started."

Stewart's eyes goggled. "The narratives?"

"Working so hard for Dakar must have been tiring. We don't want you to burn out." Green spoke now, his flat tone betraying the insubstantiality of his words.

Stewart looked at Sudgeon's expression, and saw an absolute remorselessness in his eyes. Green's eyes were gleaming, but cold. Stewart nodded slowly at them both, then to Hamish, before he turned away and walked slowly back towards the lift.

He reached the office and entered, trudging over to his desk.

"Everything definitely doesn't look all right now." Michelle spoke as Stewart traipsed across the room.

Stewart collapsed into his chair.

"I've been given the narratives to collate and check."

Their expressions immediately screwed up, like they'd simultaneously smelled something bad. "The narratives? As in, the explanation for each and every hour billed? But the first years do that. It's terrible work. And you don't even get to bill yourself for it." Jennifer spoke.

Stewart nodded. "Yeah. I hung up on Sudgeon during a phone call, then cancelled him when he tried to phone me again. He wasn't too impressed, I think it's fair to say. So now I get to do the narratives. And yes, as I can't bill, I won't be hitting any targets this month."

The girls looked appalled. "You hung up on Sudgeon?" Michelle, her voice full of stunned amazement.

Stewart nodded miserably.

"And then cancelled his call?" Jennifer now.

More miserable nodding.

"But why?" Michelle.

Stewart just shrugged, looking down. Michelle cocked her head to one side, studying Stewart.

"Guess he's not going to be inviting you to any dinner parties in the future then?"

"Guess not."

"So what now?" Jennifer asked.

Stewart shrugged again. "The narratives. Plus I'll do my report on the Dakar thing. And then I'll come back in on Monday, and keep on shovelling the excrement until someone else does something worse than what I did."

"Might take a while," Michelle said.

Stewart nodded, and got down to work.

Chapter 55

Stewart opened the door to his flat. His mind felt dull, his whole body deflated, as he hung up his coat and took his satchel into the living room, where he put it on the table.

He checked his watch. Quarter past five, the earliest he could ever remember getting back from work, ever. But on the plus side, at least neither of his flatmates would be back. Do the report, and then he could go and curl up somewhere and think about what he'd done.

He slid the notes out, sat down, and began to study them.

Stewart almost had a heart attack when there was a cough behind him. Beth was sitting on the couch, feet curled up below her, blanket covering most of her. Her face was pale, accentuating the darkness of the bags under her eyes. She was clutching a large mug of tea between two hands. The size of the mug, and the blanket covering her, combined to make her look very small and fragile.

As he looked at her, she took a deep breath.

"Hi, Stewart," she said, with a grim determination in her voice that foreshadowed the difficult conversation to come.

"What are you doing here?" he asked in amazement.

"I took the day off work. I didn't feel up to it today, so I phoned in sick. I've been reading all day." Her tone remained bleak. There was a book beside her on the couch. Stewart couldn't make out the title, but he could see the author's name: S. Dakar.

Beth took another deep breath, but before she could say anything, Stewart interrupted her.

"I'm sorry." He blurted the words out. "Beth, listen, I want to say sorry. I'm sorry for my reaction, and for what I said to you. You were right, absolutely right."

Beth's face was a combination of pain and severity, her eyes beginning to glisten in the corners.

"I know what I did was wrong. I had no right to say those things. I know that, eh, you know, the ego ... Well, fear and anger, you know ... Well, look, I just, I just felt hurt, and I lashed out. And I shouldn't have. I've felt, absolutely shite about it ever since. I mean it. Sitting in my room upstairs on my own last night, it was just going around in my head. And even worse that you were sitting down here, feeling terrible because of me. I'm really sorry."

Beth's face seemed to grow grimmer still.

"I wanted to say something this morning, but somehow, I don't know, the words just wouldn't come out." He rushed to finish as Beth opened her mouth to speak. "Listen, I want to make it up to you. What I'm about to say, I want you to know that I'm not doing this to guilt trip you into forgiving me. I just want you to know that I really appreciate you as a friend. So, anyway, I don't know if you went to the gig last night, but I ordered you a couple of tickets for another performance on Sunday night."

She gulped and cleared her throat, but the hard expression remained. "Thanks, Stewart. That's nice."

"And, look, I hope you don't mind, but I spoke with Dakar about, well, about what happened. What with him being a bit of an expert on the old feelings, and everything. And, well, he offered to meet with you, if you still wanted, for a one-to-one with him."

Beth's eyes widened. "A session with Dakar?"

"Aye. And like I said, you don't need to forgive me for this. These things are yours now, as if you owned them. Eh, yeah. Although, you know, don't get me wrong, it would be nice if you did forgive me. But if you don't want to, I get it."

Beth exhaled, and her expression broke, her whole body relaxing from its tensed position, a tired smile appearing on her face. "Stewart … Thank you."

"Right, yeah. Okay. Well, maybe we can talk about it later. And, you know, if you want to have Hamish around, for dinner or whatever, no worries. I mean, I might not stick around, you know, small talk might be a bit awkward, but I can easily head out and grab a beer. I just want you to know, it's grand. Seriously."

Beth's expression darkened again, and she shook her head. "I'm not seeing Hamish again."

"Oh. Oh, right. Eh, sorry to hear that?"

"You weren't the only one who was angry. I phoned him this morning and gave him a piece of my mind."

Stewart remembered Hamish coming into the office that morning and calling him a prick. He'd never stopped to think about how Hamish had found out. "Oh, right, yeah. Of course. Okay. Well. I'm sorry, I guess."

"Mmmmmm." She nodded in acceptance. She stopped, but something in the air told Stewart she wasn't done talking. She took a deep breath. "I didn't get a chance to tell you, but I didn't know it was Hamish at the time."

"What?"

"I didn't know who he was the night we got together. I'd seen him a few times during yoga class before, and this time, we ended up sitting next to each other afterwards when we were getting our socks and shoes back on and putting our stuff away."

"Hamish does yoga?"

"Yes."

"Hamish? Does yoga?"

Beth's eyes narrowed. "Yes."

Stewart pulled himself together. "Eh, right. Right, okay."

"He was really down about something. I asked him what had happened, and he told me that he had a chance to work with Sebastian Dakar, but that Sebastian had chosen to work with someone else. We got to talking about Sebastian's books, and what he must be like, and I mentioned that my flatmate had worked with him and how amazing it had been. I told him who you were."

Stewart's eyes narrowed. "But he didn't mention who he was."

She shook her head. "No. I think he knows you don't exactly like him. He was devastated that Sebastian asked to work with you rather than him. But anyway, we kept on talking, and after quite a few drinks, what happened, happened. I'm sorry about that. I know you don't like Hamish. I would never have done it if I'd known it was him. At least, not without talking to you first."

Stewart grimaced as he tried for a smile.

"I wanted to tell you before you saw him again, but I couldn't bring myself to do it the next morning. I already felt awful, and the thought of how upset you'd be was too much. But then you said you wouldn't be working that day, so I didn't think there was any danger of you bumping into Hamish. And then I was going to tell you last night. At the gig."

Stewart nodded once, taking in and then letting go of a deep breath.

"But why didn't you tell me you were working with Dakar again?"

Stewart sighed. "I should have. But I was planning to tell you at the Oak. I thought it would be cooler that way, I suppose, once I was in the thick of it with Dakar. Trying to impress, and all that."

Beth's face fell. She stood up and held her arms wide. Stewart looked at her for a second, then walked over to her. She hugged him tightly, Stewart returning it a bit awkwardly. They separated after a few seconds, Stewart retreating back a few paces.

"So what were you doing with Sebastian?"

"With Dakar? Well, eh, there was this murder, and—"

Beth held up a hand, and pointed to the sofa seat opposite her. Stewart smiled, a small smile, and went and collapsed into it.

He told her everything that had happened. He tried to give it to her in the order he'd encountered it himself, but he got tangled up, and things got turned around, and Beth had to ask questions to sort it all out. She was shocked by the appearance of Frank, and Dakar's shouting at Stewart. She audibly gasped when he told her he'd been arrested and handcuffed.

He didn't mention Jane's parts, instead sticking to the official story. Dakar's words about choices echoed in his head.

"And will there be a record of the arrest?"

Stewart shook his head. "They didn't write anything down. And DI Thomas told me there wouldn't be any notes made about that part."

Beth nodded her head. "That's crazy about Dakar. But I suppose everyone has a past. But what about the journalist, Frank? Any idea what he's going to do?"

Stewart shook his head again. "None. Dakar doesn't seem all that worried anymore, though. He was back to his Zen self by the time Frank was shouting at him this morning. So maybe nothing will come of it after all."

Epilogue

Stewart woke up, blinking puffy eyes against the sun streaming in through the window. It had been a nice night. He'd stayed in with Beth, watching rubbish on TV and talking about Dakar, and then Saz had come back and they'd shared some wine and beers, and all staggered off to bed. Plenty of laughter and fun, Saz even beginning to tease him about shouting at Beth. To his surprise, both he and Beth had laughed along with her.

He staggered downstairs. His watch told him it was ten in the morning. Beth was sitting at the breakfast table, in a pair of pyjamas. Stewart smiled at her as he came in, but the look of alarm on her face made him blink the sleep out of his eyes.

"What is it?"

She pointed down at the laptop in front of her, scrolling up to the headline on a news website. It screamed '*Ex-cop admits to tampering with evidence*'. And just underneath, the large photo right in the centre, a picture of Dakar was smiling out at him.

Stewart desperately read the article. It was the story about Billy Cronop. There was a claim that Dakar, a Zen celebrity, had told a journalist after the trial that he had planted the gun in Billy Cronop's coat, 'found' it there during the official search and then perjured himself at trial. The article contained some other allegations as well, matching statements, strong-arming suspects, but it all centred on the planting of the gun.

The by-line read '*Frank McPherson*'.

Stewart stood back up from the laptop, feeling dazed. And so it was done. Frank had followed through on his threat. And now Dakar was up a particular creek without anything even resembling a paddle.

"What's Dakar going to do?"

Stewart looked down at Beth, and shook his head slowly, a grimace on his face.

About the author

A former criminal prosecutor both in Scotland and at the international level for several years, Euan B. Pollock (a pseudonym) is a new author writing murder-mysteries in the classic style. He currently resides in Cambodia. To find out more, visit his website or follow him on Twitter and Facebook. His debut novel *Tricks of the Trade*, the first in the Scott and Dakar series, was published in January 2018.

Printed in Poland
by Amazon Fulfillment
Poland Sp. z o.o., Wrocław